Praise for the novels of Janet Dailey

"Dailey = magic!"
—*New York Times* bestselling author Dorothy Garlock

"The passion, spirit and strength readers expect from a
Calder story—and a Calder hero—shine through . . ."
—*Publishers Weekly* on *Lone Calder Star*

"Dailey's pacing, narrative, characterization, and dialogue
are all handled with verve and grace."
—*Publishers Weekly* on *Calder Promise*

"Dailey turns out a page-turner."
—*Publishers Weekly* on *Green Calder Grass*

"Juicy romance, the looming threat of vengeance on the
Calders and vivid descriptions of big-sky country will hold
readers' attention until the dramatic conclusion."
—*Publishers Weekly* on *Calder Storm*

"Dailey's wide following won't be disappointed."
—*Library Journal* on *Shifting Calder Wind*

"Dailey delivers!"
—*Kirkus Reviews* on *Calder Promise*

AMERICAN DESTINY

JANET DAILEY

ZEBRA BOOKS
Kensington Publishing Corp.
http://www.kensingtonbooks.com

ZEBRA BOOKS are published by

Kensington Publishing Corp.
119 West 40th Street
New York, NY 10018

All Kensington titles, imprints, and distributed lines are available at special quantity discounts for bulk purchases for sales promotion, premiums, fund-raising, educational, or institutional use.

Special book excerpts or customized printings can also be created to fit specific needs. For details, write or phone the office of the Kensington Special Sales Manager: Attn.: Special Sales Department. Kensington Publishing Corp., 119 West 40th Street, New York, NY 10018. Phone: 1-800-221-2647.

Zebra and the Z logo Reg. U.S. Pat. & TM Off.

ISBN-13: 978-1-4201-1158-3
ISBN-10: 1-4201-1158-2

Previously published under the title *Legacies*, copyright © 1995 by Janet Dailey
First Zebra Books Trade Paperback Printing: October 2009
First Zebra Books Mass-Market Paperback Printing: December 2009

10   9   8   7   6   5   4   3   2   1

Printed in the United States of America

PART I

It is well established that the Indian country west of Arkansas is looked to by the incoming administration of Mr. Lincoln as a fruitful field, ripe for the harvest of abolitionists, Free-Soilers, and Northern mountebanks. We hope to find in your people friends willing to cooperate with the South.

—Governor Henry M. Rector, Arkansas
(in a letter to John Ross,
principal chief of the Cherokee Nation)

❦ 1 ❧

Springfield, Massachusetts
May 1860

The carriage rolled up to the three-story brick home in the town's more fashionable residential district. With an agility that belied his advancing years, its driver assisted his passenger, a lovely young woman of nineteen gowned in a visiting dress in two shades of blue that flattered the honey gold of her hair and accented her blue eyes. Accepting the hand he offered, she stepped down and immediately opened a parasol to shade her face from the bright rays of the afternoon sun.

"'Tis waiting right here I'll be when you're ready to leave, Miss Parmelee," the driver informed her with a quick bob of his head.

"Thank you." Diane Parmelee flashed him an easy smile full of a potent charm that dazzled. She walked gracefully to the pedimented front porch and within seconds of her knocking, the Fletchers' Irish housekeeper, Bridget O'Shaughnessy, stood before her in a white dust cap that blended with the silver of her hair.

"How are you, Bridie?" Diane greeted her with a warm smile.

The housekeeper gaped at her in momentary astonishment.

"Saints be praised, it's Miss Diane. And all grown up, too. What a day for visitors this is. Is the captain with you?" She peered beyond Diane.

"No, my father is still at his post in Saint Louis."

"Look at me, jabbering away and leaving you standing out there," the housekeeper declared in self-reproach and waved her inside. "Come in, come in." Diane closed her parasol and stepped into the oval entry hall. The housekeeper wagged her hand in self-remonstration. "I know I should be asking after your mother, but it's mad I get just thinking about her. 'Tis not my place to be judging her, I know, but it's hard I'm finding it to forgive her for divorcing the captain to marry up with that rich Thomas Austin. 'Twas an awful thing for the captain, him being a gentleman and an officer."

Diane laughed in genuine affection. "Bridie, you haven't changed at all," she declared, unable to take offense at the housekeeper's criticism of her mother. As much as Diane regretted her parents' recent divorce, she was old enough to understand the differences that had finally pulled apart their marriage—her father loved army life and the frontier, while her mother longed for the more genteel existence and permanent home Tom Austin offered her.

"It's for certain and sure that you have," the woman countered. " 'Tis a full-grown vision of loveliness you've become. I know 'tis sorry Mrs. Fletcher will be that she isn't here this afternoon to see you, but this is the day the ladies of the Library Society have their tea."

Diane experienced a twinge of disappointment. She had always enjoyed the company of Mrs. Fletcher, who had been her confidante since her return several years before. "I had hoped to catch her at home. But I'm staying at the Wickhams'. Let me leave my card—"

"You can't be going without seeing Mr. Fletcher," the housekeeper stated flatly. "It's my hide he'll be having if you do. Come with me. It's in his study he is." Bustling off, she ushered Diane down the hall to a set of wooden doors, knocked once, and slid them open. "Begging your pardon, sir. It's another visitor that's come to see you." Without announcing Diane by name, the housekeeper stepped back to admit her.

Diane walked into the study, and Payton Fletcher moved quickly to greet her. At sixty years of age, he was a portly man with round cheeks and white hair flowing from the edges of his bald crown.

"Diane, what a delightful surprise." Both hands reached out to clasp hers in welcome. "What are you doing here in Springfield?"

"I'm staying at Judge Wickham's this summer with their granddaughter Ann Elizabeth while Mother is making a grand tour of Europe on her honeymoon. Naturally one of the first things I wanted to do after I arrived was to pay a call on my father's favorite godparents."

"We are his *only* godparents," Payton Fletcher asserted, a white eyebrow arching at her curious choice of words.

"So you are," Diane said with a teasing gleam in her eyes, then leaned forward to brush a kiss on his cheek.

"What? Oh, of course, you were making a joke, weren't you? You young people will have to forgive an old man for being a bit slow." He looked to a point beyond her left shoulder. At that instant, Diane realized someone else was in the room, and the housekeeper's phrase "another visitor" echoed in her mind. Before she could turn to look, Payton Fletcher was saying with a slightly addled frown, "You two do know each other, don't you?"

"We do." The deep, masculine register of the answering voice sent a tremor of excitement through Diane.

Its pitch was lower than she remembered, but Diane recognized it just the same. Exercising the greatest control, she slowly turned to face him, conscious of her heart thudding against her ribs.

Lije Stuart stood near the study window. He was tall, an inch over six feet, and his black hair lay ruffled along the edge of his forehead. He wore gray trousers and a dark cutaway coat tailored to fit smoothly across his wide shoulders and leanly muscled chest. His familiar face was more rugged and compelling than it had been the last time she saw him five years ago, yet it still retained the bronze cast that spoke of his Cherokee ancestry, a contrast to the startling blue of his eyes.

Born and raised at Fort Gibson in the Indian Territory, Diane had known and adored Lije Stuart her whole life. She had been a girl of fourteen when the army closed Fort Gibson and reassigned her father to a post in the East. In the intervening years, she had often wondered if she would ever see Lije again—and whether her reaction to him would be the same.

Facing him, Diane at last had her answer as the sight of him made her catch her breath. With practiced poise, she crossed the room and extended a gloved hand in greeting.

"Lije, finding you here is the most wonderful surprise." She made no attempt to mask the delight in her voice or her smile despite the mockingly demure tilt of her head.

"It's good to see you again, too, Diane." Lije's response was reserved, a habit once dictated by the difference in their ages.

But the Diane Parmelee standing before him now was no longer the lovely and innocent young girl he had known. She had grown into a woman of stunning beauty. Her face was almost mystically perfect, the kind that could rule a man's fantasies. Her hair swept back from it in a glorious, golden cascade, like an angel's. And her eyes sparkled with a zest for life. They were focused on him with an intensity that had his blood heating.

Desire flared through him just as it always had when he was around her. And, as always, Lije banked it. He took her hand. Her gloved fingers closed on his in an unusual mingling of delicacy and strength.

She gracefully made a half-turn toward Payton Fletcher. "The last time I saw Lije was at the annual May celebration held at the Cherokee Female Seminary in Tahlequah. After the May Queen was crowned, the military band from the fort played on the lawn behind the building and everyone danced— except me. My mother forbade it. She said fourteen was too young. I was totally crushed. You see, Payton, Lije had previously promised he would dance with me, and I was excited at the prospect." Diane paused and slanted Lije a sideways glance that both teased and challenged. "Do you remember what you told me?"

"That we would dance together someday when you were older."

"I fully intend to hold you to that promise, Lije Stuart."

"I can't say that surprises me." Even as Lije smiled at her statement, he envisioned her in his arms, the two of them swirling around a dance floor, their eyes locked, nothing and no one else existing. He felt that twist of desire again, and again fought it back to direct his glance at Payton Fletcher. "Diane was always a very determined young lady. If she failed to get what she wanted one way, she searched until she found another."

"I confess I do tend to be single-minded about what I want." Her eyes were on him.

"A dance is a trivial request," Lije told her.

"Ah, but great things have come from less auspicious beginnings. Don't you agree, Payton?" She turned to the older man with a confident tilt of her head.

"I do, indeed," he replied with a decisive nod. "In fact, I was just telling Lije that his education at Harvard will prove to be a stepping stone toward a promising future."

"Susannah wrote me that you were studying law at Harvard," Diane said, referring to her childhood friend and Lije's nineteen-year-old aunt. "I had hoped you would pay a call on us after we moved to Boston this past spring."

"I suspect your mother would have given me a cold reception if I had." A wry smile curved his mouth, creating craggy dimples in his cheeks.

"You shouldn't have let that stop you," she chided, acknowledging indirectly that her mother's attitude was a problem. But it was an obstacle that was literally an ocean away at the moment, one that could be dealt with later.

"Perhaps I shouldn't have," Lije conceded with the smallest of shrugs. "Five years is a long time. People change."

Diane smiled. "I have to admit I have changed from that gawky fourteen-year-old girl with freckles you last saw."

"As I recall, you only had freckles because you went riding with your father without a hat. And you were never gawky," he stated. "Even as a child, you had a beauty and a radiance that captivated the heart of every male within miles."

"And now?" She waited for his answer, her breath catching.

"And now," his glance made a slow and thorough sweep of her before coming back to hold her gaze, "impossible as it seems, you are even more beautiful."

Diane saw the attraction in his eyes. At nineteen, she was sufficiently experienced in the ways of a man to know when one was interested in her. Lije was. She wanted to hug herself with the sheer joy of knowing it.

"That, my dear, is a fact," Payton Fletcher declared. "One that I heartily echo. It was remiss of me not to tell you before how lovely you look. Lije's grandfather Will Gordon told me years ago that you can never give a woman too many compliments. I should have remembered that. It's good to see his grandson did." He glanced at Lije. "You must be sure to give your grandfather my fondest regards when you see him."

"I will," Lije promised.

"Will Gordon and I went to school together," he told Diane.

"Yes, I know."

He paid no attention to the two young people before him who, through evasive glances and silent surveillance, were taking stock of all that had changed in each other. Instead, he was temporarily lost in those long-ago days. "We had some grand times together. Many was the night Will had to carry me home."

He chuckled at the memory and shook his head. "If it hadn't been for Will, I doubt I ever would have graduated. He was the intelligent one. It's heartening to see that same intelligence in his grandson." He beamed in approval at Lije, then informed Diane, "Lije is too modest to tell you, but congratulations are in order. He has graduated from Harvard with honors."

"How wonderful! Congratulations."

"Thank you." He inclined his head.

"What are your plans now?"

"To return home and put my study of law to good use. I'll be leaving at the end of the week."

"So soon?" Diane protested. "Surely you can stay another week or two, can't you?"

"I've been gone for four years."

"What's another two weeks after four years?" She looked at him, her eyes aglow with challenge and . . . something else. "Judge Wickham is holding his annual summer party in two weeks. If you are a man of your word, you will be there to dance with me."

Payton Fletcher chuckled in approval. "Spoken like the true daughter of an army officer who has learned, to her advantage, the value a man places on his honor. You will have no choice but to stay now, Lije."

"So it would seem," Lije agreed, his eyes on her, a sizzling undercurrent flowing between them. He had never been able to refuse her anything she wanted as a child. He found it equally impossible to refuse her as a woman. More than that, he didn't want to.

The afternoon socials, shopping expeditions, luncheons, lawn parties, and teas Diane arranged enabled her to spend a good part of every day with Lije. The first week passed in a rush that culminated in an invitation from Judge Wickham for the Fletchers and Lije to dine with them at the family estate.

Dinner was a formal affair, the meal itself lasting nearly

two hours. Afterward coffee was served on the terrace. Diane strolled with Lije to its far end to view the lawn's reflecting pool and steal a few moments alone. She paused to breathe in the warm night air, attuned to the night and its magic—and to the man beside her.

"This is a grand evening. Everything has turned out so well." She glanced back at the other members of their dinner party. "Judge Wickham was very impressed with you."

"Once he recovered from the shock of learning that I was Cherokee," Lije replied dryly, a hint of censure in his tone. "You failed to inform him of that."

"Deliberately." Diane turned to face him, her eyes sparkling, her tone amused. "Not volunteering information is something I learned from my father. If they were to have any objections to my seeing you, I wanted them to voice them *after* they had become acquainted with you. I was confident that once they met you, they would recognize an intelligent and charming man who conducts himself as a proper gentleman. And tonight proves I was right. I think it would be more accurate to say the Wickhams were amazed rather than shocked to discover you are Cherokee. In fact, I think the judge admires you even more because of it." She paused to examine his reaction. "You don't look properly impressed by that."

"Should I be?" Lije countered as the warm breeze carried the scent of her perfume to him, something soft and alluring and outrageously feminine.

"Yes, you should. Judge Wickham is an extremely wealthy and influential man to have on your side. Do you remember when we were talking about your family's plantation at dinner, and Mrs. Wickham asked how your mother managed to take care of such a large house? You have no idea how relieved I was when you explained that she had servants to look after it, the same as Mrs. Wickham. I forgot to warn you—the Wickhams are staunch abolitionists. They would have been appalled to learn your parents are slaveholders."

"Many people here in the North would be. It's a subject I've learned to avoid over the last four years."

"Spoken like a diplomat." She smiled in warm approval, then paused, her look softening. "Every time I think about how fortunate I was to pay a call on Payton Fletcher on that particular day—if I had waited just a day or two more, you would have been gone, and we would never have seen each other. I would have regretted that."

"Would you have?"

A tempting glow in her blue eyes was her only response.

Surrendering to the flirtation, Lije reached for her shoulders and gently pulled her toward him. Kissing her was something he had wanted for too long.

Diane had no time to think before the power of his lips whipped through her, igniting her emotions. It wasn't the kiss, but a hard, thorough demand that kept her wrapped in his arms. She reached up to take his face in her hands as she gave, unquestioningly, what he sought from her.

Diane knew this was not a gradual smoldering, but a passion so intense and quick it seemed they were already lovers. She felt the instant intimacy and instead of being frightened, she understood that her heart had long been his. She couldn't deny him anything else.

Lije drew her closer and inhaled the warm, teasing fragrance that seemed to pulse from her skin. He reveled in the taste of her—alluring, giving, and warm. The feel of her soft, slender body created a need in him as insistent as the buffeting wind off the Plains.

She made it impossible for him to think. Soon he would forget everything but her. Lije knew her power was the kind that could make a man hunger, make him ache. It could make him weak just when he couldn't afford to lose his resolve. He had other priorities, other responsibilities.

He pulled back even as he wanted more and more of what she offered in abundance.

Diane's eyes opened slowly when her mouth was free. She looked directly at him and saw longing and caution and a glimpse of emotion that stirred her.

"I've wanted you to do that," she murmured, "for a long, long time."

Lije took a deep breath and exhaled it slowly. "I think we had better rejoin the others." At the moment he didn't trust himself to be alone with her.

"Why?" But her teasing eyes told him she knew the answer.

"I should never have touched you."

"Why?"

"It leads to more, and I'll be leaving soon."

"Not for another week, at least. Not until you've danced with me, remember?" Without waiting for a response, she linked her arm with his and directed them both back to the others.

Strings of festive lanterns lit the terrace where couples whirled in an ever-moving circle to the lilting strains of a waltz. From the tented pavilion on the lawn came the sounds of laughter, tinkling crystal, and chattering voices. But Lije was aware only of the woman in his arms, so beautiful in her white ball gown trimmed with blue forget-me-nots, her eyes aglow with happiness.

"Did you know my father taught your mother how to waltz years ago?" There was a lightness in her voice that didn't match the heady tension that throbbed between them.

"I have heard the story before."

Her glance slid to his mouth, wreaking havoc with his control. "I remember the first time my father told me about it. He made it sound so magical. I think that's when I started wondering whether it would be like that if you and I danced together." Her eyes lifted their glance to once again lock with his. "It's more than magic, Lije. Much more." She threw a quick look at the other guests. "Everyone can see it. That's why they're staring at us."

Lije spared a glance at the guests on the sidelines, noting the number of feminine eyes that watched him over the top of fluttering fans and the thinly disguised glares from many of the men. Their reactions were typical of others he had encountered during his four years in the East.

"They are staring because they are scandalized that you are dancing with a Cherokee when you could have your choice of a dozen other, more suitable partners," he told her.

Diane laughed easily. "I know them better than you do. Most of them are only pretending to be scandalized to cover their envy or their wounded egos. Especially the women. They look at you and secretly wish they could trade places with me, but they are too concerned with what other people would think."

"Aren't you?"

The curve of her lips deepened. "One of the advantages of being raised on the frontier is that polite society overlooks it when I indulge in what it would consider improper behavior in its own ranks. It's proven quite useful on occasion."

"This being one of them."

"Yes." Still smiling, Diane cast another glance over his arm at the onlooking guests as Lije guided her through a sweeping turn. "Truthfully, I suspect half the women here are waiting to see if you scoop me up and carry me off somewhere to ravish me." She looked back to him, her smile fading as their eyes met. "I have a feeling they'll be disappointed if you don't."

"We can't have that, can we?" His fingers tightened their grip on her gloved hand, a rush of heat flowed between them as the ripe man–woman tension leapt to another level.

"No, we can't." Her voice turned husky with desire.

The song ended in a flourish of notes. Lije stepped back and bowed to her, then took her hand, tucked it under his arm, and escorted her from the floor to the shadowy edges of the terrace. A moment later they slipped from the gathering, un-observed, and sought the quiet of the side garden.

Once there, Lije pulled a laughing Diane into the shad-ows of a trellised arch laden with honeysuckle. Her laughter died as she looked into his eyes. His gaze was intense, a hot, hot blue that made her throat grow dry with anticipation. He bent his head to hers, their lips met, brushed, his breath a warm caress against her skin.

With a half-smothered groan, he dragged her to him and claimed her lips in a driving kiss that was warm, hard, and demanding. Her mouth was like silk, smooth and clinging. The desire that had simmered between them all evening rushed to the surface. Lije gave full rein to it, taking his fill of her lips, but it wasn't enough. He knew it even as he felt the tremble of longing that shuddered through her. In an attempt at control, he shifted his attention to her cheek, her jaw, the delicate lobe of her ear.

"Lije," she whispered his name, going soft and pliant in his embrace. "You have no idea how much I wanted this."

"No more than I." He rubbed his lips over the blue vein in her neck that throbbed so heavy and fast.

"You don't understand," she said with a small shake of her head, then pulled back to look at him, her eyes shimmer-ing with a mixture of wonder and need. "I have adored you since I was a child. When the government closed Fort Gibson, and we had to leave, I was heartbroken." She paused and smiled, raising a hand to run her fingers along the smooth line of his jaw. "It sounds silly, doesn't it? I was only a girl. What did I know about love? That's what I used to tell my-self. But I never stopped hoping we would meet again some-day. And I was always terrified that if we did, you would be married to someone else. I'm glad you're not." Her fingers slid into his hair, drawing him down. "Kiss me again, Lije."

He obliged her and lost himself in the softness of her lips, the heat of them, the bottomless pleasure of them. Just for the moment, he thought of nothing but her—not the past with its ghosts and not the future with its vague forebodings. He knew it was madness to forget his priorities and sink into her spell. But she was all softness and strength, all trembles and demands. The scent radiating from the skin of her neck made his head spin.

"I love you, Diane." He wanted her, in his arms and in his life.

"And I love you." Her voice trembled with deep feeling. She laughed a little shakily, then bent her head to rest the top of it against his shoulder. "Who would have guessed it would all turn out so glorious?"

Gripped by a feeling of urgency, he said, "Diane, I'll be leaving soon—"

"No." Her head came up, her eyes bright with confidence. "I won't let you go."

"I can't stay—" Regret riddled his voice.

"Of course, you can. Just the other day I heard Judge Wickham mention that Senator Frederick was looking for a bright young man to fill a position he had open in his Boston office. Judge Wickham likes you. I know I could persuade him to recommend you. Don't you see how perfect it would be, with both of us in Boston?"

"Diane, no." He took her by the shoulders and held her gaze, needing to make it clear to her. "I'm going home."

She hesitated only fractionally. "Naturally you want to go home and visit your family, your parents. I understand that. Afterwards you can come back here and—"

"No."

"No?" She stiffened, then pulled away and turned from him in agitation. "Why? What on earth is there for you back there? There are so many more opportunities for you here, so much more you can do, so much more you can be."

"I have to go home. I *need* to go home." Lije didn't know how to put into words the unease he felt, the fears that never left him, the images of the past that haunted him and turned that need to return home into a compulsion. "Come with me, Diane."

"Come with you?" She swung back around.

"I want you to be my wife."

"Just like that? You can't be serious."

"But I am." His eyes frosted over at her reaction to his proposal. He hadn't intended to take her home with him, but somehow the words flowed effortlessly from his mouth— and they seemed so right.

"It's too soon to be talking about marriage. You know my mother would never give her consent if I were to go West so suddenly."

"Because I am Cherokee."

"Because you are a Stuart. She has never made a secret of her feelings toward your family."

"No, she hasn't."

"Then you see how impossible it is right now. In time—"

"I'm leaving in the morning."

"You're not being reasonable, Lije," she said angrily. "You won't listen to anything I say. It's all been so wonderful. Why do you have to ruin it like this?"

"Maybe you should have listened to your mother when she warned you a long time ago to stay away from me," he suggested in a cold, hard voice, his hurt concealed by his rising temper.

Diane retaliated in kind. "Perhaps I should have!"

Lije looked at her another long second, then turned and walked off into the night. Diane watched him for a moment, anger washing over her in waves even as tears stung her eyes. But her pride wouldn't let her run after him. He would return. She was sure of it.

❦ 2 ❧

Cherokee Nation, Indian Territory
July 1860

Lije lifted the bay into a canter. There had been few opportunities to ride back East. It felt good to have a horse between his legs again, hooves pounding clay-red dirt, air rushing over his face, and the trail open before him.

The well-worn road curled into a wooded section thick with oak, persimmon, hickory, and cedar trees, their branches arching to create a leafy canopy. Beyond the reach of the sun's hot glare, the air was cooler, filled with the rustles and stirrings of creatures moving about in the heavy growth. He rode on, the enduring wildness of the land flowing around him, getting into his bones and his mind.

All of it was familiar to him, the old sights, the old sounds, the old smells. After four years he had half-expected to return a stranger in his own land. Instead, it was almost as if he had never left.

The discovery brought a smile to his lips. He glanced back at the trailing black servant Ike. "Not much farther to Oak Hill from here."

"Just up the road a piece," Ike confirmed, riding up to draw level with Lije. They had exchanged no more than a dozen words since leaving the riverboat landing. But, as Ike recalled, Master Lije had never been the kind who liked the sound of his own voice. He had always let his actions speak for him and did more thinking than talking. But Ike's curiosity was eating away at him. He took the opening to satisfy it. "What was it like up North?"

"Not much different from here. A lot of trees and mountains and farmlands. The winters were longer and colder, the towns were bigger. More buildings, more people" He glanced sideways at Ike, a dancing twinkle in his eyes. "A lot more people."

Ike nodded, the answer echoing much of what he had already heard. "My mother told me she had never seen so many people living in one place in her whole life than she did that time she went up North with your folks. Master Blade gave my folks a pass to see some of the sights while they were in Philadelphia. Did you go to Philadelphia while you were in the North?"

"I only passed through it."

"Then you never got to see the bell they got there." Ike's disappointment was brief, replaced by memories of all the stories his mother had told him about it. Stories that he'd had her repeat to him again and again. "People are calling it the Liberty Bell. The writing on it says 'Proclaim liberty throughout all the land unto all inhabitants thereof.' That's from Leviticus, in the Bible." Ike hesitated, then asked what he most wanted to know. "Did you see any free men of color when you were in the North?"

"Very few." With eyes narrowed, Lije studied the Negro he had played with as a child. *Liberty. Free men of color.* Those words and the trace of longing in Ike's voice warned Lije that Ike was dreaming of freedom. "You better watch what you say, Ike," he warned. "These are uneasy times. A suspicious man might hear you talking about liberty and decide you might be getting foolish ideas in your head. He might even decide to do something about that."

Ike fixed his gaze on a distant point, all expression wiped from his face except for the glitter of resentment in his eyes. At that moment Lije knew that this son of Deuteronomy Jones did not share the same feeling of deep loyalty that had cleaved his father to the Stuart family.

"I didn't mean anything by it," Ike finally mumbled.

"Maybe you didn't, but it's dangerous thinking right now."

They rode out of the shade into the full glare of the sun. Lije spotted the turnoff to his grandfather's plantation and kicked the bay into a lope, eliminating further opportunity for conversation. Once more Ike fell back to trail behind.

The approach to Oak Hill Plantation was marked by a quarter-mile-long drive lined with bush honeysuckle. At the end of it stood the main house, built on the crown of a small hill and surrounded by towering oak trees. Constructed of red brick and fronted by massive Doric columns, the building possessed a quiet grace and dignity, like its owner. According to Lije's mother, the house resembled the plantation home once owned by the Gordons in what was now Georgia. Lije had been born in his grandparents' home in that faraway house, but he had no memories of it, for he had been a toddler when soldiers had driven the family away at bayonet point.

Lije had barely dismounted when the front door opened. Out stepped a slenderly built Negro dressed in a black cutaway coat and trousers with a white shirt and stiffly starched collar. A smile of welcome wreathed his face, lighting up his gentle eyes.

"Master Lije, I knew it was you the minute I saw you riding up the lane. Nobody sits a horse like you do—except maybe your father."

"Hello, Shadrach." Lije smiled at the Negro who had belonged to Will Gordon since birth. As a boy, Shadrach had made the arduous trek over the long trail from their Cherokee homeland in the East. Shadrach's sister, Phoebe, had been given to Lije's mother as her dower Negro when she married. Ike was her son—and Shadrach's nephew. "You haven't changed a bit."

Shadrach had one of those timeless faces that failed to show the passing of years. But Lije knew he had to be in his forties.

"You certainly have. That college has turned you into a full-grown man," Shadrach declared, then gestured to his nephew. "Ike, take Master Lije's horse around to the stables."

When Ike stepped up, Lije handed him the reins and moved away. Shadrach reached the front door first and opened it for him.

"You'll find Miss Eliza in the parlor," Shadrach told him.

Lije walked inside and immediately saw his grandfather's second wife walking toward him down the great hall. "Shadrach, did I hear—" She stopped abruptly, a hand coming up to touch her throat. "Lije," she murmured in surprise.

"Hello, Eliza."

Moving swiftly, she crossed the short distance between them and reached out with both hands to grasp his. "Well, just look at you," Eliza beamed. "You have grown into a handsome man. How was your trip?"

"Long, but uneventful."

"Good," she said in that crisp, no-nonsense voice that was very familiar to him. "I didn't hear the carriage. How did you get here?" Now frowning, she glanced at the door. "Where is your grandfather? Your parents?"

"I rode ahead. They'll be along directly."

"Wonderful. Come. We'll go into the parlor and chat." Deftly, she tucked her arm under his and turned him toward the arched doorway. "Susannah is still upstairs changing," she said, referring to her daughter, "but Kipp and Alex are here."

Caught off guard by the announcement of his uncle Kipp's presence, Lije stiffened, his glance shooting to the parlor doorway.

The always astute Eliza picked up on the muscles tensing

beneath her hand and tightened her grip on his arm in silent admonition. "This is a *family* occasion, Lije." The emphasis was firm. "Whatever bad blood there was between your father and Kipp belongs in the past. We must not allow it to color the present. Kindly remember that Kipp is your mother's only remaining brother. It is time to forgive what cannot be forgotten."

Lije dragged his gaze back to the tall, slender woman. "Still the peacemaker, I see" His mouth twitched with a dry smile.

"Someone in this family has to be. Heaven knows, there have been few occasions sufficiently important to warrant the gathering of all members of this family."

By *all*, Lije knew Eliza was referring specifically to his father and Kipp. Usually one or the other failed to attend a family function. On the rare times that Lije remembered both men being present, the atmosphere had been painfully strained.

"And you decided my homecoming was sufficiently important," Lije guessed.

"I believe that is obvious." She gathered up the front of her skirt hem. "Shall we go in?" Taking his agreement for granted, Eliza made a move toward the parlor. But Lije hung back, earning a puzzled look from her. "What is it?"

"Aren't you going to lecture me on Alex's innocence in all this?" he asked, eyes twinkling. Virtually from the day his cousin was born seventeen years ago, Eliza had set out to make certain that the animosity between Kipp and The Blade, as his father was called, did not extend to their sons. As the oldest, Lije had received the bulk of her lobbying efforts.

She saw the laughter in his eyes, and her lips thinned in prim disapproval. "Now you mock me."

"And you look quite beautiful," he told her. "Indignation becomes you. It brings fire to your eyes and color to your cheeks."

"What nonsense!" But for all the sharpness in her voice, Lije could tell she was secretly pleased by the compliment.

There was the tiniest hint of a smile about her mouth when she steered him into the parlor. "Kipp, look who has arrived," she announced, injecting a note of breezy unconcern.

The man at the parlor window turned, and Lije stared into the face of his uncle, his father's enemy. Wings of silver white fanned his temples, contrasting starkly with his otherwise black hair. On most people, the result would be a distinguished appearance. But Lije had never been able to look at those twin streaks of white in Kipp's hair without being reminded of a devil's horns.

This time, the sight triggered a whirl of images from the past for Lije—images of a carriage coming down the lane, his grandfather Shawano Stuart at the reins, gray hair flowing onto his collar. Suddenly, a dozen men, their faces covered with black kerchiefs, spill from the trees, hands reaching, grabbing to pull the old man down. His grandfather disappears, struggling beneath a sea of knife blades flashing in the sunlight, only to resurface, lifeless, face down in the road.

Lije had witnessed the killing of Shawano Stuart when he was less than three years old. The scene remained branded on his mind. He had never forgotten that feeling of abject terror, of being utterly powerless to help the grandfather he adored. And he had never forgotten that Kipp Gordon had been one of the masked men.

Whether justice was carried out in the killing of Shawano Stuart was considered arguable by many. Lije's father regarded it as murder, whereas his mother, Temple, saw it as a legitimate execution, however ignobly carried out.

In 1835, before Lije was born, Shawano Stuart had signed a treaty that surrendered all the Cherokee land in the East to the Federal government. Shawano, and all who signed the document, including The Blade, knew it was an unauthorized treaty, made without consent of the Cherokee people and a direct violation of the Cherokee Blood Law, a crime punishable by death. In truth, the drastic action was a desperate effort to force the leaders of the Cherokee government into negotiating a treaty with the Federal authorities and end the persecution and abuse by the Georgians that had gone on, unabated, for years.

The action cost Shawano and several other cosigners their lives. Lije's father had eluded an attempt on his life and joined others in hiding until amnesty was declared.

Time had passed, but not the memories, not for anyone who had lived during that time. Even now it silenced the words of greeting Lije might have offered his uncle. It was left to Eliza to open the conversation.

"Lije came on ahead," she told Kipp. "Your father and the others will be along shortly."

Nodding, Kipp looked him over. There was no welcome in his expression, but Lije had expected none. "You have grown more like your father." Coming from Kipp, it wasn't a compliment. "I am surprised you finished all four years of college. I thought you would walk away after the first year—as your father did."

"Perhaps I have my mother's tenacity," Lije suggested and deliberately turned to his cousin. Seventeen-year-old Alex Gordon stood off to the side, observing the exchange, his lip curling in amused scorn. He bore a surface resemblance to his father—the black hair, the high cheekbones, straight nose, and black eyes. And like Kipp, he was tall and slender. "It's good to see you again, Alex."

"Hey, Lije." A smile made a wide curve of his mouth and dented his cheeks with attractive creases. In it, Lije saw the youth he remembered—reckless, a little on the wild side, full of charm and guile. "I was about to give up on you. I thought that riverboat had probably run aground somewhere."

Lije shook his head. "The water was up, and the trip was smooth."

"Just my luck," Alex sighed in mock regret. "Here I thought I was going to get your share of the feast Granny El has prepared."

"If I know Eliza, there will be more than enough food for

everyone." Lije cast a knowing glance at his stepgrandmother. "The tables usually groan under the weight of it all."

"Naturally, this is a celebration. Speaking of which"— Eliza withdrew her hand from Lije's arm and swung toward the arched doorway—"Shadrach."

The Negro servant appeared within seconds. "Yes, Miss Eliza?"

"Bring some refreshments. I am certain Lije is thirsty after his ride."

"Yes, ma'am." He bobbed his head and withdrew.

The sound of his footsteps was almost immediately lost under the rapid tap-tapping of another pair of feet. A young woman swept into view, dressed in a gown of fawn-colored silk trimmed with Maltese lace. Ribbons caught the mass of amber brown curls and held it high on her head. Lije watched the smile break across her strong-boned face when she saw him.

"Lije," she cried in delight. "I thought I heard your voice."

"Susannah."

"It is so good to have you back." She wrapped her arms around him in a warm hug. "I have missed you, Lije. We all have missed you."

"I have missed you." Lije captured her shoulders and pushed her back from him. "Let me have a look at you" He inspected this woman who had always seemed more like a younger sister to him than an aunt. She was tall, a scant three inches under six feet. Her hazel eyes sparkled with gold flecks, reminding him of a cat. "Where is that tall, skinny girl with sticks for arms and legs who lived here when I left?" Lije shook his head in amazement at Susannah's transformation into womanhood. "You have grown into a very graceful lady while I've been away. You must have suitors lined up at your door every evening."

"What nonsense!" Susannah laughed away his comment, finding the very idea ludicrous. "No man courts a woman who towers over him like an oak tree. And if he does, you can be certain it is my father's favor he is seeking, not mine."

Lije disagreed, but he knew she would simply accuse him of being kind if he argued the point. Susannah had always found fault with her looks, convinced she was too tall and too thin; her hair, too curly; and her face, all strong bones and angles. In her mind, she was far from any definition of beautiful. But the combination had always been a striking one, never more so than now with maturity fleshing out and smoothing away all the rough edges.

"You continue to underestimate yourself, Little Auntie," he teased.

"Call me that again and I will punch you in the mouth." She narrowed her eyes in mock warning, but the laughter dancing in them erased any threat.

"Heavens, do you remember the time you gave Lije a black eye?" Eliza recalled, a smile forming at the memory.

"Very well," Susannah replied. "It was the last time he called me Auntie."

"You tried to punch me in the mouth and missed," Lije recalled.

"Only because you tried to duck."

"My eye was black and blue for weeks."

"It served you right. I am too young to be your aunt."

"But the fact remains you are."

"Then let it remain a fact and not a title," Susannah stated with an unconscious but typical air of one issuing a royal decree.

"As you command," Lije conceded with a mock bow as Shadrach returned with iced lemonade. Lije took two glasses from the silver tray and gave one to Susannah.

She took a sip. "Mmmm, wonderful."

After Eliza had taken a glass, Shadrach walked over to Kipp. "Lemonade, sir?"

"Lemonade?" Kipp eyed the pale liquid contemptuously. "Have you nothing stronger in the house?"

"If you would prefer, I could bring you some coffee, sir," Shadrach replied, cautiously respectful.

Lije glanced across the room. "Lemonade or coffee. That's your choice, Kipp. You didn't truly expect anything stronger from the mistress of this house, did you?" Eliza and her temperance group had agitated against the whiskey peddlers until they succeeded in getting Fort Gibson closed.

"To be perfectly frank, the work we did was necessary, but I regret they closed the fort." Idly, Eliza shook out her ornate fan and waved it back and forth in front of her face, keeping the summer heat at bay. "I miss the dinners and dances that were held there. And I know the young girls miss the young officers. Although I have to admit, I don't miss Captain Parmelee's snippy wife one bit." The motion of the fan quickened to a rapid tempo. "I have always admired and respected Jed, but that wife of his—" The fan went faster. "When I think of that time she forbade her daughter Diane to play with you and Lije because she didn't want her child associating with Indians, it makes my blood boil all over again."

"I think Captain Parmelee apologized afterwards, didn't he?" Susannah frowned, trying to recall.

"He did," Eliza answered, then sighed. "Poor Jed. I have never seen any man as embarrassed and upset as he was. I suspect he had cause to regret his marriage to that despicable woman on more than one occasion. It's truly amazing that Diane remained such a sweet girl. You can credit her father's influence for that."

Susannah glanced at Lije, curious to see his reaction to this comment about Diane. Diane's last letter had been full of talk about Lije, so much so that Susannah suspected a romance between the two. She was stunned to see Lije's expression—the hardness in his features and the coldness in his eyes. Not until that moment did Susannah realize just how silent he had become since the subject of the Parmelees had been raised.

"Diane wrote to me that she saw a great deal of you when you stopped to visit Payton Fletcher," Susannah said.

"Did she?" He lifted his glass and drank down a quick

swallow of lemonade. But Susannah saw the iciness of his eyes.

"How is she?"

"More beautiful than ever." But the smile that twisted his mouth wasn't kind.

The answer was too abrupt. Susannah knew at once something was wrong, something had happened. And Diane was at the core of it. How? Why? Susannah started to ask, then checked the impulse, realizing that it was quite obviously something he had no wish to discuss in the company of the others. Later she would make a point to see him in private and find out exactly what had happened with Diane.

At the parlor window Eliza waved her fan with renewed vigor. "Gracious, it has turned hot and sticky. Whatever became of that breeze we enjoyed earlier?" She peered out as if expecting to find it, then paused, stilling the fan's motion. "There's a rider coming up the lane." She leaned closer to the window. "I do believe it's Nathan. How wonderful." She was instantly all motion, bustling away from the window. "Shadrach, go fetch Reverend Cole some lemonade while I greet him."

When she left the room, Kipp grumbled, "How many others has Eliza invited to dinner? I understood this was to be a family gathering."

"Reverend Cole is like a member of the family, Kipp," Susannah reminded him. "He has been part of nearly every important occasion in our lives. Heavens, he even performed my parents' wedding ceremony—as well as The Blade and Temple's."

Lije noticed that Susannah didn't mention that Reverend Cole had also officiated at Kipp's marriage and—less than a year later—read over the grave of Kipp's young wife after she died giving birth to their son, Alex. Lije had been too young to remember much of that time himself, but he had been told that Kipp had been almost happy during his short year of marriage. After his wife's untimely death, his uncle had retreated, and his bitterness had grown deeper.

Alex lifted his glass and smiled at Susannah over the rim, a kind of taunting mockery in his eyes. "I guess that means Reverend Cole will be coming to your farewell party, too."

"What farewell party?" Lije shot a questioning look at Susannah. "Where are you going?"

"Mother hasn't told you the news?"

"What news?"

"I'll be attending Mount Holyoke this fall. Both Mother and Father are planning to accompany me on the trip to South Hadley. We leave in August."

"I return and you leave."

"I know." Some of the previous excitement faded from her eyes. "I wish—"

But Susannah had no opportunity to complete the sentence before Eliza returned with the Reverend Nathan Cole. He was a tall, spare man with a bony face and gaunt cheeks. His smile, like the man, was gentle and retiring.

"Welcome home, Elijah," Reverend Cole spoke softly, as always addressing Lije by his full given name. "It's good to have you back among us. You have been missed."

"Thank you, Reverend Cole. It's good to be back— although I just learned Susannah will be leaving us."

The reverend's attention swung to Susannah, his eyes brightening.

"Then you have been accepted at Mount Holyoke."

"I have. We leave in August."

"Will and I will accompany her on the trip," Eliza explained. "This will be the first time I've been back to South Hadley since I left to teach the children of a Cherokee family named Gordon. What's that been, Nathan? Twenty-five years ago?"

"Closer to thirty, I believe."

"I guess it has been almost that long. I was barely twenty

then and convinced my destiny in life was to teach. Little did I guess what the future would hold."

"That is as it should be." He patted Eliza's hand. "We can only hope Susannah will have as stimulating an adventure herself."

"You're right, of course. It will be good to take Susannah and visit the places of my childhood to see all the changes time has wrought. Will wants to spend some time with Payton Fletcher while we're in the area. We'll be staying with him after Susannah has settled in at Mount Holyoke." She smiled at her daughter. "You're going to like it there."

"Is that where you went, Granny El?" Alex asked.

"No. The female seminary didn't open its doors until four or five years after I had left South Hadley. That would have been in the late 1830s, I believe. But my mother taught there for years after it opened. If she hadn't passed on three years ago, she could have seen her granddaughter there." Everyone knew Eliza regretted that she hadn't returned earlier to see her mother before she died. "Now her granddaughter will be walking in the very same halls she did. I find that very fitting—though I fear Susannah's reasons for choosing Mount Holyoke have nothing to do with her grandmother's past association with it. Her favorite teacher at the Cherokee Female Seminary was a graduate of Mount Holyoke. I think it's in her footsteps that Susannah is following."

"Perhaps it's both," Susannah suggested.

"A very tactful response." Reverend Cole nodded in approval, his eyes twinkling with laughter. "A trait you obviously acquired from your father, since tact has never been a virtue your mother possessed in any great abundance."

"That is unkind," Eliza said in mild protest.

"But true, nonetheless," he replied without criticism.

"Perhaps." Eliza would admit to no more than that and adroitly shifted the attention away from herself. "As glad as we are to have you back with us, Lije, it would have been nice if you had yet another year of schooling to finish so that you would be close by during Susannah's first year away from home. I know it would have been a comfort to her. Hopefully, we can look forward to Alex joining her next year. I know Kipp wants him to study at Harvard. Of course, his marks will have to improve for that to happen."

"Please, Granny El." Alex grimaced. He was obviously not keen to embark on a lecture he had heard repeated too often over the years. "Not everyone shares your love for books and learning."

"Alexander Gordon, I will have you know an education is important. I—"

He held up a hand to stop her. "Spare me, Granny El. I've heard it all before. There are other things in life besides an education."

"Not if you want to make something of yourself. Look at Lije. He—"

"I am *not* Lije. I will never be like him." His anger came in a flash, as black and as quick as his father's. But as quickly as it was revealed, it was concealed by an easy smile. "Sorry, Granny El, but it's true."

"Of course, it's true. I never meant to imply you should be. However, that doesn't lessen the value of an education."

"Maybe I don't want to go East. Maybe I want to stay here."

Reverend Cole tipped his head toward Eliza. "I think a young lady has caught his fancy."

Alex seemed about to deny that, then changed his mind, his smile widening. "You could say that."

"Who is she?" Susannah asked. "Anyone I know?"

"You have seen her."

"Who is she? What does she look like? Don't keep us in suspense, Alex."

"Well, let's see." He paused, mischief dancing in his eyes. "She has the biggest, most beautiful eyes you have ever seen. And hair, black and shiny as a midnight sky full of stars. She is young, a bit wild, and headstrong, but—" Off to the side Kipp snorted a laugh.

"Shooting Star," Susannah murmured in sudden under-standing. "Alex Gordon, you are describing your new horse."

He laughed and dodged the slap of her hand. "Wait until you see my filly, Lije." There was pride in his voice. "She is lightning fast. I hope to have her ready to race by fall. She'll clean up at the tracks. She's going to be the fastest thing in the Nation—maybe the whole territory. I rode her today. After dinner I'll show her to you."

"I'd like to have a look at her."

"Horse racing," Eliza said in reproval. "That is not a very sound occupation, Alex."

"But a fun one, Granny El."

"You are hopeless." But there was affection in her tone.

Unlike Eliza, Lije recognized the attraction the sport would hold for Alex. Horse racing required speed, daring, and luck. The inherent thrill and danger of it would appeal to the reckless side of his cousin's nature. The higher the stakes, the better.

"You don't really want me to be any other way, now do you, Granny El?" Alex replied with confidence and charm.

"I wouldn't go that far," she began, then paused, catching muffled sounds in the grand foyer. "Is that Will's voice? I didn't hear the carriage arrive." Removing her hand from Reverend Cole's arm, she turned toward the archway.

From the hall came the rapid patter of running feet. An instant later Lije's eight-year-old sister, Sorrel, burst into the parlor. Again, Eliza experienced that momentary shock when she saw the fiery red color of the girl's hair. In her mind flashed the portrait of the first William Alexander Gordon that had hung above the mantel at Gordon Glen back in Georgia. His hair had been that color, too.

"We're here, Granny El. Alex!" Sorrel cried in delight and darted straight to her cousin. "I didn't know you were here, too."

"Surely you didn't think I would miss the chance to see my beautiful little Sorrel," he chided and playfully tugged at one of her corkscrew curls.

"If I had known you were here, I would have ordered Pompey to go faster. It's a long way from the riverboat landing to Oak Hill in the carriage. I asked Lije to ride with me, but he wouldn't." She threw Lije a pouty look, her eyes dark with hurt and resentment. "And I asked nicely, too."

"That was mean of your brother." His own glance at Lije was filled with amusement.

"You would have ridden with me if I asked, wouldn't you?"

"I would never turn down an invitation to spend time with such a beautiful young lady as yourself."

"I knew that." She beamed.

"Is that a new dress you're wearing?" he asked.

"Yes. Do you like it?" She twirled around and the scalloped hem of the tartan tiers lifted to reveal the lace edges of her petticoats.

"I certainly do. Why, in that dress, you are the prettiest girl in the Nation," Alex told her as Lije's mother walked in, her lavishly flounced gown of sapphire blue rustling softly about her.

"I wish you wouldn't fill her head with compliments, Alex. She is already too conceited for her age." But the look Temple gave her daughter was warm with a parent's love.

At forty-six Temple Stuart possessed a wonderfully mature beauty. Perhaps her waist was not as waspishly small as it had been in her youth, but she was still slender and her skin still smooth except for the attractive smile lines that drew attention to the incredible darkness of her bright eyes.

Her husband, The Blade Stuart, stood beside her, his expression guarded as he eyed Kipp across the room. There was a hardness about him now that gave a cynical twist to a smile that had formerly been gently mocking. A subtle frosting of silver laced the blackness of his hair, hardly noticeable at all unless the light was right—as it was now.

Lije's grandfather Will Gordon joined him in the doorway. He was still tall, although the weight of sixty-odd years

had begun to round his wide shoulders. The red in his hair
had been replaced by gray, but it suited him.

After a slight pause, Temple walked over to greet her
brother. "You are looking well, Kipp."

Kipp barely acknowledged her words, his gaze never leaving The Blade for an instant. Lije was stunned by the malevolence in his uncle's eyes. After four years away, he had
forgotten how virulent Kipp's hatred for The Blade was. It
came from him in waves until the room was heavy with it.
Lije caught himself wanting to move to his father's side, to
protect him from Kipp as he had done from the time he was
old enough to recognize the hostility Kipp bore him.

Before Lije could take a step, his grandfather walked casually between the two men. "Ah, lemonade." Will Gordon
lifted a glass from the tray Shadrach carried. "Just what we
need after our dusty ride. Your glass is nearly empty, Kipp.
Would you like another?"

Kipp shook his head. "This will do me."

The Blade took a glass from the tray and crossed to the
opposite side of the room. The others began talking, seemingly unaware of the tension in the room. But Lije noticed it,
just as he noticed that the two men never turned their backs
on each other.

"I had forgotten how it is between my father and Kipp."

Dinner was over, and all but Eliza, Temple, and Reverend
Cole had gone to the stables to admire Alex's black filly. Sorrel had taken one look at the sleek, long-legged horse and
wheedled until Alex gave in, hoisted her onto the saddle in
front of him, and held her snugly in place. While he took her
on a short canter around the grounds, the others strolled back
toward the house.

Will Gordon, Kipp, and The Blade walked together, with
Will Gordon firmly positioned between the two men. Lije
lagged behind to walk with Susannah, keeping both men in

view, unable to shake the old feeling that he needed to stay close to his father. With the heat of the lazy summer afternoon upon them, no one hurried. High on the branch of an oak, a mockingbird trilled its repertoire of songs.

Susannah initially made no reply to Lije's remark, then said, "If it weren't for my father, I doubt either of them would willingly breathe the same air, let alone eat at the same table."

"True." Lije nodded, aware that it was only the high regard both men had for his grandfather Will Gordon that brought them together. And Will Gordon was determined to have the wrongs of the past put aside and his family united once more.

"Actually, it's gotten better," Susannah remarked. "Remember the first time we all gathered under the same roof? It was Christmas five years ago."

"They circled each other like two snarling dogs with their hackles raised," Lije recalled.

"Remember when we sat down to dinner and Reverend Cole offered the blessing?"

Lije finished the thought. "And reminded us all of the admonition from Jesus to 'Love thine enemies.' "

"I thought Kipp was going to bolt from the table."

"Or come over the top of it."

A sigh came from Susannah, soft with sadness. "Mother says that Kipp is still convinced your father is waiting for a chance to avenge Shawano's death."

"Kipp wants him to try. He's looking for an excuse to kill him. In his eyes, my father will always be a traitor who deserves to die."

"Kipp is my brother, and I'll always love him." In truth, he was Susannah's half brother, but that was a distinction she never made. "But he is all twisted with hate. I feel sorry for Alex." She paused. A rueful smile touched the corners of her mouth. "What a gloomy pair we are. This is a beautiful day; you're home at last—we should be enjoying our time."

"I suppose we should."

"What are your plans now? Are you going to open a law office in Tahlequah?"

"I doubt it." Lije studied the dappled pattern of sunlight on the ground beneath the oaks. "The thought of sitting at a desk surrounded by books and papers is not one that appeals to me. I've had enough of that for a while."

"You could always work with your father in one of his ventures."

"I could." Lije nodded. The Blade's holdings were extensive and wide-ranging. In addition to the family plantation, he owned two buildings in Tahlequah, three riverboats, and a small fleet of keelboats. He also ran a herd of cattle on the Outlet and operated a sawmill. "I've considered asking Grandfather to use his connections and influence to have me appointed to the Light Horse."

"Lije Stuart, peace officer," she said as if imagining him in the role. "You would be good at it. You have the skills and the training in law, and you're a just and fair man. Yes, the job would definitely suit you."

"Maybe. But I think both my parents and yours would prefer that I take up lawyering—become a 'gentleman of the green bag,'" he said, deliberately using the quaintly old-fashioned term. "Fortunately, it isn't a decision I have to make right away."

Ahead of them, the trio of Kipp, Will Gordon, and The Blade strolled past the rose arbor on the plantation's back lawn. Red blooms covered the trellised vines, scenting the air with their fragrance and creating a tunnel of scarlet glory.

"Look at the roses. They're at their peak now," Susannah murmured. "Imagine how beautiful they must be at Chief Ross's home at Park Hill. The entire mile-and-a-half-long driveway is bordered with roses."

Drawn by the brilliant cascade of flowers, Susannah paused by the arbor for a closer look. A big yellow-and-black bumblebee crawled across the center of one of the blooms, its legs and wings dusted with golden pollen. Susannah touched a finger to the velvety petal on a different rose.

Lije stood back and watched as she bent her head to breathe in its perfume. A shaft of sunlight pierced the canopy of oak leaves and brushed the curly tips of her brown hair with its gold. Against the backdrop of sunlight and roses, she made a striking picture in her fawn-colored gown, tall and slender, graced with a natural pride.

More than that, she possessed a compelling honesty, a straightforwardness in both her feelings and her manner—a rare quality in a woman. She would never be a beguiling beauty, the kind whose provocative looks had a man believing more than what was said. Susannah knew nothing of a woman's tricks. Flirtatious glances and tantalizing smiles were alien to her nature.

"The garden always reminds me of Diane. We walked in it so often as children," Susannah remarked casually, though she watched closely for any reaction Lije might make.

He stiffened. Susannah studied him with sudden, sharp interest. "What is it, Lije? What happened between you and Diane?"

"Nothing."

She shook her head, refusing his answer. "Something did. Last I heard from her you two had grown closer than ever. Now, every time I mention her name, your eyes turn so bright it's chilling."

"You're imagining things."

When he would have moved away, she stepped into his path. "Don't pretend ignorance with me, Lije Stuart. I know you too well." He silently cursed her for that. "You and Diane spent a great deal of time together while you were back East."

"Perhaps we did. But the fact remains that I am here, and she is back East."

"But why? That's what I want to know."

"She's there because it's where she wants to be."

Susannah shook her head at his deliberately vague answer. "It's obvious you had a quarrel. Over what? Was it her mother?"

"Whatever was between Diane and me is over. I don't want to discuss it anymore, Susannah," he stated in a hard, flat voice. "It's time we went inside. The others will be wondering where we are."

Susannah hesitated, then chose not to pursue the subject. It was obvious Lije wasn't going to confide in her, which meant that if she wanted to get the whole story, she would have to learn it from Diane when she went East.

Together Lije and Susannah moved toward the house, neither speaking, neither noticing the pair coming through the trees behind them, and neither hearing the young voice that called out.

"Wait, Lije! Wait for us!" Sorrel shouted and broke into a run. "Wait!" But he didn't look back, and Sorrel knew she wouldn't catch up with him before he reached the house. Crestfallen, she stopped, then glanced back as Alex strolled up. "I guess he didn't hear me."

"I guess not."

"We didn't go for a very long ride. He could have waited so we could all come back to the house together."

"It doesn't look like he wanted to wait."

"I know," Sorrel nodded, the hurt setting in.

"Don't look so sad, my little Sorrel." Alex smiled at Sorrel, a calculating gleam in his eyes. "Even if your brother doesn't wait for you, you know I always will."

She looked up, all smiles again.

3

Lije waited until he was home a week before he informed his parents he intended to seek an appointment to the Cherokee Light Horse. He chose a time when the family had gathered for breakfast. Their reaction was one he had anticipated.

"The Light Horse." His mother's fork clattered onto her plate. "You can't possibly be serious about this?"

"I am." Lije calmly cut into his omelet, releasing an aromatic steam to mingle with the scents of bacon and coffee.

"But I thought—" Her glance flew to his father, seated at the head of the table, his eyes narrowed in a sharp study of Lije. "Your father and I both thought that if you chose to go on your own, you would open a law office."

"I have arranged for space to be available in one of the buildings I own in Tahlequah," The Blade informed him. "It's centrally located and more than adequate for your needs."

Lije shook his head. "I've spent most of the last four years inside walls, surrounded by books and papers and people. For now, I want something that makes some physical demands on me and offers less confinement."

"If that's your only criterion, then take charge of Grand View," Temple argued. "Heaven knows, there's more than enough work here on the plantation to keep you occupied, and it would relieve your father of some of his responsibility."

"Your overseer, Asa Danvers, is more than competent to handle the farm's day-to-day operations. I would be doing little but overseeing the overseer."

"Then take over the sawmill—or the cattle operation in the Outlet," she said, her impatience with him slowly turning to a desperate anger.

"Of what use would my education be if I did that?"

"What about the riverboats? Why—" she began, then realized his argument also applied to them and abandoned that alternative.

His father finally spoke. "You have given this a good deal of thought, haven't you?" The observation earned him a fiery look from Temple.

"Are you saying that you approve of his choice? How can you?" she stormed. "What future is there for him in the Light Horse?"

"I never said I planned to make it my life's work," Lije pointed out.

"Then why do it at all?"

"Because I have the necessary skills and knowledge to do it, and do it well."

"But why would you want to do it at all? Why would you want to spend your time tracking whiskey peddlers, thieves, and murderers; stopping brawls; or dealing with drunkards?"

"Is it better to ignore the fact that such elements exist in our Nation?"

"No, but why do you have to be the one to confront it?" She stood up and threw her napkin on the table, giving full rein to her temper. It was the first time, in Lije's memory, that she had ever unleashed it on him. The dubious honor was one she usually reserved for his father. Sorrel sat silent, all eyes and ears as she watched the back-and-forth wrangling. "Why can't you leave it to others?"

"Why?" Lije challenged, his voice growing quieter, firmer.

"Because it's unpleasant, I should leave the job for someone else to do—isn't that what you really mean? That may be the popular attitude, but that doesn't make it the right one."

She deliberately remained deaf to his reasoning. "The Light Horse doesn't have the best reputation. Some of the men are little more than vigilantes who use their authority to mete out punishment as a weapon to be used against their enemies and their enemies' accomplices."

"That's all the more reason to join and make sure that a few don't corrupt the whole system and that there is justice for everyone."

"How very noble," she said with scorn, "and how very naive. Corruption will always exist. It can never be stamped out entirely."

"That doesn't mean it shouldn't be fought wherever it is found."

"He has you stopped, Temple," The Blade said softly, the smallest suggestion of a smile edging his mouth. "Admit it."

She swung to face him, her hands clenched at her side. "How can you side with him?"

"Because his reasoning is sound."

"Sound?" The word was a strangled cry of outrage. "Am I now to fear for his safety, too?"

Without waiting for an answer, she swept from the room with her chin held high. But Lije saw the hot glitter of tears in her eyes as her parting question echoed through his mind. Rising to his feet, he swore under his breath, at last understanding the real reason she was against his decision.

"I should have remembered," Lije muttered and rubbed the back of his neck. "I never realized—"

"Nor did I." The Blade stood up and let the full weight of his gaze come to rest on Lije. "Are you still set on this course?"

Lije hesitated, then nodded. "I am." He sighed and lowered his hand. "I'd better go speak to her."

"No." The Blade motioned for him to stay. "Let me talk to her. After all, it began with me." But there was more sadness than humor in the smile he sent Lije.

Lije watched him leave, then turned back to the table and encountered Sorrel's gaze, dark with accusation. "Mama had tears in her eyes when she left."

"I know." He sat down in his chair and retrieved his fallen napkin. The omelet on his plate now looked cold and singularly unappetizing. He laid the napkin across his lap and picked up his fork.

"Why did you make her cry?" Sorrel demanded.

"I didn't mean to."

"You aren't nice at all." She scrambled out of her chair and faced him, her chin quivering and her eyes stormy. "I wish you had never come back. I wish Alex was my brother, not you!"

She ran from the room. Lije sat for a long moment, then pushed his plate away and turned sideways in his chair, hooking an arm over the back of it and sighing in regret. Regret for the hurt he had caused his mother and little sister. But Lije knew the hurt would be even greater if the feud erupted again. And if it did, he was determined to be in a position to know about it almost immediately—and to act on it, within the law. He would not stand by helplessly a second time. That was his primary motive for joining the Light Horse, one he knew he could never share with his parents.

The Blade found Temple in the parlor, pacing back and forth, pushed by the rawness of her anger and pain. She wheeled around and glared at him.

"Men." She snatched a pillow from the sofa and crushed it in both hands, her fingers curling into its plumpness. "None of you care anything about the distress you cause others."

"You know better than that."

Abruptly, she turned and crossed to the ornately carved walnut-framed fireplace. She stood before it, her gaze fixed on the intricate design of its brass fire screen.

"Of all the choices he had, why did Lije have to pick this one?"

"Because he believes it's the best one for him." The Blade walked over to her.

"It isn't fair," she said stiffly.

"I know." He smoothed his hands over her rigid shoulders and onto her arms. She tensed at his touch, then relaxed, muscles sagging as a lost and lonely sigh rushed from her.

"Every time I think back to those days in our homeland when you first advocated a treaty of removal, I remember the menace I felt when those men surrounded our house—the times your life was threatened, the times you were ambushed, wounded." Her voice was tight, on the edge of breaking. "And later, when we settled here—when Shawano and the others were assassinated and you went into hiding, I remember what it was like." Pausing, Temple turned to face him. Her eyes were dry, but it made the starkness of their pain all the more tearing. "The fear I felt every time a rider approached, certain he was bringing word you were wounded or dead. For so many, many years, I was afraid every time you left the house. Even now, my heart freezes a little when you are away and a rider comes. Moments ago, our son announced he wanted to join the Light Horse and apprehend criminals, people who may be desperate, violent men."

"I know, Temple." Reaching up, he stroked his fingers over her cheek in a tender caress.

"Do you?" She captured his hand and pressed her cheek against it. "The only thing worse than losing you would be losing our son. I don't think I could stand it."

"There would be no greater pain than that," The Blade agreed, "but I know how strong you are, Temple. You would endure it because you must. As we all must."

She drew back, her look determined once more. "But you could speak to him, persuade him—"

"I won't even try to change his mind. Lije must follow his own path. How can you expect him to choose the safe and easy way when he is our son?"

"I don't want Lije to have the life we had. I want something better for him."

"That isn't ours to choose."

"Why must you always be so reasonable?" She spun away and folded her arms tightly in front of her. He chuckled, and Temple grew testy again. "I'm glad you find me so amusing."

"I was remembering the way Lije stood up to the fire of your temper, never once flinching. I think he will have no difficulty confronting a desperate and violent criminal."

"I see no humor in that."

The Blade grew sober once more. "I expect Lije will be riding to Oak Hill shortly to ask for your father's assistance in getting appointed to the Light Horse. He knows you're upset, and he knows why you are, but he will go just the same. You may not be able to give him your approval, but don't let him leave with only the memory of harsh words between you. You will regret it, and so will he."

Wisely, The Blade didn't press the issue and turned to leave. Lije stood in the doorway. The Blade glanced briefly at Temple, then walked away, nodding to Lije as he passed him. Thinking she was alone, Temple turned and saw him.

"I sent word to the stables for Ike to saddle my horse," Lije said.

Her head came up, her chin pushed forward at a combative angle. Then she lowered it, resignation flickering over her expression. "I wish I could change your mind about this, but you are too much like your father."

"Good." Lije smiled. "That means I am forgiven."

"You sound very confident," she said, softening a little in spite of herself.

"I am."

"I have no choice." She studied him from across the room. "A long time ago I learned that Stuart men will not be controlled."

"You wouldn't want us any other way."

"Perhaps not. But you are my son, Lije. You can't expect me to be in favor of your choice."

"I understand that." There was a hint of regret in his eyes. "I'll give Grandfather your regards." He turned and walked from the room.

The sound of his retreating footsteps seemed loud in the silence. Temple heard the front door open, then close. She wanted to call him back, but her son wasn't a little boy anymore who would do what his mother said. He was a man.

As hard as it had been to remain neutral in the feud that had once so severely divided her family, she wondered where she would find the strength to accept this new development that affected her so personally.

By the middle of July Lije was appointed to the Light Horse patrol in his local district and given the rank of lieutenant and the command of four men. He spent most of his first month learning procedures, refamiliarizing himself with the area, and handling petty offenses.

Three days before his grandparents and Susannah were scheduled to leave on their trip back East, a full-blooded Cherokee on the extreme corner of Lije's district caught a man stealing his horses. Shots were exchanged. The owner fell, mortally wounded, and the thief got away.

Lije arrived on the scene, accompanied by one of his men, Sam Blackburn, shortly before the owner died. After doing what he could for the victim, he got a description of the three stolen horses from the man's wife. One was a brown-and-white paint with one glass eye; the second was their good buggy mare, brown with a white snip on its nose;

and the third was a flashy bay gelding with four white stockings and a full blaze on its face. None carried a brand, but one horse had a chipped shoe on its right hind hoof that left a print plain enough for a blind man to read. They set off after the thief, following the trail he left.

They tracked him for two days. On the evening of the second day, Lije spotted the three horses, ground-tied in the middle of an open meadow. It had the smell of a trap.

Cautiously, Lije circled one side of the meadow while his partner circled the other side. Halfway around, Lije found the tracks of the man's horse where he had exited the meadow. He followed the trail until he was satisfied the thief hadn't doubled back, then returned to the meadow for the stolen horses.

A note was tucked under the paint's halter. It read:

"Hear's them horses I stoled. I never ment to shoot nobody. It were self-defence. When he blasted at me with that shotgun and peppered my hat full a holes, it got me riled up. Never shot a man in anger afore. Never figure to do it agin. Hope he din't die."

"Look at this." Lije shook his head in amazement and handed the note to Sam. "The fool signed his name at the bottom. 'D. Russell.' "

Sam shook his head and grinned, giving the note back. "I guess he figured if he returned the horses and promised not to shoot anybody else, we'd quit his trail."

"He figured wrong." Lije scanned the hills ahead of them. "He can't be more than an hour or two ahead of us. Let's push the pace. After two nights of cold camps, I have the feeling he'll build a fire tonight. If we can get close enough before darkness falls, we might see the glow of it."

Two hours later they spotted a pinpoint of light in a patch of trees. They left the horses tied and approached the camp on foot. They found the man's horse hobbled in a grassy area alongside a creek. Its sides were still damp with sweat.

The campfire was a small one, tucked well back among the

trees. Moving with silent care, they crept closer and halted when they reached the deep shadows of the hidden campsite. A man sat close to a small fire, his body hunched forward, his head resting in his hands in a pose of weariness and defeat.

Lije motioned for Sam to cover him, then stepped soundlessly into the circle of light, gun drawn. "Are you Mr. Russell?"

The man's head came up with a jerk. "I am." He scowled at Lije, half-hidden in the shadows. "Who are you?"

"My name is Stuart—with the Cherokee Light Horse."

"God damn you." The man lunged for his rifle.

There was no time to think, only react. Lije fired. The bullet struck the man in the right shoulder, spinning him around. Even as he fell, the thief stretched toward the rifle. But Lije was already moving. Reaching it first, he kicked it beyond the man's reach. The man sagged back to the ground with a grunt of pain. Sam Blackburn came out of the shadows and retrieved the rifle.

Lije kept his revolver pointed at the thief, hammer back. "I thought you weren't going to shoot a man in anger again."

"Hell, it weren't anger." The thief pressed a hand to his bleeding shoulder wound, breathing in deep, panting breaths. "It were pure fear. I knowed you were figuring to take me back and hang me. I ain't never favored the idea of meeting my Maker at the end of no rope."

"You shouldn't have shot a man and stole his horses then." With Sam Blackburn on hand to keep the thief covered, Lije holstered his revolver and went to tend the man's wound.

"Hell, there's a lot a things I shouldn't a done," he declared, then sucked in a sharp breath, grimacing with pain when Lije probed around the wound. "Shoulder's busted, ain't it?" he said through his teeth.

"Could be." Lije nodded. "Looks like the bullet might have ricocheted off the bone and come out the top of your

shoulder. There's an exit wound anyway." Lije set about ban-
daging the man's shoulder.

First light the next morning found the trio on the trail, the
thief tied to his saddle and the stolen horses in tow. Lije
chose a route that took them past the new settlement of Kee-
too-wah, formerly Fort Gibson. If luck rode with him, Lije
thought he might get there before the riverboat departed,
taking his grandparents and Susannah on their journey to
Massachusetts.

By midday the buildings of the old fort were in sight. As
Lije lifted his horse into a canter, the hoarse blast of a steam
whistle came from the landing. It was the "all ashore" signal
that announced the riverboat was beginning its preparations
to get under way. Lije called to Sam to stay with the prisoner
and spurred his horse into a gallop. The big bay leapt forward with a fresh burst of speed.

When he topped the rise where the ground sloped to the
ledge rock, Lije saw that the gangway was still in place. A
short distance to his left, his mother and Sorrel stood by the
family carriage. Lije pushed the bay horse down the slope,
winding his way through the clusters of onlookers.

Deckhands moved to haul in the gangway. He was about
to curse his luck when he caught a glimpse of a woman in a
dark gray traveling suit talking earnestly to one of them.

He reined in short of the gangway, and there was Susannah running to meet him. "You made it." She grabbed the
bay's bridle, holding the horse while Lije swung out of the
saddle.

"You didn't think I would miss the chance to wish my favorite auntie Godspeed on her journey, did you?" he teased,
catching up the reins to his restless horse, excited from its run.

"I am too young to be your aunt." Even as she made her
standard rejoinder, her expression softened. "But I think I
would have regretted it if you hadn't called me that."

"I know." He smiled, then tipped his head to scan the
upper decks. "Where are Grandfather and Eliza?"

"On the second deck." She pointed to them. "You should see the way they've been acting," Susannah declared. "They are like a couple going off on a belated honeymoon. It's really been quite touching."

"They've been looking forward to this trip."

"They have," she agreed, then paused, her hazel eyes softening on him again with pleasure. "No one else thought you would make it today. Temple said you were off tracking down some murderer. But I knew you would be here."

"I almost didn't make it."

"True."

A captain's mate stepped up, claiming Susannah's attention, a look of poorly disguised impatience on his face. "Begging your pardon, miss, but we're ready to shove off now. If you're going with us, I suggest you come on board."

"Of course. Right away." She turned back to Lije with regret. "I have to go now. You better write to me, Lije Stuart."

"I will," he promised.

She hesitated a split second, then asked, "Is there any message you would like me to take to Diane?"

His expression instantly hardened. "Give it up, Susannah. It's over."

But she caught the flicker of pain in his eyes that he wasn't quick enough to conceal. "For your sake, I hope not." In a rare display of affection, Susannah pressed a quick kiss to his cheek and whispered, "Be careful, Lije." Then she gathered up the front of her skirts and hurried up the gangway onto the boat.

Lije watched for a moment, then swung onto the saddle and backed his horse away from the loading ramp. With a last wave to Susannah and his grandparents, he reined the bay around and rode back up the slope to the family carriage.

"You were late," Sorrel declared with a haughty little lift of her chin. "You almost didn't get to see them before they left."

"It was close." Lije dismounted, his spurs making a small clinking sound when he stepped to the ground.

"Are you all right?" Temple ran her gaze over him, a mother's concern in her eyes. Behind her stood his uncle Kipp and his cousin Alex, but there was no sign of his father.

"Yes."

With that worry disposed of, her attention turned critical of the dust and sweat that caked him. "Lije Stuart, you are as ripe as one of our workers after a day in the fields." She raised a scented hankie to her nose to combat the rank odors coming from him.

"Make that nearly three days and you'll be closer to the truth." Belatedly, Lije slapped at the legs of his trousers, raising little puffs of dust. "It's nothing that a bath and clean change of clothes won't cure, which will be the first thing on my agenda when I get home tonight." He glanced beyond them in an idle search. "Didn't Father come with you?"

"He had business in Fort Smith. He plans to meet the boat when it docks there."

"What happened to that horse thief you were after?" Kipp wanted to know, a touch of smug challenge in his question. "Did he get away?"

"No. We caught him last night." Catching the clatter of hooves on the hard-packed ground, Lije looked back as Sam Blackburn rode in, leading the prisoner and the stolen horses. He halted close to the carriage, nodded first to Lije and then to the others, but didn't speak. "We're on our way to the district courthouse with him."

Kipp stared at the prisoner. "I heard the man he shot died the next morning."

"He did." When Lije glanced at his uncle, he caught a flash of metal on the man's coat lapel. It was a small lapel pin, fashioned in the shape of two crossed pins. Lije instantly had a nagging feeling that the pin had some significance—that it had been described to him before. He couldn't recall when, or by whom, or what it represented. But there was an identical pin on Alex's lapel.

"What will happen to him?" Sorrel asked, all round-eyed.

"He will be kept under guard until his trial, which will probably be tomorrow or the day after." The Cherokee Constitution guaranteed that every citizen of the Nation would receive a speedy and fair trial.

"Will they hang him?" she asked in a near whisper, showing a child's mixture of morbid curiosity and apprehension.

Lije hesitated, searching for a way to spare his little sister some of the harsher realities of life. But Alex, feeling no such compunction, interjected, "If he is judged guilty, he will likely be hanged the same day."

"Is that true?" She looked at Lije and unconsciously moved closer to their mother.

"He has to be found guilty of stealing and murder first." But in the Cherokee justice system, sentences were carried out as swiftly as the trials.

The rasping toot of the steam whistle collectively turned their attention away from the prisoner to the riverboat as it maneuvered away from the landing, seeking the river's channel. Arms waved in farewell to its passengers.

With the departure of the paddle wheeler, there was no more reason to linger. Kipp and Alex were the first to say their goodbyes, leaving Lije with his mother and little sister.

"We will see you tonight then?" his mother said after Lije had assisted her into the carriage.

Lije nodded. "Have a bath and a hot meal waiting for me."

"I will."

"Can't you come home with us now?" Sorrel protested.

"He has to take the prisoner in," Temple explained for him. She cast one last, smiling glance at Lije, then signaled to their Negro driver to proceed.

The driver flicked his whip over the backs of the team and urged them forward with the reins. Lije stepped back from the carriage's wheels and waited for it to rumble past, then looped his reins over the bay's neck, and climbed into the saddle once more.

"Ready?" Lije said.

Sam Blackburn nodded, but the prisoner simply looked at him, a little pale and glassy-eyed with pain and despair. Lije took the reins to the prisoner's horse, and they set out. Nothing more was said until the settlement was a good mile behind them. "If you met a man wearing an insignia of crossed pins on his coat, what would it tell you, Sam?"

Sam shot him a quick, measuring glance, then looked straight ahead. He took his time answering. "It would tell me the man has joined the Keetoowahs."

"The Keetoowahs?" Lije frowned.

"It's a secret society. Its members are mostly full-bloods, but it is led by the missionary Evan Jones."

"The abolitionist." Lije now recalled hearing that the insignia of crossed pins indicated the wearer belonged to an antislavery group operating within the Nation. At the time he had been troubled that the Northern movement to free the slaves had spread into the Nation. He knew firsthand how zealous some of its believers could be. But that wasn't what troubled him now. "It makes no sense that my uncle Kipp belongs to it. He cares nothing about Negroes. In fact he owns several field-workers himself."

"The members also claim they seek to preserve the old traditions of the Cherokee."

There were many old traditions in the Cherokee culture, but Lije could think of only one that Kipp would seek to keep alive—the Cherokee Blood Law, which called for the death of any Cherokee who signed away tribal lands—as Lije's father had done all those years ago. Alex would naturally go along with his father.

"Hatred is an ugly thing, Sam. It always starts out small, as a little seed of resentment that is held close and fed with bitter thoughts. If it isn't cast out, it puts down roots and begins to grow. And the more years it's nourished, the bigger it grows until a man is blinded by it—until he can see, hear, and feel nothing but his hatred."

Sam grunted an acknowledgment but made no comment. Silence stretched between them before Sam broke it with a seemingly idle remark. "I heard Stand Watie has asked your father to join the local chapter of the Knights of the Golden Circle."

This was another secret organization that was ostensibly proslavery. Stand Watie was the brother of the late Elias Boudinot, a signer of the so-called Phantom Treaty, just as Lije's father had been. And just as Shawano Stuart had died at assassins' hands, so had Elias Boudinot.

Lije felt this news travel through him like a chill down his spine. Like the American states, the Cherokee Nation was slowly beginning to separate into opposing camps with slavery as their banner. But they were banding together along old lines, ones that had divided Major Ridge and his supporters of the Phantom Treaty from those loyal to principal chief John Ross, who had fought against the treaty right up to the moment of removal, that eventful day the Cherokees were forced to move westward.

A black cloud darkened the sky. In the distance thunder rumbled. A storm was coming. Lije saw it clearly.

∽ 4 ∾

Springfield, Massachusetts
The first week of September 1860

The maple trees on the Wickham estate still wore their summer green colors, but there was a slight nip in the air that warned of autumn's approach. As the carriage swung onto the long drive that led to the brick manor house, Susannah sat forward in eager anticipation of greeting her friend Diane Parmelee once again.

She and Diane had known one another for as long as Susannah could remember. As a child, she had looked on Diane Parmelee as her best friend. She still did, even though they hadn't actually seen each other in five years.

Smiling, Susannah thought back to the girl she had known at Fort Gibson. Beautiful Diane with her honey gold hair, china blue eyes and a face that could only be described as exquisite was petite and, in short, everything that Susannah was not. Yet she had adored Diane, and the two had seized every opportunity to see each other . . . until that day outside the sutler's store at the fort.

The memory of that incident still sprang vividly into her mind. It stunned her now as it had done so long ago. . . .

* * *

Susannah heard a young girl's laugh, rising like the notes of the musical scale. Glancing up from the marbles game in progress, she saw her nine-year-old friend Diane walking toward the sutler's store, holding her father's hand. Susannah's joy was instant.

From the moment Susannah had learned they were going to Fort Gibson, she had hoped and hoped she would get to see Diane Parmelee. Most times she did. The sutler's store was close to the officers' quarters where Diane lived. If the weather was nice, she could usually find Diane playing outside. Excitedly, Susannah tapped Lije on the shoulder. "Look. Here comes Diane."

"I see her," he said without looking up, the shooter marble resting in the crook of his forefinger, his thumb cocked behind it as he took aim at one of Susannah's marbles.

"How could you? You haven't even looked."

"I saw her when she came around the corner with Captain Parmelee. I always see things before you do." He let the shooter fly. It cracked against her marble, knocking it out of the circle.

"Why didn't you tell me?"

He shrugged. "That was your best green marble. Now it's mine."

Susannah ignored the baiting gleam in his eye. The loss of her favorite marble suddenly didn't seem important, not with Diane approaching. Hurriedly, Susannah straightened from her crouched position and waved to her friend. Diane waved back and said something to her father. He smiled and nodded, releasing her hand to let her run ahead.

As the girl drew closer, Susannah experienced a small twinge of envy. Diane was the perfect picture of little-girl fashion. Her dress was pale violet, trimmed with purple ribbons. The delicate lace of her petticoats peeked from beneath the skirt's hem. Violet and purple ribbons trailed from the straw hat she wore. Her hair was curled in shiny gold ringlets, framing a face that always reminded Susannah of a china doll with its big, blue eyes, thick lashes, pointy chin, and perfectly shaped mouth. She knew she suffered by comparison, her rose pink dress hanging loosely on her scrawny frame, her hair a mass of unruly curls, and her arms and legs all bony and thin. As always, when confronted by Diane's undeniable perfection, Susannah lifted her chin a little higher.

"Susannah, I didn't know you were here today." The joy in Diane's expression gave Susannah a feeling of importance and worth. "Have you been here long?"

"Not long," Susannah assured her, then discovered Lije was now standing beside her.

Diane gave him a sidelong look through her lashes, a small smile of pleasure touching the corners of her mouth. "Aren't you going to speak to me, Lije?"

"How are you?" he said, his expression guarded, his eyes intent in their study of her.

"Very well, thank you." She rewarded him with a big smile. "If I had known you were going to be here, I would have come to the store with Mama. Did you go by our quarters to see if I was there? Papa and I went for a walk." She swung her smile to the captain as he joined them.

"Susannah, Lije, it's good to see you." Captain Parmelee acknowledged their presence with a nod.

Susannah unconsciously stood straighter, mimicking his erect posture.

"How do you do, Captain Parmelee?" Her words were formal, but her smile was easy.

She had known Captain Parmelee all her life. He had known her since the Gordons lived in Georgia. Over the years she had heard endless stories about him. Her favorite was the time in Washington, D.C., when he first met her half sister Temple and taught her the waltz. It had painted a vivid picture in her mind, one that had taken on a romantic overtone after Susannah overheard her mother, Eliza, remark that she suspected Captain Parmelee was still half in love with Temple, even though he was married to someone else.

"What are you children doing?" Captain Parmelee asked.

"Playing marbles," Susannah said to draw attention away from the sudden tightening of Lije's jaw. She knew he didn't like being called a child. He thought twelve was too old to be called that.

"Who's winning?" Diane glanced down at the game in progress. "Lije is. He always wins."

"He's older," Captain Parmelee offered in consolation, then turned his gaze on Lije. "Is your mother here?"

Lije nodded. "She and Eliza are in the store."

"I see." He half-turned, his attention drawn to the store's entrance.

"Do you play marbles?" Susannah asked Diane.

"Not very well," she admitted with regret.

"I could show you," Lije volunteered.

"Would you like to play with us?"

Diane turned eagerly to her father. "Please, may I, Papa?"

"How can I refuse when you look at me with those big, beautiful eyes?" he teased, and Diane giggled. "You stay here and play with Lije and Susannah while I go inside and see if your mother has finished her shopping."

"I hope she hasn't. But if she has, maybe you can find something else for her to look at," Diane suggested impishly.

The captain laughed and shook his head in mock dismay, smiling ruefully. "I'll see what I can do."

"Thank you, Papa. Thank you ever so much," she declared, all aglow with her success.

"Be careful not to get that pretty dress dirty, or your mother will have my hide."

"I'll be careful, Papa," Diane promised.

"You children have fun." He moved off toward the sutler's store, his stride lengthening.

Susannah took his previous admonition seriously. "If you

tuck the back of your skirt behind your knees when you crouch down, your dress won't touch the dirt," she said and proceeded to show Diane the proper way.

Diane copied her actions and carefully arranged the front of her skirt over her knees. Soon all three were crouched around the collection of marbles on the ground.

"Do you know the rules?" Lije asked.

"Some of them." Diane nodded. To Susannah's surprise, Lije showed no exasperation with Diane's lack of knowledge of the game. Patiently, he explained everything. "The object is to knock the other person's marbles out of the circle."

"But I don't have any marbles."

"You can have some of mine," Lije volunteered.

"May I have that blue one? It's ever so pretty." Diane pointed to one that Susannah knew was Lije's best marble.

"Sure," he said without hesitation.

Susannah stared at him in amazement, then realized he was certain to win it back. Taking his lead, she gave some of her own marbles to Diane. Once the marbles were evenly divided, Lije demonstrated the use of the shooter marble. Diane watched in dismay as he pocketed a red marble of Susannah's that he had successfully knocked out of the dirt circle.

"You get to keep the marble you hit out of the circle? But that means I could lose my blue one. You are so much better at playing this game than I am. I won't have a chance."

"I'll use my left hand to shoot the marble instead of my right. I'm not as good with that hand."

"That would be the fair way," Susannah agreed.

Lije proved to be adept with his left hand, but not nearly as accurate. He missed with his next shot. Susannah took her turn, but out of courtesy to Diane, she didn't aim at the blue marble. She scored twice and missed.

"You can try now," she said to Diane.

Diane held the shooter marble in almost the correct position. But there was no snap to her thumb, and the shooter more or less rolled off her finger.

"That was a practice shot," Lije said quickly. "Since you're just learning, you can try it a couple more times before it counts—only make sure you flick your thumb, like this." Again he demonstrated the technique. Again Diane tried to emulate it without success. She retrieved the marble and tried again; the result was no better. "Here, let me show you."

Lije came around the circle. Taking her hand, he molded her fingers and thumb in the right position, then had her try it without the shooter. Finally, he had her use the marble again. This attempt was slightly better.

"Let's try it again," he said. "This time you hold the marble, and I'll shoot it. I want you to feel the way my thumb rakes across your finger."

He shifted closer, angling his body to curve against her right side, his left hand resting on her shoulder, one knee on the ground for balance. Again he took Diane's hand and cupped it in his, molding it in the proper position.

As soon as the shooter was in place, Lije leaned down until their faces were nearly cheek to cheek. "We'll aim for that yellow marble."

Something—some sound, some vibration of the ground, some movement in the outer range of her vision—penetrated Susannah's absorption in the pair. She looked up and instantly froze at the sight of Captain Parmelee's wife bearing down on them, a look of pure hatred on her face.

"Cecilia!" The shout came from Captain Parmelee. Susannah had a brief glimpse of him outside the sutler's store, his arms laden with wrapped parcels, his expression one of shock and consternation. Then his wife was on them.

"You filthy, horrible creature. What are you doing touching my daughter," she screamed, her hands grabbing Lije like talons, ripping him away from a startled Diane and flinging him to the ground. She instantly seized Diane and pulled her upright, dragging her close as she turned a murderous glare on Lije. "Don't you ever put your dirty hands on her again."

She shook with rage. "Do you hear me? Don't you ever come near her again!"

"But, Mama," Diane protested, near to tears, "Lije and Susannah are my friends. We were play—"

"Shut up!" She gave Diane a hard shake that frightened her into silence. "They are nothing but dirty little Indians. You are never to play with them again. Not ever!"

"Cecilia." Jed Parmelee arrived on the scene. "For God's sake, what are you doing? That's Temple's son and—"

"Do you think I don't know who it is?" She spat the question. "Do you think I don't know he's the offspring of that vile, loathsome bitch-dog? I will not have that dirty Indian trash putting his hands on my daughter again. Do you hear? I will not have it!"

She stalked off, dragging Diane with her.

In her mind Susannah could still see the tears running down Diane's cheeks and the look of sorrow and dismay on her face. She remembered how heartbroken she had been after the incident, certain she would never see her dearest friend again. But less than a month later, Diane and her father had ridden up to Oak Hill, Diane on her palomino pony and Captain Parmelee on a cavalry mount.

Jed Parmelee had made the visit seem a casual thing, claiming that he and Diane had been out for an afternoon ride and decided to pay a call on the Gordons. Since the day was mild, refreshments were served outside near the rose arbor. Everyone had acted as though the incident had never occurred, except Susannah; she had hung back, unsure of her welcome.

Finally, Diane had approached her and politely asked to be shown the roses. When they reached the arbor, Diane had squared around to face Susannah, her expression drawn in serious but earnest lines.

"I promised my mother that I would never play with you or Lije again," Diane informed her. "From now on when we see each other, we may talk or go for walks or sing songs, but we must never ever play together."

Susannah frowned in confusion. "But isn't that the same thing as playing?"

"No. My father says that sometimes it's best to make a strict interpretation of orders. And playing means games like marbles and dolls and jump rope and hide-and-seek. My father says it would be terribly impolite not to talk to you. And my mother wouldn't want me to be impolite," Diane insisted, her mouth curving in a conspiratorial smile.

"Then, we can still be friends?" Susannah asked, half afraid to believe it.

"Of course." Diane smiled. "My mother only said we couldn't play together. She never said we couldn't be friends."

Looking back, Susannah could see it was that fine distinction Diane had drawn, with her father's help, that had enabled their friendship to endure. She was grateful it had been made.

The carriage rolled to a stop with a slight lurch in front of the Wickham mansion. The driver came around to help her out. Susannah thanked him and walked up to the front door. She glanced at the bell key and hesitated, gripped by a sudden attack of nerves. It had been five years since she'd last seen Diane. Even though they had corresponded during all that time, it wasn't the same as meeting each other face to face again. People change, and friendships with them. Perhaps theirs had changed, too.

There was only one way to find out. Susannah turned the key and listened to the muffled ring of the summoning bell. A butler in full livery opened the door and surveyed her with a jaundiced eye.

"May I help you, miss?" he inquired with doubt.

"Miss Susannah Gordon to see Miss Parmelee. She's expecting me," Susannah replied on a note of authority.

"She is, indeed." With a faint bow, he opened the door wider. "Please come in, Miss Gordon. I will inform Miss Diane of your arrival."

"There's no need, Billings." Diane's voice came from the second-floor landing. Susannah glanced up as Diane descended the grand staircase in a gliding rush, the skirt of her striped blue-green silk dress flowing behind her. "I saw the carriage drive up and knew it had to be bringing you, Susannah." She reached the foyer's marbled floor and crossed it, her hands reaching out to clasp both of Susannah's in welcome. "It's been years and years since I saw you last. And look at you—how tall and lovely you are."

Susannah laughed, relieved to see that Diane was as warm and generous as she remembered. "Tall is certainly accurate."

"Lovely is, too—although I suspect you are one swan who will always perceive herself as a homely duckling," Diane declared in amused reproof, then turned, instructing the butler, "Billings, take Miss Gordon's cape and bonnet, and ask Mrs. Kincannon to fix us some tea."

"Would you like it served in your quarters—"

"Heavens no." Diane laughed, and it was the same happy, melodic sound that Susannah remembered from her youth. "With all my trunks scattered about my sitting room, there is barely enough space to turn around. We'll have our tea in the parlor."

"Very good, miss." He nodded and took Susannah's cape and bonnet from her, then withdrew.

"The parlor's this way." Diane caught her hand and led her in its direction, just as she had done when they were girls.

Curiosity got the best of Susannah before they reached the room. "What are your trunks doing out? Are you going somewhere?"

"I leave for Boston tomorrow. Mother and Mr. Austin return from their honeymoon trip the end of this week, so I'm going back to make sure everything is in readiness for their arrival." She ushered Susannah into the parlor, a large room with towering walls and a mixture of furniture, high-backed chairs with deep seats and wide arms and squatty soft chairs of velvet with hassocks to match before them. Diane sat down in one of them and motioned Susannah to sit in its twin. "You don't know how glad I am that you came today. I was afraid we might miss each other. So tell me, how are your parents, your sister Temple, and The Blade? Their little girl Sorrel, does she still have that glorious red hair she had as a toddler?"

They chatted for a time about family and mutual acquaintances, catching each other up on the latest news. Not once did Diane give any indication that she was suffering any of the pain Susannah had glimpsed in Lije. She laughed and gossiped with Susannah as if nothing had ever happened. Susannah was almost ready to believe that it might have been one-sided except for the way Diane avoided any reference to Lije.

"So what are you going to do when you go back to Boston?" Susannah asked at last.

"I don't have any real plans, but I imagine my mother will keep me busy while she looks for a suitable husband for me," Diane replied in her typically careless voice. "She thinks it's time I was married."

Taking a chance, Susannah said, "Something tells me that Lije hopes she doesn't succeed."

Diane's smile faded. "I wasn't aware Lije thought about me at all," she said, rising from her chair and crossing to the window.

"He still cares about you, Diane."

Tensing, she swung around, a flare of hope in her eyes. "Did he ask you to tell me that?"

To Susannah's regret, she had to say, "No."

"I should have guessed that." Diane turned away again, her shoulders slumping a little even as her chin came up.

"What happened between you, Diane?"

"I don't want to discuss it."

"That's what Lije said when I asked him. Why? What did you two quarrel about?"

"It doesn't matter."

"It does to me," Susannah insisted. "I care about both of you. You sounded so happy in your letter. I'd like to help if I can. Did your mother come between you?"

There was a long moment of silence before Diane finally replied, "Only indirectly. You see," she began with a rush, turning to argue her case to Susannah, "Senator Frederick had an opening in his Boston office. It was a tremendous opportunity for Lije. I was certain I could persuade Judge Wickham to recommend him. But Lije wouldn't even consider it."

"You wanted Lije to live here in the East." Susannah wanted to make certain she understood Diane correctly.

"Yes. After all, there are so many more opportunities for him here—especially if Judge Wickham chose to champion him. If Lije became a success, Mother couldn't possibly object to him. But Lije rejected the idea out of hand. He was going home, and that was that. He was unreasonable— absolutely and totally unreasonable."

"To be honest, Diane, I can't imagine Lije ever agreeing to live in the East."

"I should have known you would take his side," she accused stiffly.

"It isn't a case of taking sides," Susannah told her. "It's simply that I know Lije, I know what he's been through, what the family has been through. He's strongly protective of his father, Diane. He always has been, and I expect he always will be." She stood up, needing to emphasize her point. "Diane, he was a little boy when he saw his grandfather killed by a group of men in black masks. He adored his grandfather, but there was nothing he could do to help him. He was too young, too small. He had to simply stand there and watch. He's never forgotten that."

"It was a terrible experience, I know, but it happened a long time ago," Diane argued.

"But it still colors his thinking."

"Then he should understand that my family is important to me, too," Diane countered. "My mother has her faults. I don't deny that—but she is still my mother. I care about her."

"And you should," Susannah agreed. "But as much as I wish I could say otherwise, I don't think the day will ever come when your mother will approve of Lije—no matter how successful he might become."

"I don't know why we're discussing any of this," Diane said with impatience, but Susannah noticed Diane didn't disagree with her comment. "Lije has made it clear that he doesn't care anything about my feelings. So why should I care about him?"

"You don't mean that, Diane."

"That's where you're wrong, Susannah," Diane stated, her temper flaring. "I do mean it."

Susannah made another attempt to reason with her, but Diane only grew more adamant. Rather than create a rift in their friendship, Susannah changed the subject.

Privately, she had hoped she would have something positive to write Lije, something to give him hope. But now that she understood the nature of their quarrel, she saw nothing that would remedy the situation. Unable to offer him any encouragement, Susannah decided not to mention her meeting with Diane at all when she wrote him.

❦ 5 ❧

Campsite off the Texas Road
November 15, 1860

Twilight streaked the western sky with swirls of magenta and violet that grayed to purple where the sky spread over the rest of the land. The shadows grew longer and thicker, blackening the ground. A whispering wind carried the chill of approaching winter on its breath as it stirred the few leaves still clinging to the blackjack trees.

High above, the first evening star winked dimly while below, the glow of a small campfire threw its faint light against the darkness that gathered beyond its circle of stones. Wisps of aromatic steam rose from the large tin mug on the fire's edge and scented the air with the smell of coffee boiling.

Lije rescued the mug from its bed of hot embers and set it on a flat stone to steep. Automatically, he retreated from the fire, forsaking its feeble warmth to settle back against his saddle, his heavy coat fastened all the way to his neck, his thick leather gloves covering his hands. The air was so cold he could see his breath.

He tore off a chunk of beef jerky from his saddlebags and slowly chewed it. Silence built around him, broken only by the occasional crackle of the fire or the stomp of his horse. He idly scanned the shadows. This was the time when the ghosts of the night came out, when the rustling wind reminded him of the whisper of silk, when he saw the golden lights of her hair in the campfire's dancing flames, when the heat of the fire caressed his skin like the warmth of her breath. With jaws rigid, he reached inside his coat to once again confront his ghost. He pulled out his latest letter from Susannah and shifted closer to let the firelight play over the words penned in Susannah's precise hand.

Dearest Elijah,

It was with great eagerness I read your letter of October 10, advising me of my parents' safe return. It was most assuring as I did not receive Mother's letter until three days later.

The first snow has already fallen here. As you warned me, winter is an early visitor to the North. I confess, at times, I long for home and our crisp autumn days that often linger 'til December. But I am quite happy—

Lije skipped the next few paragraphs that described her teachers and the new acquaintances she had made, and stopped when he reached the part that began:

I hesitate to write this, but perhaps it is best that you know. At Payton Fletcher's invitation, I spent this past weekend at his home in Springfield. His grandson Frank Austin Fletcher, whom I believe you knew at Harvard, was also in attendance. Business had recently required that Frank spend time in Boston. As Frank was aware of our prior acquaintance with the Parmelees and the time you spent in the company of Diane Parmelee when you were here, he believed I would be interested to know that Diane has become—and I quote his words—"the belle of Boston." According to

*him, her list of admirers grows longer with each pass-
ing day. He claims they crowd about her like "bees
around a jam jar." But it seems she has singled one out.*

*Frank had the "honor"—his words again—of sit-
ting next to Diane at a party. He said she asked after
you and seemed quite piqued to learn you had made
no inquiries after her. Later that same evening, the
guests raised their glasses in a champagne toast to
celebrate the announcement of her engagement to
John Albert Richards. Frank said that Diane's mother
was almost delirious with joy over her choice for a husband. I am told Mr. Richards is considered quite handsome by the ladies, and his family is reported to be
worth millions. Frank was certain you had met Mr.
Richards when you were here.*

Lije abruptly folded the letter and shoved it back inside his
coat pocket. He remembered the man well from Harvard. John
Richards was a rude, insufferable snob. The instant he had
learned that Lije was from the western frontier area and
Cherokee, he regarded him with nothing but contempt. He
was sure Diane's mother would get along splendidly with
her future son-in-law.

In the darkness behind him, the big bay horse trumpeted
a loud breath, catching some suspicious sound or scent in
the night and alerting Lije to it. Lije came to his feet and
stepped into the shadows with catlike swiftness. He moved
with caution, gathering up the rifle propped against his saddle and padding softly back to where his horse was picketed,
his hearing now tuning in the night sounds.

The bay had its head up, its ears pricked forward, its attention fixed on some point in the deepening darkness directly opposite them. Lije slid a hand up the rope to the bay's
halter. Something was out there. He could see it in the horse's
tension and flaring nostrils, opened wide to sift through the
night scents and identify the object.

"Easy now, Jubal," he murmured low. "What do you smell out there, fella?"

Lije knew it could be anything from a skunk or a coyote on the prowl to another rider. A second later he detected the soft footfall of a horse approaching the campsite at a slow walk and felt the bay's chest swell to whicker a greeting. He clamped a hand over its nose to silence the call.

The muffled hoofbeats stopped. Then came the faint creak of saddle leather rubbing together. "Hello the camp," a voice called lazily from the darkness, announcing his presence as common range courtesy required. "I'm coming in."

Lije saw nothing but a wall of shadows. "Come ahead, but come slow."

There was another groan of leather, followed by the slow, but steady, clop of a horse. A black shape came out of the shadows, gradually taking on the form of a horse and rider as it drew closer to the fire. The rider stopped his horse inside the circle of light and rested both hands on the saddle horn. The man's hat was pulled low, the brim throwing a shadow over his eyes. A day's growth of beard darkened his cheeks.

"I've been smelling your coffee for the last half mile," the man said, falling into that slow, Texas way of talking. "I thought I might share your campfire for the night. I'm tired of my horse's company. He never listens to what I say and talks way too much," he said.

The horse shifted, swinging its hindquarters about. The firelight played over the brand on its hip. "Your horse is wearing the Rocking Lazy L brand," Lije said from the shadows.

"He better be." The angle of the man's head changed slightly as he tried to locate Lije's position. "I ride for the Rocking Lazy L down in Texas. The name's Lassiter. Ransom Lassiter."

"What brings you up this way?"

"I bossed a herd of longhorns north earlier this year. I'm on my way back home," he said. "You're asking an awful lot of questions. I'd feel easier about answering them if you'd step out where a man could see. You know who I am. It would be kinda nice to know who you are."

"Fair enough." Lije walked into the firelight, carrying the rifle at his side, the butt hooked under his arm and the barrel aimed at the ground. "The name's Lije Stuart. I'm with the Cherokee Light Horse."

"I guess it comes natural to be suspicious of strangers in your line of work."

"It pays to be cautious." Lije inspected the stranger, taking in the thick film of trail dust on his clothes. The dust, as much as the spurs on his boots, the wide-brimmed hat, leather chaps, and the tally book poking out of his vest pocket, told Lije the man was a Texas drover. But Lije saw nothing about the stranger to put him on his guard. The man was his own age, in his early to mid-twenties, with shaggy brown hair framing lean, strong features. His eyes held a glint of humor in their gray depths, and there was something close to a smile on his lips. "Light and spread your bedroll wherever you like."

"I'm obliged." Ransom Lassiter swung out of the saddle. "If you have any coffee to spare, I'll swap you a tin of peaches for some. Mine got ruined at the last river crossing when a couple a snakes came swimming up and my horse objected to their company."

"Smart horse," Lije observed dryly, a small smile showing. "Toss me your cup and I'll boil you up some coffee."

Ransom Lassiter dug a dented cup out of his saddlebags and lobbed it to him, then set about unsaddling his horse and bedding it down for the night. Moments later he came back to the fire, toting his saddle, gear, and a rifle.

"Did you trail your herd to Kansas City or Westport?" In the last year both towns had been the favored destinations of most herds driven out of Texas.

"We planned on taking them to Kansas City, but we never made it," Rans Lassiter admitted as he lowered his saddle to the ground and dropped his bedroll beside it. "The minute we hit the Kansas border, we were met by a bunch of farmers with shotguns. We didn't have a sick animal in the entire herd, but they refused to let us pass. They claimed they had lost too many cattle to Texas fever and they weren't going to lose any more. So we turned east and walked those long-horns all the way to Saint Louis." He took a tin of peaches from his grub sack and handed it to Lije, then retrieved his mug of boiling coffee from the fire's embers. "I heard Lincoln got elected."

"He did." The elections had been the previous week.

"It begins now." Rans Lassiter sighed and pushed his hat to the back of his head, revealing gray eyes that shined like polished pewter in the fire glow. He sank to the ground and leaned against his saddle, using it for a backrest and stretching his long legs out, his dusty and scarred leather chaps dragging the dirt. "The Southern states will start seceding."

"There's no need." Lije took his knife and proceeded to cut open the peach tin. "The office of the president has neither the power nor the authority to abolish slavery. Even Lincoln has acknowledged that. And Lincoln's party holds a minority in both the House and the Senate. He will be like Tyler, Pierce, and Fillmore before him; anything he tries will be futile. All the Southern states have to do is sit tight."

Lassiter's mouth curved in an amused smile that seemed characteristic of him. "It's clear you don't understand the gentlemen of the South. They promised to secede if Lincoln was elected. It is now a matter of honor. They said they would do it; now they must."

"Wiser and cooler heads might prevail." Lije stabbed a portion of peach and lifted the dripping fruit from the tin.

Lassiter chuckled. "When the choice is between wisdom and honor, honor will always prevail in the South."

"It could be." Lije recalled reading a report that delegates from South Carolina were to meet this week to discuss secession. It had been South Carolina's threat of nullification that

Andrew Jackson had faced during the Cherokee's trouble with Georgia. Back then, Georgia had threatened to join with South Carolina. With two states in rebellion, Jackson had not allowed them to unite. In South Carolina's case, he had ordered warships to the Charleston harbor to assert federal authority over the state, while in Georgia's case, he had appeased the state by refusing to protect the rights of the Cherokee to their lands. But Jackson wasn't the man who occupied the chair of the president now. Perhaps the time for further skillful avoidance of a confrontation had already passed.

"My father believes that no president will take military action if any of the states secede," Lije said. "He feels the president will rely on diplomacy and intermediaries to come up with a solution that will ultimately reconcile the two sides."

"Maybe." Rans blew on his coffee. "Many of the Cherokee own Negroes. Where do your people stand on this?"

"Our principal chief John Ross has said it's none of our affair, that it's for the whites to settle. He advocates neutrality, insisting that the Nation is too far removed from the arena of conflict for it to reach this far west." Lije smiled, remembering something else. "The other day I overheard one of our cooks tell Ike that the war clouds hanging over the North and South were too heavy to tote across the Kansas."

"Who's Ike?"

"One of our Negro servants. We were boys together." His smile faded as Lije recalled his conversation with Ike his first day back and the longing in Ike's voice when the subject of freedom had been raised. Until that moment, it had never occurred to Lije that Ike wanted to be free, and it had troubled him ever since that Ike resented being a slave. They had been friends and playmates all their lives. But Lije was no longer certain he could trust Ike. The discovery brought a feeling of loss with it.

"It strikes me the Indian Territory sits in the middle of things. You got Texas to the south and Arkansas to the east.

Both of them are going to side with the South. To the north sits Kansas, and you touch a corner of Missouri. Both of which are mostly Union. I don't see how you can stay neutral when you serve as the perfect supply route—and one side or the other is going to want to control that. You can bet no Texan will want to see a wide open road all the way to its border for some Union army to come marching down. And that's what you've got cutting right through the heart of your land. No, the Indian Nations will have to choose sides, or they'll be caught in the crossfire."

"You talk as if the war has already started." Lije plucked another peach from the tin.

"It's coming."

"Maybe," Lije said between chews. "My grandfather says other nations, such as Switzerland, have maintained a neutral position while wars were waged around them."

"You know"—Rans Lassiter sat forward, crossing his legs and resting his elbows on his knees—"you have talked a lot about what your father believes, what your chief and your grandfather say, but you haven't offered one opinion of your own. I'd like to know what you think."

"I think . . . if there is a war, the Southern states will lose."

Lassiter's head came up, his expression stiffening in offense. "You sound mighty damned definite about that."

"You asked."

"What makes you so certain that will be the outcome?"

"The South has no means to sustain a war. The North can put more men in the field than you, more guns, more cannons, more everything. You will be out-supplied and outnumbered, with Union gunships closing your harbors from resupply."

"Sounds like you spent some time thinking about this."

"I spent the last four years back East in Harvard. When the first rumblings of secession and war began, it was a topic of considerable debate. If you analyze the situation coldly, without passion, there is no chance the South will win."

"Maybe." Rans smiled. "But I think you have forgotten that David felled Goliath with one well-aimed blow. It could be the war won't last long enough for all those other things to come into play."

"I think it will."

Rans tipped his head in disagreement. "A lot of people in the South believe those Yankees don't know how to fight—just one Southern boy could whip ten of them."

"Do you believe that?"

"I seem to recall that those Yankee boys whipped the British twice." Rans glanced sideways at him, a sparkle of humor in his gray eyes. "Of course, they did have some Virginians fighting with them. One of the best was George Washington. The South does know how to grow leaders."

Lije chuckled, liking the Texan. "What do you think, Lassiter?"

For once the Texan was serious. "Like you, I think the Southern states would be up against some long odds. But I am Texan, born and bred. As Texas goes, so will I go." He lifted his head, his glance sober and reflective. "And you, Lije Stuart?"

"The same—as the Cherokee Nation goes, as my family goes, so will I." But Lije knew it would never be that easy for him. There was already one division within the Nation, a splitting along the old lines of feud between the Ross and Ridge parties. Lije raised the tin and drank the liquid in it, but it no longer tasted sweet.

Rans Lassiter drained his mug. "Good coffee," he announced and laid back against his saddle, removing his hat and placing it over his face. Lije did the same. For a long time all was still, with only a few night sounds and the snap of a dying fire. Then Rans spoke, his hat partially muffling the idleness of his words. "I wonder if Texas will still be in the Union by the time I get home."

* * *

It was. But on December 20, 1860, South Carolina seceded. Within forty days, the states of Mississippi, Florida, Alabama, Georgia, and Louisiana followed. The six states met on February 1, 1861, to form their own congress and declared themselves to be the Confederate States of America, choosing Jefferson Davis as their president. Texas joined this new Confederacy of Southern states on March 16, the same day Governor Sam Houston refused to swear an oath to the Confederacy on the grounds that it violated his oath to the United States. He was removed from office.

On April 14, Confederate guns opened fire on the Union garrison at Fort Sumter in Charleston Harbor, South Carolina. Two days later the Union forces at the fort surrendered. On the following day President Lincoln called for seventy-five thousand volunteers to put down the insurrection. Virginia, Arkansas, and Tennessee immediately voted to secede.

War was inevitable.

6

"Will Gordon, what on earth are you doing?" Eliza stared aghast at her husband.

He ignored her and continued to push at the cork, using his thumbs to work it free from the bottle. It released with an explosive pop and rocketed straight to the ceiling. Alex was there with a glass to catch the liquid that foamed out. Shadrach waited with more glasses on a tray.

"Will Gordon, that is champagne." Eliza swept into the room in high dudgeon.

"Indeed, it is." Will gave his grandson Alex a conspiratorial wink and filled a second glass with the bubbly wine.

She stopped short of him, hands on her hips. "You know very well I will not allow intoxicating spirits in this house."

"Today can be an exception," Will replied smoothly and passed a glass of champagne to his son Kipp.

"It is high time there was something stronger in this house than tea and lemonade," Kipp grumbled under his breath, earning a glare from Eliza.

"This is, after all, a special occasion," Will went on.

"I am very aware it is your birthday," Eliza began.

"My sixty-sixth birthday." Will inserted the reminder, his glance warm with affection and playful chiding. "An event sufficiently remarkable to warrant a bending of the rules, I should think. Shall I pour you a glass?" he asked, an impish twinkle in his cinnamon brown eyes.

When she hesitated on the verge of refusal, Alex leapt in. "Come now, Granny El. You take sacramental wine at Communion."

"That is different."

"Even if it is, one glass of champagne will not condemn you to perdition," he reasoned. "Besides, you know you cannot refuse to drink a toast to Grandfather's continued good health."

"Alex Gordon, that is unfair," she protested.

"Of course it is." He grinned.

"Eliza?" Will held an empty glass in one hand and the magnum of champagne in the other.

She sighed in ill-pleased surrender. "A little sip. No more than that." She watched closely as Will poured barely more than a swallow into the glass. She steadfastly ignored his smile when he handed the glass to her.

Kipp raised his glass. "To your health, and to many more years of it."

"Hear, hear." Alex lifted his glass in an echoing salute.

Eliza, alone, was slow in raising hers. "I should have thought you would wait until Temple and The Blade arrived to join in the toasting."

"We will simply drink another toast when they get here," Alex told her and took a healthy sip of champagne.

"Not I," Eliza declared and raised the glass to her mouth. She tipped it, intending only to wet her lips with the celebratory wine. But in her caution, she inhaled the fizz, which immediately ignited something that fell between a sneezing and choking fit. Will came to her aid, slapping her soundly on the back, all the while struggling to contain his laughter. "It was not amusing," she told him when she had recovered.

"Of course not." But, like Kipp and Alex, he was still fighting back a smile. "Next time, though, I suggest you drink the champagne rather than inhale it."

"I prefer to do neither." She set her glass on Shadrach's tray.

"Do you remember that gala dinner we attended at the fort a few years after we arrived here?" Will asked. When Eliza ignored his question, he confided to Kipp, "One of the officers poured almost an entire bottle of whiskey into the punch when no one was looking. Your stepmother thought it was the most unusual punch she had ever tasted—and kept going back to refill her cup."

"I was merely trying to ascertain the ingredients."

Will chuckled. "You should have seen her face when I told her it was laced with whiskey."

Eliza tried to be angry with him for resurrecting that memory, but she found herself laughing as well.

"Did you get a little tipsy, Granny El?" a laughing Alex wanted to know.

"Not in the least," Eliza insisted, struggling to regain her composure.

"But she did feel quite wretched the next morning, as I recall," Will said.

And Eliza found herself laughing again, in spite of herself "That was quite an experience," she admitted, then sighed a little wistfully. "They did have some grand parties at Fort Gibson."

"With the firing on Fort Sumter by the new Confederacy of the South, we may soon wish there were still Union troops at the fort," Kipp remarked.

"Their civil war does not concern us," Will stated crisply.

War. North. South. That was all anyone talked about lately. Eliza remembered too well all the threats of secession by Georgia and the terrible turmoil of that time thirty years ago before the removal of the Cherokee. Back then she had been an avid participant in any political discussion, quick with her opinions and combative in defense of her beliefs. But she no longer found such talk stimulating.

The memory of the detention camps, the long trail, and those first years of bloodshed and struggle before they built Oak Hill into the vast plantation it had become, was much too fresh. She knew the pain and suffering, the deprivation and poverty, the illness and death that could result from war. Whether it was fought with rifle and sword or with lawyers and writs, the devastation to a people was the same. Cowardly or not, she didn't want to hear such talk.

"Did I tell you, Alex, that we received a letter from Susannah this week?" she asked, turning to him. "She asked about you. She is anxious to learn when you will be leaving for Harvard."

"I haven't decided whether to go."

"But you have never been East. The trip will be an adventure for you. I know I shall never forget the experience of my first train ride when we went East with Susannah."

"What difference does it make if I wait another year before going to college? The East will still be there. So will Harvard, if that's where I decide to go." Before Eliza could respond, Alex turned to Will and a new topic. "I raced my filly last week," he told him. "She showed her heels to all of them and won pulling away. She is definitely the fastest thing around. She could make your Firestorm look like an old nag."

"And The Blade's stallion, too," Kipp inserted with a jeering curl of his lip.

Beyond glancing at his father, Alex took little notice of the remark. "Maybe after dinner, we can have a match race. Shooting Star against your Firestorm."

"You seem very confident," Will observed.

"I am."

"What is the wager?"

"Will!" Eliza objected that he would encourage Alex to gamble.

"Now, Granny El, I will make a wager that even you will like." Alex smiled. "If my filly loses, I will go to college at the end of summer."

"And if your filly wins?" Will asked.

Alex hesitated, the grooves in his cheeks deepening as his smile widened. "I have admired that navy revolver of yours ever since you got it last year."

There was a brief raising of eyebrows when Will heard his response. For a moment, he said nothing, then nodded. "Very well. The revolver it is—if your filly wins."

"Men," Eliza declared. "If I live to be a hundred, I doubt I will ever understand your fascination with guns and fast horses." But she knew much of her current objection to the former came from all the talk about civil war in the United States.

Shadrach came to the archway. "Miz Temple and Master Stuart are here, Miz Eliza."

As he stepped aside to admit them, Sorrel ran up. "You forgot me, Shadrach. I am here, too."

"My mistake, Miss Sorrel." Shadrach bowed to her in apology, then faced the room once more, eyes twinkling, smile suppressed. "Miss Sorrel is here as well," he said as Temple and The Blade walked up. The Blade paused, his glance searching out Kipp's whereabouts.

Without waiting for them, Sorrel dashed into the room, straight to her grandfather. "I made you a present, Grandpa." She smiled up at him, every inch the miniature coquette in her party dress of white organdy trimmed with blue rosettes and silk ribbons. "But Mama says I mustn't give it to you until dinner."

"If that is what she says, I have no choice except to wait 'til then, do I?" Will smiled back.

"Do you want to know what it is?"

"Sorrel." Temple hushed her as Will laughed.

"Whatever it is, Sorrel," he said, "I know it will be my favorite present because you made it for me."

"Did you hear that, Mama?" Sorrel turned, proud and excited.

"I heard." She smoothed a hand over Sorrel's flame red locks and absently straightened a blue ribbon twined through them.

"Where is Lije?" Eliza frowned. "Don't tell me he was called away?"

At that moment Lije came through the archway. "I am here, Eliza."

"Good." Will reached for the magnum of champagne. "Now if we can get Shadrach to bring more glasses—" But Shadrach had already anticipated the need and returned with three more on his tray.

"Champagne?" Temple arched a startled look at Eliza.

"Yes, champagne in this house." Eliza shook open her fan and waved it at her face, her expression drawn in disapproving lines. "An exception for this one special occasion, he says. The man is absolutely impossible today. Anyone would think he was turning sixteen instead of sixty-six."

The Blade sent Will a knowing look. "I think Eliza worries that this rush of youthfulness might not last until you retire this evening."

Eliza heard Will's chuckle and saw the smiles the others tried to hide. Heat flooded her face. "Such things should not be said in mixed company." She waved her fan with renewed vigor, trying to cool her cheeks even as the suggestion curled deliciously through her. Will saw it and laughed outright, earning him a sharp, "Behave yourself, Will Gordon."

"If I must," he murmured with a nod of mock acceptance and poured champagne into the glasses. Shadrach passed them around.

"A toast to you, Will." The Blade lifted his glass.

"Where is mine?" Sorrel demanded. "I want some ch-champagne, too."

"Absolutely not," Eliza declared quite emphatically.

"But I have never had it before." Sorrel saw at once that her grandmother was not about to relent and appealed instead to her grandfather.

"May I have some, please, Grandpa? You said it was a special occasion."

He glanced at Eliza and smiled at Sorrel with genuine regret. "I think not."

With a determined set to her chin, she turned away and fixed her attention on Lije, giving him her sweetest, most confident smile. "You will share yours with me, won't you, Lije?"

He smiled faintly and shook his head. "Your grandmother is right, Sorrel. You are too young for champagne. You will have to wait until you are older."

"That isn't fair." She folded her arms, pushing her lips in a mutinous line. "I only wanted to taste it."

"Sorry. Another time."

Before Sorrel could renew her protest, The Blade raised his glass and proposed a toast to Will. Lije echoed the sentiment and took a sip of his champagne. Out of the corner of his eye he caught a slight movement and glanced sideways in time to see Alex motion for Sorrel to come stand by him. When she did, he bent down and whispered something to her. Her expression turned triumphant, then just as quickly changed to something prim and decidedly secretive.

"How is that new riverboat of yours doing?" Will asked The Blade as Alex and Sorrel strolled over to the parlor window.

"She ran full her last trip," The Blade replied. When the pair paused in front of the window, Alex stood slightly behind Sorrel, partially shielding her from the view of the others. "I only rode her as far as Little Rock, but we bested the *Nancy May*'s time by three hours."

Alex passed Sorrel something. Lije couldn't be certain, but he suspected it was his glass of champagne. An instant later, he had a glimpse of it as Sorrel tipped her head back to take a sip. Immediately, she drew back and pushed something at Alex, who laughed softly.

"A time like that will gain you more customers," Will remarked.

"While you were in Little Rock, did you meet with the governor and Boudinot's son?" Kipp challenged. The thinly disguised venom in his voice pulled Lije's attention back to the adults. "Everyone knows they are trying to force our Nation into making an alliance with the new Confederacy."

"I spoke with the governor . . . briefly," The Blade admitted coolly.

Eliza closed her fan with a snap. "Must we discuss such matters today?"

"What matters are you talking about?" Alex came wandering back to the group.

"The ones we are not going to discuss," she said crisply.

Lije obliged her by changing the subject. "I expect you will be leaving for college soon, won't you, Alex?"

"That will be decided this afternoon after dinner," Alex replied, sliding a quick smile at his grandfather.

"Will you sit beside me at dinner, Alex?" Sorrel asked.

"There is no one I'd rather sit beside than you, Sorrel," Alex promised.

More than an hour later, Shadrach entered the kitchen and handed the silver tray with its solid silver coffee service to one of the maids. "They have retired to the drawing room. You and Sally get the dishes cleared from the dining room table."

He waited to make certain they did his bidding, then pulled a kerchief from his pocket and blotted the perspiration from his brow and neck. Taking advantage of these few moments' respite from his duties, he shrugged out of his day coat and hung it on a wall peg. Next to it was another black coat with a top hat and a pair of white gloves on the shelf directly above it, part of his nephew Ike's livery uniform as the Stuarts' driver. Glancing over his shoulder, Shadrach smiled at the young man seated at the kitchen table, taking pride in the way his sister Phoebe's son had grown.

Ike was an intelligent and handsome man. Tall like his grandfather and namesake, he was leaner, without the bulging muscles his grandfather had acquired from working at a blacksmith's forge. Although lighter skinned than Shadrach's father, Ike had the same honed jaw and cheek and long, straight nose that came to a point like an arrowhead, the line of the nostrils flaring back.

Shadrach walked over to the big metal coffeepot and poured a cup. "Where is your father, Ike?" He had expected to find him sitting at the table, eating with his son.

"Outside I guess," Ike sat with both elbows resting on the table, a fork in one hand, a piece of fried bread in the other. "Keeping watch, I imagine. You know how Master Blade is whenever that brother of Miss Temple's around."

But he didn't look up from his plate when he spoke, his answer barely audible. That wasn't like his nephew. Frowning, Shadrach sat down on the long bench opposite Ike. Lifting the cup to his mouth, Shadrach blew on the scalding hot coffee and quietly studied his nephew. From the looks of the plate, Ike hadn't eaten more than three or four mouthfuls.

"Doesn't look like you're very hungry."

Ike shot a quick glance at him, then again lowered his head to stare at the plate, the fork in his hand now idle. "It's too hot outside today, I reckon."

"Or else you have something on your mind. Want to tell me about it?" Calmly, Shadrach took a sip of the coffee and waited, noting Ike's increased tension and vague agitation.

Ike leaned forward, resting all his weight on his forearms and casting an anxious glance at the kitchen staff to see if they were listening. "Haven't you ever wanted to be a free man, Uncle Shad?" His voice vibrated with the effort to keep it low—and the intensity of his feelings.

Shadrach stiffened. He had expected Ike to confide in him about a woman or maybe the new overseer at Grand View, but not this. "You aren't thinking of trying to run away, are you, Ike?"

Resentment and hurt flashed across Ike's face as he tossed the piece of bread and his fork onto the plate, indifferent to the clatter he made. He pushed back and rose to his feet. "I should have known you felt just like them," he muttered and headed for the door.

Stunned by the underlying anger, Shadrach was slow to follow him outside. Ike stood at the far end of the kitchen's sheltering overhang, his hands on his hips, the stance mirroring his frustration as he stared at the milky blue sky.

When Shadrach started toward him, Ike glared. "Go away. Just go away."

Shadrach hesitated, then continued forward. "Your question took me by surprise, Ike."

"Yeah." He expelled a short laughing breath that reeked with bitterness.

"Would you like to hear my answer?"

"Why? I know how much you think of your mistress. I've heard the story a thousand times about Miss Eliza teaching you and my mother, the way she used to leave lessons and books out for you after your own mammy refused to let you go to the school. You feel the same loyalty toward her that my father feels toward Master Blade."

"Loyalty has got nothing to do with being a slave. It's something you give freely because it's been earned—not because you'll feel the lash of a whip otherwise. Slave or free, I would feel the same toward Miss Eliza. And every slave in this world has his dreams of freedom, Ike, and don't you ever think otherwise. But a slave has only got two ways to get his freedom—he can either earn enough money to buy it, or serve his master the best he can and hope that he will be rewarded with his freedom. Running away isn't being free. It's just running, trading one life of fear for another."

Ike lowered his head. "What about this war everybody is talking about, Uncle Shad? Do you think they will really send armies into the South to free all the slaves?"

"That's what everybody says, and I think it might happen."

Ike heard the hesitancy in his uncle's voice as if he, too, was uncertain whether he should believe freedom could come to them. Somewhere nearby a lark sang. Ike gazed at the plantation, the manor house, the orchards, the distant slave cabins, and the fields of tall corn and cotton. He tried to imagine what it would be like to be free. This was the only life he had known. Every morning he had awoken to the sound of the horn blowing, summoning the slaves to work. Every day, he had done what he was told to do. He had never owned anything in his life, not even the clothes on his back.

"If you were free, Uncle Shad, what would you do?" he wondered.

"I would teach." The answer came quick and strong. Surprised, Ike glanced at the slender wisp of a man who was his uncle. There had never been any size to him. And Ike had never thought of him as being strong. His mind was quick—and filled with many stories and much knowledge, but strong? No, Ike had never thought of him that way. Now he saw his uncle's strength—there, in his face as he dreamed. "I would build a schoolhouse and I would teach as many children as the building would hold. I would free them from ignorance because it enslaves."

Ike said nothing. Instead he let his uncle's words ring in the summer air, quietly spoken yet no less fervent. Dreams. There had to be more than dreams.

❧ 7 ❧

Lije stood with the others on the shaded front veranda that served as an impromptu grandstand for the afternoon's match race. The irregular course followed a narrow dirt lane that swung away from the house, curved between two fields, and circled back to the front of it, with the iron ring post serving as the finish line.

"Can you see them yet? Can you see them?" Sorrel bounced up and down with excitement, straining to catch a glimpse of the racers.

"Not yet." Lije scanned the dirt track between the fields. "They should be making the turn at the fields about now. We should see them any minute."

Too impatient to wait, Sorrel dashed off the steps and into the center of the temporary race course. Temple took a step off the veranda. "Sorrel, you come back here this instant."

"I will, Mama. I will." But she continued to peer down the road. Just as Temple started after her, Sorrel turned, all excited. "Here they come! Here they come!" she cried, running back to the veranda.

The sound of drumming hooves reached Lije first; then he saw the two horses racing toward the house, both riders bent low. The sleek black filly was in the lead, stretched out flat and driving effortlessly. On her heels pounded a bright red chestnut. The chestnut surged forward in a burst of speed.

"He's catching her," Will murmured, intent on the racing pair. "He's catching her."

"Come on, Firestorm," Eliza urged, her earlier objections to the race forgotten in the excitement of it. "Come on, boy."

"Run, Shooting Star. Run!" Sorrel shouted in counterpoint.

Off to the side, Alex muttered directions to the jockey. "Stop holding her back. Let her have her head. Let her run."

As the two horses thundered closer, the black filly seemed to flatten out a bit more and shot into the lead. The chestnut tried to answer the challenge but ran out of ground. The duo swept past the finish line with the filly a half-length in front.

In the aftermath of laughter and congratulations that carried the others off the veranda to wait for the racers to canter back, only Lije noticed the one-horse shay coming down the lane. He studied the vehicle, unable to make out its two occupants, but he felt sure he recognized the bald-faced roan pulling it.

Stepping off the veranda, he moved to his father's side just as his ever-alert servant Deu came up. "Someone's coming down the lane, Master Blade."

As his father turned to look, Lije added, "If I'm not mistaken, the horse and shay come from Johnson's Livery."

"I think you are right." The Blade pulled a cigar from his pocket and lit it, but his attention remained on the vehicle. The two blowing racers trotted back to the group, distracting the others.

"Can you see who it is?" Lije asked.

"Not yet."

"I think there are two people," Deu said.

As the horse and shay drew closer, Deu's observation was confirmed. The vehicle's hooded top kept the faces of its occupants in shadow, but it was clear there was a man at the reins, accompanied by a woman in a gown of lavender.

The sharp *clip-clop* of the roan's hooves and low rumble of the shay's wheels soon attracted the notice of the others.

"We have visitors, Eliza," Will remarked.

She turned with a frown. "Who on earth would come calling today?"

Curious, the others gathered around. Instinctively, The Blade glanced over his shoulder to locate Kipp. But he was on the far side of the group, holding the bridle of his son's filly, absently stroking its black muzzle.

When the driver halted the shay in front of the house, one of the grooms dashed forward to hold the roan's bridle. Lije watched as the man climbed out of the vehicle and straightened to stand tall and erect, his golden beard shot with silver. Lije jerked his gaze to the shay's passenger, recognition jolting through him.

"Why, it's Jed Parmelee," Eliza murmured in surprise as Jed came around to the passenger side and extended a helping hand to his female companion. "But who is that with him?"

Lije knew the answer to that even before the gloved hand appeared and the first dainty foot peeked from beneath the hem of her lavender gown. He steeled himself against the sight of her as Diane Parmelee stepped to the ground and raised her lavender-and-lace parasol. She lifted her head, her glance instantly seeking him out. He found himself staring into the bewitching blue eyes that had haunted him since he left Massachusetts. A smile played across her lips, warm and faintly enigmatic. Lije tried to be indifferent to her, but her mere presence reached deep inside, twisting him in knots as it always had. Sheer pride kept him from joining the others when they went to welcome the pair.

"Jed Parmelee, what a wonderful surprise. I almost didn't recognize you without your uniform," Eliza declared, then turned to his daughter. "This surely can't be Diane. Haven't you grown into a lovely young lady? Your father must be very proud of you."

"I hope he is, Mrs. Gordon."

"Eliza. I insist you call me Eliza."

There were more greetings exchanged, but Lije paid little attention to the chatter of voices until his grandfather voiced the question uppermost in his own mind. "What are you doing back in this area, Jed?"

"Visiting old friends," he replied.

"If we are welcome, that is," Diane added, looking straight at Lije.

"What a thing to say," Eliza exclaimed. "You are always welcome at Oak Hill. Surely you know that."

"I wasn't certain. Lije has yet to speak to me." Again Diane held his gaze, her look bold and lightly challenging, yet filled with confidence.

All attention shifted to him. He sensed the knowing speculation in his father's glance and ignored it. Emotions ran raw through him, too many to unravel. He wanted her, he hated her, he loved her, and most of all, he resented her coming here and putting him through this hell again.

"A visitor is never turned away from the door of a *Cherokee*." Lije stressed his heritage, but kept his voice level, his feelings pushed out of it.

Something flickered in her eyes. Irritation, he decided, certain it couldn't have been hurt. In any case it was too quickly veiled by the lowering of her lashes for Lije to identify it. When she raised them again, her eyes were clear of any reaction.

"I will remember that." Something in her voice told him that he had just given her something she could use to her advantage.

"We were about to have refreshments on the side lawn. It's shady there, with a bit of a breeze. You will join us, won't you?" Eliza invited.

"We would be delighted." Jed Parmelee inclined his head in acceptance.

For a fraction of an instant, Lije had the opportunity to make his excuses and leave. But there was cowardice in such an action, a tacit admission that she still had the power to disturb him. Lije would not give her that satisfaction.

When the general exodus began to the side lawn, Lije trailed along. He stayed slightly apart from the others, refusing the tea cakes Shadrach brought around and drinking the minted lemonade without tasting a drop of it. He rarely looked at Diane, but he was conscious of her every movement, her every breath.

She was the center of attention, the warmth of her smile captivating everyone from Sorrel to Will Gordon. Lije hadn't expected it to be any other way.

"Susannah wrote that you were living in Boston with your mother," Temple remarked.

"I was," Diane replied from her seat on the ornamental iron chair, looking utterly flawless and utterly feminine. "But, with all this talk of war and the call to arms, I naturally wanted to see my father again."

"Naturally." Will Gordon nodded his head in approval.

"What a pity Susannah isn't here," Eliza said with regret. "I know she would so like to see you."

"How is Susannah?"

"I had a letter from her only last week," Eliza replied and proceeded to relate, in detail, the current happenings in her daughter's life.

"I miss the walks Susannah and I used to take." Diane rose from the chair with a grace that came as naturally to her as breathing. "You have no idea how many times I've longed to come back—to see this country and all of you. I was born here in the Nation. I grew up here. Yet, sometimes it seems I have been away much longer than six years."

The ring of sincerity in her voice made Lije turn his head and cast a skeptical glance in her direction.

A sense of nostalgia seemed to settle over everyone else, holding them all silent for a moment. "Those were simpler times," Eliza murmured.

"Indeed." Will Gordon echoed the sentiment.

Diane drifted toward Lije, then paused and swung back to face the others. "Would you think me rude if I stole Lije so he could show me some of our childhood haunts?"

"Of course not. You two go right ahead." Eliza waved her hand, sending them on their way.

No one considered that he might object. But Diane had known that all along, Lije realized. She also knew he couldn't refuse her in front of his entire family. He said nothing when she moved to his side and slipped her hand through the crook of his arm. He felt a little jolt at the contact and steeled himself against the disturbance.

"Shall we?" She tipped her head, slanting him that familiar look that both promised and withheld.

His answer was a smooth lift of his hand, indicating that she choose the direction they would take. She turned slightly, drawing him with her. Together they set out in the direction of the rose arbor. Lije made no effort to break the silence between them, letting it build along with his own tension.

"The arbor was always one of my favorite places," she murmured when they reached it. She withdrew her hand from his arm and moved closer to examine a fading rose. "It's a shame so few are in bloom now."

"Why are you here, Diane?" His voice was without emotion, but there was no less demand in it.

She tilted her head to one side and studied the changes a year had wrought in him. The ardent glow was gone from his eyes, leaving them cool and impenetrable. There was a new hardness ridging his jaw, a new harshness in the cut of his cheekbones. For the first time Diane doubted her ability to command the situation, but it only lasted a moment.

"Why?" Diane tipped her head to the side, letting the parasol frame it. "To beg your forgiveness, of course."

He released a short, humorless breath. "I can't imagine you begging for anything."

"I admit my experience is limited."

"What do you want with me? What new game are you playing now?"

"It's no game," she replied, quite seriously, but Lije was beyond hearing it.

"Go home, Diane. Go back to your fiancé and all the rest of your fine friends."

"Then you did learn of my engagement," she said in a pleased voice, turning fully toward him now. "I was very angry with you for a time, Lije. In fact, I accepted John's proposal of marriage purely out of spite. I think I secretly hoped you would come charging back to rescue me when you learned of it. Of course you didn't. So I had no choice but to rescue myself." Her smile widened at the memory of it. "You would have enjoyed seeing Mr. John Albert Richards's face when I told him I would never marry such a rude, arrogant snob as he."

"Is that what really happened?" he challenged. "Or did he reject you?"

A look of hurt flashed across her face. Briefly, she tipped her head down, then threw it back with regained poise. "I have my share of faults, Lije Stuart, but lying has never been one of them."

Silently, he looked at the pride and determination in her expression and felt the weakening of his resolve. He looked away. She had made a fool of him once; she would not do it again.

"You have plenty of other beaux, Diane. Go console yourself with them." He started walking, needing to release some of the coiled energy inside him. She instantly fell in alongside him.

"I am afraid they have all gone off to war," she said with airy unconcern. "So you see, I'm quite alone now."

"That is your problem."

"You are being extremely difficult, Lije Stuart," she declared, impatience in her voice.

He stopped and swung about. "Just how did you expect me to react? Did you think I would rush to your side when you stepped from the carriage?" he said with scorn, then taunted, "Or perhaps you thought I would sweep you into my arms and confess that I still loved you."

"That would have been nice," she said, a teasing twinkle in her eyes.

"This time you are the fool," he stated and watched the light in her eyes dim. He told himself he was glad. "You can't always have what you want, Diane."

"Even when I want you?" she asked softly.

He hardened himself against it. "Tell me, Diane," he challenged, "Does your mother know you're here?"

"She knows." The simple answer didn't begin to describe the vicious words she had exchanged with her mother, the hateful things that had been said and were not soon to be forgotten. But her gaze remained clear and direct as Diane deliberately injected a light note into her voice. "She informed me that if I came, I would never be welcome in her house again, that I was no longer her daughter."

He arched an eyebrow. "Am I supposed to believe that?"

She smiled dryly. "I assure you she was quite sincere." The lazy breeze brought the sound of a woman's laugh to them, and Diane looked back to the cluster of people on the side lawn, easily picking her father out of the group. He was the one with silver-gold hair watching Temple Stuart with thinly disguised adoration. "It was never really you my mother hated, Lije," she said thoughtfully. "You—or for that matter, anyone of Indian descent—are merely a symbol of whom she truly hates, and that is your mother. I think she always knew my father was secretly in love with Temple even before they were married. In her mind, your mother was a rival for his affections. It never seemed to matter to her that your mother saw him only as a friend. She became twisted with jealousy, and that jealousy eventually turned into hatred. I thought when she left my father and married Mr. Austin, she would get over it. She hasn't. Now, I doubt she ever will." When Diane turned back, she found Lije watching with a new wariness.

"You can put away your bag of women's tricks, Diane. I am wise to them now."

"You never gave me a chance to come to terms—"

"It's a bit late for coming to terms, isn't it? More than a year has passed. Or had you forgotten that?"

"I hadn't forgotten," she shot back. "You aren't the only one with pride, Lije Stuart."

"Pride? Is that your excuse? But then, it does fit, doesn't it? After all, you were too proud to marry a Cherokee."

"That wasn't it at all."

"Wasn't it?"

"No!" She stopped, recognizing that she would never reach him through anger. She sighed and lowered her head. "We are fighting again, just as we did that night. It didn't begin that way." She drew on that memory when she looked up, letting it shine through her eyes. "Do you remember the way we waited until no one was watching before we slipped away— the way we laughed when we ran down the path to the garden. You caught me there and gathered me into your arms. Do you remember, Lije?"

"I remember." But it was the sight of her upturned face as much as the memory that trapped him in her spell again.

Her lips glistened in age-old invitation, and Lije found himself falling into the old pattern of wanting her, needing her. It angered him even as he pulled her against him and brought his mouth down on hers, seeking to punish her for the ache that wouldn't go away. He ground his lips against hers in a searing kiss, but her lips were unexpectedly gentle beneath his and the dimension of the kiss changed.

Slowly, softly, his lips responded to hers. Her mouth felt so warm, so right. Needs he thought he had finished with sprang fresh and strong. He felt the tremulous movement he knew women used as seduction. It caught him back from the edge. Even as need continued to crawl through him, he released her and stepped back.

"You still want me, Lije." There was a whisper of relief in her voice.

But it was the shine of triumph in her eyes that he sought to crush. "I wanted you that night, too," he reminded her in a voice that was flat and cool. "But when I asked you to be my wife, you turned away and chided me for getting too serious."

"I confess I was very selfish that night." Diane moved closer, confident again. His words were cold to her, but he wasn't. She had no reason to fear on that score. The kiss had shown her that. Now she had only his pride to surmount, which would not be easy. But then, she'd had a difficult time swallowing her own, but she had managed it. He could, too.

"You see," she continued, lifting a gloved hand and running her fingertips along the edge of his lapel, ignoring his stiffness, "I wanted to find a way that we could be together without alienating my mother. I thought I could do that if you stayed in the East and became a success. Then you jumped to the ridiculous conclusion that I was hesitating because you were Cherokee. You were so certain of that you wouldn't listen to anything else I said."

He clamped a hand over her fingers, but he didn't push them away, merely stilled their movement. His hard expression never altered as his gaze made a feature-by-feature study of her face. "Do you truly expect me to believe that's the reason you refused me, Diane?"

"I never refused your proposal, Lije," she corrected.

"Is that right?" he mocked. "Then, can you explain why it's taken you over a year to come up with this interesting clarification?"

"You aren't the only one who suffers from an excess of pride, Lije. After all, I was the one wrongly accused. As far as I was concerned, it was your place to apologize. When you made no effort to contact me—when you left without so much as a goodbye"—The muscles in her throat constricted, choking off her voice. She paused and looked away, unable to let him see how deeply she had been wounded. She struggled to regain that pretense of lightness—"it hardly endeared you to me."

"You say it all so easily."

"Easily?" She let a spark of anger show. "It is never easy to take the first step, especially when you stand there still determined to believe the worst of me."

His eyes narrowed in their study of her. "I don't know what to believe."

"Lije Stuart," she said in exasperation. "My mother has closed her doors to me; I have traveled across half a continent to straighten things out between us and let you know I still love you. If you still want to marry me, I accept. What else am I to do to prove myself to you?"

"I don't know." His fingers tightened on her hand.

Diane pressed her lips together in a firm line. "My father expects to remain in the Nation no more than a week. If I leave with him, I won't come back. When you finally do make up your mind, you have to come to me. I will not humble myself twice. Not for you or any man."

"I don't recall asking you."

He took perverse satisfaction in the hurt that flashed through her eyes an instant before she jerked her hand from his grip.

"I think it's time we rejoined the others," Diane stated crisply.

"I agree."

This time she didn't take his arm. They walked separately back to the rest of the group, connected by sizzling undercurrents of tension and the memory of harsh words said long ago in anger.

Observing their approach, Jed Parmelee rose from the garden bench and offered the seat to his daughter. "You two weren't gone long." He divided his questioning look between them.

Diane ignored it and sat down, arranging the drape of her skirt with practiced ease. "No, we weren't."

Lije paused beside his mother's chair. She glanced up at him. "I just suggested to Jed that he and Diane stay at Grand View while they are here. I thought it was a wonderful idea, don't you agree?"

"Visitors are always welcome at Grand View," he conceded.

"We wouldn't want to impose," Jed began.

"You wouldn't," Temple quickly assured him.

"Diane tells me you plan to stay a week," Lije inserted, again concentrating his attention on Jed Parmelee.

Jed hesitated a split second, his glance darting to Will Gordon and sliding away just as quickly. "Approximately a week, yes."

The hesitation coupled with the inadvertent glance at his grandfather made Lije suspect that Jed Parmelee might have another purpose for coming here. "I am curious, Captain— where is your uniform?"

"Packed away for the time being."

"Given the outbreak of hostilities, isn't it unusual for an officer to be granted a furlough at such a time?"

Jed looked at Lije with new respect and a glint of admiration. "It would be—if I were on furlough."

"But you're not."

"No. I was sent here. Unofficially, of course," Jed added, then directed his explanation to Will Gordon. "We know the Confederacy has made overtures to the five civilized tribes with the hope of persuading them to make an alliance with the South. I am here to determine, if possible, the position the Cherokee intend to take in the coming conflict."

For a long moment, silence ruled the group. The Blade leisurely tapped the ash from his cigar onto the lawn, apparently indifferent to the glaring look Kipp sent him. But it was Will Gordon's reaction that Jed was most interested in.

"Our Nation has a treaty with your government." Will chose his words with care. "We intend to adhere to it. Chief John Ross has stated on numerous occasions that he desires to have the Cherokee Nation remain neutral."

A short, contemptuous sound came from The Blade. "The man is a weather vane. As usual, he waits to see which way the wind blows."

"What do you mean by that?" Jed threw him a sharp look.

"He means"—Kipp spoke up instead—"that Pike has promised Stand Watie a commission in the Confederate army and has offered to supply the necessary arms and ammunition to outfit a regiment for Watie. I believe The Blade returned so quickly from his recent trip so he could join the regiment Watie intends to form."

The Blade ignored the accusation. "Neutrality is impossible, Captain. You know that or you wouldn't be here."

Diane frowned, a hint of alarm in her expression. "Why is it impossible?"

"Because the Union states of Kansas and Missouri lie north of us," Lije replied. "The rebel states of Arkansas and Texas occupy the land to the south and east. Already the Choctaw, Chickasaw, and Creek Nations have expressed a willingness to make an alliance with the South. The Cherokee Nation is fast becoming an island in the midst of a Confederate sea."

"But where do your sympathies lie?" Jed pressed.

The Blade held up a hand to stave off the question. "Before I answer that, let me ask you a question, Captain."

"Very well." He nodded.

"Our treaty with your federal government calls for protection. Where are your troops? Texas forces hold all military outposts in the territory except for Fort Gibson, which is still in the hands of the Cherokee. How do you propose to defend us should the rebel army invade?"

It was one of the questions Jed had dreaded. "We can't at the moment. We don't have sufficient forces to send. But we will."

"In other words, your government has abandoned us."

"That isn't true." But, in essence, it was, and Jed damn well knew it.

"Let me remind you of something else, Captain," The Blade continued. "We have long been a nation of slaveholders. And the intent of your war is to abolish slavery."

"If there is a major conflict, it will be waged to preserve the Union. The president has no authority to abolish slavery. Nor does he wish to do so, as he has stated repeatedly." But that long-used argument had already proved itself futile when the Southern states seceded. Jed tried another tack. "I can't believe the Cherokee will align themselves with the South. Have you forgotten the way your people were treated by the Georgians?"

"I haven't forgotten," The Blade told him. "Neither have I forgotten the events that led up to it, including your President Jackson's stated intentions of removing all Cherokee to lands in the West. And I heard an echo of those same words from your current administration in a speech that contained the statement, 'The Indian Territory south of Kansas must be vacated by the Indian.'" He paused for effect. "It seems, Captain, that we are expected to abide by the terms of our treaty with you, yet you are allowed to ignore them at will. Rhetoric no longer impresses us, Captain. Only action does."

"Action," Kipp snarled from his side of the group. "Do you mean like Watie's attempt last week to raise the Confederate flag in the public square at Tahlequah? You know he seeks to usurp Ross as the principal chief."

"Ross is an old man," The Blade snapped, for the first time his composure breaking to reveal the anger beneath. "He has never been a leader, only a follower—like a leaf blowing before the strongest wind."

"You must understand, Captain," Will inserted quickly

"What the Cherokee seek is peace. We have no wish to be drawn into your war—by either side."

"And that is the wind currently blowing," The Blade mocked.

Jed sensed there was more than a degree of truth in The Blade's words. During the years he was stationed at Fort Gibson, he had learned one thing about John Ross. As determined as Lincoln was to preserve the Union, Ross was equally determined that the Cherokee Nation would remain united as well.

"And if the wind changes?" he asked, already guessing The Blade's answer.

"Then Ross will change his position."

"Don't listen to him, Captain!" Kipp sprang forward to confront The Blade, his hands clenched into tight, trembling fists at his side.

The faint tension that had been present now became a charged current. In two silent steps, Lije was within reach of the pair, ready to intervene if the situation turned violent.

Kipp was blind to his presence, blind to everything except the man before him, the man he hated above all others. "He accuses Ross of being a weathercock, but he is the one who changes before the wind. We have pledged to honor the treaty he and others forced upon us, but he seeks to abandon it."

"The Federal government has already abandoned it," The Blade declared. "Didn't you hear Parmelee admit it has no troops to protect us? Lincoln's administration has already stated it wants all Indians removed from this territory. It did not give us this land; we are here at its sufferance only. But the Confederacy has promised us free title to the land, representation in its Congress, and the protection of its armies. And its soldiers are here in the territory, ready to defend us."

"Are they here to defend us—or to overthrow Ross and install Watie in his stead?" Kipp accused, his face mottled with hatred. But it was his hands Lije watched. His hands and their nearness to the bulge in his jacket.

"If they did, this Nation would finally have a leader."

"A traitor, you mean," Kipp snarled.

"That is enough, Kipp," Will Gordon ordered in a quiet but firm voice.

Kipp hurled an angry look at him. "He would have Parmelee believe we are a Nation of traitors. But there are only a few among us. We have a treaty and we will honor it. We will not sell out!"

"Are you accusing me of being a traitor?" The Blade demanded hotly. "If you are, why don't you come right out and say it? Or can't you do that without a black kerchief around your neck?"

The reference to the cloth Kipp wore as one of the executioners of The Blade's father, Shawano Stuart, sliced through the last thread of Kipp's restraint. He muttered a curse in Cherokee as his hand flew toward the bulge in his jacket.

But Lije was a half second quicker, seizing his forearm in an iron grip and checking its upward movement. "Don't, Kipp," Lije warned as the man froze in shock at finding Lije so close to him. Kipp's mouth curled in a snarl of contempt, and the muscles in his arm flexed in resistance to his hold. "I would hate to charge my own uncle with assault, Kipp," Lije added.

"Kipp, my God." Eliza was on her feet, a hand at her throat while Temple looked on in horror.

Suddenly Lije felt the pressure of a gun muzzle in the center of his back. He stiffened in surprise, his blood suddenly running cold.

"Let go of his arm, Cousin," Alex murmured behind him, his tone lazy and smugly amused, and Lije cursed himself for not keeping track of Kipp's son. "I said let my father go." Alex jabbed him with the muzzle.

"Alex, no." The plea came from Diane even as Lije slowly and reluctantly opened his fingers, releasing Kipp.

"Good work, Son." Kipp rubbed his arm where Lije's hand had been, his eyes dark with malicious glee as Lije remained motionless.

"You better step back here with me," Alex told his father.

"You should have stayed out of this, Alex," Lije said grimly.

"I did—until you stepped in, Cousin." Alex eased the pressure of the gun against Lije's back.

Recovering, Will Gordon stepped forward. "Put that gun away, Alex, and do it now. I will not permit this sort of behavior at my home."

"Tell *them* that," Alex challenged, but Lije no longer felt the revolver at his back. He stole a glance over his shoulder to make certain Alex had moved away, then made a slow pivot around to face them, careful to keep his hands in plain sight. "I never guessed your navy revolver would come in so handy when I won it from you, Grandfather."

"If I had known you would use it this way, I would never have agreed to the wager. Now, put it away." Will Gordon placed himself directly in front of the pair. Lije shifted slightly to keep both Kipp and Alex in view but remained silent, unwilling to say anything that might provoke Alex, who appeared to be enjoying it all a little too much.

"I think I will keep it handy, Grandfather, while Father and I depart from this delightful gathering," he replied, still smiling. "You are ready to leave, aren't you, Father?"

"Yes. I can no longer stand the company of traitors." Kipp threw a last glaring look at The Blade before he turned and stalked off in the direction of the stables.

Alex backed away a few steps, slowly lowering the revolver, then turned and started after his father. For a moment everyone kept their place. Then Sorrel broke the grip of stillness that claimed them.

"Alex, come back!" Sorrel ran after him, but Lije caught her before she had gone more than a few steps. "Let me go! I don't want Alex to leave."

"It's best that he does, Sorrel," Lije insisted, easily thwarting her attempt to pull free. "You can see him another time."

"But I want to see him now!" she stormed. "He was going to push me on the swing. Push me real high. He promised."

"I'll take you later and push you on the swing—"

"No, you won't," she denied. "You'll be too tired or too busy just like you always are. You're just like Papa. You're never home and when you are, you never have time for me." Her chin quivered, her lower lip trembling as she sniffed back her tears. "Alex is the only one who does things with me. He's the only one who likes me."

"That isn't true." He crouched down to her level.

"Yes, it is!" She sobbed now in renewed anger as Temple hurried to them. "It's your fault Alex left. Why did you have to hurt Uncle Kipp?" Then she turned roundly on their father. "Why did you have to argue with him? I hate you. I hate both of you!"

She broke free and ran toward the house. Temple looked at Lije, her eyes dark with regret. "She didn't mean that," she said, and sent a quick apologetic glance at The Blade as well, then went after Sorrel. In the heavy silence that followed, Lije heard the soft swish of a woman's skirts near him and turned. Diane stood before him, the alarm fading from her eyes, but not her concern for him. She lifted a hand, as if to reach out to him, then drew it back.

"Are you all right, Lije?"

"Yes." From the stable area came the hard pound of hooves. Lije watched as Kipp and Alex galloped briefly into view, then cut across a field and disappeared from sight.

"The old feuds." Diane paused and shook her head, her expression troubled and confused. "When we left Fort Gibson six years ago, there was peace between the two factions."

"It was more like a truce," Lije corrected. "The growing hostility between the North and the South has created an atmosphere of distrust again and stirred awake the old hatreds. Agents on both sides exploit that for their own ends."

Jed Parmelee turned to Will Gordon. "I am responsible for this, Will. I'm sorry."

Will denied that with a shake of his head. "The incident is regrettable, but you are not to blame. Tempers are running high on both sides. It takes little to ignite them."

"Perhaps." But Jed Parmelee appeared unconvinced. He turned to The Blade. "I hope you will understand that, under these circumstances, I'll have to reconsider your invitation to stay at Grand View. My mission here is a delicate one. It might be jeopardized if it's perceived that I'm choosing sides in your old disputes. It will be best if I keep my room in Tahlequah. Diane, of course, remains free to accept your invitation."

"I would like to stay," she told The Blade. "But only if you're certain my presence won't create problems for you."

"It will be no problem for us. However," he cast a considering glance at Lije, a trace of amusement tugging at the corners of his mouth, "I can't speak for my son on that score."

Her laugh was low and musical. "I hope to cause your son a great many problems."

"You may not have as many opportunities as you might wish," Lije informed her. "My work with the Cherokee Light Horse occupies much of my time."

"The Light Horse," Diane echoed in surprise. "That was what you meant when you told your uncle you didn't want to charge him with assault. I thought you planned to open a law office."

"I did," Lije admitted. "When I returned, I realized the Nation had a greater need for peacekeepers." He paused and looked in the direction Kipp and Alex had taken. "But today I only succeeded in widening the conflict," he said, thinking of Alex.

"That was inevitable," The Blade stated. "You couldn't see

Alex's face when he was holding that gun on you. Believe me, he was enjoying the sense of power it gave him."

"I never should have agreed to the wager," Will murmured.

"It would only have postponed this moment," The Blade told him. "It was coming. I think we all know that."

Lije privately acknowledged the truth of his father's claim. Events were moving too swiftly. It had become impossible for anyone to control them, not only in the American states but in the Cherokee Nation as well. He wondered whether Diane realized that.

﹒ 8 ﹒

By week's end telegraph keys chattered from one end of the continent to the other, spreading the news of a Confederate victory at Bull Run near Manassas, Virginia. Although the Union army's defeat could hardly be called a decisive one, it dealt a crushing blow to the Union cause within the Cherokee Nation and gave credence to the South's claim that the Northerners had no stomach for a fight.

Lije's father said as much at dinner that night, on one of the rare occasions when Lije was able to join his family for the evening meal. Diane was notably quick to take exception to his remark.

"May I remind you that one battle does not make a war, Mr. Stuart," Diane chided, all lightness and charm as she disagreed with her host.

"But one battle can win a war," he replied.

"Perhaps, but that isn't the case here," Diane countered with a confident smile as the black serving maid returned to the dining room with their dessert course. "As you know, our officer corps was severely depleted when so many of our best military commanders defected to the South. It will require some time to reorganize our commands."

"Assuming the South gives you the time."

She smiled, taking no offense at his remark. On the contrary,

Diane appeared to enjoy the verbal sparring. "Don't underestimate the will of the Union army, Mr. Stuart."

"I don't. But neither do I overestimate it."

"Well put, Mr. Stuart," Diane conceded and dipped her spoon into the delicate floating island. She tasted it, then made an appreciative sound in her throat. "This is delicious, Mrs. Stuart."

"Thank you. I—"

"Mama had Essie Lou fix it for me," Sorrel broke in. "It's my favorite."

"It was my mother's favorite dessert, too," Diane recalled. "While we were at Fort Gibson, she always served it when she entertained." She paused, her expression turning thoughtful and reflective. "Isn't it odd the things a person remembers? The winter before the fort was closed and we left, a regiment stopped for a few days to rest their horses. They were on their way to a garrison somewhere in Texas, I believe. I remember the regiment was under the command of Colonel Albert Johnston—the same Johnston who is now a general in the Confederate army. And his second in command was Colonel Robert E. Lee. My father told me that this last April, Lee was offered the command of the new Union army, but he refused it and subsequently joined the rebel forces. He's in charge of the Army of Virginia now. He seemed a very kind and gentle man to me, with a quiet dignity you couldn't help but admire." She smiled at the memory. A moment later, her smile widened. "There was another officer with them, too—Stuart was his name. J.E.B. Stuart. He was very dashing and gallant. My mother was quite charmed by him, I remember. And as you all know," she said, her eyes sparkling with laughter, "my mother is a woman not easily charmed by anyone."

The others laughed. Sorrel was the loudest, anxious to be accepted as an equal by the adults at the table even though she didn't understand the humor in Diane's remark. Lije managed only a forced smile. Where Cecilia Parmelee was concerned, he had lost much of his sense of humor. When the laughter died, Diane's mood sobered again. "So many of the officers I met at the fort have joined the rebel cause— Lee and Longstreet, Lieutenant Hood from Texas, and Captain Kirby-Smith."

"Speaking of rebels," Lije glanced at his father, "I hear Stand Watie has organized a band of guerrillas. I am told he's offered its services to the Confederate army even though Chief Ross's order forbids any Cherokee from participating in the warfare on our borders. Is it true?"

"Yes." The Blade carefully avoided meeting the sudden, sharp look Temple sent him. "They have made their headquarters in the vicinity of old Fort Wayne."

"But surely such action compromises Chief Ross's position of neutrality," Diane remarked in mild reproof.

"Neutrality will be impossible," The Blade told her. "If the fighting comes this far west, the Cherokee Nation will become a battleground."

"Must we talk of war and fighting?" Temple protested with thinly disguised irritation. "Surely there are any number of more pleasant topics that can be discussed."

"You're right. I apologize," The Blade said, but his smile teased her. "I'm afraid I acquired the bad habit of discussing politics at the table from you." Unable to deny it, Temple flashed him an angry look. His smile widened even as he swung his attention to their houseguest. "Believe it or not, I had no interest at all in politics before I met my wife. Now she objects to it. I suspect mainly because my views seldom coincide with her own, which can make things very awkward at times."

"But never dull." Diane smiled back.

"No, never dull," he agreed. This time when he glanced at Temple, he saw the little smile she was trying to conceal, and he knew he was forgiven.

Temple turned to their daughter. "Sorrel, have you told

your father of the entertainment you've planned for him after dinner?"

Sorrel leaned forward, eager to claim center stage. "I learned two new songs on the piano, and I am going to do them for you tonight."

"You play them beautifully, too," Diane told her. "I was listening while you practiced today."

The Blade frowned and took his watch from his vest pocket to check the time. "I sent word for Asa Danvers to come to the house at half past eight," he said, referring to the plantation's overseer. "He left a message that he needed to see me."

"You're always too busy for me." Sorrel slumped in her chair.

"No doubt his business with Mr. Danvers is very important, but I don't think there is any need for you to be upset, Sorrel," Diane said. "I'm certain your mother can arrange to have our coffee served in the music room. That way you can play for us while we drink our coffee, and your father will still be able to keep his appointment with Mr. Danvers."

Sorrel sat up. "Can we, Mama?"

"Of course." Temple immediately summoned the maid.

The Blade glanced at Diane Parmelee with a mixture of gratitude and reluctant admiration. He had been fully prepared to dislike Jed Parmelee's beautiful daughter. But Diane possessed that rare combination of beauty, intelligence, and wit. He could now see the attraction she held for his son, although he doubted Lije had spoken more than ten words to her tonight. In fact, Lije had spent almost no time in her company since she had arrived.

Candles flamed brightly in the music room, casting their light into every corner. Lije stood behind his mother's chair and watched his sister at the piano, her head bent over the keys in studious concentration.

He never once allowed his glance to stray to Diane, but her profile filled his peripheral vision. He was aware of the attentive way she watched Sorrel, the small smile of approval that curved her lips, and the shine of her hair in the candlelight, the same golden color as the flames. It was as if there were no one and nothing else in the room. The pressure of it worked on nerves that were already stretched taut.

Restlessness surged through him as he waited, with jaws clenched, for Sorrel to finish her mini-recital. The instant the last chord faded into silence, he left the others to praise his sister's efforts.

Once outside, he walked to the edge of the wide veranda and stopped to light a cigar. He puffed on it and leaned a shoulder against a tall, white pillar, struggling to relax. A full moon hung low above the trees, a large and lustrous pearl against the velvet blackness of night over which had been strewn a scattering of diamond-bright stars. But he found no enjoyment in the sight or the evening silence. All his senses were turned to the sounds coming from inside the house.

When he heard the door swing wide behind him, Lije steeled himself not to turn. Light footsteps approached. He took another puff on his cigar and watched the blue smoke dissolve into wisps.

"I wondered where you had gone." Diane stopped near him, the sweep of her full skirt brushing his leg.

"I needed some air." The small ease the cigar had given him was gone. He flipped it into the night. His gaze followed the crimson arc it made as it fell.

"It's a lovely evening," she remarked. "You don't mind if I join you."

Raw and tense, Lije straightened away from the pillar and swung his gaze to her. "You already have."

"Yes." Diane tipped her head and slanted him one of her patented, provocative looks. "Do you mind my staying here?"

"No." But the admission was a grudging one, made as he faced outward again.

"I wondered," she said. "I have seen so little of you this past week."

"I warned you it would be that way."

"So you did, but I have the feeling that you deliberately arranged to spend as little time with me as possible."

Again he was the object of her knowing glance. "I hope you didn't expect me to dance attendance on you."

"The way you did back East, you mean?" Diane guessed.

This time he leveled his own glance at her. "Yes."

"By that, am I to infer that you intend to ignore me completely from now on?" her voice teased.

"Diane," he began, his patience exhausted. .

"You remember my name." She rounded her eyes in mock surprise. "Now that is reassuring."

In spite of his better judgment, Lije found himself smiling. "Why are you doing this, Diane?"

"Why are you avoiding me?" she countered.

He sobered slightly. "When you have been badly burned, you're careful about getting too close to the fire again."

"But isn't the cold much worse?" She stood before him, as serious now as he was, her eyes reflecting the same needs and wants that tormented him.

The nights of restlessness and frustration had him on edge, teetering on the brink. Lije was never sure who made the first move. One moment they stood apart; in the next they were wrapped together.

His lips hovered above hers, threatening, promising. She couldn't tell. She didn't care. It was their taste she wanted, no matter how harsh, how demanding. Reaching up, Diane drew his face down to hers. She felt his body, hard and confident, against hers. She tasted his lips, soft and urgent.

There was fire. There was heat. He took all she gave, then more. It might never be enough. She could make him blind and deaf with needs. Knowing it, Lije couldn't stop it. The way she touched him, so sure, so sweet while her mouth was molten fire. Desire boiled in him, rising so quickly he was weak with it before his mind accepted what his body couldn't deny. He held her closer, rough against smooth, hard against soft, flame against flame.

Whatever doubts he'd had, Lije never doubted the want. He hadn't always understood it, the intensity of it, but he had never doubted it. Such mindless passion was pulling at him now.

When at last she buried her face against his jacket, he felt the tremors that shook her and gathered her closer still. "Do you have any idea how much I love you, Lije?" she murmured against his collar. "I would have hounded you shamelessly until you took me back."

The chuckle came from low in his throat. He cupped her face in his hand and tipped it up so he could look at her. "Now you tell me."

"Aren't you going to say it, Lije?" she whispered, her eyes focusing on his lips. "A woman likes to hear the words."

"I love you." His voice was thick with the powerful emotions that lived within him. "I never stopped loving you."

"Show me," she insisted with a boldness that took Lije by surprise. When she saw his stunned expression, Diane laughed softly in delight and turned inside the circle of his arms, wrapping them tightly around her middle and letting her head fall back against his shoulder. "Do you see how brazen I have become with you? I would gladly anticipate our wedding night. That shocks you, doesn't it?"

"To the core." The mere mention of marriage had sobered him and forced him to look ahead at the choices each would have to make. Choices that could tear them apart.

"Will your family think it improper if we marry quickly?"

"That will depend on how quickly." He chose not to mention the problems ahead of them. Instead, he took his pleasure in the moment—in the silken texture of her hair against his cheek and the fresh scent of her skin. "My mother will certainly object if she isn't given time to plan a large feast for us."

"And Father will want to be part of it," she said and released a long sigh.

Beneath it, Lije caught the soft crunching of footsteps. "Someone's coming." He released her and stepped away even as he spotted the overseer approaching the house.

Her soft laugh mocked his show of discretion. "Are you concerned for my reputation?" she teased.

Before he could reply, Lije was greeted by the overseer. "Evenin', Mr. Stuart. Ma'am." He doffed his hat to Diane, the bald crown of his head gleaming white in the moonlight.

"Asa." Lije nodded to him.

The overseer paused by the steps and glanced back into the moonlit darkness. "Saw a rider turn into the lane. Seems a bit late for company."

Lije stiffened in instant wariness and scanned the tree-lined road. There was something moving in the deep shadows that cloaked it. Distance muffled the thuds of the horse's hooves, making them faint but audible now that his hearing was attuned to them.

"Go tell my father we have a visitor," he said to Diane on a deliberately casual note.

"Of course." Unhurriedly, she went inside to deliver the message.

Common sense told Lije that a man riding straight up to the house was no cause for alarm, but an inbred sense of caution pushed him off the moon-bathed veranda and onto the shadowed lawn.

"You make an easy target, Asa," Lije warned the overseer. "You better move out of the moonlight."

The man scurried away from the steps, taking cover near some tall shrubs. "You figure this fella means trouble?" he called softly.

"He could," Lije acknowledged in an equally low voice and fell silent. As the horse and rider drew closer, they became a solid black shape against the darkened lane. When they crossed a patch of moonlight, Lije had a long glimpse of the man's silvered beard. Recognizing the rider, he relaxed.

"Do you know who it is?" The Blade's voice came from the open doorway.

"It's Parmelee." Lije went forward to meet him. The Negro Ike trotted out to take the captain's horse when he dismounted. "You're out late tonight, Captain."

"I just came from your grandfather's." Jed handed the horse's reins to Ike. When he glanced toward the house, moonlight played over the grim set of his features and the network of tired lines in his face. "Is Diane inside?"

As Lije started to say she was, Diane glided from the house. "Papa," she cried and rushed down the steps to meet him halfway. Lije deliberately hung back to give them a moment of privacy. When he did, Ike shifted closer. "Is it true, Master Lije?"

"What?" Lije frowned at the interruption.

Ike avoided his glance and rubbed a hand over the horse's velvet nose. "I heard there was a big battle back East, and the Yankees lost."

"That's true." Lije regarded him curiously.

"I guess that means the war's over."

"Not yet," Lije replied curtly and moved off to rejoin the others, fully aware it would simplify a great many things if it were over now.

"This is such a wonderful surprise," Diane declared. "I had no idea you would be coming tonight."

"It was a last-minute decision," Jed told her, the corners of his mouth lifting in a wan smile. "I just received word that I'm to return immediately and make a report on my findings here."

"So soon," Diane said in dismay.

He nodded. "There is little to be gained by staying longer. I met with Chief Ross this afternoon at Park Hill. Despite our recent defeat in Virginia, he remains firm in his policy of neutrality for the Cherokee. Under the present circumstances, that's the best we can expect."

The Blade made a scoffing sound, which Diane ignored. "That's good news, Father. Now there is something that I want to tell you"—she stopped and moved to Lije's side, taking his arm—"or I should say, that *we* want to tell you—all of you," she added, including Lije's parents in her sweeping glance, her face radiant with happiness. "Lije and I plan to marry."

Lije noticed the sharp, probing glance his father sent him at the same moment that his mother gasped, "How wonderful!"

Jed Parmelee's reaction was more subdued but no less genuine than Lije's mother's as he took Diane's hand and wrapped both of his around it. "I couldn't be happier, Diane," he murmured. "I know how much you wanted this." Turning, he offered his congratulations to Lije. Then Temple came up to hug them both.

"Are you going to have a wedding?" Sorrel wanted to know. "May I be in it?"

Diane laughed at her eagerness. "Of course, you may. We'll make you a beautiful new dress to wear for the wedding."

"A yellow one? I like yellow."

"Then yellow it will be," Diane promised, still all smiles.

"Did you hear, Mama? I get a new yellow dress." Sorrel beamed with satisfaction, then suddenly swung back to Diane, demanding, "When is the wedding?"

This time Diane hesitated, her glance running to her father. "We wanted it to be soon, but . . . with you leaving tomorrow and—" About to mention the war in the East, Diane stopped, then brightened with a new thought. "Christmas. Everyone knows the war will be over long before Christmas. You'll have time to obtain a furlough so you can be here to give me away. And a Christmas wedding will be beautiful with garlands of holly and mistletoe strung everywhere."

"And it will give us ample time to make your gown," Temple stated, starting to make plans. "On his last trip to Fort Smith, The Blade picked up a recent issue of *Godey's Lady's Book*. We'll go through the fashion plates and see if there's a gown you like that we can copy."

"And one for me, too," Sorrel inserted

"Of course." Temple smiled, then looked at the others. "Shall we all go inside? We have so much to talk about, to celebrate." Taking their agreement for granted, she hooked her arm around Diane's and set off for the house. "The last time I was in the mercantile store in Tahlequah, they had a bolt of white brocade in the back room. It would make a beautiful wedding dress."

As the men started to follow, the overseer, Asa Danvers, stepped from the shadows. "Can I have a word with you, Mr. Stuart? It's important."

Something in the curtness of the overseer's voice had Lije pausing along with his father. Jed Parmelee continued toward the house with the women.

"Very well," The Blade agreed. "We'll go into my study."

"If it's all the same to you, I'll say my piece right here," Danvers told him. "I'd just as soon not be under the same roof as that Yankee captain." This time there was no mistaking the man's hostility as he turned and spat in contempt.

"What is it you want to say?" The Blade challenged while Lije stood by, curious now to hear the answer.

"It's like this," Danvers began. "It's all well and good for the Cherokee to stay neutral while the South fights for its rights. But I got family in Arkansas. It's where I was born. So I'm handin' in my notice. Soon as I get my wife and kids to her sister's farm north of Fort Smith, I figure on joinin' up and fightin' for the cause."

"How soon will you be leaving?"

"Soon as I can get packed and loaded."

"I'll have your wages for you in the morning."

The man nodded and turned to leave, then swung back. "That Abe Lincoln can talk all he wants, but there ain't no damn way I'm ever gonna believe that some damn nigger is equal to me. It just ain't so!" He jabbed his finger in the air to enforce his contention.

When The Blade said nothing, the overseer hesitated, then stalked off. Lije noticed Ike standing off to the side with the captain's horse. His head was flung up in proud defiance, the skin stretched taut across his features, his eyes hot with anger and resentment.

Diane called from the house, "Lije, are you coming in?"

"I'll be right there," he replied, again feeling the probe of his father's gaze.

In silence they set off for the house, but the silence didn't last. "This engagement of yours," The Blade said quietly, "is it wise?"

"That remains to be seen." Lije had his own doubts on that score. "I heard today that Stand Watie invited you to join his band of guerrillas."

"He did."

"Are you going to accept?"

"I haven't mentioned it to your mother yet, but I was considering it," he admitted. "It would make things very awkward for you and Diane, though, with Jed an officer in the Union army."

"Very awkward," Lije agreed, aware he would then be faced with a decision of his own, and there was only one choice he could make.

"We both know your mother would be opposed to the idea of my joining in the fight. To be honest, it's the thought of how she'll worry about my safety that makes me hesitate. I have caused her a great many anxious hours during the years of our marriage. She will think it's unfair to cause her more. Perhaps I'll wait," he said. "With luck, all the fighting may be confined to the East."

"And with luck, it will be over by Christmas," Lije said, echoing Diane's words as they climbed the steps to the veranda.

The weeks following Jed Parmelee's departure were busy ones. Much of Diane's time was occupied with wedding plans and preparations, while Lije had his hands full trying to keep some semblance of order in his district. The Confederate victory at Bull Run had led to repeated clashes in the Nation between Watie's Knights of the Golden Circle, who now called themselves the Southern Rights party, and Ross's supporters in the Keetoowah Society—the so-called Pins Indians who had taken the name of the Loyal League. Every day Lije saw the division within his Nation deepening.

Late one evening in the middle of August, Lije returned to the family plantation. He bypassed the darkened windows of the house and rode straight to the stables. Heat lightning flashed along the horizon. Nearby an owl hooted, and its haunting call seemed to reinforce the sense of foreboding that gripped him.

The yellow glow of a lantern spilled from one of the stalls. Spotting it, Lije pointed his tired horse toward it, his muscles tensing in automatic wariness. The light moved as he approached the stall door. A man stepped out, the lantern held high to throw its light on Lije.

"Is that you, Master Lije?"

Recognizing Ike's voice, Lije relaxed a little and walked his horse into the light. "It's me." He halted his horse by the hitch rail and swung out of the saddle, conscious of the fatigue that tugged at him. "What are you doing here so late?"

"One of the colts got tangled in some briars. Some of the gashes were deep. They festered up pretty bad. I thought I better check on him."

"How is he?" Lije unbuckled the cinch and pulled the saddle off.

"He's pretty sweaty, but he drank some water. I think he'll pull out of it." Ike hooked the lantern on the iron bar outside the stall door.

When Lije lifted the saddle onto the hitch rail, he spotted a suspicious-looking bundle on the ground. He shot a look at Ike, his jaw hardening in anger. "What's that, Ike?"

"What, sir?"

"That bundle on the ground outside the stall."

Ike glanced at it, then back at Lije, a glimmer of resentment showing in his eyes. "What do you think it is, Master Lije?"

"It looks like it could be your belongings, Ike. You weren't thinking of going somewhere, were you?"

"Where would I be going, Master Lije?"

"Nowhere," Lije snapped, then fought to rein in his temper. "What's this all about, Ike? No one here has ever whipped you or put you in chains. You have always been treated well."

"Yes, sir," Ike nodded. "I been treated as good as any of your horses. I got me a clean straw bed, food, and water. Now and then I even get me a friendly pat."

"Dammit, Ike—" He took an angry step toward him.

"If you were to take a closer look at that bundle on the ground, Master Lije, you'd see it was rags I used to tie a poultice on the colt's leg." He waited while Lije threw another glance at the pile of cloth.

"You could have told me that when I first asked you," Lije said in irritation. "Why didn't you?"

Ike shrugged, not answering. "Guess you'll be wanting me to take care of your horse now."

"Yes." Lije gathered up the trailing reins, but he didn't immediately pass them to Ike when he reached out to take them. "Don't get any foolish ideas in your head, Ike."

"Like what?"

"Like running away." Lije watched for a reaction and saw

none. "If you did, Ike, I would be the one who came after you. And I know how you think, Ike. I would track you down. Dammit, it's my job, Ike. I would have to do it, whether I liked it or not."

"I reckon that's so." Ike nodded.

Lije studied him a moment longer, then handed over the reins and moved away, heading for the house. Heat lightning again streaked across the night sky, briefly illuminating the path through the trees. The grass beneath his feet was parched and yellow from the summer-long drought. It crackled like brittle paper with each step.

The air was sultry, the faint breeze providing little relief Although he had traveled no more than twenty yards, Lije could already feel the perspiration gathering between his shoulders. He thought longingly of a bath, but that would mean rousting the servants to carry the water—and possibly waking other members of the household. Possibly waking Diane.

He didn't want to see her tonight, not with the uncertain news he carried and its potential ramifications. Tonight he would content himself with merely washing off the day's accumulation of dust and sweat. He would leave the bath for tomorrow. Maybe by then there would be more information.

Sighing, Lije lifted his gaze to the house and the sweep of the columned veranda that encircled it. A pale, wraithlike figure floated across the lawn toward him. He slowed his steps, cursing softly in Cherokee when he recognized Diane, clad in a loose-fitting nightdress of white longcloth, her hair unbound, flowing past her shoulders.

She ran straight to him and wrapped her hands around his neck to pull his head down. "I thought you would never come home, Lije."

The soft fervor of her voice assaulted him an instant before he tasted the honeyed warmth of her lips against his mouth. A shudder coursed through him, an oath ripped out, then he was responding demanding, exciting. Nothing was clear to him as his lips raced crazily over her face. Reason dimmed in desire. There was only Diane and his growing hunger for her.

Home. She said it as if she would always be here waiting for him. But would she?

Made irritable by the unanswerable question and the rawness of the needs she aroused in him, Lije roughened the kiss. But she wasn't frightened by its demanding pressure. Instead, she strained closer. But it wasn't enough, and they both knew it.

Breathing hard and fighting to control it, Lije lifted his head to look at her. Boldly, she returned his look, then let her lashes sweep down before tracing the outline of his lips with her fingers.

"My, but you are a hungry one tonight," she murmured a bit breathlessly.

"Very." His voice was husky.

Her lashes came up, letting him see the impish light that danced in her eyes. "Then it's a good thing I sent Phoebe to the kitchen to fix you something to eat."

But he didn't smile as she had expected him to do. Her reference to Phoebe came too close on the heels of his exchange with Phoebe's son Ike.

Diane misread the sudden sobering of his expression. "Don't tell me you have already eaten?"

"No."

"Then what is it?" It was a careless question that expected no serious answer. And Lije tried to oblige her.

"Nothing," he said, but he wasn't convincing.

Her eyes narrowed sharply "Something is wrong. What happened today?"

He hesitated, then admitted, "There's been word of a battle in Missouri."

"Missouri. My father—" Stopping, Diane lowered her head and dragged in a long breath, then looked up, showing the steely composure befitting the daughter of an officer and a soldier. "Where was it?"

"At a place called Wilson's Creek, southwest of Springfield."

"What happened?"

"A Union force of roughly five thousand men attacked a combined Confederate army of twice that number. After some fierce fighting, the Union army was forced to retreat to Springfield. There are reports of heavy casualties on both sides."

"My father's regiment," she began with the same forced calm. "Was it involved?"

His expression softened with regret. "I honestly don't know. I waited, hoping to get more definite information. The initial reports made mention only of a Union general named Sigel who commanded some artillery."

"Then we don't know whether his regiment took part in the battle." She stared at the front of his shirt. "Maybe they haven't ordered him back into the field yet. Maybe he was still at headquarters making his report. Maybe—" Her voice broke, and she closed her eyes. She offered no resistance when Lije gently pressed her head to his chest. "What if he's wounded, Lije?" she whispered. "What if—"

"Sssh. We don't know that."

"No. No, we don't," Diane repeated in an attempt to cling to the hope it offered. "I don't know what I would do if anything happened to him," she declared with an expressive little shudder of dread.

"I know," he murmured in comfort. "We'll find out more details tomorrow."

"Yes." She pushed back from him, her head down as if ashamed of her actions. "I know I shouldn't worry, but . . ."

"He's your father. I would think less of you if you weren't concerned about him."

Diane touched his cheek in gratitude, then reached down to take his hand. "Let's go to the house. Phoebe will have your supper ready."

Hand in hand, they walked to the house, neither speaking.

Late the following day they learned that Captain Parmelee's regiment was not part of the Union forces engaged in the battle at Wilson's Creek.

But the fighting had moved west.

And the Southern newspapers heaped praise on Stand Watie and his rebel guerrillas involved in the fight for their capture of the Union artillery. In the eyes of the press, Watie was a hero.

The Confederate victory and Watie's new status put pressure on the principal chief John Ross to abandon his stated position of neutrality. More and more, it appeared that the South was going to emerge victorious from the war. If the Cherokee Nation did not become its ally, then it would be regarded as a foe.

The wind was blowing strongly from the South.

PART II

We are in the situation of a man standing alone upon a low naked spot of ground, with the water rising rapidly all around him. He sees the danger but does not know what to do. If he remains where he is, his only alternative is to be swept away and perish. The tide carries by him, in its mad course, a drifting log. It perchance comes within reach of him. By refusing it, he is a doomed man. By seizing hold of it, he has a chance for his life. He can but perish in the effort, and may be able to keep his head above water until rescued or drift to where he can help himself.

—John Ross,
principal chief of the Cherokee Nation

❦ 9 ❧

The black filly tossed her head and pranced sideways with excitement, eyeing all the saddle horses, single buggies, and wagons banked along the street racks around the town square. "Full of fire and ready to run, are you?" Alex grinned and held the filly to her dancing walk. "Too bad it isn't race day."

He rode past the two-story brick hotel, filled to capacity like the rest of the town. Children raced in and out of the alleys between buildings while women strolled from store to store to see what the merchants had to offer. But there were few men to be seen along the walks. They were crowded around the east side of the square where the government buildings were located.

Alex pointed his horse in the same direction. He had traveled no more than a few yards when a familiar voice called his name. Glancing around, he saw Sorrel crossing the street, accompanied by her grandmother, mother, and their Negro serving maid Phoebe. Alex started to nod a greeting and ride on. Then he noticed Diane Parmelee in the group. He smiled when he recognized the woman who was the daughter of a Yankee captain and his cousin's future bride.

He rode over to them. "Good afternoon, ladies." His glance flicked to the packages and bundles of goods in their arms. "It appears you have already bought out the stores. Where are you bound to now?"

"The dressmaker's shop," Eliza replied while Diane Parmelee watched him with cool eyes. Alex smiled, certain she was remembering the time when he had held a gun on her precious fiancé.

"I'm having a new dress made to wear in the wedding," Sorrel informed him. "Mrs. Adair has to measure me first, though. Would you like to come with us?"

"It sounds very entertaining, but I think I'll go find out if we have finally joined the Confederacy," Alex replied and caught the small smile that touched Diane's lips. "You surprise me, Miss Parmelee. I never thought you would find the prospect so amusing."

"Considering how unlikely it is that such a thing would come to pass, I—"

"But it will come to pass," Alex interrupted smoothly. "Didn't my dear cousin tell you that this meeting today is for the purpose of making an alliance with the Confederacy?"

She tipped her chin a fraction higher. "He informed me that the rebel government had made another proposal. But they have done so countless times in the past. From what I was told, there is nothing new in it that would cause Chief Ross to abandon his position of neutrality."

"But the circumstances are different this time. The South is winning the war—and making a hero of Stand Watie in the process. Chief Ross can't continue to sit on his hands if he wants to remain chief. That's why he has thrown his support to the South." Alex smiled at the mixture of doubt and dismay in her expression. "Good day, ladies." He touched a hand to his hat in a mock salute and rode off, chuckling to himself.

Diane looked from Temple to Eliza. "What he said—is it true?"

Eliza pressed her lips together in deep disapproval. "As much as I regret it, yes. Chief Ross intends to support making an alliance with the South."

"But why?"

"We are faced with a Hobson's choice, Diane," Eliza replied. "Either we make an alliance or face military occupation."

"Is that the threat the South made?" she demanded, indignant and showing it.

"My dear, they didn't have to put it into words," Eliza told her. "Such things are always couched in diplomatic terms that make their true meaning implicit. The Cherokee have lived under a soldier's bayonet before. It's not an experience we care to repeat. Therefore, we will bide our time and wait for the Union army to put down this rebellion of the Southern states."

"This is difficult for you, I know," Temple inserted, reaching out to press a hand on Diane's arm in a gesture of comfort and compassion. "Sometimes it's very hard to avoid taking sides in an issue, especially when everyone else around you is."

"I know." But Diane wasn't listening. Too many other thoughts and questions were tumbling through her mind. Why had Lije not made the gravity of the situation clear to her? From the way everyone talked, she had assumed a position of neutrality was the only possible option, considering how divisive opinion was among the Cherokee. Had she been so wrapped up in their wedding plans that she hadn't listened properly? The longer Diane thought about that, the more uneasy she became. And with the uneasiness, the first seeds of anger were sown. Anger and a sense of betrayal.

When Alex reached the east side of the square, he spotted his father in the crowd of men outside the Council Building.

Dismounting, he tied the filly to a hitching rack and worked his way through the throng to his father's side.

The instant Alex touched his shoulder, his father spun around, his hand instinctively reaching inside his coat for the .31 caliber pocket revolver he always carried. Alex drew back, a smile widening the line of his mouth at how jumpy his father had become. Admittedly, the frequent and violent clashes between Watie's supporters and the members of his father's society of Pins Indians had given him cause. Alex knew of at least three killings that had occurred.

"You should never come up behind a man like that," his father growled in irritation.

"Sorry."

"You should be. Where have you been? Ross is about to address the convention. I thought you wanted to hear him."

"I do." Alex followed his father to the meeting area.

It was jammed with people. Most were dressed in the frock coat and white shirt of a planter while some wore the hunting shirt and turban of the mountain Cherokee. Kipp immediately scanned the gathering, not stopping until he located The Blade. His Negro servant was at his side, and Lije stood nearby.

Distracted by The Blade's presence, Kipp didn't hear the beginning of Ross's address. With gritted teeth, Kipp watched The Blade, noting how smug he looked standing there, listening to Ross speak the words that would ally them with the Confederacy, words that accomplished the very thing The Blade had wanted. Hatred rose up like a bitter bile in his throat. Kipp swore to himself that The Blade would live to regret this day. He would see to it. Somehow. Some way.

When a resolution for making an alliance with the Confederate States of America was put before the convention, it was greeted with cheers of approval and passed by acclamation. As they filed out of the meeting house, Kipp suddenly found himself face to face with The Blade. His son Lije stood at his side.

The Blade smiled and pulled a cigar from his pocket, lighting it and calmly exhaling the smoke. "It seems we have aligned ourselves with the South."

"No. We have prevented you and your cohort Watie from making your own treaty with the Confederates and usurping Ross's authority, just as you did years ago," Kipp retorted contemptuously.

"Perhaps this time it *is* a fear of losing his power that prompts Ross," The Blade murmured, then lowered his glance to the bulge in Kipp's coat. "But now you will have an opportunity to use that pistol you always carry, won't you?"

Surprise and the dawning of an idea robbed Kipp of the chance to make a suitably cutting reply before The Blade moved off. He stared after that wide set of shoulders, as always partially blocked by the Negro servant who had become his shadow over the years. In the heat of battle, no one would know who fired the shot that killed a man. No one. The idea grew in Kipp's mind, taking root in the fertile soil of his hatred for The Blade.

Lije glanced sideways at his father. "It wasn't wise to bait Kipp like that."

"Kipp doesn't need baiting," The Blade replied in dismissal.

Outside the meeting house, The Blade paused to relight his cigar. Lije halted beside him and idly swept his glance over the slowly dispersing throng. Among the many shades of dark clothing, he caught a glimpse of deep rose and focused on it. Diane stood alone in the square directly across from him, her pink parasol raised to break the glare of the sun as she scanned the faces of the departing men. Lije knew she was looking for him, and he also knew why.

"Diane is waiting for you," his father observed.

Lije nodded grimly. "I know. I won't be long." He moved away.

When she saw him crossing the dirt street, she took a step toward him, then stopped and waited for him to reach her, a fine tension in every line of her body. He read the anxiety and confusion written in her expressive eyes.

"Is it true?" she asked, already braced for his answer. "You have joined the Confederacy?"

"It isn't official. A treaty has yet to be signed, but Ross has the authority to do so now."

"Why didn't you tell me?" Diane demanded. "Why didn't you make it clear the outcome of this meeting would be different? Why did I have to hear it from your cousin Alex?"

Alex. Lije had no difficulty at all imagining the enjoyment Alex had derived from being the one to enlighten Diane. He battled back the surge of anger.

"What would it have changed if you had known?"

"Nothing, I suppose," Diane admitted in frustration. "But it wasn't fair to keep it from me. I am not a child to be protected from unpleasantness."

"No," Lije agreed and sought to end this discussion. "Where are Mother and Eliza?"

"At the dressmaker's shop. I had an appointment to be measured for my gown. Sorrel—"

"I'll walk you there." He took her arm and turned in the direction of the dressmaker's shop near the Masonic Building. "From now on, stay close to them. It might not be wise to venture off by yourself anymore."

"Are you suggesting it's no longer safe for me to walk down a public street?"

"It's widely known that your father is an officer in the Union army, Diane. And we have now aligned ourselves with the South. You may not be treated as kindly as you once were." Lije didn't know if there would be more to it than that, and he didn't care to find out.

She fell silent after that. When they reached the shop entrance, she turned to face him. "What will happen now, Lije?" she asked. "What will you do?"

"What I must," he replied, deliberately evasive.

"I—"

Sorrel came bounding out of the shop. "Hurry, Diane. Mrs. Adair is ready to measure you. I'm all done. She said my dress will be the most beautiful one she has ever made."

"That's wonderful, Sorrel. Now go tell Mrs. Adair I'll be in directly."

Sorrel frowned. "But she's waiting for you."

"You'd better go in," Lije told Diane.

"Where are you going?"

"My father and I have to meet some people. I'll see you tonight." He managed a smile before he walked away. His expression soon hardened with the thing he had to do and the knowledge of what it might cost him.

A copper sun clung to the rim of the western horizon. Its lengthening rays washed the plantation's white columns with amber light as Lije returned home, accompanied by his father and the Negro servant Deuteronomy Jones. Ike waited to take his horse. Lije dismounted and handed over the reins, then glanced at the house, half-expecting to see Diane emerge.

As the horses were led away, The Blade joined him. "I know the trouble this will cause with Diane."

Lije nodded, aware his father spoke from personal experience. "I saw it coming. I had hoped it could be avoided, but . . ." He shook his head, the line of his mouth turning grim again. The moment he had dreaded was now here. There was no turning from it, no way to make it easier.

Gripped by that bleak knowledge, Lije entered the house. Temple crossed the grand foyer, smiling a welcome. "You are home earlier than I expected. I thought I would have to delay dinner tonight."

Lije glanced past her. "Where's Diane?"

"She went up to her room. I—"

But Lije didn't wait to hear more, going directly to the staircase that curved to the second-floor bedrooms. He climbed the steps one at a time, his movements unhurried and deliberate. When he reached the top, the door to the guest room opened, and Diane came out. She had changed into a summer-green dress that intensified the blue of her eyes and the yellow gold of her hair. Lije stopped and watched her approach, studying the perfection of her features, the subtle allure of her smile, and the knowing glow in her eyes that radiated a warmth he seemed to feel in his blood.

"I hoped I would have a chance to speak to you before dinner, Lije." She stopped before him and reached up to straighten and smooth the lapel of his coat, an intimate and wifely gesture that subtly staked claim to him. "I was short with you today and that was wrong of me. Joining the Confederacy was not your doing. I know that. But it was extremely upsetting, coming as it did with no forewarning."

"I had hoped it wouldn't come to pass." The truth of that statement was in the flatness of his voice.

When she tilted her head, inviting his embrace, the urge was strong to gather her into his arms and love this moment away. Seemingly of their own volition, his arms circled her waist, but he held her loosely, stirred by the fragrance rising from her flaxen hair. He breathed it in, memorizing its scent and a thousand other details about her.

"I shouldn't have said there were no forewarnings," Diane said and sighed with easy ruefulness. "There were numerous indications—the things your father said, the changing attitudes of others—but I refused to believe them, pretended not to hear all the many hints that were made. Looking back, I can see all of them now. But, today, the idea of rebel soldiers riding freely through the countryside—"

"That is why it will be best if you go back to Saint Louis where your father is posted." Lije was blunt with her. Deliberately.

"Without you?" Startled, she looked up, her lips parting

in surprise. Recovering, she released a half-irritated laugh. "What a ridiculous thing to say. You don't honestly believe the arrival of rebel troops will make me leave here. Admittedly, their presence will be offensive, but I'm not about to flee from it."

"And if there are rebel soldiers living under this roof?"

Diane drew back, shock draining the color from her face. "What are you saying? Will rebel troops be quartered here?"

"Chief Ross has agreed to raise two regiments for the Confederacy. Watie has again asked my father to join his ranks. This time he agreed. He is now organizing a company to serve under Watie, which he will command."

"Your father," she murmured with a mixture of regret and anguish. "Lije, how awful for you—"

He cut across her words, his voice hard. "I have resigned from the Light Horse to join my father's company. I—"

Before he could say more, Diane pulled back, recoiling from him, the heat of anger and accusation in her eyes. "How can you join the rebels? Don't you know what this means?"

"Yes." His reply was clipped.

"You can't. You can't or you wouldn't do this." She came back to him, pressing close, her chin lifting in silent determination. "You love me, Lije. I know you do. We can go away together—we can go back East, far from the war and the fighting."

"No." He kept his arms at his sides. Her reaction was exactly what he had expected. But that didn't make it hurt any less.

"But there's no reason for you to be involved in it," she argued.

"I believe there is."

"You can't." Her fingers curled into the cloth of his frock coat as her expression registered his resolve. "Don't you realize it's only a matter of time before Union troops will be sent to drive the Confederates out?"

"I know, that."

"You know that?" Diane was incredulous. "But my father could be among those troops. You could be fighting him."

"Would you have me fight my father instead?" Lije challenged.

"Why must you fight at all? Why must you put me through the torture of having my father on one side and you on the other? It isn't fair."

"I'm sorry. It's what I have to do."

His reply stopped her, but only for an instant. "But what of your grandfather and your mother? You know their sympathies are with the Union. They won't approve of this either."

"But they don't have enemies who are eager to kill them."

"The old feud," Diane murmured tightly. "That's what this is about, isn't it? It has nothing to do with the North or the South." When he didn't answer, Diane unleashed her frustration. "All that started long before you were born. You had no part in the feud. It has nothing to do with you."

Lije disputed that. "I saw my grandfather Shawano die at the hands of assassins. I won't stand by and watch my father killed."

"Just because your uncle Kipp—"

"My uncle is only one of many who would like to see my father dead . . . just as my father is one of many they would like to see dead. This war gives them a license to kill. Given the opportunity, they will use it. When they do, there will be reprisals. For many Cherokees, your war between the North and the South will become nothing more than an excuse to settle old scores. I must weigh in on my father's side."

Diane stared at him, her body stiff with resentment and her eyes bright with tears. "There's nothing I can say, is there? You don't care what this does to us. You don't care how I feel."

"I care—but that won't change my decision."

"Don't you see what you're doing, Lije?" she said tightly. "You are choosing the past over our future together. You are more concerned with settling old scores than you are with building a new life with me."

"It may seem that way."

"It *is* that way."

"I can't take the chance of the past repeating itself."

"Then—this ends it between us, Lije. I can't marry a man who would go into battle against my father, not because he believes in the rebel cause—I might have respected that— but because of some ancient feud that began before you were ever born!"

He nodded slowly. "I will arrange for your passage on the keelboat scheduled to leave for Fort Smith at the end of this week. From there you can travel by overland stage to Saint Louis."

"My trunks will be packed by morning. I would prefer not to remain in this house another day. If your grandparents cannot take me in, then I will stay at the hotel until the boat leaves." Diane crossed to her room, then stopped, her hand on the door. "You must know the South will lose this war," she said without turning.

"It's very likely."

She walked into the guest room and closed the door, shutting him out. Lije stood motionless, conscious of a sense of loss that pumped him empty. Slowly, he turned and walked back down the steps, alone.

Diane gathered another armload of undergarments from the tall chest of drawers and carried it to the bed. One by one, she folded them and placed them in a trunk. Every movement was carefully calculated, carefully controlled, a defense against the storm tide of emotions that threatened to rip her apart. Tears burned the back of her eyes, but she wouldn't give in to them. She had learned, to her pain, that Lije Stuart was not worth shedding one tear over.

There was a knock at her door. Diane dropped a camisole

and whirled around to face the door. "Who is it?" She held herself still, wanting it to be Lije.

"Diane, it's Temple. May I come in?"

A shudder of disappointment nearly fractured her control. She scooped up the fallen camisole and turned back to the trunk. "Of course, come in." She didn't look around when the door opened and Temple walked in. "I expect Lije told you I'm leaving—that we have broken our engagement." She spoke curtly, needing the sharpness to keep the pain from surfacing.

"Yes," Temple said quietly. "I hoped we might talk."

"Perhaps you should speak to your son. He's the one who refuses to listen to reason." Diane laid the camisole in the trunk and picked up a cotton slip.

"I was once in a similar situation years ago," Temple said. "Like you, I thought my only choice was to walk away. I was wrong. I don't want to see you make the same mistake I did, Diane. Loving a person means that the time will invariably come when you strongly disagree with him, but that's when you have to hold on to your love even more tightly. You have to love each other in spite of that."

"I know you mean well, Mrs. Stuart. But the circumstances are different. You see, I was more than willing to compromise, more than willing to meet him halfway. But your son refused to make any concession."

"This was a difficult decision for him—one he didn't make lightly. Try to understand—"

"But I do understand, Temple. I understand very well. Lije chose the past over me." It was clear to Diane that Lije didn't love her. How could he when he cared nothing at all about her feelings? He wanted her, he desired her, but he didn't love her. That, in the final analysis, was the only conclusion she could reach.

* * *

An early morning fog drifted through the trees, turning the air cool and heavy with its dampness. Here and there, light rays splintered through its filmy web to sparkle on the dew-wet grass. It was only a matter of time before the rising sun burned off the thin layers of mist.

A stable hand led another horse over for Lije's inspection. The slow, steady thud of its plodding hooves echoed loud in the morning stillness, the sound carrying just as it had earlier when Lije heard the rumble and clatter of a horse-and-wagon team pulling up at the house—one sent to transport Diane to his grandfather's home at Oak Hill. Lije knew, any moment now, the wagon would be leaving with Diane.

With one ear tuned for the sound of the departing wagon, Lije signaled the stable hand to trot the roan horse so he could watch how the animal moved. The roan had traveled no more than a few yards when Lije heard the telltale click of a hind foot overreaching to strike a front hoof. He ordered the horse stopped to determine the cause of this gait defect.

When he saw no fault in the roan's conformation, he walked over and checked its feet. Finding the problem, he told the stable hand, "Make sure he gets reshod."

As Lije moved to the roan's head, he caught the sound of footsteps and the rustle of petticoats coming from the path that led to the big house. He turned, half-hoping . . . But it was his mother who approached the stables through the swirls of mist. He turned back to the roan and took a snug hold of its lower jaw, then rolled its lips back to examine its teeth, deliberately taking his time about it.

Temple halted behind him. "They're bringing down the last of Diane's trunks, Lije. She will be leaving soon."

"I know." The inspection complete, Lije waved to the stable hand to take the horse away.

"Aren't you going to tell her goodbye?" Temple persisted.

"Everything was said last night." He waited for the next horse to be brought out.

"You will regret this, Lije."

He nodded. "We both regret it, but that changes nothing."

Temple studied her son's profile, pained by the hardness she saw in his cheek and jawline—and by the feelings he kept deeply repressed. Like Diane, Temple strongly disagreed with the decision her husband and son had made, but unlike her, Temple would not estrange herself from them because of it. Not this time.

She touched his arm, wishing she could take away his pain. "Maybe after the war," she said, seeking to give him hope.

"Maybe." But Lije wouldn't look that far ahead.

Stand Watie, commissioned a colonel in the Confederate army, had made old Fort Wayne the headquarters for his regiment of Cherokee Mounted Rifles. By the time Diane left on her journey to Saint Louis, Lije and The Blade Stuart had reported for duty at the old fort, along with the company they had raised.

A second regiment of Home Guard was also organized, to serve the South under the command of John Drew. Lije wasn't surprised to learn that Kipp and Alex had joined it along with a large number of Pins Indians.

On October 7, 1861, the treaty between the Cherokee Nation and the Confederate States of America was signed at Park Hill, officially making the Cherokee an ally of the South—and the Union their mutual enemy.

But there was little action that winter except the inglorious pursuit of a large band of Creeks, loyal to the Union, who were trying to reach the safety of the Kansas border. The rest of the forces marched and drilled in preparation for a planned spring campaign to sweep through sympathetic Missouri and capture Saint Louis. The campaign was to be launched from northern Arkansas.

❦ 10 ❧

Grand View Plantation
Cherokee Nation, Indian Territory
March 11, 1862

Wisps of smoke curled from the chimneys of the Doric-columned mansion nestled among the trees. Weariness, bone-deep and mind-numbing, gripped him as Alex stared at the smoke. Smoke meant fire, warmth, and food. He kicked the black filly into a trot and tugged on the reins of the horse in tow.

The jarring gait drew an immediate groan of pain from the man on the second horse. Alex instantly checked the filly's pace and glanced back at his father. He was slumped low on the horse's neck, his body shifted to one side, straining the ropes that tied him to the saddle. His gaunt face was pasty and grayed with pain beneath the battle grime, his dirty jacket torn and blood-soaked.

Drawing back level with him, Alex carefully eased Kipp onto the saddle seat. "We're almost there. Another hundred yards. No more than that."

"Where?" Kipp made a weak attempt to rouse himself "Where are we?"

"Temple's." Alex had decided not to try to reach Oak Hill.

His father had drifted in and out of consciousness ever since his wound started bleeding again.

"Should have killed him." Kipp began rambling, "charged that . . . battery, my chance then . . . I should have . . . killed him."

"Don't talk. Save your strength."

But Alex knew what his father was talking about. As clearly as he could see the house before him, he remembered the moment when he saw his father take aim at The Blade. In the confusion of their charge on the Union battery emplacement, his father had hesitated—no more than a second. Then the horse in front of him went down, shot out from under its rider, and the opportunity for a clear shot at The Blade had been lost.

That memory was only one in a series that were stored in Alex's mind, filling him with sharp, vivid impressions. He wiped the palm of his hand on the leg of his breeches, remembering how sweaty it had been when they formed up behind that rail fence in Arkansas near a place called Pea Ridge. There were a thousand of them, Watie's regiment on foot and his on horseback, along with a squad of Texas cavalry, all lined up to charge the Union battery. It had consisted of three guards, supported by a detachment of Union cavalry. Between the enemy fire and the thundering rush of blood in his head, Alex hadn't heard the order to charge.

The noise, he remembered that—the gobbling war cry of the full-bloods, the eerie rebel yells of the Texans, the rapid drumming of hooves, the explosion of gunfire, and the boom of the cannons. And the smells too, he remembered them— the acrid powder smoke, rank horsehide, sweating flesh, and most of all the smell of fear.

In a strange way, he had seen everything around him, yet he hadn't been able to focus on anything. His recollection of the charge, the skirmish around the batteries, was made up of disjointed images—a horse somersaulting to the ground; men reeling backward; faces contorted in expressions of savage desperation; blood oozing between the fingers of someone's hand clutching a wound; a riderless horse fleeing in panic, empty stirrups flapping against its sides; and a cavalry officer in blue leveling his gun—at him.

Even now Alex couldn't remember pulling back the hammer of his navy revolver or squeezing the trigger. He could only remember the jerk of the revolver in his hand, the officer recoiling to his left, and the revolver jerking again and again until the man tumbled from the saddle.

But that was after they had captured the guns, when the exhilaration of victory was screaming through him—the exhilaration and the soaring sense of power. The fleet black filly had carried him to the front of the charging line; he had routed the enemy and put fear in their faces. The sight and smell of blood hadn't been revolting like some had said. When he reloaded his revolver, Alex remembered laughing at the discovery that his hands weren't shaking, but cold and steady.

The filly stopped. For a split second, absorbed in his recollections, Alex didn't know why. Then he saw the white columns immediately before him and the wide veranda beyond that circled the mansion.

Dismounting, he dropped the filly's reins and walked back to his father. He was unconscious again. Where the hell was everybody? Hadn't anyone seen them ride in? Then he spotted a slave approaching the house from the stables.

"Boy! Hey, boy!" he shouted and began loosening the rope that held his father in the saddle. "Come here and give me a hand." When the young black man broke into a lazy trot, Alex snapped, "Dammit, I said get over here and help me. Now!" The slow trot turned into a loping run.

Together they dragged his father from the horse and carried him into the house. Alex paid no attention to the lavish furnishings, taking note only of the tuneless plinking of a piano coming from the music room.

"Temple! Aunt Temple!" He halted in the grand foyer dominated by a sweeping staircase to the second floor.

The piano exercises ceased, followed quickly by the sound of running feet. "Alex!" Ten-year-old Sorrel raced toward him, smiling in delight, then faltered, the smile fading. "Uncle Kipp," she uttered in alarm. "What's wrong with Uncle Kipp?"

Just then Temple appeared, and Alex addressed his answer to her. "He's been shot."

"No." As quickly as it came, the expression of shock left her face. "Take him upstairs to my room. Sorrel, go tell Phoebe to bring my medicine, bandages, and some hot water."

"But—"

"Don't argue with me!" Temple flashed. "Just do as you're told and be quick about it." She grabbed her daughter by the shoulders and gave her a push toward the rear of the house, then hurried after Alex and Ike as they carried Kipp up the steps to her second-floor bedroom. After they laid him on the bed, Temple carefully lifted aside his jacket to expose his torn and bloodied shirt. "When did this happen?"

"Two . . . no, three days ago," Alex replied. "I dug the bullet out. But it's started bleeding again."

Kipp moaned when his sister gently pulled the blood-soaked bandage away from the wound, revealing the jagged and fiery red hole. With an effort, Temple steeled herself not to react to the sight, reminding herself of the number of blacks she had treated with injuries more horrible than a bullet wound. Except this was her brother.

"We heard rumors all the Cherokee regiments had pulled out to meet a Union force. What happened?"

"There was a battle . . . over in Arkansas along Telegraph Road near the Butterfield stage stop at Elkhorn Tavern. It went on for three days." Raking a hand through his hair, Alex moved away from the sofa, a drawn, tired look on his face. "We should have won. There were over sixteen thousand of us. Someone said the Union army had less than ten thousand. The first day, I thought we would beat them. We took one of their artillery emplacements. Some of the full-bloods called the guns 'the wagons that shoot.'" He inserted a humorless laugh and gazed at the ceiling. "But we couldn't move the guns to the rear because we didn't have any battery horses. So we burned the wooden carriages. Then they started shelling us, and we had to take cover in the woods."

Phoebe hurried into the bedroom carrying a kettle of hot water, cloth for bandages, and Temple's medicine basket. "Is he hurt bad, Miss Temple?"

Temple shook her head uncertainly. She was aware that both her daughter and Ike stood inside the room, but at the moment her concern was split. "Lije and The Blade, do you know if they're all right?" She glanced at her nephew while Phoebe poured hot water from the kettle into the china wash-bowl and cooled it with water from the matching pitcher.

"I don't know." Alex avoided her gaze. "The last I heard, Watie and some of his men had taken up a position on the ridge behind the tavern to observe enemy movements. General McCulloch and General McIntosh were both killed on the second day of fighting—General Slack was wounded and had to be taken from the field. There was so much confusion," he said. "We were pinned down in the woods with shells and shot exploding all around us. All the supplies and ammunition were back at Camp Stephens on Little Sugar Creek. Finally, we made our way back there. That's when Father was shot—when we were retreating. Our regiment had scattered. I couldn't find any help. I knew I had to get him out of there. I had to get him home."

When he turned to check on his father, Sorrel gasped loudly. "Alex, there's blood on your neck. You've been hurt!"

In vague surprise, he reached up and felt the side of his neck, wincing slightly when he touched a dark, blood-caked line. Sorrel rushed to his side, but he impatiently dismissed her concern. "It's nothing. Only a crease."

"It needs tending just the same." Not to be deterred, she took his arm and pushed him backward onto the plushly up-holstered seat of the bedroom's mahogany armchair. "Now you sit there while I clean it for you."

Temple stole a look at the two of them as Sorrel busied herself with wetting a cloth. Her mothering brought an amused smile to Alex's face.

"I don't think it will require a bandage," Sorrel informed him, assuming a very adultlike air, when she finished washing the wound.

"I don't either." Alex hid a smile.

She sighed and gazed at him proudly. "I'll bet you were very brave, Alex."

"Brave?" That hint of a smile faded, a hardness taking over his expression. "I might feel brave if we had won. We should have. We would have." Alex insisted forcefully, "if the Confederates had kept their promises to us. But the weapons they issued us—old shotguns and muskets, pepper-boxes for pistols, flintlocks—that's what most of them were. Half of them wouldn't fire. And the other half, you wondered if they would blow up in your face. We were no match for the Union troops with their modern rifles and revolvers. Some of the full-bloods elected to fight with bows and arrows and tomahawks rather than use the worthless guns they were given, and I don't blame them. Father and I were lucky. We had our own guns. I wouldn't be alive if it weren't for the navy revolver I won from Grandfather."

He paced as he talked, his hands moving all the time. Temple was unnerved by the wildness in his eyes, but she recognized that he needed to talk and she let him, keeping her own hands busy applying a poultice and bandage to Kipp's inflamed wound.

"Where is the money they were supposed to pay us? We haven't received it or the uniforms or warm coats they promised either. As for food—when there is any—it isn't fit to feed a field nigger." Alex paused and issued another harsh, humorless laugh. "On our way back to Camp Stephens, we met a wounded soldier from the Missouri brigade. He said when they captured the Union supply camp, they found barrels of flour, hams, oysters, sardines, lobsters, canned fruits, cheese, and coffee. Except for some skinny squirrels I killed, all we had to eat this last week was parched corn." Holding back none of his bitterness and frustration, Alex swung around to face her. "Dammit to hell, we weren't even supposed to be in Arkansas. It states in our treaty that we aren't required to fight outside the borders of the Indian Territory. What the hell were we doing in Arkansas?"

Unexpectedly, the rage seemed to vanish, leaving only a bitterness in his dark eyes when Alex looked at his father. He walked slowly to the bed.

"We never should have made a treaty with the Confederates," Alex muttered. "More and more are saying that. My father said it from the beginning, but nobody would listen to him. They wouldn't be hungry and cold now, or armed with worthless guns. They wouldn't have been beaten at Pea Ridge and forced to run."

Temple finished tying Kipp's bandage, then pulled the quilt over Kipp's shoulders. "Warmth and rest are the two things he needs now." She smoothed the front of her apron. "Get this mess cleared away, Phoebe, and have Caesar get a fire started in the fireplace. When you go downstairs, tell Dulcie to fix Alex something to eat. Ike, you take care of their horses."

"Right away, Miss Temple." With a quick bob of his head, Ike backed out of the bedroom into the second-floor hall.

The minute he was out of sight of his mistress, Ike stopped and thought back on everything Miss Temple's nephew had said about the battle. If Master Blade and Lije had been there, then his father had too. He never went anywhere without Deu. Had he been hurt?

Ike tried to be worried about him. Part of him was. But the rest . . . the rest of him was excited by the news that the Union army had won the battle. They might be marching into the Nation this very minute to free all the slaves. The thought filled him with a kind of exultation. He ran down the stairs, his feet barely touching the steps.

* * *

A week later word reached Grand View that The Blade, Lije, and Deu had emerged from the battle at Elkhorn Tavern relatively unscathed. By then, Kipp had recovered sufficiently from his wound to rejoin his company. Two weeks later, it was part of the detachment sent to John Ross's home at Park Hill to guard the principal chief, the Nation's governmental documents and records, and its funds.

Ike waited in vain for the Union troops to arrive. Instead of pursuing the retreating rebels, the Union army remained at the battle site. Ike had to face the fact they weren't coming. At least not yet.

☙ 11 ☙

Fort Davis
Indian Territory
July 1862

When The Blade returned from an officers' briefing, the hard set of his features warned Lije the news was not good. Following the rebel defeat at Pea Ridge in Arkansas, Lije's regiment under Cherokee colonel Stand Watie had become the advance guard along the northern border of the Indian Territory, with orders to gather information on Union troop movements and to raid and harass the enemy whenever and wherever possible. Lije's regiment was now stationed at Fort Davis on the south bank of the Arkansas River—within sight of Fort Gibson, a scant three miles away.

The Blade passed Lije without a look or a word and went straight to his tent. Deu waited for him under the canvas-topped ramada that provided relief from the unstinting glare of the July sun. The Blade took off his hat and shoved it at Deu, then picked up the bucket of drinking water and poured some into a tin pan. He set the bucket back on the ground and bent over the tin pan, scooping up the tepid water in his hands and splashing it over his face and neck.

Lije walked over. "What's the situation?"

The Blade straightened and took the clean bandanna Deu handed him, his glance running momentarily to Lije. "Yesterday the Union flag was raised over Fort Gibson." He mopped his wet face with the bandanna, blotting the excess water from it. "Today we learned Ross was arrested at Park Hill and immediately released on parole. The entire detachment sent to guard Ross and the government documents deserted en masse to join the Federals."

Kipp and Alex had been part of that detachment, which meant they were now on the Union's side.

"You expected that would happen," Lije reminded him.

"I expected it," his father admitted with a grim nod. "The Union is now actively recruiting Cherokees. Already, they have one regiment and they are seeking to fill the next. In all, it's expected that some twelve hundred will join them, most of them deserters from our own ranks."

"The number doesn't surprise me," Lije said. "Even though most Cherokees favored the idea of neutrality, many also leaned toward the Union."

"Do you see the irony in all this?" The Blade turned his sharp gaze on Lije, a bitter humor slanting his mouth. "For years they have condemned me for signing the false treaty that brought our people to this land. Yet they urged Ross to sign a treaty with the Confederacy. Now, at the sight of the first Union soldiers, they turn their backs on it and rush to join them. Their treaty was false, and they know it. But knowing it will only make them hate me more—me and all the others of the old Treaty party who remain loyal to the Confederates." He looked to the north at the heat waves shimmering in the distance. "This war is now openly one of old grudges and new."

Once Lije had believed the War Between the States would be over soon. Now he realized the Cherokee Nation was beginning a war that would likely continue long after the American Civil War ended. He thought of Diane with a deepening sense of pain and regret. There was no chance for them now. None at all.

"One thing about it," Lije said, searching for something positive in all this, however twisted it might be, "you won't have Kipp at your back anymore. From now on, you'll be facing him across the battle lines."

"There is something to be said for that," The Blade agreed in a desert-dry voice. "Maybe now I'll lose that twitchy feeling in my spine."

The Union troops didn't remain in the area long. Lack of rain and intense summer heat had burned the grass throughout most of the Nation, leaving little forage for their horses. The wagon train with much-needed supplies and provisions had failed to arrive from Baxter Springs. And the commanding officer of the Union expedition had been arrested by the second-ranking officer and charged with either being insane or plotting treason. The combination of these factors prompted the Union army to withdraw from the territory near the end of July, leaving behind a portion of two regiments of the Indian Home Guard to protect the area.

As soon as the Confederates learned the white troops had pulled out, rebel units crossed the Arkansas to test the strength and the resolve of the two Cherokee brigades that remained, brigades composed mainly of soldiers whom the South regarded as turncoats. During the first week of raids and skirmishes, damage was inflicted by both sides.

The big bay horse snorted and shied from Lije's examining touch. "Easy, Jubal. Easy," Lije crooned and threw a quick glance at Deu to make certain he had a snug hold on the bay's head.

After that short flare of resistance, the horse soon settled and stood quietly, putting no weight on its left front leg, its head hanging low, its ears drooping, its eyes dull. Lije watched

Deu take an extra wrap on the lead rope, then slid his own hand down the bay's wither toward the shoulder wound, all the while listening to the distinctive grunting breaths of an animal in pain.

Releasing a troubled sigh, Lije stepped back and nodded to Deu to relax his hold on the horse. "It looks worse today than yesterday. Maybe if we put a poultice on it."

"If my boy Ike were here, he'd have Jubal running around on all four legs in no time," Deu said. "He always did have a healing touch when it came to horses."

Lije offered a distracted nod of agreement, then turned, catching the familiar clatter of shuffling hooves, rubbing leather, and jingling chains that signaled the return of a patrol from across the Arkansas. It was a Texas troop, led by a man on a zebra dun, gold lieutenant's bars sewn on his gray jacket. There was something familiar about him. Lije studied him a moment, then smiled inwardly when he recognized the drover who had shared a campfire with him on the eve of the war.

"Lassiter, isn't it?" he hailed the man. "Ransom Lassiter from the Rocking Lazy L."

The Texan reined in and frowned, then smiled crookedly and leaned forward to rest his arms on the front of his saddle, a weariness lining his features. "Lije Stuart, what I wouldn't give for a taste of that coffee you had." The lazy drawl was the same, but that familiar glint of humor was gone from his gray eyes. The war and the fighting had done that, Lije realized. It had taken away the laughter and the softness, made it a memory they reached for now and again. All of them. And after only one short year of fighting.

"Wouldn't we all," Lije agreed.

"What happened?" Rans nodded at the drooping bay.

"Gunshot. Nothing vital was hit. I dug the ball out two days ago, but he's still going down."

"Good-looking horse," Rans said, his glance traveling over the bay. "He's got some thoroughbred in him, doesn't he?"

"He does," Lije confirmed.

"We're going to need horses like that one," he said, then looked again at Lije. "One of my boys used to live with the Comanche. Nobody knows more about horses than the Comanche. If you want, he can take a look at yours, see if there's anything he could do for it."

"I'd be obliged."

Rans turned in the saddle and shouted down the line, "Kelly!"

"Sir!" A private in Confederate gray reined his horse out of the column and cantered forward. He had a boy's build and youthful features, and the beard stubble of a grown man on his cheeks.

"See what you can do for the lieutenant's horse," Rans ordered. The private threw him a half salute and walked his horse closer to the bay, then dismounted. Lije moved aside to let him examine the horse's shoulder wound. "Looks like your horse wasn't the only one shot." Rans glanced pointedly at the bandage tied high on Lije's left arm.

"Just a crease." Lije shrugged it off, the action setting up sharp twinges. He ignored them, just as he ignored the dull throb that took their place.

"It's a good thing nobody is going to be asking you to raise your arms in surrender anytime soon," Rans observed, his mouth twitching in a near smile as he straightened in the saddle. "Both Yankee Indian brigades have pulled out. Your chief, John Ross, went with them, along with his entire family and most of his valuables."

"Ross is gone?" Lije frowned in surprise.

Rans nodded. "Headed for Kansas. Word is that he took the government records and documents with him, and all of the funds."

"For safekeeping, no doubt," Lije guessed, aware this news would upset many—most of all his commanding officer, Colonel Stand Watie.

"No doubt." Rans lifted the dun's reins. "I'd better go make my report. Send Kelly on to camp when he's through." He started to signal the patrol forward, then checked the movement. "You know what else I heard?"

"What?"

"The Union army in Kansas is recruiting coloreds. Sounds to me like the North is getting desperate."

Piano music drifted softly into the library. The lazy melody matched the August breeze that wandered through the open French doors and caused the candle flame to sway ever so slightly. Shadrach turned the page of Rollin's *Ancient History* and changed the tilt of the book to allow more light to fall on the printed words.

A whisper of movement came from outside the open doors. He paused to listen, but it didn't come again. The Negro dismissed it as the rustling of the evening breeze. He read another sentence, then heard it again—the sound, very light, very careful, a suggestion of stealth in it. Someone was out there. And it wasn't Master Will or Eliza.

Slowly and quietly, Shadrach closed the book and inched it down alongside him, pushing it between the arm of the chair and the seat cushion. He didn't know who was out there, but he didn't want some rebel to catch him looking at a book. There had been reprisals against Union sympathizers, now that the Union troops had withdrawn from the area. It was well known that Will Gordon was a staunch supporter of Ross. Add to that the fact his son and grandson had joined the Union army, and the Gordons were a prime target. Shadrach sensed there was trouble ahead, worse than in Georgia.

It could be it was outside this very minute.

"Psst. Uncle Shad," a voice whispered from the darkness.

Frowning, Shadrach rose from the chair and walked to the doors. He could see nothing but a sliver of moonlight filtering through the trees into the formal gardens.

"Ike?" he called back softly. "Is that you?"

"Yeah. I gotta talk to you."

Shadrach glanced at the library doors that stood open to the hall. From beyond them came the lilting strains of a waltz on the piano. "Stay there." He gestured to his unseen nephew, then walked quietly to the doors and pulled them together, leaving a small gap so he could hear Eliza if she summoned him.

He went back to the French doors and motioned for Ike to come inside. A dark figure stole from behind a bush and darted through the opening, crouching low. The minute he entered the library, Ike stepped sideways so he couldn't be seen from outside, a furtiveness in his every action and look.

"What are you doing here?"

"I'm leaving for Kansas." Ike spoke low and quick. "They're recruiting coloreds into the Union army up there, and I'm going to join. I can't stay around here waiting for them to come free us. I have got to go fight . . . and help it come about. I wanted to tell Ma what I was doing, but . . . she wouldn't understand. She would no more think of leaving the Stuarts than she'd think of shaving all the hair off her head. She acts like they're family. She's your sister. I thought . . . maybe you could explain to her where I'm going and why."

"Are you sure they're taking coloreds into the army?" Shadrach was skeptical.

"I'm sure. They're trying to raise a whole regiment. They're gonna give us guns, teach us how to shoot, and everything. They're even going to give us uniforms just like regular white soldiers."

"Where in Kansas?"

"Leavenworth. I figure if I travel at night and hide in the daytime, I can make it without being caught. I don't know how long it will take, but—" He stopped and eyed Shadrach warily. "Why?"

"Because I'm going with you." When had he decided

that? Shadrach was as stunned as Ike to hear the words come out of his mouth. The idea was crazy. It was mad. They probably wouldn't make it, but . . . by God, he was going to try.

"Are you sure? I mean . . ." Ike stammered in confusion and surprise.

Shadrach suddenly noticed Eliza wasn't playing the piano anymore. He held up his hand to silence Ike and cocked his head toward the doors. He could hear two sets of footsteps. "Wait outside." He lowered his voice to a whisper, then moved swiftly to the doors. He stepped into the hall, partially closing the doors behind him as Eliza and Will walked arm in arm toward the staircase.

"Miss Eliza."

Both paused and turned. "Shadrach, I didn't realize you were still here," Eliza declared. "We won't be needing you anymore tonight. You—"

"Please. May I have a word with you, Miss Eliza?"

"Of course." She hesitated, then turned to Will. "I'll be along directly."

Smiling, Will nodded and continued to the stairs while she walked down the hall to join Shadrach. Reaching him, Eliza paused and glanced after her husband, watching as he negotiated the steps, moving slowly and stiffly.

"His rheumatism is acting up again," she murmured in concern. "I can't seem to convince him that he needs to take things slower at his age. Will doesn't like to be reminded he's getting older." When he disappeared from view, Eliza turned to face Shadrach, clasping her hands together in front of her. "Now what was it you wanted to talk to me about?"

A smile tugged at the corners of his mouth. That stance, the crisp authority in her voice—she was the schoolteacher again, addressing one of her pupils. For a brief moment Shadrach felt the pull of nostalgia as memories of those few short months he'd spent in her classroom as a boy grew strong within him.

"There are many things I've wanted to say for a long time,

Miss Eliza. But, first of all, I want to thank you for giving me the greatest gift a person can receive . . . an education. I know the risk you ran teaching a slave—"

"I have never thought of you as a slave, Shadrach," Eliza cut in. "I have always looked on you as a friend."

"I know you have. And I'm grateful for that. You always treated me like I had a mind and feelings and dreams. Not many have done that, except . . . maybe Reverend Cole."

"Just what is this all about, Shadrach?"

"It's about me . . . and my dreams. You've always been special to me, Miss Eliza. You opened up a whole new world to me. Maybe it isn't good to teach a slave, because he gets dissatisfied with his life. It starts him to thinking that he is as good as anybody else. He starts wanting things."

She drew back slightly. "What are you saying?"

"I'm saying . . . that I'm leaving. Running away never made any sense to me before. But now, I'm running to something. They are recruiting colored soldiers in Kansas, and that's where I'm going—to join up."

"You can't." Shock, dread, fear, confusion—so many things went through her head that Eliza wasn't sure what her reaction was.

Shadrach smiled a little sadly. "After all you have done for me, I couldn't leave without telling you goodbye. It wouldn't have been right somehow. I would appreciate it if you would explain things to Master Will. He's been good to me, and I wouldn't want him to think that it was anything against him."

"When . . . when are you leaving?"

"We're going tonight."

"We?"

Shadrach hesitated. "I'm going with Ike."

"Don't you know how dangerous it will be?" Eliza protested.

"Yes."

At that moment Eliza knew there was nothing she could say to dissuade him. Oddly enough, she didn't want to. It was crazy, but she felt proud of him. Shadrach was as much of a friend to her as the social barriers between a white woman and a black man would allow.

"You and Ike will need a pass," She walked briskly into the library. "Try to avoid the patrols if you can. I am not certain how much they will respect a pass . . . especially now." Hurriedly, she scratched one out, then folded the paper and handed it to him, for an instant letting their fingers touch. "Be careful, Shadrach."

"I will. Tell Phoebe I will look after Ike."

Eliza nodded. "You were the very best pupil I ever had. I will miss you greatly." When her eyes filled with tears, she felt self-conscious, then noticed that his, too, were moist. Suddenly it was all right.

"I will miss you, too, Miss Eliza. If the good Lord is willing, maybe someday you can come visit the school I'm going to have . . . when we're all free."

"I would like that."

Then Shadrach was gone, slipping out through the French doors. Eliza walked over to them. There, in the patch of moonlight, she could see two figures moving quickly toward the Negro quarters. It struck her as ironic that the first time Shadrach had come into her life, he had been outside a window. Now, the last time she saw him, he was outside a door— a door she had opened for him.

❦ 12 ❧

Two weeks and not a word. Eliza wondered if Shadrach had made it to Kansas. She tried to convince herself that he and Ike were all right. Otherwise, she would have heard something. To her relief Will had agreed to say nothing about Shadrach's absence. She had feared Will would want to post a notice that his slave had run away and offer a reward for his return. She should have known Will would understand.

"It's a beautiful day."

Eliza glanced at her husband. There was a look of contentment on his tired and drawn features. She was glad he had agreed to her suggestion that they sit in the garden after dinner, instead of returning directly to the fields. Here, amidst the deep shade of the trees, the south breeze blew strongly, giving an illusion of coolness to the sweltering heat of midday.

"It is hot." Eliza held the collar of her dress away from her neck, trying to give the air a chance to reach more of her skin.

"It's beautiful and hot," Will conceded, then breathed in deeply. "Can you smell the scent of peaches in the air? They should be ready to pick soon. I must check the orchard later this afternoon."

"You are supposed to be relaxing, not thinking about work," she chided.

"Oh? And what were you thinking about so seriously a moment ago? I saw that worried little frown." Behind the teasing light in his eyes, there was a desire for an answer to his question.

"Susannah." For the life of her, Eliza didn't know why she mentioned their daughter instead of Shadrach, although Susannah had been on her mind a great deal of late. "It has been a long time since we heard from her. I try not to worry. I know she is safer in the East. I only hope we have convinced her to remain there until this war ends. But you know how headstrong she can be at times."

"Just like her mother."

"Will," she said in quick protest.

"It's true." Smiling, Will reached across the iron bench and took her hand, linking their fingers together. "You are an unbelievably headstrong woman, Eliza. You always have been. I remember the time you absolutely refused to leave Gordon Glen . . . and the trail you didn't have to walk, but you did. I remember the teacher who always tried to pretend she was prim and proper. Then I would catch her wading in the creek with the children—no shoes, no stockings, and her skirts up. You haven't changed, Eliza."

"I haven't waded in a creek in years," she retorted in a half-hearted denial.

"Look at you now. The mistress of Oak Hill sitting with her skirts up to her knees letting the breeze blow up her legs."

Made suddenly and self-consciously aware of the sensation of air on her legs, Eliza looked down at the material bunched in her lap, the strip of broderie anglaise that edged her drawers, ending just below her kneecaps, and the white bareness of her legs below that. "It's hot," she offered in her own defense, then looked at Will, and laughed. "Perhaps I haven't changed."

"I hope you never do. I love you just the way you are."

"And I love you, Will Gordon." She clasped his hand a little tighter and felt the answering pressure. She leaned over and kissed him, their lips moving familiarly against each other and clinging for a tender moment before Eliza drew back. After twenty years their passion might not be as intense, but she knew their love was stronger. And that, after all, was what mattered.

"It feels good to sit here with you," he stated.

"For me, too."

She was glad now she hadn't told him about the milk cows that had been stolen from the pasture sometime in the night. She almost had at dinner, but Will had looked so tired she decided not to bother him with it. After all, there wasn't anything he could do about it. They were gone, no doubt stolen by Confederate troops in the area. Before he had gone over to the Union side, Kipp had complained often about the lack of adequate food, warm clothes, and ammunition in the Southern army. Eliza wasn't surprised that the rebels had begun foraging on their own. By now, those cows had probably been butchered, cooked, and eaten, which was a shame; they were good milk cows.

No, she didn't regret her decision not to tell Will. There was time enough to do it later. Right now this peace and quiet was what he needed.

"Miz 'Liza? We's gots the dishes all done." The call came from the house, the voice belonging to Lucy, the maid Eliza had placed in charge of the house staff.

Sighing, Eliza realized how much she had come to rely on Shadrach. Now that he wasn't here to direct the staff, no one seemed to know what to do next.

"I will be right there." Reluctantly, she untwined her fingers from Will's and flipped her skirt and petticoat over her knees. When she stood up, he started to rise, too, but fell back, wincing and pressing a hand to his left shoulder. "I wish we could go to the oil springs at New Spring Place," Eliza murmured. "Your rheumatism always seems better after you've bathed in that green oil."

"Maybe after the harvest is over." Again Will made a move to stand up. "No, you stay here and finish your cider." Eliza glanced at the half-full glass in his left hand.

"All right." Will settled back against the bench.

Although surprised by his ready agreement, she didn't question it. She was glad he was taking advantage of these few minutes to rest. He did it too seldom.

As Eliza walked away, Will watched her, a tall willow of a woman with curly hair and gold-flecked eyes. How strange that in his mind he could still see her so clearly—the way she had been when he first saw her, alarmed but not afraid. He couldn't remember a time when she had ever been afraid.

Absently, Will glanced at the house, studying the white-columned veranda and the neat layers of red brick—brick made right here in their own kiln. The house sat on the crown of a hill, surrounded by towering trees. Lately, the house reminded him more and more of Gordon Glen, his old home back in what was now Georgia. Everything did: the gardens; the row of Negro cabins tucked in the grove of trees; the layout of the buildings; the orchards; the fields of cotton, corn, and indigo; the pastures of cattle; even the clay red soil of the land. The only thing lacking was the sight of peacocks strutting over the lawn. Maybe the next time he went to see John Ross, he would buy a couple of peahens and a cock. No, he couldn't do that. John Ross had left. Gone east, into exile.

He wanted to get up, but he felt too heavy, too tired to move. Then he heard the distant tinkling of music. Was that Eliza playing the piano? It had to be. The tune sounded like his favorite nocturne, the one she always played for him. Smiling, he leaned back against the bench and closed his eyes.

The glass of cider slipped from his loose fingers and fell, crashing against the bench leg and spraying cider onto the grass.

"Will? Will, wake up." Marveling that he could sleep so soundly on the hard iron bench, Eliza gave his shoulder a shake. At her touch, he slumped sideways. "Will," she murmured in vague alarm and bent over him, her hands clasping his wrist. She couldn't find a pulse. "Dear God, no." The first sob rose in her throat. She pressed a fist to her mouth to force it back, but it came through. And more followed. "No, no, no, no," Eliza sobbed over and over again as grief drove her to her knees.

That was the way the housemaid Lucy found her, kneeling beside him and weeping softly, her head resting on his legs, her hands clutching at him. Uncertain, Lucy ventured closer, not wanting to believe what her eyes told her.

"Miz Eliza, Master Will—is he—" She couldn't say the word. He looked too peaceful.

Slowly, very slowly, Eliza pulled herself away from him and rose to her feet, struggling against the heaviness that weighted her heart and her body. She kept her back to the woman, needing to keep her pain private a little longer.

"Will is dead." The words came from that deep cavern of emptiness she felt inside. Eliza made no attempt to wipe the tears from her face as she stared at the gentle man who had been her husband, her lover, and her dearest friend. "Tell Shadrach—" She stopped, remembering that Shadrach had left. Suddenly, her mind was crowded with the hundred things that had to be done, things Shadrach would have seen to if he were still there. Now it was left to her. "Old Tom should be at the stables. Have him get someone to help carry Will into the house."

Lucy hurried away. Alone again, Eliza realized this was the last private moment she would have with her husband.

She bent down and kissed him for the final time. "I love you, Will Gordon," she whispered tightly. "Always and forever."

Two days after Will's death, Lije and The Blade arrived at Oak Hill. A heavy stillness enveloped the house and grounds as if the summer wind had ceased its blowing out of respect for the owner's passing. The black cloth draped around the front door told Lije more clearly than the message they'd received that his grandfather would never again step out of the house to welcome him.

When one of the Negro maids admitted them, Lije found himself missing Shadrach's familiar presence in the house. He hadn't been at all surprised to learn Ike had run off to join the Union's new colored regiment, to the utter shame of his father, Deuteronomy. But Shadrach—Lije still couldn't visualize that slender Negro donning a uniform and taking up arms.

"You came." The relieved words came from his mother as she crossed the great hall to meet them, reaching out a hand to each of them, her dark eyes haunted with grief. "I didn't know if—I wasn't sure—" Her voice threatened to break and Temple stopped, her mouth trembling in a forced smile. "You are both all right? You're both safe."

"We're fine," The Blade assured her.

"I couldn't stand it if anything should happen to you. Not now, not after losing my father," she declared stiffly.

"I know." He gathered her close. For a moment, she allowed herself to accept the solace he offered. Then she drew back. "There was no warning. No warning at all. He was sitting alone in the garden. He was fine when Eliza left him."

"Where is Eliza?" Lije asked.

"She's in the parlor with him."

Lije started for the parlor, then noticed a very subdued Sorrel standing by the archway, pressed close to the wall.

Guiltily, he realized he had never given a thought to his younger sister. His concern had been solely for his mother and Eliza. That changed when he saw the hurt and confusion in her expression.

He went to her. Before he could speak, Sorrel announced, "Alex and Uncle Kipp aren't here. Granny El sent a message to tell them about Grandpa, but she doesn't know whether they got it. She said even if they did, they probably wouldn't come because it's too dangerous for them here." Her eyes accused Lije of being to blame for that.

"These are dangerous times for everyone, Sorrel."

"It isn't right that Alex and Uncle Kipp aren't here."

"A lot of things happen that aren't necessarily right."

"Grandpa always tried to make things right. Now he's gone, nobody will." She turned quickly, hiding the tears that spilled down her lashes, and fled down the great hall.

Once Lije had objected just as passionately to life's injustices. Like Sorrel, he had been young, and he hadn't understood why people couldn't stop hating and killing each other so his father could come home. He still didn't understand it, even though it was once again tearing his family apart.

Sobered by the thought, he turned toward the parlor. Inside, the room's furniture had been rearranged to accommodate his grandfather's casket. Eliza sat beside it, one hand resting on the Bible in her lap and the other on his coffin, her head bowed in silent grief.

She glanced up absently when he entered the room. "Elijah." A small smile of welcome lifted the corners of her mouth, but it couldn't erase the sadness that clouded her eyes. She looked past him. "The Blade," she began, "is he with you?"

"He's with my mother." Lije sat in the chair next to hers and gathered her hand in his.

"Temple has been so worried about both of you."

"I know. How are you, Eliza?"

Tears sprang into her eyes, but she only shook her head

and gave him another brave smile. "It was so quick—and he looked so content." She glanced down at the Bible in her lap. "I wish Reverend Cole could be here."

"Where is he?"

"In Kansas—at Baxter Springs, administering to the refugees from the various Indian Nations who have gathered there." Her attention strayed back to the casket. "Perhaps Kipp will see him there. Nathan would want to know about Will."

"Yes, he would."

The Blade entered the parlor, accompanied by Temple, and offered his condolences to Eliza.

In the awkward, emotional moment that followed, Temple glanced around the room. "Where's Sorrel?"

"I believe she went out to the garden." Lije kept his reply casual.

"I hope she doesn't wander too far from the house." Temple went to one of the parlor windows to look. "There are too many raiders about, too many acts of reprisal taking place now that the Federal troops have left." She turned back to the room, her glance turning to The Blade in silent appeal. "I have tried to convince Eliza that Oak Hill is a prime target. Everyone knows Father's sympathies were always with the North. Now that Kipp and Alex have gone to the Union side, it won't be safe for her to stay here alone. She needs to come live with us at Grand View."

"It would be wise, Eliza," The Blade told her.

"Wise or not, I'm staying here." There was a sharpness to her voice that matched the sharpness of her grief. "This is my home. Will and I built it together. Susannah was born here." At the mention of her daughter, Eliza paused, suddenly distracted. "The letter to Susannah, I must remember to post it," she said, then sighed. "Goodness only knows whether it will reach her. The mails have become so unreliable with all this fighting going on."

"Give it to me," Lije said. "I'll see that it gets through to Susannah."

"How—" Temple broke off the question, a look of dread entering her expression. "You'll be going north again to raid, won't you?"

Lije was careful to avoid a direct answer. "Our regiment has the assignment of patrolling our northern border, and the South is not without friends in Missouri. One of them will see that it gets into a mail pouch bound for the East."

Tears welled in her eyes as Eliza reached out and squeezed his arm. "Thank you."

When Lije rode away from his grandfather's graveside, the letter to Susannah was in his saddlebag. Within a week, his regiment received its orders to move out. The direction was north.

⊸ 13 ⊶

Fort Scott, Kansas
November 1862

A blustery northwest wind swept off the Kansas plains, raising a cloud of dust that swirled around the train depot. Diane shook the worst of it from the skirt of her dove gray suit and glanced idly around the waiting room. When a hand touched her elbow, she turned and looked into the smiling face of her escort, Major Adam Clark, the post surgeon.

"Why don't you have a seat while I find out when the train is due?" He gestured toward the wooden bench along one wall. "Hopefully, it won't be running too late."

"Hopefully," Diane echoed the sentiment and turned toward the bench.

But after riding in the dubious comfort of the post's ambulance wagon, Diane wasn't eager to sit again. Instead, she wandered over to the potbellied stove and held out her gloved hands to the toasty warm heat radiating from it. A short, middle-aged man in civilian clothes stood on the other side of the stove. Although his face was familiar to her, it wasn't until he smiled that Diane recognized the clerk from the local mercantile store.

"I'm sure glad Charlie fired up this stove," the man declared. "It's a cold wind blowing out there today."

Diane nodded in agreement, the memory of its sharp bite producing a small shudder. "Winter is just around the corner, I'm afraid."

"You're right about that." He glanced out the nearest window. "It won't be long before that wind will be blowing snow instead of dust." He paused and eyed her curiously. "Are you headed off somewheres?"

"No, I'm here to meet Reverend Cole. He'll be arriving on the train."

"Reverend Cole." He frowned, trying to place the name. "He's the missionary with them Indians encamped over near LeRoy, ain't he?"

"Yes."

"I thought so. He's been in the store a time or two. I take it he's a friend of yours."

"I've known him since I was a little girl." Truthfully, it had only been within the last year that she had grown close to the elderly minister. Diane was careful not to delve too deeply into the reasons behind that. Pride wouldn't allow her to admit that she sought out Reverend Cole as a means to learn the latest news about Lije. She always anticipated Nathan's reports on his condition and whereabouts.

Their engagement was ended. It was over between them. Diane was determined to build a new life for herself, a new future—one that excluded Lije. She had thrown herself into the effort by working, striving, and fighting, all the while smiling to hide the pain of rejection. And yet . . .

Adam Clark joined her, a quick smile carving attractive, masculine dimples in his cheeks. "The train should be rolling in any time now."

"Wonderful." Diane smiled back. "I truthfully thought we would be in for a long wait."

"I wouldn't have minded," he said casually, his manner

offhand, but the warmth in his eyes suggested his interest in her was anything but casual.

It wasn't the first time Diane noticed the way Adam Clark looked at her. As always, she pretended she didn't. "I'm afraid I'm not as patient as you are."

"Patience is a necessity in my profession," he reminded her. "As much as we might wish it otherwise, every physician quickly learns the healing process can't be hurried."

"No, it can't," she agreed, realizing that in his own subtle way, he was telling her that he knew she hadn't fully recovered from her broken engagement, and that he was willing to bide his time until she was heart-whole again. She warmed to him, touched by the understanding he had shown for her.

"Say," the store clerk spoke up, "ain't you the doc from the fort?"

"I am." Adam Clark pulled off his leather gauntlet and extended a hand in greeting to the clerk. "Dr. Adam Clark, originally from Abilene."

"Josiah Hubbard," the store clerk identified himself and shook hands. "Pleased to meet you, Doc—Sorry, I guess I should be calling you Major," he said, glancing at his insignia of rank.

"Major is the army's idea, not mine," Adam replied with a wry smile. "I answer quicker to Doc than I do to Major Clark."

"Say, Doc, you wouldn't happen to have a good poultice for carbuncles, would you? My missus has been plagued with them lately." The store clerk went on to describe at length his wife's problem.

Diane took advantage of the distraction to make a covert study of the young army physician, his previous assertion of patience still fresh in her mind. She judged him to be somewhere in his early thirties, of average height and build. His hair was thick and dark, a mass of curls he kept trimmed close to maintain a neat appearance. He had the fine features of an artist and gentle eyes that inspired trust. His teeth were pearl white and evenly spaced, set off by a rich and carefully groomed dark mustache. His bearing was one of a man quietly confident and capable.

Search as she might, Diane could find no surface resemblance to Lije. She should have been glad about that. Instead, she grew irritated that the image of Lije remained so vivid in her mind. She had only to close her eyes to see his strongly boned face, the black of his hair, and the blue of his eyes. It angered her that merely thinking about him could produce again a whip of emotion, which should have dimmed long ago—along with the hurt.

"Sounds like the train is about to pull in." The clerk's announcement broke across her thoughts, making Diane aware of the long, muffled sound of a whistle, signaling the train's approach to the station. "Sure been good talking to you, Doc."

"I hope I was some help." Adam Clark nodded to the man in farewell, then turned his attention to Diane. "Shall we go outside and wait on the platform?"

In answer, she took his arm and headed toward the door. "You must get tired of everyone parading their aches and pains before you, wanting free medical advice."

"I don't mind—unless I'm with someone. Then I would prefer more pleasant topics—such as the way your eyes light up when something amuses you."

She laughed. "Is that a clinical observation, Doctor?"

"A compliment. Most definitely a compliment. Do you mind?"

Although inwardly on guard, Diane feigned a breezy unconcern. "Why should I mind?"

He gave her a long considering look as he opened the door onto the station platform. "Because I'm not sure you're ready to accept a compliment from me," he replied in all candor.

Diane replied in kind, "To be honest, I'm not sure I am either."

"That, in itself, is a hopeful sign." He ushered her outside, where the clatter and rumble of the arriving train eliminated further conversation.

The whipping wind swept the smoke and steam from the train onto the platform. Diane turned to avoid the brunt of its sting as the locomotive wheezed to a stop, the cars clunking against one another in a chain reaction. The cloud of steam and smoke lifted, swirling away on the wind, giving Diane a clear view of the disembarking passengers.

Reverend Cole was the third person off the train. She spotted his tall, bony, stoop-shouldered frame the instant he stepped down. Smiling a welcome, Diane went forward to meet him. He nodded briefly to her, then turned back and offered a helping hand to the woman behind him.

Diane stared in astonishment. "Susannah! What are you doing here? I thought you were back in Massachu—" Her delight in seeing Susannah vanished in a dawning rush of sorrow and sympathy. "Your father. Reverend Cole told me of his passing in August. Susannah, I'm so sorry."

They hugged and Susannah fought back a few tears. Then Diane remembered her manners and introduced Susannah to Adam Clark. "Susannah, I would like you to meet Major Adam Clark, the post surgeon. When I mentioned to Major Clark that I was coming to meet Reverend Cole, he remembered he had a shipment of medical supplies due to arrive on the train and offered to drive me." Both Diane and Major Clark knew that he could have easily arranged for the shipment to be picked up by one of his subordinates. But he had used it as an excuse to spend time in her company. "Major, this is one of my dearest friends, Miss Susannah Gordon. Susannah and I have known each other since childhood."

"I'm glad to meet you, Major Clark."

"The pleasure is definitely mine, Miss Gordon," he replied and nodded to Reverend Cole. "I hope you had a good trip, Reverend."

"I did."

"I still can't believe you're here, Susannah," Diane declared, then explained to Adam, "The last time I saw her, she was back East attending the female seminary, Mount Holyoke."

"You've traveled a long way, Miss Gordon."

"A very long way."

Diane turned to Reverend Cole. "Did you know Susannah was coming?"

He shook his head. "I was as surprised as you are when I boarded the train and saw her sitting in the car." He paused, then added, "Susannah is on her way home to Oak Hill."

"*Now?*" Diane protested, her attention swinging to Susannah. "But such a trip is so very dangerous these days."

"So Reverend Cole has told me more than once," Susannah said with a quick smile that suggested her decision had been the subject of considerable discussion between them on the train. Then her expression grew serious. "But I can't bear the thought of my mother being alone. She needs me . . . now, more than ever before."

"Susannah, you really should wait until the area is more secure. A woman traveling alone—"

"Reverend Cole has agreed to accompany me. In fact, he insisted on it." Susannah smiled. "We plan to leave tomorrow morning at first light. Hopefully, I'll get to see Kipp tonight—"

"His company went out on patrol. I saw them ride out this morning. I doubt they'll be back before you leave."

"I would have liked to have seen him. Alex, too."

"Isn't there some way I can talk you out of this, Susannah?"

"None at all," she replied, then hesitated, her gaze darting between Major Clark and Diane. She searched Diane's face for a clue as to the relationship between the two, but guessing nothing, finally asked, "If I should see Lije when I get home, is there any message you want me to give him?"

Diane thought she had been braced for the sound of his name. She was wrong. The instant she heard it, a longing leapt up, sharp and strong and unmistakable. She crushed it, almost as quickly.

"You can tell him . . . I hope all is well," Diane said in a voice deliberately flattened of emotion.

"Is that all?" Susannah prodded gently, conscious of the major's intent appraisal of her friend's response.

"Yes, that's all."

"Diane, I know it's difficult for you, your father fighting on one side and Lije on the other, but—"

"If it were only that, Susannah. But it isn't. Lije is obsessed with that stupid feud."

"Try to understand, Diane—"

She broke in, needing to end this discussion, "I understand very well."

Reverend Cole, sensing Diane's uneasiness, changed the subject. "We'd better go to the baggage car and claim your trunks, Susannah. The train won't stop here for long."

"You're right, of course," Susannah admitted. "And heaven knows we have a lot to do if we want to leave in the morning."

They started toward the baggage car. Anxious to make amends for the sharpness of her previous words, Diane said, "When you finish the preparations for your trip home, you and Reverend Cole will come to dinner, won't you? When I left, my father's striker was already busy preparing a special meal for us."

"Of course, we will," Susannah assured her. "You have no idea how good a home-cooked meal sounds after all this traveling—not to mention the company."

"Good." But Diane knew she faced the prospect that Susannah might again bring up the subject of Lije at dinner. Thinking quickly, she glanced at Adam Clark. "You will join us for dinner as well, won't you? I meant to ask earlier."

"I'd be delighted," he told her as they arrived at the baggage car. When Susannah went to point out her trunks to Reverend Cole, Adam Clark tipped his head toward Diane and asked in a low voice, meant for her hearing alone, "Am I right in assuming that Miss Gordon is related to your former fiancé?"

Diane nodded, uncomfortable with his question and struggling not to show it. "Susannah and his mother are half sisters."

"And my role at dinner tonight—am I to play the ardent suitor, or merely that of one of your father's fellow officers?"

"Am I so transparent?" Diane smiled her chagrin, aware that he had seen through her invitation and knew she planned to use his presence to keep the dinner conversation away from any discussion of her broken engagement.

"You must remember I'm a trained observer," he said a little wryly, the gentleness of understanding in his eyes.

Her smile softened. "I do like you, Major Clark."

"If I'm to be convincing tonight, I suggest you call me Adam."

"Very well . . . Adam."

Later, as they loaded Susannah's trunks in the ambulance wagon, Diane stole a glance at Adam Clark. She knew it was unfair to use him this way, but she took solace in the fact that he was willing, no doubt secretly hoping that one day she would regard him as more than a friend. In truth, she felt safe with him, confident she wouldn't have to fend off unwanted advances, that he would demand of her no more than she was willing to give.

But try as she might, Diane couldn't imagine loving anyone other than Lije. The thought made her angry. Surely in this new life she was building for herself, she could find a new love, couldn't she?

The problem was—she didn't seem to want one.

৩ 14 ৫

Small, yellow-tipped flames danced above the campfire's white-hot embers. In the iron pot suspended above them, a stew of rabbit, potatoes, and onions released its appetizing aroma into the night air. Susannah Gordon stirred it, then swung the pot away from the fire's center and crouched down in front of the fire again.

The air had a sharp autumn nip to it, and overhead, a canopy of stars winked brightly to compete with the light of a sickle moon. Drawing the wool shawl more firmly around her shoulders, she stared at the campfire, not focusing on the flames themselves, but rather the charred ends of the sticks that lay on the outer circle.

The partially burned wood reminded her of the homesite she had seen that day. Blackened timbers, charred rubble, and gray ash piled like autumn leaves were all that remained of the house that had once stood there. A neighbor said the rebels had burned it.

Back in Massachusetts, the newspapers had carried few reports of fighting this far west. Rather, the stories in recent months had dwelt mainly with the second battle of Bull Run and the bloody clash at Antietam. Arriving at Fort Scott in Kansas, Susannah hadn't understood why so many families had fled the Indian Nations and taken refuge there.

But today, after riding past field after field lying fallow; after crossing pastures empty of livestock and overgrown with weeds; and after observing homes abandoned, most ransacked, some burned to the ground, all the stories she'd heard at Fort Scott became real for her. Talk of Confederate guerrilla bands terrorizing the countryside, pillaging and looting and burning—striking with the swiftness and devastating force of a lightning bolt before vanishing—had seemed impossible. She hadn't believed it was as bad as they said. Now she did.

Something rustled in the dead leaves behind her. A second later, a twig snapped. Susannah stiffened, alarm shooting through her as she glanced toward the sound, conscious of the light weight of the small derringer in her dress pocket. A month ago she had laughed when Frank, Payton Fletcher's grandson, had given it to her for protection, well aware that when he thought of the Indian Territory, he conjured up images of the Plains tribes that lived along its western boundaries.

To pacify him, she had packed the derringer away in her valise and forgotten all about it until tonight—until she had seen what war could do to a land and a people. Now it was tucked in her pocket, and she wasn't laughing. Now she wished she had paid more attention when Frank had tried to show her how to shoot it.

A tall, lanky man emerged from the darkness, carrying a bundle of broken branches and dead limbs in his arms. The diffused glow of the campfire touched the white of his clerical collar. Susannah relaxed, smiling at the fear that had momentarily frozen her.

"The horses are settled for the night. I picked up some firewood on the way. I thought we might need it before morning comes. Mmmm, that stew smells good, Eliza." He stopped on the edge of their camp, his head dipping self-consciously.

"I am sorry, Susannah. Sitting there, you looked so much like your mother, I—"

"I understand, Reverend." She had lost track of how many times Reverend Cole had slipped and called her by her mother's name since they started this journey. He meant no offense by it. Actually Susannah found it, and his insistence on accompanying her home, quite endearing. She was glad of his company.

"Your mother has always called me Nathan." He moved within the circle of light and laid the bundle of wood on the ground near the fire.

"I know." Susannah spooned a generous portion of stew onto one of the tin plates, added a chunk of skillet bread, then handed the plate to him, her glance falling briefly on his fingers, long and on the bony side of slender like the rest of him.

He sat down on an old log, rolled close to the fire, and balanced the plate of stew on his lap, then waited until Susannah had fixed a plate for herself and joined him. With bowed head and clasped hands, he began speaking the words of blessing for the food they were about to eat, just as he had done before every meal they had shared.

Susannah clasped her hands in prayer and bowed her head, turning it slightly to study him. Noble probably wasn't the word most people would use to describe Nathan Cole, but that was the way she thought of him. Noble and kind and good—with the gentlest eyes she had ever seen in a man. Most ministers she knew preached about the wrath of God, but not Reverend Cole. He didn't fear his God; he loved Him. And it was that love that shone in his face and softened his severely angled features and gaunt cheeks. The lines she saw around his eyes and mouth all came from smiling.

"The stew is excellent. Aren't you going to try it?"

Startled by his gentle inquiry, Susannah realized she hadn't heard him finish the blessing. "Sorry, I was . . . thinking."

Hastily, she picked up her fork and speared a chunk of rabbit meat.

"About what?"

"About Mother." Which was half-true. "Wondering if she is all right."

"Your mother is a strong woman. I'm sure she is just fine."

"Of course."

"At times I find it odd the way the past seems to repeat itself," he remarked thoughtfully. "Did you know that I accompanied your mother when she traveled to Georgia all those years ago? Neither of us could have guessed that she would eventually marry the man whose children she had come to teach. I performed the wedding ceremony myself outside the walls of Fort Gibson. Now, here I am, making another trip with her daughter, who looks so like her mother—tall and graceful with the same shimmering gold in her eyes."

Susannah knew the reverend had once been in love with her mother. "Did she need as much moral support as I do?"

"In some ways, more," Nathan admitted. "She was facing the wilderness—the unknown. You are going home."

Watching him, Susannah was almost positive he was still in love with her mother. The look in his eyes when he talked about her, the way he kept talking about her, made her long to ask. If she were really like her mother, she would. But Susannah wasn't quite as outspoken as Eliza.

"Remember those temperance meetings Mother used to have at Oak Hill . . . and in Tahlequah, too. You were always there. Mother would play the piano, and we would sing those songs. What was that one? I can't remember the words, but it went—" She began to hum the notes of the melody, hesitantly at first, then as her recollection of the tune became clearer, with increasing confidence. "I know! It was—"

But the title didn't come out of her mouth. Frozen in shock, Susannah stared at the armed men on the opposite side of the campfire. Ghostlike, they had materialized out of nowhere, without a whisper of sound. But there was nothing ghostlike about the weapons they carried. Fear turned her mouth dry when Susannah saw the gun barrel pointed at her.

A ragged, shabbily clad lot confronted her, their faces dark with rough beards, slouch hats pulled low, leaving only their eyes to glisten from the shadows of their faces—the way an animal's eyes glowed in the darkness.

"Who are you? What are you doing here?" Even as she found her voice to make the sharp demand, one of them moved silently into the circle and picked up the old shotgun Reverend Cole had left propped against a jagged tree stump.

"We could ask you the same questions," came the drawled answer.

Susannah was so busy counting that she wasn't sure which of them had spoken. There were six men whom she could see, but there was no telling how many more were out there in the darkness.

"I am Reverend Nathan Cole." Nathan stood up, smiling that benign smile of his that knew no enemy. "And this is . . . my ward, Miss Susannah Gordon. We're on our way to her home. As you can see, we have camped here for the night." He indicated the fire and the wagon behind them.

"And where might your home be?" The man in the center, the tall, lean one with narrow hips, was the man who spoke. The voice had a deceptively soft drawl to it, like velvet sheathing steel.

They were obviously rebels; thinking fast, Susannah replied, "My home is not far from my sister's—Mrs. Stuart of Grand View, although I am not entirely sure it's any of your business."

"Mrs. Stuart. Would that be the wife of The Blade Stuart of the Cherokee Mounted Rifles?" The man tipped his head at an inquiring angle. For the first time his face was illuminated by the firelight, and Susannah was able to distinguish his features—the slope of his lean jaw, the high ridge of his cheekbones, the smooth slant of his forehead, and the gray of his eyes.

"It would be. Now that we have answered your questions, would you be so good as to answer ours?"

Unexpectedly, he swept off his hat and made a mockingly gallant bow. His eyes changed from the color of dark steel to glittering silver. "Lieutenant Rans Lassiter of the Texas Brigade, at your service, ma'am." There was a flash of white teeth as he smiled, almost tauntingly. "And these are my men, plus a few more out looking to see if you have anyone else with you."

"We don't."

"She's right," a man's voice drawled behind her. Susannah turned on the log, again startled by the sight of yet another man appearing out of nowhere. "It's just the two of 'em. They got their horses picketed over in those trees."

"I told you." Susannah looked back at the lieutenant. His hat once more covered his brown hair and shadowed his face.

"So you did, but when we're scouting an area, we have a duty to check on such things, ma'am." He walked into the light. "We smelled your smoke about a mile back . . . and the stew even farther than that."

"We have some left. You're welcome to it," Reverend Cole offered.

"Thank you, Reverend." Lassiter nodded to his men, indicating they should help themselves.

Susannah stared in amazement as they swarmed around the pot, producing plates out of nowhere. Within seconds they scraped it clean and sat hunkered around the fire, shoveling the stew into their mouths and sopping up the juices with chunks of skillet bread. They were ravenous, Susannah realized. She looked at her own plate, suddenly guilty at the way she had picked at her food—especially when she noticed there hadn't been enough for Lieutenant Lassiter.

She hesitated, then offered her plate to him. "I'm not hungry."

He held her gaze for an instant. "I guess it shows we haven't had a decent meal in a good while. You'll have to forgive our manners, Miss Gordon." He smiled crookedly, a glint of rueful humor in his gray eyes. "Or should I say, our lack of them."

"No apologies are necessary, Lieutenant." She felt ill at ease when he took the plate from her. Part of her regretted feeling sorry for them. They were Confederates. For all she knew, they might be the very ones responsible for the desolation she'd seen, and here she was feeding them.

"I gotta be honest with you, ma'am," one of them said as he wiped up every drop of juice with his last bite of bread. "This is the best meal I've et since I had Sunday dinner at Momma's house just before I left." He popped a piece of bread into his mouth and chewed it with his mouth open, looking around at the others. "Wouldn't ya jus' love a cup of real coffee now . . . and maybe, a ceegar?"

At the wistful nods of agreement, Reverend Cole spoke up again. "We have some coffee in the wagon. Would you like us to brew some?"

"Would we? Whoo-eee! That's like askin' does a kid like Christmas!" The man laughed.

"I'll fix the coffee." When she stood up, Susannah felt the men's eyes traveling up all five feet, eight inches of her. She thought she had become used to being stared at because she was tall. She was wrong.

She walked to the rear of the wagon and set the coffeepot on the ground beside her feet, then rummaged through Reverend Cole's supplies for the coffee. Something clunked softly against the side of the wagon when she reached inside. The derringer; she had nearly forgotten about it.

"What else you got in that wagon?"

She jumped when a voice spoke beside her. "Didn't anyone ever tell you it isn't polite to sneak up on people?" she snapped angrily. At almost the same instant, she found the coffee. Picking up the pot, she swept back to the fire, thinking the man would follow. But he didn't.

"Hey! Looky here!" He shouted and held up some cans.

"They got tins of peaches . . . and tomatoes." He tossed them to his buddies and went back to his search. "Hell, they got a lot of food in here."

When the men flocked around the wagon, Susannah started to protest, then glanced uncertainly at Reverend Cole. He smiled back, letting her know it was all right. She hesitated a moment longer, then put the coffee on to boil and listened to their excited talk. They acted as if they had found a treasure.

One of the soldiers opened a tin with his knife and stabbed out a peach half. He shoved it whole into his mouth, ignoring the juice that dribbled down his whiskers and onto the front of his ragged shirt. Even Lieutenant Lassiter took part, although he still held himself slightly aloof from his men.

"What d'ya suppose is in this trunk?" The one named Kelly hopped into the wagon bed next to Susannah's trunk, then waved to another man. "Come on up here, Hayes. Give me a hand."

"No." Susannah moved quickly to the wagon. "That is mine."

No one paid any attention to her. "I got first dibs on any shoes."

"Leave it alone. That trunk doesn't belong to you." Everything she owned was in that trunk—her clothes, her few pieces of jewelry, her books—everything. Taking food was one thing, but stealing her property was another. Out of desperation, Susannah fumbled in her pocket and pulled out the derringer. Holding it with both hands stretched in front of her, she aimed it in the general direction of the two men atop the wagon. "I said that doesn't belong to you. Get away from my trunk."

"I think you boys better listen to her." Slowly and carefully, Rans Lassiter set the tin of peaches on the wagon bed. "She has a gun—if you want to call it that."

"And I will shoot if I have to," she insisted boldly, secretly hoping the mere sight of the weapon would make them leave her things alone. "Get away from my trunk . . . and the wagon."

"Didn't anyone ever tell you, Miss Gordon, that it isn't polite to point a gun at someone?" Rans Lassiter moved directly in line with the end of the derringer and started walking forward—slowly and deliberately. "It's definitely bad manners." ·

"Don't come any closer," she warned, fighting the sudden spate of nervousness.

"I have to." He smiled. "If you shoot, I want you to be sure you're close enough to hit what you're aiming at. Those little guns aren't very accurate at a distance. You don't want to miss with your first shot."

"I said stay where you are!" She pointed it at the ground in front of his feet, closed her eyes, and pulled the trigger. Nothing happened.

She opened her eyes in astonishment and looked at the gun. In two springing strides, Lassiter crossed the space that separated them and seized her wrists, forcing them up into the air. Susannah struggled frantically to keep control of the derringer.

In the next second, she was hauled roughly against him. But it wasn't the impact of being suddenly crushed against the hard length of him that stole the breath from her lungs, but the discovery of his face so close to hers—so close she could feel the stubble of his short beard. He was no more than an inch taller than she was; his gray eyes looked almost directly into hers. She could see the black pupils ringed with silver. And his mouth was a mere breath away.

She froze, numbed by a thousand sensations all clamoring to make themselves known—from the jutting angle of his hipbone pressing into her stomach to the solid wall of his chest flattening her breasts. Her heart stopped beating for an instant, then went racing off like the wheels of a locomotive trying to find traction.

Dear God, what was she thinking of? She was a woman

alone with men who claimed to be soldiers. And she had never seen a more disreputable-looking lot. Reverend Cole wasn't a young man. If they chose to assault her—to rape her—he couldn't protect her. What had she gotten herself into?

Susannah stared at the strong, tanned fingers that held her right wrist. She still clutched the derringer. He hadn't wrested it from her yet.

She felt the warmth of his breath on her neck. She was suddenly more tense than before. "Perfume," the lieutenant murmured. "It's been a long time since I smelled perfume on a lady."

"Kindly let me go," she ordered, fully aware that she was in no position to make demands.

She watched as his fingers slowly slid up her hand and closed over the derringer. The roughness of them reminded her of the rasp of a cat's tongue. She let him take the gun from her, and he loosened his hold. She stepped quickly back from him.

"In this part of the country, Miss Gordon, if you're going to carry a gun—more importantly, if you're going to point it at someone—you better know how to shoot it."

She could feel the heat rising in her cheeks. She could well imagine how humorous he thought this was and refused to meet his gaze, knowing those gray eyes would be laughing at her. Instead, she stared at the weapon in his hand, watching as he deftly and familiarly checked to see whether it was loaded.

"Before you pull the trigger, you have to cock it. Like this." With his thumb, he pulled back the hammer. "See how it's done."

"Yes," she snapped.

Gently, he eased the hammer back into place. Then, with a slight movement of his hand, the derringer lay in his callused palm. "You better hang onto this, Miss Gordon. Next time you may need it. But try to remember how to use it." She looked up in disbelief, doubting that he truly intended to give it back to her. He smiled, ever so faintly. "And don't shoot at the ground. This thing only carries one bullet."

There were snickers behind him. Self-consciously, Susannah took the derringer from him and shoved it inside the pocket of her skirt.

"Kelly, Hayes, out of the wagon." Still looking at her, he lifted his voice to bark the order, then turned to face them, his tone becoming light. "I have the feeling the lady wouldn't appreciate you two going through her things. Although you might look quite fetching in petticoats and bonnets."

Guffaws of laughter followed his remark, accompanied by a few ribald comments, spoken low out of deference to Susannah. She heard parts of them and shut her ears to the rest. Someone mentioned the coffee, and they drifted back toward the fire. Wanting to avoid them, she busily set about cleaning the dishes.

Almost immediately, Reverend Cole came over to her. "Are you all right?"

"Yes. And you don't have to say it. I know it was a stupid thing to do."

"We have all done one or two of those in our lives, Susannah. Do not be too hard on yourself."

"That isn't easy." She managed a smile, then darted a quick glance at the men lounging around the campfire, drinking coffee and trading stories. "Maybe it's the war. It seemed so far away when I was in New England. I keep remembering the burnt-out houses we passed. And I keep wondering if these men were responsible."

"No, some were set by Yankee torches."

Susannah stiffened, recognizing Rans Lassiter's voice behind her. "I didn't know." She tried to pretend she wasn't surprised that he was there.

"It's easier to blame us Johnny Rebs. But the Yankees have their night riders. And then there are the others . . . bushwhackers like Quantrill. You can never be sure which side they're on. It usually depends on what there is to be looted."

"Quantrill was one of the men who led the attack on Independence, Missouri, in August, wasn't he? I read about it in the papers."

"He's somewhere in Arkansas now, but the way he drifts in and out of the territory, you can't be sure. If a man ever rides up on a black stallion, dressed fancy, with a plume in his hat, you keep that derringer handy, Miss Gordon. It's said he has an eye for the ladies."

"I appreciate the warning."

"This is good coffee, the first we've had in a long while." He swirled the liquid in his tin cup, then drank it down. "Only two things I know that could beat it—a bottle of good whiskey or a beautiful woman. A man could get drunk on either." The way he looked at her made Susannah feel warm all over, but this time not from embarrassment. He pulled his gaze away. "You and the reverend better get yourselves a cup before we drink it all."

He turned and walked back to the fire, pausing on the edge of the circle and listening to the talk, but taking no part in it.

"He seems lonely," Susannah murmured.

"And young," Reverend Cole added. She glanced at him in questioning surprise. "He can't be more than twenty-six or twenty-seven."

"He has to be older than that. His eyes—"

"His eyes are old from all he's seen . . . the things he's gone through. I saw the same look in the eyes of some of the young Cherokee men who walked that long trail from Georgia. His eyes don't have that bitterness though, just the soberness of hard experience. He still knows how to smile. That is precious, Susannah. There was a time when I thought your father would never smile again. So many didn't."

She had heard the stories of the suffering many times, but Reverend Cole made it seem real. Maybe because he looked so sad . . . so sorry. She slipped a hand into the crook of his arm. "Let's get some coffee."

"Yes, before they drink it all." He deliberately repeated the lieutenant's words in an effort to lighten the atmosphere.

The rebel called Kelly pulled a harmonica out of his pocket and began playing "Dixie." Three soldiers jumped to their feet and began dancing, sashaying around each other, lifting their feet high, and laughing while the rest clapped hands in time with the music and sang.

The instant the hymn of the South ended, the man struck up another lively tune. A scrawny red-haired man grabbed Susannah's hand and pulled her into their makeshift circle. In the next second, another hooked her arm in his and swung her around, passing her on to the next.

Rans watched her as she swung from partner to partner, skipping, swirling, laughing, her skirts flying and revealing her ankles—and the inch-and-a-half high heels on her boots. She wasn't as tall as he'd thought. And he already knew she wasn't as skinny as she looked. He had felt the fullness of those high breasts against his chest, breasts that would more than fill his hand.

He silently cursed the direction of his thoughts and looked down at the coffee dregs in his cup, but the attempted distraction didn't work. He had to watch.

Why didn't he admit it? He was jealous. There she was dancing with his men, supple and graceful in their arms, the gold in her eyes glittering with happiness. Yet, when he had held her, that gold had been fire sparks and her body had been as rigid as a stone statue, but a statue with perfume on her neck. And the perfume wasn't the cheap kind a whore used to smother the smell of her sweat and another man's semen. Rans knew the difference.

Susannah Gordon was a lady, and he was tired of the bar whores and camp followers.

This war hadn't turned out to be what he thought when he

first joined up. There had been little glory in the battles and skirmishes he'd fought, only a helluva lot of blood and desperation.

For him, the war had been mostly patrols like this—rides that amounted to burning and looting. Their orders were to cut off the enemy's supplies, destroy their hay and grain fields. He was supposed to make it impossible for them to grow food for themselves or for their animals; he was to make it impossible for the enemy to forage.

Perhaps he hated Quantrill and his ilk so much because he hated himself. After all the fighting and killing, he wanted to feel good inside. She could help him do that.

He heard her peal of laughter, all throaty and warm. It twisted through him, knotting him up into one big ache. Several of his men were singing. He hadn't paid much attention to the song Kelly was playing until he heard the words to it.

> "... The sun so hot I froze to death.
> Susannah, don't you cry.
> Oh, Susannah, oh, don't you cry for me."

He swore again and rubbed the knotted muscles along the back of his neck. When he brought his hand away, Rans accidentally brushed his jaw and felt the sharp stubble of beard growth. He hadn't shaved in three days or bathed in anything other than river water in over a year.

What was the matter with him? Instead of standing around like some damned schoolboy resenting the fun everyone else was having, why didn't he go over there? He wanted to dance with her, hold her in his arms. What was stopping him? He was Ransom Lassiter. His family owned one of the biggest damned ranches in Texas.

He set his cup on a log and walked around the fire ring to the dancers as the song ended. He flashed one warning glance at his men. They stepped back, leaving the path clear to Susannah, their laughing eyes turning silently speculative and knowing. At first she didn't see him, then she turned, the full light from the fire falling on her.

For an instant, Rans could only stare at her smiling lips, parted as she drank in air. Her eyes sparkled with life and her cheeks glowed with high color. A few curling wisps had escaped the neat chignon during the spirited dancing. He liked the hint of dishevelment it gave her. It crossed his mind that she would look that way after he had made love to her, only her lips would be swollen from his kisses.

When he saw her smile start to fade, he made a mock bow. "I believe this is my dance, Miss Gordon." She pressed a hand to the base of her throat as if it would help her to breathe. He wished to hell she hadn't. The action pulled his glance to the deep rise and fall of her breasts, and the material of her gown straining to cover them and succeeding instead in outlining their jutting roundness. "Make it a waltz, Kelly, so the lady can get her breath back." He knew she wanted to plead exhaustion, but he didn't give her a chance.

His hand was at the back of her waist before she could raise an objection. On the very first note, Rans spun her away, the pressure of his hand smoothly guiding her through the steps. Susannah tried but she couldn't seem to break contact with his compelling gray eyes. They held her captive, half-veiled as they were by his sooty lashes and smoldering like hot charcoal.

Around and around, they whirled. With each turn, she was spun closer and made even more aware of the brush of his legs through the thickness of her skirts. Yet she had to hold on to him. She had the impression he knew that. Did he also know all the crazy things she was feeling—like the curious fluttering in her stomach?

"I'm not altogether sure you want me to catch my breath, Lieutenant," she accused, conscious that it was still coming in a shallow rush. "I think you're trying to steal it."

"Could I?" His softly drawled question was like a lover's caress. Her pulse accelerated at an alarming rate.

"Lieutenant, I—"

"Rans. We aren't too formal in Texas."

"I see." She swallowed, trying to rid herself of the tension that strung her nerves on a thin thread.

"Do you?" His glance went to her throat, reminding Susannah of the perfume she had automatically dabbed behind her ears this morning—the perfume he had remarked on earlier. "I don't think you realize how tempted I am to forget you're a lady."

She looked away, suddenly noticing how far they were from the fire. Darkness was all around them. "That isn't something a gentleman would say." He was no longer spinning her in graceful circles. They were practically dancing in place, going through the motions of the waltz steps, but barely moving at all.

"No? The gentlemen you've known must have been fools. Or else they were blind."

"I don't think—"

"Good. I don't want you to think. I only want you to dance with me."

Again Susannah was guided into another sweeping turn. She stepped on something. It rolled, throwing her off balance and twisting her ankle. She stumbled against him. Immediately, both of his arms went around her to catch and steady her. Susannah found herself again literally face to face with him; only this time their lips were actually touching. It was like a lightning bolt jolting through her. Looking into his eyes, she couldn't make herself move in any direction.

"You don't need to be afraid of me, Susannah." He whispered the assurance, his lips moving against hers to form the words. She hadn't realized her own lips were so sensitive, yet she could feel every feather-light touch against them. "Don't be afraid."

A warmth—a pressure spread over her mouth. Dear God, he was kissing her, and she was afraid—afraid of the things she was feeling. She pushed away from him and took a quick step back. She gasped at the sharp twinge of pain that shot from her ankle.

"Are you all right?"

"Yes." Tentatively she put her weight on it, testing its strength. Luckily, she felt nothing more than an achy soreness. "I turned my ankle. That's all." Suddenly, he scooped her off her feet and cradled her body in his arms. "What are you doing? You can't intend to carry me?" Didn't he realize how big she was? At five feet eight, she was no lightweight.

"That is exactly what I'm going to do." There was a splash of white in his dark beard when he smiled at her. "Put your arms around my neck."

There really wasn't anywhere else to put them. But when she felt the rippling bulge of his shoulder and neck muscles, Susannah wasn't too sure this was a good idea, although she had to admit he didn't seem to be struggling under her weight.

"This isn't necessary," she murmured. "I can walk."

"But I don't want to find out you can," he drawled, his gray eyes glinting with mercuric brightness. "I'm enjoying this too much."

"Stop it." Susannah knew he didn't mean it, not really. Anything in skirts would look good to him.

"Susannah, are you all right?" Reverend Cole hurried forward to meet them.

"I turned my ankle. If the lieutenant would put me down, I could walk it off. But he is too busy playing the gallant and chivalrous Southern officer to listen."

The lieutenant's jaw tightened, his mouth disappearing altogether in the shadow of his dark beard. He stopped abruptly and let her feet swing to the ground, his eyes changing back to the hard gray color of flint. Aware he was angry, she moved away, walking gingerly but without difficulty.

"My men and I will bed down over there in the trees for

the night, Reverend. I've thrown out a picket, so you and Miss Gordon should be safe here in camp. I would put out the fire, though. No sense advertising where you are to any bushwhackers who might be roaming around." His glance flicked briefly to Susannah. "In the morning, we'll escort you home."

"Thank you, Lieutenant."

"We owe you for the food and the coffee." He turned on his heel and walked away, followed reluctantly by his men. Susannah watched him, conscious of the strong regret she felt at his leaving.

"A man's pride is a fragile thing, Susannah." Reverend Cole came over to stand beside her. "Sometimes it is the only protection he has. But it can be easily wounded. Men may appear insensitive—invincible even—but I assure you, my dear child, we aren't."

"You think I was churlish."

"Nothing cuts the ground out from under a man quicker than a woman's tongue." He walked over to the fire and began scattering the coals.

❧ 15 ❧

The next morning, they rose at first light. After a cold breakfast, Susannah stowed their camp equipment and bedrolls in the wagon while Reverend Cole harnessed the team. Finishing her chores before he did, she went over to help. Then she saw Lieutenant Lassiter crossing the small clearing toward her. He looked different in the daylight. Then she realized why. He had shaved.

Last night he had looked like the roughest kind of outlaw. This morning he looked like a man of purpose and pride.

She stared at his hard, lean features, finding not a hint of softness in them. Last night she had sensed the strength in his face. Now it was positively potent.

When he reached her, Rans took off his hat and raked a hand quickly through his hair. "If my actions offended you yesterday evening, Miss Gordon, I apologize. I—"

"You cut yourself." Without thinking, she reached up and wiped the small trickle of blood from the nick along his jaw, at the same time letting the rest of her fingers lie against the side of his neck near the pulsing vein.

In the blink of an eye, he grabbed her hand and roughly jerked it away from his face, then continued to hold it, his fingers digging in, nearly cutting off the circulation to it. "I wouldn't touch a man like that again, Miss Gordon."

"Why?"

"Why!" The word exploded from him.

A second later her arms were pinned to her sides and her lips were crushed against her teeth by his mouth. And yet she felt no pain, only searing pleasure. His lips didn't stop moving over hers and rolling back, nuzzling, coaxing a reaction Susannah could never have anticipated.

This wasn't a suitor's awkward bussing. This was a lover's kiss. She had always wondered what it would be like. Now she knew. Inside, she felt all molten and raw.

He broke the kiss long enough to say gruffly, "That's why." Then he pulled her against him, rubbing his mouth over her cheek, breathing hard, and trembling. "I wanted to kiss you like that last night. Hell. I wanted to do more than that, Susannah. Remember, I warned you that a man could get drunk on a beautiful woman. And when a man is drunk, he forgets the niceties of courtship. There isn't the time to woo a woman in the middle of a war. Do you understand?"

"This is insanity," she whispered, breathing in the soapy smell of his cheek. "I don't even know you." She turned anyway, finding his lips once more and kissing him. If it was insanity, she wanted more of it, much more.

"Lieutenant!"

They quickly moved apart at the sound of the shouted call and pounding hooves. Kelly rode into the clearing, leading a saddle horse. "Chavez is back. Said it's all clear. We're ready to ride as soon as the preacher is." At that moment Reverend Cole led the harnessed team of horses into the clearing.

"Be right there." Rans turned back to Susannah and smoothed the crumpled brim of his hat, then set it on his head, holding her gaze all the while. "The name is Rans. Ransom Lassiter, and don't you forget it."

"I won't." The promise was easy to make. Susannah knew she would find it impossible to forget him.

On the way to Oak Hill, Susannah's thoughts were divided between concern for her mother and an awareness of the man on the zebra dun riding alongside the wagon. He rode with the ease of a man who had spent most of his life in the saddle, balanced and relaxed, moving with the horse, not against it. Looking at him, Susannah could almost believe this was nothing more than a pleasant morning ride for him—if it weren't for that watchful air he never lost, one that said if trouble came, he would be ready for it. And Susannah suspected his reaction would be as swift and deadly as the situation demanded. The thought should have frightened her, but it didn't.

A dozen times she had considered what might have happened last night if Rans Lassiter had been a different sort of man. He and his band could have stolen the wagon and all its supplies, terrorized and abused them, and neither she nor Reverend Cole could have stopped them. They had both been at their mercy. Yet, never once had Rans Lassiter or his men acted in a way that was deliberately threatening. Almost from the outset she and Reverend Cole had been treated with a rough sort of respect.

She was grateful for that. But it wasn't gratitude Susannah felt when they stopped at midmorning to rest the horses and Rans lifted her from the wagon. Gratitude didn't heat the blood or make her breath catch in her throat. His glance held hers for a long second before he moved away to attend to the horses.

Not until he had sentries posted and the horses watered did he return to the wagon where Susannah was helping Reverend Cole water the team. "We'll move out in about ten minutes, Reverend."

"We'll be ready."

Susannah felt Rans's attention focus on her as the stoutly muscled gray horse lifted its nose from the leather water bucket she held for it. "I'll carry that for you," Rans said when she lowered the bucket.

The bucket was far from heavy. Susannah knew his offer was an excuse for him to linger. "Thanks." She waited while he emptied out the little bit of water left. "We keep the buckets tied back here by the water barrel." She walked over to the wagon to show him. "You mentioned you knew my brother-in-law, Captain Stuart—"

"*Major* Stuart," Rans corrected as he fastened the leather bucket in its place. "He was promoted six weeks ago."

"I hadn't heard," she admitted. "I was wondering . . . if you know him, perhaps you know his son, Elijah Stuart, as well?"

He nodded, his mouth twisting in a smile. "Lije and I have shared a campfire before." He pulled the knot tight, then turned, a touch of amusement in his inspecting glance. "You don't look old enough to be his aunt."

"I'm not." She smiled, remembering the way Lije always teased her about it. "How are they? My sister will want to know."

"They were fine the last time I saw them." His glance centered on her lips for one tantalizing instant, then came back to her eyes.

Again Susannah felt warm all over and turned her face into the crisp breeze that warned of winter's approach. "Where are they? Do you know?"

"Not for certain."

She looked down at the ground. "Even if you did, I'm sure you are under orders not to reveal the location of Confederate troops. Such information could be useful to the Union army."

"It could."

"There is something I should tell you." Resolve lifted her chin.

"What's that?"

"My brother Kipp and his son, Alex, are both fighting on the side of the Union." With that confession made, Susannah looked to see his reaction. It was as if a shutter had come down, closing away his thoughts. "It's common knowledge in the Nation that my father was loyal to the Union."

"And where do you stand?"

"My sympathies are with the Union as well," she admitted, and tipped her chin a little higher. "I deliberately gave you the wrong impression last night by referring so quickly to my brother-in-law, Major Stuart. I saw you were rebels and I thought—"

He cut her off. "I can guess what you thought." There was something grim in his expression, but the steady regard of his eyes never wavered. "What makes you think you're safer now than you were last night?"

A brief ripple of alarm traveled through her, then vanished. "Because I trust you now," she said simply and truthfully.

He shook his head, a sudden grin splitting his mouth. "Is that answer supposed to appeal to my honor as an officer and a Southern gentleman? If it is, you've made a mistake, Susannah. Where you're concerned, I don't have one honorable thought in my mind." Reaching up, he rubbed his thumb over the curve of her cheek and mused, "Not a single, solitary one."

She trembled a little, but not from fear. "You don't frighten me."

He glanced up, capturing her gaze. "No? You frighten the hell out of me, Susannah." The line of his mouth softened as he lowered his hand, then turned, saying over his shoulder, "Be ready to leave in five minutes."

Reverend Cole halted the team in front of Oak Hill's columned mansion. Nothing stirred. It looked as empty as the fields they had passed. Worried, Susannah climbed down from the wagon without waiting for assistance.

Then the front door opened, and out stepped her mother, a little older than she remembered, a little thinner, but still tall and beautiful. Susannah picked up her skirts and ran to meet her.

"Susannah? What are you doing here? You're supposed to be back East."

"I came home." She hugged her.

Eliza drew back to look at her and lifted a trembling hand to smooth a tangle of curls back from Susannah's face. "You received my letter about your father. Lije said he would see that it got through the lines."

"It did. I—" Her glance was drawn to the front door as a fresh sense of loss swept over her. "I wish I had been home. I wish—"

"I know." Eliza gave her shoulder a comforting squeeze, her own eyes misting over. A horse snorted, reminding them both they were not alone. "Now, who do I have to thank—" The sight of Reverend Cole patiently standing a few yards away stole the rest of her words as she drew in a sharp breath of surprise. "Nathan."

"Eliza," He came forward and folded his long fingers around her outstretched hands. "You look as lovely as ever."

"I can't believe this," she declared, then divided a questioning glance between the two of them. "How on earth did you two—"

"You mentioned in your letter Reverend Cole was at Fort Scott," Susannah explained.

"I tried to convince Susannah to wait until the Texas Road was safer to travel, but she was determined to come home, no matter the risk. And the good lieutenant here," he looked back to where Rans Lassiter stood loosely holding the reins to the dun horse, "was kind enough to escort us these last few miles."

"Mother," Susannah drew her forward. "I want you to meet Lieutenant Ransom Lassiter of the Texas Brigade. Lieutenant, this is my mother, Mrs. Eliza Gordon."

He pulled off his hat and took the hand Eliza offered with a slight bow. "A pleasure, Mrs. Gordon."

"You have my gratitude, Lieutenant Lassiter, for seeing my daughter safely to my door."

"And you have mine, Mrs. Gordon, for having such a lovely daughter. She made the ride to your home much too short."

His casually drawled words couldn't mask his interest in Susannah. Eliza noticed the way his gaze lingered on her daughter, as well as the color rising in Susannah's cheeks. "You understand, Mrs. Gordon," he continued, his gaze still on Susannah and a smile hovering at the edges of his mouth, "it's been a long time since any of us have been in the company of a lady capable of blushing. It makes it easy to forgive her Yankee leanings and to regret the war that has hardened hearts and minds."

"Violence of any kind is always regrettable," Eliza replied.

"But sometimes unavoidable," he interposed.

Eliza lifted an eyebrow. "Men tend to believe that."

He laughed in his throat, his head dipping a moment. "It is obvious your daughter gets her spirit, as well as her beauty, from you, Mrs. Gordon."

"I hope her manners aren't as poor as mine have suddenly become. Please, you and your men come in. Let me fix you something to eat—"

He held up a hand to stave off her words. "As much as I would like to accept your invitation, we have to be going. It might not be a good idea for my men to discover your Yankee sympathies. And they might if we stayed. Besides, we have neglected our duties long enough as it is."

His glance flicked to Susannah as she struggled to hide her dismay. She hadn't expected the time for goodbyes to come so quickly, or the ache of regret to be so poignant.

Try as she might, Susannah was hard-pressed to explain her attraction to the rebel officer, but she couldn't deny its existence. She remembered the way Rans had kissed her that morning—and the way she had kissed him back—and suddenly she wanted to throw herself into his arms once again.

Instead, she waited patiently while he took his leave first from her mother, then from Reverend Cole.

"You and your men will be in our prayers," Nathan told him.

"We will need them, Reverend," Rans said, a wry slant to

his mouth. His attention swung at last to Susannah, his gray eyes darkening a shade. "Keep a place reserved for me on your dance card, Miss Gordon."

"If you wish." She inclined her head in careful agreement.

"I wish." His look implied far more than simple confirmation. Nodding to her, he touched his hat, then prepared to mount.

"Lieutenant." She stopped him. "Will you give Lije a message for me?"

"If I can. There's no guarantee our paths will cross," he told her.

"Of course, but—if you do see him, tell him I saw a young woman he knows. Diane. She's at Fort Scott, with her father."

"I'll give him the message." He climbed into the saddle and signaled his men to move out.

As he swung his horse toward his men, he began whistling. After a few seconds Susannah recognized the song and its opening lyric, "Oh, Susannah, oh, don't you cry for me." She released a short laugh and pressed a hand to her mouth as tears sprang into her eyes.

Rust brown leaves swirled around the legs of the Confederate horses and mixed with the dust churned up by the shuffling hooves. The brooming November wind swept it all back, pelting the trio who watched the departing rebel patrol.

"Come. Let's go inside." Eliza's arm curved around Susannah's shoulders. Reluctantly, she submitted to its gentle pressure and turned toward the house, her heart heavy with a sadness she didn't want to explore. "The lieutenant seemed quite taken with you."

"It isn't likely I'll ever see him again though, is it?" Susannah voiced the thought that kept drumming in her head.

"Only God and time will tell," Eliza replied with a slight sigh.

A cautious Lucy held the front door open for them, her glance continually darting after the rebel patrol. Susannah looked back one last time at the collection of riders. They were halfway up the lane, trailed by a low cloud of rolling dust and tumbling leaves and framed by the arching branches of winter-bare trees. She thought she saw Rans riding at the head of the company, but they were too far away to be sure.

Inside the house, Susannah paused and loosened her grip on the wool shawl, letting it slide down about her shoulders. As she turned to say something to Reverend Cole, her glance fell on the shotgun propped against the wall by the door.

"Lucy, go put the kettle on for tea," Eliza instructed. "And tell Ebediah to see to Reverend Cole's wagon and team. They will—"

"Mother, what is this?" Susannah indicated the shotgun by the door.

Unruffled by the demanding tone, Eliza replied, "That's your father's shotgun, of course." She walked over and picked it up, then proceeded to unload it with an expertise that had Susannah gaping. "Surely you haven't been in the East so long that you fail to recognize a shotgun."

"I know what it is, Mother," Susannah said, recovering. "But what is it doing by the door? And when did you learn how to handle a gun?"

"Shortly after your father died I had our neighbor old Mr. Johnson show me." She tucked the shells in her apron pocket. "I had no choice. With all the marauders about, my workers were too afraid to go into the fields to harvest the few crops we were able to raise—unless I stood guard with this." She indicated the shotgun she cradled quite naturally under her arm, its muzzle pointed at the floor.

"Do you know how to shoot it?" Susannah continued to regard her mother with amazement.

"I know how to shoot it. That isn't to say I could hit what I aimed at—unless it was very, very close."

Susannah looked to Reverend Cole to see if he found this news as startling as she did. He smiled, his eyes a-twinkle. "Perhaps your mother can instruct you in the use of your derringer."

"A derringer?" Eliza's expression mirrored Susannah's previous incredulity. "What are you doing with such a thing?"

"It's for protection," Susannah began defensively, only to stop when she heard Reverend Cole chuckle. A moment later all three of them were laughing.

"If we don't laugh at what we have become, then we must cry at the dire situation we find ourselves in," Eliza finally said as she led them all into the parlor. "Sometimes I wish that we had packed up and gone North at the outbreak of the war when so many other families fled the area. But Will wouldn't hear of it. Soldiers had forced him from his home once, years ago, then ransacked and looted it before destroying it. I know he couldn't bear the thought that history would repeat itself here at Oak Hill. It's why I can't bring myself to leave, even now, after all that's happened."

"Is it so bad, Mother?" Susannah frowned, troubled by the note of despair she had detected.

"Marauders have driven off all the livestock, save for one old mule and a milk cow that I hid away in that little glade by the creek. They have trampled or burned most of the crops. The few stores we have left, I put in the old root cellar. So far they haven't discovered its existence, but I expect it's only a matter of time before they do." She sighed and cast her gaze over the parlor. "The silver and tea service, all the small things of value in the house, I buried behind the stables."

Reverend Cole nodded in approval. "A wise precaution, Eliza."

"You said marauders. Do you mean the rebels have done this?" Susannah couldn't help thinking of Rans.

"Rebels, jayhawkers, the lawless rabble that has no loyalty to either side—they have all done damage here in the

Nation." Eliza went on to tell them of raids on neighboring homes, beatings of Northern sympathizers, and the acts of reprisal committed by Union soldiers during their brief sojourn in the Nation, the robbings and the killings.

Susannah thought of her sister and asked, "What about Temple?"

"Her circumstances are not much better. She, too, has lost livestock and crops, though she does enjoy the protection of The Blade's name." She paused and looked at Susannah, a quiet anguish in her eyes. "As happy as I am to see you, I wish you had remained in the East, far from all the fighting here."

"I couldn't let you stay here alone, Mother," Susannah said, aware that she was only beginning to understand how protected she had been from the brutality of war. She would understand even more in the coming weeks and months.

Reverend Cole remained at Oak Hill for two more nights; then he continued on, intent on distributing what remained of the food and supplies in his wagon to the numerous destitute families in the area.

In late November the warm autumn weather ended, and the cold and freezing rains of winter moved across the Cherokee Nation. The weather matched the apprehension and gloom that claimed the countryside and all its occupants.

During December word filtered into the Nation of a major battle across the border in Arkansas at a place called Prairie Grove. The initial reports claimed that a combined Confederate force of eight thousand men had attacked a Union force of only six thousand southwest of Fayetteville. Federal reinforcements arrived in the middle of the day-long battle to thwart the hopes of a rebel victory. With yet more fresh Union troops expected to reach the battle site in the morning, the Confederate army slipped away in the night, leaving its campfires kindled to fool the enemy.

Susannah wasn't able to learn whether any of the Texas Brigade took part in the fighting, or whether her brother Kipp's regiment was there.

On Christmas Day Temple arrived at Oak Hill to bring them the news that both Lije and The Blade had emerged from the battle unharmed. She had learned—she wouldn't say how—that they were somewhere south of the Arkansas River. Susannah rejoiced with her and privately wondered whether Rans Lassiter was also safe, and whether he had given Lije her message about Diane. With head bowed, she listened to Reverend Cole's prayer for an end to the fighting and offered a fervent "Amen" when he concluded.

But the year ended with another Union foray into the Nation. Federal troops briefly reoccupied Fort Gibson, crossed the Arkansas River, and attacked and burned the Confederate stronghold of Fort Davis, driving the rebels deeper into the Choctaw Nation.

Again the Union force didn't stay to guard the area. It withdrew to its winter headquarters at Fayetteville, Arkansas. With the Yankees in northern Arkansas and the Confederates wintering at Camp Staration in the Choctaw Nation, the Cherokee Nation was left unprotected.

The sharp cold stung her face the instant Susannah stepped out of the detached kitchen into the cold February morning. She glanced up at the high blue sky and the bright sun that had failed to raise the frigid temperature more than a few degrees. She shivered and pulled the wool scarf up to cover her nose and mouth.

The crunch of heavy footsteps on the frozen ground came from her right as Ebediah trudged toward the kitchen, steam rising from the pail of fresh milk he carried. He had on the heavy winter coat that had been her father's, but he still looked half-frozen. Susannah made a mental note to speak to her mother about having one of the younger workers milk the cow in this cold weather. Ebediah was too old; he looked too fragile.

Privately, she wished her mother would give all the slaves their freedom. But as her mother had reasoned, with the war still raging, they would have nowhere to go, no food to eat, and little chance for survival.

How would any of them survive? Susannah wondered. Two eggs were all that had been collected that morning. With no corn to feed them, the hens had stopped laying, yet she knew she should be grateful they still had any chickens.

As she turned toward the house, Susannah heard the distinctive pounding of hoofbeats like a distant rumble of thunder. She paused and looked toward the road beyond the fallow field, her heart lifting just a little at the sight of the band of riders. But no one rode a zebra dun. She felt the first glimmer of alarm.

Taking no chances, Susannah called to Ebediah, "There are riders coming. Dump that milk on the ground. If they find out we have a cow, they'll search until they find it."

He hesitated no more than a heartbeat before he tipped the bucket and emptied the warm milk onto the cold ground. Susannah ran into the house to spread the alarm.

But Eliza had already spotted the riders from the dining room window. She met Susannah at the bottom of the staircase. "They're coming up the lane now. Come with me. We haven't much time." She ran up the steps straight to her bedroom. "In the bottom drawer of that chiffonier is an old petticoat. Bring it to me."

"Why? What do you want with an old petticoat?" Susannah asked as she knelt down to retrieve it from the drawer. When she lifted it out, she was surprised at its weight. "This is heavy. How much lead have you sewn into the hem to weigh it down?"

"Not lead, my dear." Eliza placed a hand on Susannah's shoulder to steady herself as she stepped into the petticoat.

"Four hundred dollars in gold. I took it out of your father's strongbox and sewed it into this old petticoat for safekeeping. You'll have to tie it tight or it will fall right off."

"Gold." Susannah pulled the strings tight, smiling in admiration of her mother's cleverness.

"I left a few dollars in the strongbox so they would find something." Eliza shook her skirts out to cover the petticoat. "Now let us hope our visitors are not the sort who molest women."

Just as they finished, the stamp and snort of horses could be heard in the drive directly in front of the house. "They're outside." Susannah looked at her mother.

Eliza smiled a nervous smile and squared her shoulders. "Let's go greet them."

When they reached the stairs, the front door burst open and a dozen shabbily clad men poured into the house, brandishing pistols and rifles. Eliza froze, for an instant transported back to that long-ago day at Gordon Glen when Union soldiers had swarmed into the house.

"What is the meaning of this?" Susannah demanded.

Recovering, Eliza lent her voice to her daughter's. "Who do you think you are, barging into my home?" She saw the ruffians falter and turn their startled, unshaven faces up to stare at them. "Did you not see the brass knocker on the door? It was put there to be used."

"Oh yeah?" One of them swaggered. "Maybe we wasn't sure you'd open the door to us."

"Who are you?" Susannah swept her gaze over the motley group. One wore a Union army jacket, and another had a Confederate forage cap. "What regiment are you with?"

"What regiment?" one of them repeated and guffawed. "Why, I guess you could say we're with our own regiment."

"Are you in charge of this rabble?" Eliza moved down the steps, and Susannah stayed right with her.

"I guess I am."

"Then kindly explain what it is you want here," Eliza stated.

"If it's food, I will be happy to share the few supplies in my storeroom with you. No man is ever turned away from Oak Hill hungry."

"Now, that's right nice of you to say that, ma'am." He grinned. "I like generous women myself. I tell you what, why don't you just hand over the keys to that storeroom of yours, and we'll help ourselves to everything we need."

And they proceeded to do just that. Susannah and Eliza stood helplessly by while they scattered through the house taking anything and everything of value, emptying trunks and drawers, ripping the trim from bonnets and dresses, leaving nothing untouched.

Late that evening, Susannah and Eliza arrived at Grand View with the few belongings they were able to salvage loaded in a field cart drawn by an old mule. Their slaves walked behind it, leading the milk cow.

When Temple came out, Susannah faced her with forced calm. "They took everything," she said, and cast a worried glance at the vacant look on her mother's face. "All the supplies, blankets, quilts, sheets, all the sewing things—buttons, thread, pins, needles . . . I don't know how many thousands of other things."

"Eliza." Temple reached out to her in sympathy.

Eliza breathed in shakily at her touch and lowered her head. "When we left . . . Oak Hill was in flames."

"No." Temple whispered and looked to Susannah.

"It's true. They set fire to the barns, everything. They laughed the whole time."

"Let's get your mother inside where it's warm."

Together they helped Eliza out of the cart and guided her into the house.

☙16☙

Sweat trickled down his face, stinging the corners of his eyes. Lije wiped at it with one hand while relentlessly scanning the narrow road leading away from the creek. The dense woods surrounding him broke the glare of the white-hot sun overhead. The musky smell of damp earth and wet wood was strong in the heat of the summer day as he watched and listened for the approach of the Union supply train bound for Fort Gibson, which had been retaken by Federal forces in April. But the roar of the rain-swollen creek behind him masked any sound.

Lije watched the billowing dust on the horizon, a long, tan cloud that hung over the Texas Road. Wagons rolled beneath it, the supply train stretching some two miles in length, flanked by a full regiment of infantry, supported by an artillery unit, with a regiment of cavalry scouring the point, flanks, and rear of the train.

The supply train was expecting trouble. Behind Lije, on the other side of Cabin Creek, sixteen hundred Confederates were dug in, waiting to give it to them.

Anytime now, Lije thought, the column's advance scouts would be arriving to check out the ford at Cabin Creek.

He made a quick visual check of his men, picketed along the wooded bank. Their watchful stances showed they were equally alert, the muggy heat and the fatigue that were their constant companions temporarily forgotten.

A coldness worked along his nerves and tension sharpened his senses, but Lije knew better than to wish for an end to the waiting. Two years of fighting had taught him the waiting would be over soon enough.

Then it came—the sharp report of a musket cracking above the sound of the creek's swift-running water.

His head snapped around as he homed in on the sound. The Union's advance guard hadn't come down the Texas Road; instead they approached the ford from the side.

He snugged the rifle butt to his shoulder and took aim. A clot of smoke blossomed to his left. Lije fired. The enemy was engaged. Instinct and experience took over; there was no time to think, only to act and react.

The clang of ramrods merged with the whine of bullets, the snapping of branches, and the roar of blood pulsing in his head. The splashing of water told him the first of his men had waded into the swollen creek. Lije shifted position to fire again. Sighting down the gun's barrel; he searched the blue ranks for an officer, hoping to slow the skirmishers' charge and gain time, enabling his men to cross the creek safely. A Union major would do nicely. As he centered his sights on one man, another officer moved into his line of fire.

Recognizing the distinctive streaks of silver in the man's hair, Lije stared at the man in shocked disbelief. Kipp. His uncle was part of the advance detachment. Was Alex with them?

Another volley ripped through the leaves, and Lije fired blindly and backed up, reaching the bank and crossing the creek. The Union guard pressed its attack. As he neared the opposite side, rebel guns opened up, giving him cover fire. Fighting the tug of the current, Lije scrambled upward and rolled into a trench. He stayed still long enough to catch his breath and count his men, then went to make his report to The Blade.

"I lost six," he told him. "Two, maybe three dead. The other three missing. Wounded, maybe captured." Dripping water and sweat, Lije sagged back against the slope of the trench and mopped his face with his shirtsleeve, his energy flagging now that the high-charged action was over. "Kipp was with the advance guard."

The Blade looked across the way. "Then he is in front of us."

Wryness tugged at a corner of Lije's mouth. "Has General Cabell arrived with his men? Or Cooper?"

Both Lije and The Blade knew that these forces were needed to capture this supply train. Thus far, not a single supply train had gotten through since May. Without this shipment, Fort Gibson would fall, and the South would once again control the whole of the Indian Territory.

"Not yet. The high water may be delaying them."

Lije nodded, his gaze shifting to Deu, who approached them carrying two tin mugs. "I fixed Master Blade some broth," Deu said. "I thought you might like some, too, Master Lije."

"I would." Lije took the cup, the steamy aroma awakening the hunger pangs his morning meal of hardtack and jerky hadn't appeased. He sipped it, the flavorful broth mixing with the powder grime from the cartridges that clung to his lips. He looked to the north side of Cabin Creek—the Union side. "What's their strength?"

"Our scouts identified the Third Indian Brigade, reinforced with units from Gibson, the Second Colorado Infantry, a company of Kansas artillery, and"—The Blade paused, his glance traveling after the departing Deu—"the Kansas First Colored Volunteers."

Lije understood his father's hesitation. Deu's son Ike was with that regiment. So was Shadrach. And Jed Parmelee was one of its officers.

"Damn." The soft curse of regret spilled from him.

Across the way, the Union horse artillery lumbered into position on the north bank, a twelve-pound howitzer supporting lighter cannons.

"Take cover." The needless order traveled through the rebel ranks.

An artillery bombardment began, a mix of solid shot and deadly canister shell. Under cover of the barrage, Union soldiers moved to the bank and took depth soundings of the creek. Once the findings had been obtained, they broke off the artillery assault and pulled back, leaving a heavy guard posted on the north bank.

"They'll make camp for the night and wait for the water level to drop," The Blade guessed.

"Maybe that will give Cabell and Cooper time to get here," Lije said and moved off to check for casualties.

The precious supply train withdrew two miles to the rear and set up camp in a section of open prairie along the Texas Road. The main Union force camped well back from Cabin Creek, out of range of the Confederate position.

Outside his tent, Jed Parmelee idly puffed on a cigar and scanned the bivouac area. Campfires dotted the scene, bright flickers of light against the gathering darkness of early evening. Voices murmured in subdued conversations while someone somewhere played a lonely song on a harmonica.

"Would ja be wantin' any more coffee, Major, suh?"

Jed glanced absently at his black striker. "Maybe later. I think I'll take a walk around now, Johnson."

"Yes, suh, Major. I'll keeps it hot fo' ya."

Seeking no company, Jed wandered to the edge of the bivouac and lifted his head to study the glitter of the evening's first stars. Searching out and identifying the constellations had always been a relaxing exercise for him, but tonight his quiet contemplation was interrupted by a whisper of sound, a soft rustle of grass indicating the lightness of a carefully placed foot. Jed pivoted, half-expecting to be challenged by a sentry. But the silhouette of a soldier remained silent and motionless.

"Who's there?" Jed challenged.

"Corporal Gordon," came the lazy reply an instant before the man stepped closer, out of the deep shadows into the range of the camp's reaching light. "Alex Gordon, Major Parmelee. You may not remember me that well, but you know my father, Kipp Gordon. Of course, you know my aunt, Temple Stuart, very well."

Jed stiffened at the slyness that invaded the latter remark, but he couldn't deny the vivid image of the dark and beautiful Temple that leapt instantly to his mind. His gaze narrowed on the man's rather smug grin.

"I remember you, Corporal Gordon." The last time Jed had seen him, Alex had been holding a gun on Lije Stuart. "What are you doing so far from your company's camp, Corporal?"

"Just enjoying a little night air," Alex replied. "I've been teaching some full-bloods the finer points of playing dice—and making some easy money in the process. I decided I'd take a little stroll before I turned in—see how your coloreds are doing after learning they'll make up the main attack force tomorrow. They seem awful quiet to me."

"Do they?" Jed didn't like the tone of his voice, or the hint of jeering contempt that laced it.

"You should have heard my father when he learned our units were to be held in reserve to guard the flanks. He did everything but get down on his knees and beg to be part of the attack." Alex paused. "That's Watie's men over there."

"I know." Jed nodded.

"Which means The Blade is there, too. My father had visions of making my aunt a widow before tomorrow is over. He hates the idea that somebody else might deprive him of the pleasure of killing The Blade." His smile took on a mocking twist. "I think he knows you would like to see The Blade dead, too."

"He is mistaken," Jed snapped.

"Is he?"

"You'd best get back to your company, Corporal."

"Good hunting to you tomorrow, sir." Alex raised his hand in a careless salute. "That is, if your coloreds actually make it across the creek tomorrow."

Jed heard the note of skepticism and clamped his teeth around the cigar, making no reply. Still wearing a smile, Alex turned and walked back into the shadows.

Sighing, Jed turned back to the bivouac, the peace gone from the night. His glance traveled over the black faces of the men gathered around the campfires, observing the tension in them, the hints of apprehension. It was always like this on the eve of battle—this waiting, haunted by the specter of what tomorrow might bring.

But more so for these men, Jed realized. Tomorrow they would go into battle for the first time. Jed felt the tension, all right, but it was familiar to him—just as all the sights, sounds, and smells of a battle were. To be honest, he wasn't sure how these Negro soldiers would react tomorrow. But one thing he did know—he had never commanded men more eager to become soldiers.

There, by one of the campfires, Jed spotted the familiar figure of Will Gordon's former butler, Shadrach. He recalled the surprise he'd felt when he recognized Shadrach among the black recruits. Like so many ex-slaves, he had assumed the surname of his former master.

In his mid-forties, Shadrach had been easily the oldest of the recruits. Uncle Shad, that's what everyone called him— officer and soldier alike. He was only one of four blacks in the entire regiment who could read and write. At night, it was said, Shad held classes in the barracks to teach others.

From the looks of it, he was at it again. Jed approached the campfire where a handful of black soldiers crowded around the slim Shadrach Gordon. Drawing closer, Jed saw that Shadrach wasn't showing the men how to make the letters of their name. He was writing letters for them. Letters home. Sobered by the discovery, Jed halted in the shadows, out of reach of the firelight.

"Tell her I be fine and for her not to be worryin' about me none," the black on Shadrach's right said, then watched closely while Shadrach made the marks on the paper. When Shadrach finished, the man hesitated, then shrugged uncertainly. "I reckon that's all. If'n you could just sign it Cuffy, then I'll make my mark under it so's she know it's from me."

Shadrach handed him the pen, and the man called Cuffy drew an X on the paper with painstaking care. Someone threw another log on the fire. As the flames shot up greedily, the sudden flare of light fell on Jed. Instantly, two soldiers scrambled to their feet and came rigidly to attention, their hands held in a stiff salute that would have done credit to a West Point cadet.

When the others started to follow suit, Jed stepped into the circle of light, flicked an answering salute, and checked the rest. "As you were, men." They relaxed, but not completely. An enlisted man never relaxed completely in the presence of an officer. "You wouldn't happen to have any coffee left?"

"Yes, suh, Major, suh." In a flash, a tin cup of steaming coffee was offered to him. "It be clean, suh. I ain't drunk out of it."

Jed started to comment on that, then thought better of it, and simply nodded. "Thank you, Private."

"You're welcome, suh."

With the cup, he gestured to the paper in Shadrach's hands. "Writing letters home, I see."

"Uncle . . . I mean, Private Gordon here, writ one to m' wife for me," Cuffy admitted. "She can't read, but she's workin' for dis white family. And I figured she could have them read it to her. I . . . I thought the letter might be some comfort to her in case . . . well, in case."

"I wrote my daughter, Diane, earlier this evening," Jed admitted. "I have been meaning to write for over a week now, but tonight I decided I . . . shouldn't put it off any longer. Of course, Diane says every time she receives a letter from me, she knows there's been a battle somewhere. Every soldier, regardless of rank, thinks of his family on a night like this."

"I reckon that's true," Cuffy smiled almost gratefully.

Jed took a sip of the hot brew. "This is good coffee."

"Uncle Shad made it," someone said.

"I thought as much." He let his gaze seek out Shadrach across the fire.

That man had the gentlest, brightest eyes of any man he'd ever seen. There was a quality in Shadrach's eyes that was almost childlike in its trust. Yet there was intelligence, too. Very definitely intelligence. Right now, Jed suspected Shadrach knew exactly what he was doing here among the men. In his own way, Jed was trying to assure them that all soldiers experienced the same doubts, fears, and apprehensions they were feeling tonight.

"There is nothing a soldier likes better than good coffee," Jed remarked idly.

"That's a fact, suh," someone agreed.

"The fact is—you are good soldiers." He stared at his cup, feeling the silence grow heavy around him. "There are a lot of people who think you don't deserve to wear that blue uniform."

"What do you think, Major Parmelee?" Shadrach asked.

"Tomorrow morning when we start across that creek, it isn't going to matter what I think. Only what you think—what all of you think. You will answer the question yourselves." Unhurriedly, he downed the rest of the coffee, then handed the empty cup back to its owner. "Good luck . . . and good hunting."

After the major left the campfire, the only sound for several minutes was the crackle of flames. Ike stared into them, hunching forward over his upraised knees. "What do you suppose it will be like tomorrow, Uncle Shad?"

"Noisy," came a dry response.

Someone laughed softly. "It'll be that, shore 'nuff."

"Well, I'll tell you one thing," Cuffy spoke up. "Red or white, them rebs ain't gwine to like seein' no blacks with guns. No sirree, tomorrow morning, they ain't gonna show us no mercy. No mercy at all."

"Only a slave runs," a voice said from the darkness. "And I ain't a slave no more. I'm a soldier."

"Hear, hear," Shadrach murmured in quiet agreement.

At first light, Lije spotted the First Kansas Colored Volunteers marching in a long column down the dusty Texas Road to the banks of Cabin Creek. There, they fanned out in double-rank formation while behind them battery horses and their outriders galloped, hauling the cannons and caissons to their assigned positions.

A moment later the artillery opened up. The ground vibrated with the impact of another solid shot, close this time. Lije rolled over onto his back and looked down the line at the men hugging the wall of the trench. As yet, General Cabell hadn't arrived. Neither had Cooper.

Cradling his rifle across his chest, Lije looked up to the sky to watch for more black balls. Farther down the line, a canister exploded in a sharp puff of smoke above the entrenchments, hurling thousands of metal balls through the air in a downpour of deadly black hail. Lije shuddered, hating the damned canisters.

He fixed his gaze on the morning sky and studied its soft blue color, the same clear shade as Diane's eyes. Diane. He had tried not to think about her, to block her from his mind and his memory. But at odd moments like this, in the midst of an artillery bombardment, her image came to him. Diane with her golden hair and knowing eyes.

He knew there was no point in looking back. Right now there was no point in thinking at all. Clasping his hands over the rifle, he breathed in the morning air, the smoke, and the musty smell of the earth at his back.

He wondered how Ike would do in the fight to come—and thought back to the days when they had hunted pheasant and squirrel together. The boy could shoot. Ike wasn't a boy anymore. Oddly enough, he wanted Ike to do well today. Idly, he recalled the hunger for freedom he'd seen in Ike's face and wondered if Ike knew the Cherokee Council in exile had passed an emancipation law this past February, freeing all slaves owned by the Cherokee.

A silence lengthened and stretched into an eeriness after the thunder of so many guns. Lije rolled to his feet in a crouch and peered over the top of the trench. Men moved into position on the opposite bank.

"They'll be coming now," he told his lieutenant. "Have your men ready."

Across the creek, a cavalry company approached the north bank on foot. A major on horseback stood in his stirrups and raised his saber, the sunlight glinting on its steel blade. Lije saw at once it wasn't Jed Parmelee. Parmelee was too experienced; he would never have presented such a blatant target of himself.

"Charge!" The order rang through the new stillness.

As one unit, the company rushed forward, scrambled down the steep bank, and waded into the chest-high water, the men's weapons and ammunition held above their heads. The major rode into the creek with them, waving his saber and urging them forward.

Lije moved along the trench, cautioning, "Steady now.

Hold your fire. Hold. Hold." He watched and waited until the bluecoated soldiers passed the halfway point and neared their positions on the south bank, then barked the order, "Now!"

All up and down the south bank, rebel guns opened fire, unleashing a murderous enfilade. The major's horse screamed while two bullets struck its rider, and the Yankee officer reeled from the saddle, pitching into the water.

"Fire at will!" Lije shouted.

Lije regrouped his company at the rear entrenchment, the prairie at their backs. He looked at the advancing blue wall of infantry and the cavalry units galloping up to charge his position. Even as he gave the order to fire, Lije knew they wouldn't be able to fight off the Union attack, not without reinforcements, not without Cabell's artillery.

As the blue wave rolled forward, Lije lifted his revolver and fired. Amidst the smoke haze he had a glimpse of an officer with a gold-and-silver beard. Jed Parmelee, there, among the colored infantry. In the next second, he spun out of view, whipped backward by the force of a bullet. From his gun? Someone else's? Did it matter?

"They're running!" someone whooped down the line.

Wiping the sweat from his eyes, Ike saw the rebel forces falling back from the heavy charge, their resistance disintegrating into a disorderly retreat.

"We did it!" Ike thrust a victorious fist in the air. "Man, oh, man, we showed 'em all!"

"Ike, over here. Quick!" Shadrach called to him. "It's Major Parmelee. He's been hit."

Off to his right, Major Parmelee sagged against the slender support of Shadrach's arms, his knees buckling even as he struggled to keep them under him. His left arm hung limp at his side, the sleeve and shoulder of his uniform dark with blood.

Ike rushed over, saw the grayness in his face and the glaze of shock in his eyes. "Major, you got to sit down, sir. You're bleeding bad."

Jed tried to push aside their assistance, but the loss of blood had weakened him, stealing his strength. "Be fine in a minute." The words were slurred. "Go. Get back with your company. Break that rebel line."

"It broke, sir," Shadrach told him. "The rebs are running south as fast as they can, and the cavalry's making sure they don't change directions."

Jed turned his head and tried to focus his eyes on Shadrach. "Running?"

"Running like all the furies were after them, sir."

Farther out on the prairie, a bugler blew Recall, summoning back the troops giving chase to the fleeing rebels. Hearing it, Jed lifted his head, his eyes brightening for a moment. Then he sagged against Shadrach.

"I will rest a minute," he said.

Carefully, they lowered him to the ground. Over his shoulder, Ike shouted, "Hey, Cuffy, go get the surgeon for the major."

A white captain from one of the companies in the regiment arrived and took charge, ordering the pair back to their unit. Ike stole a glance over his shoulder as they moved away.

"How bad do you think it is, Uncle Shad?"

"I'm not sure," he answered with a shake of his head. "The major lost a lot of blood."

"Will he lose his arm?"

"I don't know."

✣ 17 ✣

"Look at how dry this soil is." Eliza shook her head in dismay at the dust and clods of dry dirt that fell from the carrots she pulled. "If it doesn't rain in the next day or two, we'll have to haul water from the river."

"It's going to rain, Granny El," Sorrel assured her, making slow work of thinning the beet row. "You can hear it thundering in the distance."

"Thunder?" Susannah lowered her hoe and threw a skeptical look at the blue sky overhead. "There isn't a single cloud to be seen. You're imagining things, Sorrel."

"No, I'm not. Listen. You can hear it thundering far off."

Smiling, Susannah lifted the hoe to chop at another weed growing near the potato plant. "I'm afraid you're indulging in a bit of wishful thinking. You don't like the prospect of hauling—" She stopped and cocked her head to the side, catching a long, low rumbling sound. "Mother, Temple, do you hear that? What is it?"

"I told you—it's thunder." Sorrel stood up and shook the dust from her skirt.

"It can't be." Temple listened closely to the low, steady rumble. "It doesn't stop or change."

"Could it be cannon?" Susannah wondered. "There were rumors of fighting north of here two days ago. They thought the supply train from Kansas had been attacked."

"That's it." Eliza pushed to her feet.

"What?"

"Praise the Lord, it's the supply train," Eliza declared. "And it's coming down the Texas Road. That's what we're hearing—the rumble of hooves and wagon wheels."

In that flash of an instant, Susannah knew her mother was right. "It got through!" She dropped the hoe and grabbed Temple's hands, laughing and crying at the same time. Soon all three women were laughing and hugging and crying, rejoicing at the news.

A puzzled Sorrel looked on. "Why are you all so happy about the supply train?"

Temple clasped a hand over her mouth, too overwhelmed with relief to answer. In the last few months they had carefully refrained from sending Sorrel to the food cellar. They hadn't wanted her to see how empty it was, how close they were to having no food for the table. Without the fresh vegetables from the garden, the milk from the cow, and the eggs from the few hens they had left, their situation would have been dire indeed. As it was, they were luckier than most, especially the hundreds of starving families gathered around the fort for refuge.

Grand View had been spared the ransacking and looting that had devastated most of the homes in the Nation, thanks in part to a tacit agreement by both sides that Grand View should be regarded as neutral ground. To the rebel forces, it was the home of their Major Stuart. To the North, it was the residence of the widow and daughter of Union loyalist Will Gordon. Marauders remained their only worry thus far.

Susannah went over to her niece and slid an arm around

her shoulders. "The Union wagons will be carrying food and supplies."

"We'll have sugar again," Temple said, smiling through her tears. "Maybe cornmeal. And coffee. Real coffee."

"And thread," Eliza added. "Maybe some cloth to make you a new dress, Sorrel. You've outgrown all your old ones, the way you've been shooting up like a weed." She glanced at the girl, noting that she was not only growing up but filling out as well. Sometimes Eliza had the feeling that Sorrel was turning from child to woman right before her eyes.

"And bacon," Susannah inserted on a wistful note. "We haven't had any bacon since last winter. Can't you just smell it sizzling in the skillet?"

"Listen" Temple looked in the direction of the Texas Road, which passed within a half mile of their property. "It's getting louder now. The wagons must be closer."

"This is a cause for celebration," Eliza declared.

"Let's go see it," Sorrel said, catching their excitement.

Susannah laughed. "You just want an excuse to stop working in the garden."

Sorrel grinned, an impish light in her eyes. "Don't you?"

Susannah laughed again and directed a glance at Temple and Eliza.

"It would be a sight to see, wouldn't it?"

"Indeed, it would," Eliza agreed with a decisive nod. "Phoebe is at the wash shed. Sorrel, you go fetch her. If we are to put work aside, then it's only fair that we all do."

The supply train was an awesome sight. Traveling in a dust cloud created by more than three hundred wagons drawn by mules and oxen, with their military escort of cavalry, infantry, and artillery, it extended several miles in length. The steady din of rumbling wheels, clattering hooves, and marching feet seemed unceasing.

As the first of the cavalry rode past, Sorrel grabbed Temple's arm and pointed. "Look, Mama. There's Alex!"

"Where—" Temple started to ask, but Sorrel rushed to the road's edge, waving and shouting to attract her cousin's attention. A second later Temple spotted Alex amidst a group of riders, then saw Kipp on the outside flank of the same group. She hurried forward to greet him, catching at his horse's rein when he pulled up. "Kipp, it's been so long since I've seen you. How are you? I—" she began.

"Fine—no thanks to your husband and the traitors he rides with," Kipp snarled.

Her smile of welcome faded. Temple wanted to shudder at the hatred she saw in his eyes. A man rode past, a bloodied bandage wrapped around his head. She felt sick.

"What happened?" Susannah came up beside her.

"They were lying in wait for us at Cabin Creek, but their little ambuscade failed." He dug blunted spurs into his horse and sent it lunging forward, forcing Temple to step back.

"What about The Blade . . . and my son?" Her voice trailed off as she acknowledged that her question would go unanswered. Temple pressed a fist to her stomach and struggled to control the rush of fear.

"They're all right, Temple." Susannah glared at Kipp's back. "Both of them. I know our brother. If they weren't, he would be gloating now."

"Yes . . . yes, he would." But that knowledge couldn't alleviate all of Temple's anxiety. It was something she lived with. Always.

A wagon drawn by a team of mules clattered past them. More followed, the train of wagons stretching back to merge with the dust haze. A straggly line of infantry trudged alongside the wagons, flanking the train. Fatigue showed in their dusty, sweat-streaked faces. Some stiffened, squaring their shoulders to march a little smarter as they passed Temple and Susannah, but most were too weary to give them more than a passing glance.

A cavalry captain galloped forward from the rear of the train and swerved his horse around the pair, acknowledging them with a nod and a bowing sweep of his hand. The touch of gallantry in the gesture reminded Susannah of Rans Lassiter. She wondered where he was, what he was doing—if he was safe. And then she felt foolish. He probably hadn't spared a thought for her.

A ruddy-faced infantry sergeant paused long enough to warn them, "Beggin' your pardon, ladies, but ya best be steppin' back a bit before one of these cavalry boyos runs ya down."

"Of course." Temple looked around for Sorrel and finally spotted her standing back with Eliza and Phoebe along the edge of the wide Texas Road. They were all smiles. Temple tried to summon a smile of her own when they rejoined them, but it was a miserable attempt. It suddenly seemed very long ago that she was as happy as they were that the supply train had nearly reached the fort. The news that Lije and The Blade had possibly been involved in an attack against it had changed everything. "Now that we've seen the train, it's time we went back and finished our tasks."

"Wait." Phoebe strained forward, hope blooming in her expression. "Do you see those soldiers coming? They are coloreds. Miss Eliza, do you suppose my Ike is with them?"

"And Shadrach," Eliza added quickly.

"They told you they were running off to join the Union army. Maybe . . ." Phoebe left the sentence unfinished and ran to meet the approaching Negro troops. The others followed, Temple drawn by the thought that Ike or Shadrach might be able to tell her something about Lije or The Blade. Phoebe wasted no time, asking each man as he passed, "My son Ike, do you know him? Ike Jones. He left to join the army."

Man after man shook his head. A few offered the hope, "Maybe he's with one o' the other companies back a ways."

And Phoebe would move on to the next man, repeating her question, sometimes adding, "My brother Shadrach joined up, too. Do you know him?"

Finally one soldier perked up at the name. "Shadrach. You mean—Uncle Shad. He be teachin' me t' read an' write."

"That would be Shadrach." Eliza insisted. "It has to be."

"Last I saw, he was a couple wagons back." The man gestured over his shoulder.

"Shadrach will know about Ike," Phoebe murmured on a sob and ran down the line to find him. Three wagons back, she saw Ike and forgot all about her brother as she flung herself at her son with an exultant cry.

Sorrel pointed. "Mama, it's Ike. Phoebe found him."

"I see." But it was a second face beyond Ike that Temple fastened her attention on.

"Miss Eliza, Miss Temple," Shadrach called to them, a smile wreathing his face.

Temple was a step slow to follow when Eliza and Susannah hurried to meet him. "Shadrach, it's so good to see you again," Eliza declared, smiling through her tears. "My, don't you look fine in your uniform. How are you?"

"I am fine, Miss Eliza. Just fine."

"Will would be so proud if he could see you."

His bright smile faded, his eyes darkening in sympathy. "Major Parmelee told me about Master Will. I am sorry, Miss Eliza. I wish—"

"I know." She briskly wiped the tears from her cheeks and pushed her chin out, refusing to dwell on her grief.

Taking the cue, Shadrach turned to Temple as she joined them. "How have you been, Miss Temple? Your brother Kipp is with the train, somewhere up ahead, I think."

"I saw him. He said the train was attacked at Cabin Creek. He said it was General Watie's regiment."

"That's true. But I checked, Miss Temple. Your boy Lije and The Blade weren't among the rebel dead and wounded we found after the fighting stopped. If they were with General Watie, they got away clean."

"Thank God," Temple murmured in relief.

"Is Major Parmelee still attached to your regiment?" Susannah scanned the trio of mounted officers as they rode past.

"Yes, but . . . the major was wounded during the fight at the creek. Hit in the arm."

There was a look of worry in Shadrach's eyes. Susannah saw it. "How serious is it?" she asked, her mind flashing back to accounts she'd read in eastern newspapers that told of hospital tents set up near battle sites, blood-splattered surgeons with their bone-cutting saws, the screams of half-drugged patients.

"The surgeon thinks he was able to save it . . . unless gangrene sets in."

Eyes closed, Susannah offered a fervent, "Dear God, no."

"Where is he now, Shadrach?" Temple asked.

"He's bedded down in the back of one of the wagons, along with some of the other wounded. They're giving him something to keep him asleep so he doesn't feel all the jostling of the wagon."

"Thank God," Eliza murmured.

Shadrach glanced after the other Negro soldiers, nearly out of view. "I have to catch up with my unit now." He took a step in that direction. "We should reach Fort Gibson tomorrow."

"We'll see you there when we come for supplies," Eliza promised and waved as he jogged after his company.

There was no more reason to linger by the roadside. As one, they turned and started back to the house, sobered by the things they had learned.

"I can't stop thinking about Jed." Eliza shook her head in dismay. "I pray he doesn't lose his arm."

"Diane will be sick with worry when she learns of this," Temple declared with a sigh. "The poor girl."

"Susannah? Susannah, do you hear me?" Eliza's sharpening voice finally broke through her abstraction.

"Sorry, Mother. I wasn't listening. What did you say?"

"Tonight we must make a list of supplies we need," Eliza stated. "And I promised Nathan the next time we came to the fort, we would bring any old clothes we have, blankets, household items, anything that might be of use that he could distribute among the destitute families who have sought refuge there. We need to gather those things together as well."

"I have lots of dresses that are too small for me. We can take those," Sorrel declared.

"And your shoes," Temple added. "Don't forget your old shoes."

Sorrel nodded absently, her thoughts already running off in another direction. "I hope I can see Alex when we go to Fort Gibson."

"Alex," Temple murmured in irritation. "I swear he is all you ever talk about."

"But I never had a chance to talk to him at all today," Sorrel said in her own defense. Then her face brightened with a sudden thought. "I think I'll wear my green dress with the little sprigs of violets on the trim. I look quite grown up in that. I wonder if he'll recognize me. Do you think he will, Mother?"

"I expect he will." It was Temple's turn to reply absently.

"You look sad, Mother. What's wrong?"

"I was thinking about Major Parmelee—thinking it could have been your father, that he could be the one in the wagon, his arm . . ." She swallowed back the rest of the words.

"Jed's arm will be fine," Eliza assured her.

The hospital, like the rest of Fort Gibson, overflowed with soldier and civilian alike. Every inch of space was occupied by the ill and the injured, leaving little room to walk among them. Susannah stepped through the open doorway and paused, assaulted by fevered moans, labored wheezings, and faint whimperings that filled the air. She made the mistake of taking a quick, deep breath and inhaled fetid odors intensified by the sweltering July heat. She coughed and quickly raised a hand to block the rank smells.

Beside her, Temple murmured, "I knew conditions had deteriorated here at the fort, but I never realized . . ." Her voice trailed off as she stared at the crowded row of cots draped with mosquito netting.

An orderly emerged from behind one of the tented cots, a battered basin in his hands. His face was unshaven and gaunt with fatigue. His glance swept over them in quick assessment.

"If you're lookin' fer the surgeon, he's restin'. If it ain't serious, go see one of the assistant surgeons in the tent outside." He started to turn away, then swung back, brightening a little. "Or if you come t' help—"

"We came to see Major Parmelee," Susannah said, hurriedly averting her gaze from the greenish yellow pile of pus-soaked bandages in the basin.

"The major? He's down this way. Follow me, and I'll show you where he's at." He took off to lead the way.

"How is he?" Temple asked.

"Good, considering," the orderly tossed the answer over his shoulder.

"Considering what?" Susannah wanted to know.

"His arm—they didn't have to—" Temple began.

"Amputate?" he finished the question. "Naw. The doc did a piece of work saving it. But that ball sure tore the he—tore the dickens out of his arm. Chewed up a bunch of muscle, it did. Even if it heals up right, I ain't sure how much use he'll have of it, but he's got his arm." He stopped and used the basin to gesture at a partitioning screen. "He's in the cot on the other side. His striker's there, lookin' after him."

At the orderly's less than heartening prognosis, Susannah glanced at Temple. A crippled arm—the anxiety of it was there in her sister's eyes.

"It could be worse, Temple," she offered in a low voice.

"I know." Temple swept her skirts to one side and stepped around the isolating partition. Susannah followed.

A summer breeze drifted through the opened window to the right of the hospital cot, its dusty freshness providing a respite from the rank odors that permeated the rest of the ward. A Negro private rose quickly from the straight-back chair situated close to the cot, his bright glance darting from Temple to Susannah.

"I was jus' feedin' the major some soup. He ate nearly all of it." He set the bowl and spoon on a wooden box under the window. "Nobody said the major was gonna be havin' visitors. If you's jus' gives me a minute, I be gettin' the major fixed up here." He returned to the cot and swept away the cloth he had tucked under the major's chin. Taking a corner of it, he gently wiped around his mouth. "The major be some tuckered out from eatin' all that soup, but he be gettin' stronger every day now."

In Susannah's opinion, the man on the cot looked anything but strong. His eyes were closed; his face, pale as chalk; his breathing, shallow; and his left shoulder and arm, swaddled in bandages.

"Major." The private leaned over the cot and placed a hand on the undamaged right shoulder. "Major, suh, you gots visitors. Some ladies to see ya, suh."

His head moved slightly, his eyelids fluttering open. "Johnson," came the weak, but unmistakable voice of Jed Parmelee.

"Yes, suh, it's me, suh. You gots visitors."

"Visitors?" Jed licked his dry lips and shifted his head a fraction on the hard pillow, his dull glance searching. "Who . . . Diane?"

Temple moved to the opposite side of the cot and laid a hand on his right arm, a determined smile on her lips. "No, it's me, Jed. Temple."

"Temple." His eyes brightened, life and light springing into them. It was a reassuring sight. "Been worried about . . . you."

"We have been worried about you," she countered. "Shadrach told us you have been wounded."

His head moved in a faint nod even as his mouth curved in a slow smile. "Arm. Told that sawbones . . . had to save it. Needed two arms to waltz with . . . beautiful lady."

"He be ramblin' a bit, Miss," the private inserted quickly. "They give him morphia for the pain. Sometime he don't make no sense."

"This time, he is." Temple's voice softened with remembrance.

"First time, Temple," Jed spoke with slow care. "Remember . . . showed you. . . ."

"Yes, you taught me how to waltz a long time ago."

He nodded his head. "Do it again . . . war ends . . . soon now." His bright gaze swung to his striker. "Tell . . . news."

"Yes suh, Major," the man replied, then looked at Temple, his expression aglow with excitement. "We jus' found out— the same day the major wuz fighting them rebels at Cabin Creek, over in Pennsylvania, Gen'ral Meade wuz whippin' old Bobby Lee at a place called Gettysburg. An' the very next day, Gen'ral Grant tooks Vicksburg. The No'th gots the whole Mississippi River in its hands now an' cut the South right in half. The war be over soon foh sure."

"Let us pray that it is." But Susannah found it difficult to be as positive.

Frowning, Jed Parmelee raised his head an inch. "Who—"

"Susannah is here with me," Temple explained.

The lines faded from his forehead as his hand lifted, fingers curling. "Susannah."

She moved closer to the cot, her fingers reaching to take his right hand. "My mother sends her regards, Major. She's with Reverend Cole. She said she would come see you before we left."

"Diane . . . tell her not to worry. I'll . . . be fine."

"I'll write a letter and tell her I've seen you and assure her that you're on the road to recovery."

"Please." It came out in a whisper, his eyelids growing heavy with fatigue.

"Be best if the major rests a bit," his striker suggested. "Talking wearies him some."

"Of course," Temple bent closer. "You sleep now, Jed. We'll come back another day when you're stronger." His mouth twitched in a near smile as his eyes drifted closed, his breath evening out. Temple straightened. "Thank you, Private."

"Johnson, ma'am. Private Johnson," he said, and moved quickly to escort them from the partitioned area. "Don't be worryin' 'bout how puny the major looks. The way he be eatin' he'll get his color in jig time. An' the next time you come, the major be up and about."

"I hope so," Temple murmured none too certainly.

"Don't be a-frettin' 'bout him none. I looks after him. The major, he be a good man."

"A very good man," Susannah agreed. "Thank you, Private Johnson."

"Yes'm."

Outside the hospital, Susannah paused, a sick feeling in her heart. "Did you take a good look at his arm, Temple? He'll never regain the use of it."

"But he lives. What is the loss of an arm when it could have been his life?" Her eyes blazed with a light that was too hot, too bright. In that instant, it was obvious Temple was not thinking of Jed Parmelee, but of The Blade and her ever-growing fear that the war would take him from her.

There were no words of reassurance Susannah could offer. In silence they crossed the compound, threading their way through the crush of army vehicles, soldiers, and refugees to the sutlery where they met up with Eliza and Sorrel.

"How is Jed?" Eliza wasted no time on preliminaries.

"Weak, but lucid. He didn't appear feverish at all," Temple replied. "It's been five days since he was wounded. I think the danger of complications has passed."

"That is good news."

"Where's Phoebe?" Temple looked around for her maidservant.

"She's still fussing over Ike—to his utter embarrassment." A smile edged the corners of Eliza's mouth.

"And scolding Shadrach for running off and leaving Granny El," Sorrel added, then paused, her eyes aglow with excitement. "I saw Alex. He was amazed at how much I've grown up. He said I was turning into a beautiful young lady. Mama, he looked so handsome in his uniform."

"I'm certain he did."

"Do you know what else he told me?" Sorrel declared, making a lightning switch to wide-eyed and solemn. "He said the rebels are massing across the river, that you can see their tents from the top of the buildings here at the fort. They're that close."

Temple whipped around to stare in that direction, straining to see the distant bank through the people and buildings that blocked her view. "So near," she murmured, and Susannah knew she was referring to her husband and son, not the presence of the rebel troops.

"Alex said you can see their campfires at night scattered all over. He said the whole rebel army is gathering over there, and our Union spies say they're getting ready to attack the fort, that there's six thousand or more of them. Everybody is afraid because we don't have enough soldiers to fight that many. They've asked for reinforcements, but they don't know if they'll get here in time. Everybody could be killed."

Susannah pressed her lips together, irritated with Alex for alarming Sorrel with rumor and speculation. "He should never have told you such things."

"I'm glad he did." Sorrel stiffened at the implied criticism of her cousin. "I hate the rebels. I wish they were all dead."

Temple swung back around. "You shouldn't say what you don't mean, Sorrel. If you want to wish for something, wish for the war to end, but don't wish for the death of all the rebels—because you'll be wishing for the death of your father and brother. And you don't want that."

Sorrel flung up her head in sudden and angry defiance. "They don't care what happens to us, so why should I care what happens to them? Look what they've done. Look at the homes they've burned, the people they've killed, the food and crops they've destroyed. People are sick and starving because of them. They deserve to die for what they've done."

The instant Sorrel uttered her bitter and vindictive denunciation, Temple lashed out, her hand striking Sorrel's cheek with a resounding slap. "Don't you say that." She grabbed her by the shoulders and shook her hard. "Don't you ever say that again, do you hear? The Confederates are not responsible for all the destruction and devastation around here. The Yankees have done their share of looting and burning, too—and the bushwhackers. If you want to blame something for the misery and suffering, blame the war. *Blame the war!*"

When she started to give Sorrel another shake, Eliza stepped in. "Temple, no," she softly reproved.

All in one motion, Temple released her daughter and swung away, her body taut and trembling. "How on earth did I raise such a child? How did she get this way? Alex, Alex, Alex," she said in a low, angry voice. "He is all she ever talks about—and it should be Lije. It should be Lije."

Sorrel glared at her, still stiff and smarting from her mother's physical and verbal slap. "I am not a child anymore to be talked about as if I weren't here. I have feelings, too!"

"Of course, you do." Susannah moved quickly to Sorrel's side, sliding an arm around her waist and steering her a few steps away. "But so does your mother."

"I don't care what she feels."

"Now you are talking like a child," Susannah admonished. "Sorrel, you are old enough to understand how thoughtless and cruel it was for you to say you wished your father and brother were dead. You don't really want them to die, do you?"

"No," she admitted in a small, subdued voice, eyes down-cast.

"You hurt your mother very deeply when you said that. There is enough pain and suffering already without you adding more."

"I know. But Alex said—"

Susannah stopped her. "It doesn't matter what Alex said. You must learn to think for yourself."

"He wouldn't lie to me," Sorrel insisted.

"But he might not know the whole truth."

Behind her, Susannah heard Temple offer a fervent "I pray to God that Jed is right and the war ends soon."

Susannah added a silent prayer of her own.

☙18☙

Fort Gibson
Cherokee Nation
July 11, 1863

Three days later Jed Parmelee recovered sufficiently to move out of the hospital ward to his own quarters on the post. His soldier-servant Private Johnson opened the door when Temple and Susannah came to see him the following day.

The striker broke into an instant smile. "The sight of you is sure goin' to cheer the major's heart."

"How is he?" Temple studied the Negro's face, watching for the smallest reaction.

"See foh yo'self." He swung the door open wide, ushering them into the main room's half-shade.

Jed sat in a chair, a blanket draped over his legs despite the day's heat. His uniform blouse was loosely buttoned, revealing the bandages that strapped his left arm to his side, creating an unnatural bulk around his middle. His face still had that drawn look of pain, but much of his color had returned, just as his striker had predicted.

The instant he saw them, Jed gripped the arm of his chair

with his good right hand and pushed himself upright, paling slightly with effort and swaying for an unsteady second.

"Jed, no. Don't." Temple rushed forward, certain he would fall.

But he took the gloved hand she would have used to guide him back onto his chair and raised it to his lips. "I am quite capable of standing, Temple. This wound has stolen much of my strength, but it has not made an invalid of me."

She smiled in relief. "I'm glad to see that, but I hope you will humor me by taking your seat again."

"Of course." Jed released her hand and offered no objection when she took his arm, supporting him as he lowered himself into the chair. "Please, have a seat as well." He gestured to the worn sofa against the wall, the only other piece of furniture in the room except his chair and the wooden crate beside it. "Our comfort is Spartan here, but it's better than what the hospital offered."

"Definitely." Susannah sat on the sofa next to Temple and automatically arranged the smooth fall of her skirts. "I wrote Diane that you were doing well, but it's clear I'll have to write again and tell her how much you've improved."

"I have started three letters to her myself." Jed rubbed his hand over the bulge his bandaged arm made under his blouse. "The doctor tells me it's unlikely I'll regain the use of it, but one-armed officers have served in the army before." He paused, lost in the privacy of his thoughts for a moment before he roused himself. "Johnson, fix some tea for the ladies. And bring a plate of that shortbread you made."

"Yes, suh. Right away, suh." The striker left the room, disappearing into the back quarters.

"I hadn't expected you to visit again so soon," Jed said, then frowned in sudden concern. "Are the roads safe for you to travel?"

"We were well protected," Susannah assured him, smiling easily. "From the moment we turned onto the Texas Road, we were within hailing distance of a full regiment of Union soldiers. They marched into the fort right behind us."

"It must be General Blunt with reinforcements," Jed said in satisfaction. "God willing, we'll go on the offensive now and hit those Johnny Rebs before they can regroup." Temple stiffened at the impatience in his voice, the hint of irritation that it might not happen. He caught her faint movement and immediately sighed his regret. "My apologies, Temple. I didn't think."

"That is not quite true. You did think—like a soldier, which is what you are." She sat with unnatural stillness, her hands folded in her lap.

"Still . . . with the war and all"—he chose his words with care, making reference to The Blade and Lije—"I would have understood if you hadn't come to see me."

Temple shook her head. "This war has torn apart too many families, severed too many relationships. I would hate to see our friendship become another victim of it."

"So would I." Jed nodded slowly. "So would I."

There were voices outside the door and the scuffle of footsteps. The latch clicked and the door swung open. Major Adam Clark, the army physician Susannah had met with Diane at Fort Scott, walked in, a carpetbag tucked under one arm, a valise gripped in his other hand. He turned back to look at someone behind him.

"Here we are." He stepped aside as Diane swept through the doorway, a hand tugging at her bonnet strings, a film of travel dust dulling the coffee brown color of her dress.

"Thank you, Adam." She reached up to pull off her bonnet and saw Jed in the chair. She faltered an instant, relief leaping into her eyes, the lines of tension smoothing from her face. "Well, Father, how wonderful to see you sitting in that chair." All smiles, she pulled off her bonnet and glided to him, her glance flicking to Temple and Susannah. "And entertaining guests, too, I see." Bending, she kissed his cheek, then straightened. "I didn't expect to find you two here, but I'm glad you are. It's good to see you again, Susannah."

"It's good to see you, too, Diane," she said, and meant it.

There was the smallest hesitation, the smallest hint of tension when Diane turned to extend a greeting to Temple, the woman who would have been her mother-in-law. "How are you, Mrs. Stuart?" she inquired, none too certain of her reception.

"I will be much better when you call me Temple, as you always did," she replied gently.

Diane's smile was quick and full of gratitude. "How are you, Temple?"

"That's much better."

She glanced back at her escort as Adam Clark set her bags down. "Temple, I'd like you to meet Major Adam Clark, the physician assigned to General Blunt's regiment. This is Mrs. Stuart, Adam, and I know you remember meeting Susannah at Fort Scott."

"I do indeed," he confirmed, nodding to them. "Ladies."

"How are you, Major Clark?" Susannah searched for some indication that the relationship between Diane and the doctor had progressed beyond friendship. She didn't see one, but she knew it wasn't from lack of desire on the part of Adam Clark.

"Fine, thank you." His attention swung to Jed as he examined him with a clinical eye. "It's good to see you up and about, Major Parmelee."

"It certainly is," Diane chimed in, then directed her question to Temple and Susannah. "So tell me, has Father been behaving himself?"

Before they could reply, Jed caught Diane's hand to keep her by his chair. "Diane, what are you doing here?"

"What a silly question," she chided, still smiling. "I came to see how you were. You surely didn't think I would stay at Fort Scott after I was informed you were badly wounded. I half-expected to find you at death's door. I'm delighted to be wrong."

Jed dismissed her concern with an impatient shake of his head. "But how did you get here?"

"General Blunt was kind enough to escort me"—she paused, her eyes taking on an impish glow—"though, naturally, he was unaware of it. The minute I learned the general was marching to Fort Gibson, I threw some things in my bags and arranged to travel with a refugee family who planned to follow closely on the army's heels for protection."

"You are very resourceful," Jed said with pride.

"The daughter of an army officer has to be," Diane said with a laugh, then sent a brief, searching glance to the back quarters. "Where is Johnson? He is still with you, isn't he?"

"He is," Jed began, only to be interrupted by the striker's return.

"There you are, Johnson." Diane saw the enameled tray he carried and the mixed assortment of cups. "And you made tea. Wonderful."

"I thoughts I heard your voice, Miss Diane, and I adds a extra cup fo' you. But I didn't know the major was with you. I'll fetch another."

"Don't bother," Adam Clark told him. "I can't stay. I'm sure my services are needed at the dispensary. I'll stop by later this evening and see how you are. Ladies," he said, taking his leave of them before walking away.

Diane watched him for a moment, then pushed the wooden crate away from her father's chair and maneuvered it into position in front of the sofa. "You can set the tray here, Johnson."

"Have a seat, Diane." Temple shifted to make room for her on the sofa.

"After bouncing on that wagon seat for days, I prefer to stand," she insisted with a laugh. Jed chuckled. It was the first sound of genuine amusement Susannah had heard from him. She silently marveled at the way Diane brought life and laughter to every corner of the drab room. There was no doubt she would be excellent medicine for Jed. "Please, you pour, Temple."

"If you wish."

The striker placed the tray on the crate. "I'se sorry we ain'ts got no pretty cups fo' you to sip from, but the tea be hot."

"I noticed there are many things we don't have," Diane observed. "No curtains at the windows, no rugs on the floor, no pictures on the wall. I can see I'm going to be very busy these next few days trying to make this place presentable."

"Believe me, you won't recognize these quarters when Diane finishes with them," Jed declared. "As I said before, she is very resourceful."

"At an army post, that means I am an excellent scavenger." After the tea was poured, Diane picked up two cups and carried one to her father, turning it so he could grip it by the handle.

"You will have to be," Susannah said, "especially here, where even necessities are hard to find."

Diane sobered. "Yes, there are so many people all crowded together. The sanitary conditions are deplorable—refuse everywhere, open latrines. I shudder to think what the rations have been, as isolated as this post is, and as tenuous as its supply line is." She stood beside her father's chair, her hand resting lightly on his shoulder.

He smiled up at her. "Diane was very active in the women's relief organization in Kansas. Naturally, she did more than tend the sick, write letters, and collect bandages, clothing, and food items. She was extremely quick to draw the post commander's attention to any deficiencies in cleanliness, diet, or ventilation."

"I did make a nuisance of myself on occasion." Again her smile was back, making light of her contributions.

"And you worked hard, too."

"When it was necessary."

"With so many families living at the fort for protection, the needs are endless," Temple admitted. "Many lack even the basic necessities of food, clothing, and shelter. We brought all our spare clothing and blankets to Reverend Cole last week, but it was so little. And the crowding . . . there is so much sickness and disease, it's been difficult for the fort surgeon to cope."

"No single person can solve all the problems here. But several people working together can make a difference, and at least improve the situation," Diane stated. "Naturally, the first thing that has to be done is identify the points of concern. After that, steps can be taken to correct them. For that, you need a lot of hands willing to help." She paused, her glance running over Temple and Susannah in quick assessment. "I know it's a struggle merely to survive right now, but if you could spare a few hours every other week or so . . ."

"Listen to her," Jed declared, amused and proud. "She isn't here five minutes and she's already recruiting volunteers."

"Father is right." The corners of her mouth turned up in a rueful smile. "Forgive me. But there are so many things I am powerless against that when I do find something I can do, I tend to charge right in. It's a failing of mine."

Susannah laughed. "It's a laudable one. I, for one, will be happy to help whenever and however I can."

"We all will," Temple added.

"Good." Diane beamed with pleasure. "After all, it has nothing to do with the North or the South. It's about helping those who are suffering, those who are living in intolerable conditions."

Temple nodded. "I know Eliza has often lamented her inability to ease the work load Reverend Cole has taken upon himself, especially with the orphans."

"How is Eliza? And Sorrel?"

They chatted for a time about family, each of them skirting any talk of war that might lead to an inadvertent reference to Lije or The Blade. All the verbal tiptoeing soon created a strain.

Before it became too noticeable, Susannah sought a diversion and found it in Jed's empty cup. "Would you like some more tea, Major?"

He glanced at his cup as if surprised to find it empty. At the same time Susannah noticed the first signs of fatigue around his eyes and mouth.

"No, I don't believe so," he said and leaned forward to return his cup to the tray.

"I'll do that, Father." Diane took it from him.

"I think it's time we were on our way," Susannah said. "We don't want to overtire you, and we do have a long ride home ahead of us."

Jed made a half-hearted protest that clearly revealed his flagging energy, a fact that both Temple and Diane noted.

"We'll come again," Temple assured him, rising.

"I'll walk you to the door." As she moved away from his chair, Diane glanced back at her father. Already he had abandoned his pose of alertness, his chin drooping, his body sagging against the chair. All her earlier concerns for him rushed back.

At the door, Temple turned to say goodbye. Diane held up a silencing finger and motioned both of them outside. She stepped out after them and closed the door nearly shut.

She came straight to the point. "I couldn't ask him. His arm, how serious is it?"

Temple hesitated, then admitted, "It's possible he'll never regain the use of it, but it could have been worse, Diane."

"Of course." She bowed her head stiffly. "I was told the supply train was attacked by Watie's regiment. Is it true?"

"Yes, but—you can't blame Lije for this, Diane," Susannah protested.

She lifted her head, her eyes cool, pain hidden in their depths. "Then he was there."

Susannah wanted to lie, but all she could do was shake her head. "Don't do this, Diane."

She turned back to the door, her hand reaching to push it open again. "Please come visit Father again. Don't let my being here stop you."

"We would never do that. We've been friends too long," Susannah told her. "That will never change, no matter what."

Diane looked back, gratitude welling in her eyes. "Thank you."

Back inside, Diane directed a quick glance at her father and paused. His eyes were closed; a small grimace of pain showed in his expression. Her glance slid to the empty blouse sleeve pinned to his shoulder.

She was suddenly dangerously close to tears, but there was no time for weeping now. No time to dwell on what-might-have-beens and what-ifs.

Turning, she gave the door a hard push. It closed with a solid thud, the sound rousing her father as she had known it would. She swept back into the room. "I swear, it is hot enough outside to boil an egg in its shell. On days like this, everyone would be wise to follow the example of the Mexicans and take a siesta."

Jed raised an eyebrow. "Are you hinting I should lie down?"

She grinned and bent down to give him a peck on the cheek. "I always knew you were a clever man. As for myself"—she straightened, holding onto her carelessly bright air—"I have a thousand things to do, but the first order of the day is to bathe. Just as soon as you lie down to rest, Johnson can start bringing me buckets of water. Heaven knows, I will need them. I feel like I have half the dirt from the Texas Road on my skin."

Jed chuckled, then caught at her hand and gave it a squeeze. "I love you."

"I love you, too, Daddy." She wished she were six years old again so she could crawl onto his lap and know the comfort of his arms around her, soothing all her troubles away.

But she was no longer a child. Her troubles were not so easily banished.

Lije was the cause of the ache inside that wouldn't go away. He was the memory that haunted her, never leaving her alone. God help her, she still loved him. And she hated him because of it. She desperately wanted to forget him.

Someday, she promised herself.

ಅ19ಎ

Soldiers in Union blue swarmed over the wagon, rummaging through its contents, throwing out most of what they found. The afternoon rang with the clang of metal pots and iron skillets, splintering wood, hoots of discovery, and the crash of breaking china. Alex pushed his forage cap to the back of his head and looked on with indifference. The wagon and its contents belonged to John Meynard, a Cherokee long known as an advocate of the rebel cause.

Meynard's wife ran up to the black mare and clutched at Alex's leg. "They're destroying everything. Make them stop. Please. It's all we have."

Unmoved by her frantic plea, Alex cast an idle glance in the direction of her husband, who stood stony-eyed before Kipp. Blood still ran fresh from the gash along Meynard's temple where Kipp had pistol-whipped the man for refusing to reveal information about rebel troops in the area.

Again, Alex heard the man's sullen voice say, "You are the only soldiers we have seen today."

The man was lying. Like his father, Alex was convinced

of it. For days now the countryside had been rampant with rumors that a large Confederate force had crossed the Arkansas River and was headed north. At a farm two miles down the road, an old man and two young boys claimed they had seen a band of twenty or thirty rebels ride past their cabin around noontime. The old man had also insisted that he'd seen a large dust cloud to the west, and he swore it wasn't made by a passing buffalo herd.

If the dust were the main body of the Confederates, then the band of riders was its scouting patrol. And if it had been on the road or anywhere close to it, these people had to have seen it.

Over at the wagon, flour billowed like white smoke from the sack that one of the soldiers held upside down. Cackling, the man gave the sack a final shake and tossed it on the slick black pool of wagon grease that puddled next to an over-turned bucket.

Again, the woman pleaded with Alex. "Not our food. We have children to feed."

Alex glanced at the runny-nosed girl clinging to the woman's skirts. A boy of seven stood beside the yoked oxen, his cheeks streaked with tears, his chin trembling, and his eyes glaring his hatred and fear.

"Stop them, please."

When the woman pressed closer, the black mare snorted and danced sideways to escape the contact. Alex made no attempt to check the movement.

"If you want us to stop, you'd better have your husband tell us what we want to know."

She looked at her husband, hesitated, then let her shoulders sag in defeat. "We saw no rebels," she said in a wooden voice, then turned and watched in stricken silence as a heavy wooden trunk fell from the back of the wagon. Its lid snapped on impact, spilling clothes and blankets. She jammed a fist against her mouth, smothering the involuntary sound of protest.

Alex saw that the clothes on the ground were of good quality, better than what the family had on. He took another look at the well-fed oxen, all splattered with mud. Deliberately?

Alex knew John Meynard had been a prosperous farmer. Not as wealthy as The Blade Stuart, perhaps, but he and his family had lived very comfortably. But their farm was now in Union domain, and like so many other Confederate sympathizers, they were fleeing south to friendlier territory. They could not take everything they owned, but they had packed all their valuables.

Grinning, Alex dismounted and dropped the mare's reins. "Hey, boys," he called to his compatriots in the wagon box. "Haul everything out of there and start ripping out the floorboards. It could be they're hauling rebel gold."

As the men fell to the task with a vengeance, Alex watched the woman's reaction out of the corner of his eye. She smothered another sob of protest but showed no alarm. He shrugged at his luck—or lack of it—and walked over to the water barrel lashed to the side of the wagon.

The instant he reached for the barrel's lid, the woman rushed up. "What is it you want? What are you doing?"

After her previous pleas, Alex was amused by her sudden vehemence. "A hot day like this makes a man thirsty."

"You want water, I'll get it for you." She fumbled in her haste to gather up the drinking gourd that hung from the barrel.

Suspicious of her offer, Alex grabbed her wrist, stopping her. "I'll get my own." When she looked up, he saw the panic in her eyes and smiled, his suspicions growing. "What's in the barrel?" he asked softly.

"Water, of course." She dropped her gaze, looking anywhere except at him.

"I think I'll take a look for myself."

"No," she moaned and squeezed her eyes shut.

He maintained his grip on her wrist and lifted the lid to peer inside. There, in the shadowy bottom of the wooden keg, was a dark cloth bundle, almost invisible if he hadn't looked closely.

"What have we here, I wonder?" Grinning, Alex propped the lid up and plunged an arm into the water.

His groping fingers quickly closed around the bundle and felt the flat, round shapes of coins. He winced at the prick of something sharp. A lady's brooch, maybe? After a furtive look to make sure no one other than the woman watched him, Alex pulled the bundle out and tucked it inside his blouse. Laughing softly, almost silently, Alex jerked her closer.

"Your idea was sound," he told her in a low taunting voice when she strained away from him. "Water is plentiful now. It isn't something anyone would bother to steal. But you gave it away."

With a sob she pulled free and ran a few steps away, then paused and clutched the little girl closer to her skirts. Alex laughed.

"Hey, Corporal." A soldier poked his head around the wagon's canvas cover. "There's nothing under this floor but ground."

"Too bad," Alex shrugged, smiling at the cool wetness of the bundle against his skin.

A sharp, cracking thud ripped the air. Alex turned as the husband fell to the ground, blood pouring from the freshly split flesh along his ear and cheek. Kipp stood over him, his revolver aimed at his head.

"By God, I'm tired of your lying!" Kipp raged.

"John! No!" the woman shrieked and ran toward her husband, only to be halted when Kipp swung his gun at her.

"Get back." He snarled the order, then threw an impatient look at Alex when he walked up. "We've wasted enough time here. The fool knows where those rebels went, but he won't talk."

"Ask her." Alex jerked a thumb at the woman. "She knows."

"No." She shook her head, fear leaping into her eyes.

"Where'd you see them? Where'd they go?" Kipp pointed

his gun at the man on the ground. "Answer me, or you'll be a widow."

"Dear God, no." She reached out a hand to Kipp in mute appeal, then saw the futility of it and sobbed helplessly, "You're animals. Animals!" She paid no attention to the whimpering little girl reaching up, begging to be held.

Alex glanced from the unconscious man on the ground back to the woman. "She doesn't seem to care much about saving him, does she?" In one step, he grabbed the child by the hair and yanked her away from the woman at the same time that he drew his revolver and pointed it at the screaming girl. "Talk or she dies."

"Please, God, no. Don't hurt her." The woman sank to her knees, her hands outstretched to the child. "Don't hurt my baby."

"Talk!" Alex barked again and cocked the hammer.

"We saw them!" she screamed and broke into sobs. "Don't hurt my baby. Please, please."

"Where? When?"

"Three hours ago. Four. I don't know," she gulped back another sob. "It was at the creek. They were in some trees by the bank, watering their horses."

"How many?" he said above the little girl's whimpering cries.

"Twenty—I'm not sure. Oh God, let her go."

"Where were the rest of them? The main body?"

"We didn't see any others—"

He tugged sharply at the girl's hair roots and ignored her fresh wail of pain and the little fingers that pried at his hand. "Where?" When the sobbing woman started to shake her head in denial, Alex pressed the muzzle to the girl's head. "Talk!"

"No!" She clutched at her throat. "We never saw them, but—John—John thought they were farther west. There's a town . . . to the north. He . . . he said they would circle wide of it. Please."

Satisfied that he had all the information he could get, Alex started to ease the hammer forward. Then his father broke in. "What regiment were they with? Who was commanding them?"

She shook her head, her mouth opening for a speechless second. "I—" She pressed a hand to her forehead, trying to think. "John . . . John knew one of them. He said he rode with Colonel Watie."

"The man he knew—what was his name?" Kipp demanded with sudden and savage intensity.

"I think it was . . . Stuart. He used to be with the Light Horse. That's all I know, I swear it. Ple—"

Kipp had already heard all he needed to hear. "Let's go." He strode off, shouting to the rest of his men. "Mount up!"

Alex shoved the girl at the woman and hurried to his horse, holstering his revolver. She gathered the child up in her arms and ran sobbing to her husband. Alex threw them a glance and swung into the saddle, smiling to himself. Meeting up with the Meynards had proved to be profitable—in more ways than one.

The Blade loped his horse across the prairie. Deu, as always, rode with him along with an escort of three men. The main body of his troop, some one hundred strong, was a good four miles behind him, and Lije was somewhere ahead of him with his scout patrol.

It was the *somewhere* that bothered The Blade. Lije had pulled out this morning at first light. He should have reported back hours ago. Had he run into a Union patrol? The Blade had heard no sounds of gunfire, though he knew he might be beyond the range of such sound.

Again, The Blade regretted that he had placed Lije in charge of the scouting detail: He trusted Lije's judgment and instincts, but having a son under his command weakened a man, made him worry about one instead of the whole. Yet

Temple would never forgive him if anything happened to Lije.

Where the hell was Lije?

He pointed his horse toward a hill. He knew this particular countryside well. He was only hours from Grand View. From home. But he couldn't let his thoughts dwell on that. Last night he had dreamed of Temple turning witchlike to love him. Even now he had only to close his eyes and . . .

He shook his head to dismiss the vision from his mind and galloped his horse up the hill. At the top, The Blade reined in and surveyed the surrounding land from the hill's vantage point.

"Here you are, Master Blade." Ever anticipating his needs, Deu handed him an old, battered spyglass. All the regiment's equipment was as inferior as that damnable Mexican gunpowder. Roughly twenty percent of Watie's men had no weapons at all. The rest had old muskets, flintlocks, or, worse, Texas rifles, which were just as likely to blow up in your face as fire. The promised uniforms had never arrived. Few of the men had a change of clothes; many were in rags or blue uniforms they'd stolen off a dead Yankee. But they were fighters, every one of them. They knew nothing of military discipline and protocol, but they knew how to fight. If they could only get their hands on some of the Union's new repeating rifles . . .

The Blade sighed and lifted the spyglass to begin a slow, thorough search of the area to the east and north, but he saw no sign of the patrol. On the chance that Lije had circled wide, he checked the northwest quadrant. Still nothing. He lowered the glass, a grimness thinning his mouth.

"Riders." One of his escorts pointed to the narrow dirt road a half mile distant that ran through the valley on their right. "It looks like our patrol." He stood in his stirrups and waved.

Turning, The Blade saw the mounted group. Just as he spotted them, the riders swung left and galloped straight for the hill. At first glance, he thought it was the scout patrol except—they had been coming from the south.

He raised the spyglass and cursed. "Yankees." He pushed the spyglass at Deu and caught up the reins. "Scatter! Now!" He pulled his revolver to snap off a shot as the others sank spurs into their horses. He saw Deu pull up to wait for him. "Go on! I'm right behind you."

He fired at the onrushing riders and started to wheel his dancing horse after the others, then hesitated. The Yankee in the lead was Kipp. He swore as the first bullets whined around him. He fired another round, trying to slow them.

Something slammed into his left shoulder. The impact nearly spun him out of the saddle. He grabbed at the horse's mane, conscious of a hot, stabbing fire high on his left arm. With his spurs, he jabbed the horse into a gallop, fighting the numbness that claimed his left side.

When he reached the flat of the prairie, he looked back. Kipp had topped the hill and was now racing after him, whipping his horse mercilessly. Another rider was a short distance behind him. Alex? He couldn't tell.

His horse started to slow. The Blade kicked it, then felt the animal laboring, its gait roughening. He looked down. Blood flowed from a small hole above its right shoulder. It had been hit as well. He spied a small thicket of brush just to his left and spurred his horse toward it.

"A little farther. You can make it," he said as much to himself as to the horse.

Gamely, it galloped on, bloody foam now spraying from its nostrils. Fifteen feet from the thicket, the horse stumbled and went down, pitching The Blade forward. He landed heavily on his left side. Pain exploded through his body.

Roll. Instinct told him to roll into the thicket.

The next time he opened his eyes, he found himself tangled in the undergrowth. Had he passed out? He didn't know. He wasn't sure. Horses. He could hear them. Fighting off the swamping blackness, he staggered and crawled into the thicket, ignoring the clawing branches and slicing thorns. The gun. It was still in his hand.

Don't go deeper into the brush, instinct warned again. Kipp will expect that. Get to the edge.

After crashing through the brush like a half-crazed, wounded animal, The Blade now crept with caution and care, moving as noiselessly as possible. The pain in his arm had receded to a fierce throb. He could think now without the blackness swarming around him. A single layer of brush separated him from the tall prairie grass. He paused and crouched low to get his bearings.

Hoofbeats drummed the ground to his right and stamped to a halt. "We have him now!" It was Kipp's voice—not twenty feet away. The Blade turned to face it. Through the thick leaves he could see the legs of the horses, then the blue pants of two riders. Was it Alex with Kipp?

"He's in that brush, I tell you. He's there, I can smell him. Come out, Stuart!" Suddenly, there was a cracking report of a revolver. Instinctively, The Blade ducked, but the bullet pierced the brush well away from him. Kipp was firing blindly.

"Come out, Stuart! Or do I have to come in there and drag you out like I did your father? You're a snake and a traitor. You should have died long ago. This time you will. Come out!" Again he fired.

At the mention of his father, The Blade involuntarily tightened his grip on the revolver in his hand, his thumb automatically going to the hammer, his forefinger gently hooking itself around the trigger. With great stealth, he wedged his way through the last layer of brush into the tall grass.

"This is your last chance, Stuart!" Kipp challenged. "Either come out and die like a man—or I'll come in and kill you like the snake you are!"

The Blade straightened slowly, bringing the revolver up to bear. Neither Kipp nor Alex noticed him. Both concentrated their attention on the broken branches in front of them, their guns aimed at it.

"Are you looking for me, Kipp?"

Kipp swung around, a snarl of rage claiming his face. As his pistol lifted to take quick aim, The Blade squeezed the trigger of his own cocked gun. It bucked in his hand. Kipp yelped, the fingers of his right hand splaying, dropping the gun as a red stain spread quickly down his right forearm. He grabbed the wound and started to bend to retrieve his gun.

"Try it, Kipp. Go ahead and try it," The Blade pulled back the hammer again. Alex was behind Kipp, his line of fire blocked by his father. "Throw your gun into the grass, Alex." The Blade never took his eyes from Kipp. "I don't want to kill you."

There was a movement behind Kipp. Then the sunlight glinted on blue steel as the gun arched through the air and landed somewhere in the grass near The Blade's fallen horse. Moving slowly and keeping the revolver pointed at Kipp, The Blade worked his way to their horses, his left arm hanging limp at his side.

"What are you waiting for?" Kipp jeered. "Why don't you kill me? You've wanted to do it for years. This is your chance. Pull the trigger, Stuart. Come on, shoot me."

"Be glad you are Temple's brother, Kipp." The chestnut's reins were still looped around its neck. It snorted suspiciously when The Blade came up on its right side, but the horse continued to stand quietly. Keeping the gun pointed at Kipp, The Blade put a foot in the stirrup, then quickly and fluidly swung into the saddle.

"You are a coward, Stuart. All traitors are. Your father was."

"I never met a man who deserved to die as much as you do, Kipp." Unexpectedly, the horse tossed its head, breaking his concentration for an instant. When he looked again, Kipp was pulling something from inside his jacket—a pocket revolver. Reacting instinctively, The Blade fired. Kipp backed up a step and pressed a hand to his stomach. The gun slipped to the ground as he pitched forward.

Alex rushed to his father. "He's dead." The rage of anger and grief twisted his face. "He didn't have a gun!"

Alex's words barely reached The Blade. Weakness was setting in. He had to get out of there while he still had the strength. The chestnut struck out across the prairie at a fast trot.

Alex came to his feet, yelling. "You murdering bastard! You'll die for this!"

Furiously, Alex searched through the trampled grass near his father and found the gun his father had dropped. Quickly, he raised it and sighted down the barrel, cocking the hammer. He squeezed the trigger without flickering so much as an eyelash. The resounding report echoed and reechoed across the prairie. He smiled when The Blade slumped in the saddle. The startled chestnut broke into a canter.

Alex turned back to his father's body, the smile fading. "I killed him for you," he said.

Then, with gentle care, he picked up his father and cradled him in his arms. He carried him to the ground-hitched black mare. She shied briefly at the smell of death, but Alex crooned to her. None too certain, the mare let him lift the body onto the saddle and snorted her dislike for the burden.

Deu galloped more than two miles before he realized The Blade wasn't behind him. Worried, he rode back toward the sound of scattered gunfire. Ahead, he saw the returning scout patrol had surprised the attacking Yankees, putting them to rout. With the Yankees in full flight, they broke off contact. Although he didn't see The Blade among them, he did see Lije splitting off from the others to meet him.

Lije reined in his lathered horse. "The whole damned countryside is crawling with Union patrols." He looked past Deu. "Where's the major?"

"I don't know. I thought he was right behind me."

Lije rose up in his stirrups to scan the sweep of prairie. Nothing. An uneasiness gripped him. "Something's wrong." He kicked his weary horse into a jaded canter. Deu joined him.

A half mile farther on, they spotted a chestnut horse grazing in a hollow, a rider slumped over its neck. "Master Blade was riding a bay," Deu said when they rode closer. "But that's his coat. I've patched it too many times not to recognize it."

It was the longest two hundred yards Lije had ever crossed. When they reached him, Lije peeled out of the saddle before his horse came to a complete stop. Deu was right behind him.

The chestnut horse moved off a couple steps, then fell to grazing. Lije got a sick, cold feeling in his stomach when he saw the spreading blood stain on the back of his father's coat. He approached the horse slowly, talking softly, not wanting to spook it. The instant he had the reins in his hand, he moved to his father's side and lifted his head. There was a groan and fluttering of the eyelids.

"He's alive," he said, hope lifting.

"Lije?" The voice was weak, the word faint.

"I'm here. Deu is with me. Don't worry, we'll take care of you."

"Kipp . . ."

A muscle leapt visibly in Lije's jaw. "What about him? Did he do this?"

"S'dead," The Blade mumbled, the words stringing together. "Killed 'im . . . can't tell . . . Temple . . . hurt . . ." His voice trailed off in a wavering sigh, a limpness stealing over his muscles.

"He's lost consciousness." Lije battled back the need to rage and curse. Dammit, he should have been with him! He should have been at his side. This was his fault.

"Master Blade will be all right. We'll take care of him," Deu said, but he sounded as worried as Lije.

But Lije knew if his father was going to live, words weren't going to save him. And no doctor traveled with their raiding party.

"Find Duncan," he told Deu. "Tell him what happened, and tell him we're taking my father home."

❦ 20 ❧

"Eliza," Temple whispered, shaking her stepmother's shoulder. "Eliza, wake up."

"Mmmmm, what?" Eliza stirred, drowsily lifting her head. "What is it?"

"There's someone outside. I saw him from the bedroom window." The minute she saw Eliza's eyes snap wide open, Temple stepped back from the bed. Eliza threw back the covering sheet. "It might be a deserter or a runaway slave looking for something to eat. I only saw one, but there might be more. I don't know." She turned toward the open doors to the second-floor veranda and listened for a moment. The walnut stock of the Colt navy revolver felt smooth and oddly cool in her hand. "I sent Phoebe to wake Susannah and Sorrel. I'm—"

"I'm already awake," Sorrel said from the bedroom doorway. "Why are you two whispering anyway?"

Temple swung around to angrily whisper, "Sssh, not so loud. Someone's outside."

"Who?"

"We don't know."

As Eliza pulled on her cotton wrapper, Susannah rushed into the room, with Phoebe at her heels. "Temple, we can't find—There you are," she said when she saw Sorrel near the door.

"All of you stay here," Temple ordered. "I'm going downstairs and find out who is out there."

"Not alone, you're not," Susannah retorted.

Temple started to argue with her, but she recognized that stubborn tone. "Very well, come along," she murmured irritably and moved into the hallway.

Just as she reached the top of the staircase, she heard the front door open. With greater care, Temple started down the steps, clutching the gun tighter, her palms sweating. She looked back once, reassured by the sight of Susannah one step behind her.

In the heavy silence, every little sound seemed magnified, the swish of her nightdress, the soft pad of Susannah's feet behind her, the creak of a floorboard. Suddenly, she saw a figure outlined by the paleness of the foyer wall. It was moving toward the stairs.

Gripping the gun in both hands, she raised it and pointed it at the dark shape. "Who are you? What do you want?" she demanded. "Speak up quickly, or I will shoot."

"It's me. Lije."

"Lije!" On a surge of joy, Temple lowered the gun and lifted the hem of her nightdress to run down the steps. "It's Lije," she called back to the others. "Phoebe, light the candles. Hurry." Almost immediately, light flared behind her, spraying a dim glow that reached to the bottom of the staircase where Lije stood. Temple ran straight to him. "You're home. I can't believe it." She went into his arms and laughed when she discovered the gun was still in her hand. "I thought you were—It doesn't matter what I thought." She drew back and reached up to stroke his cheek and run her fingers into the sides of his hair. "Look at you—your hair, it's positively shaggy. When did you cut it last, for heaven's sake? But you look wonderful. So wonderful."

She kept chattering away, her face shining with happiness.

Lije thought of all the worry and grief and fear she had known for so many years. It should have made her bitter and unlovely. But it hadn't. His mother was too strong, too indomitable. She would need that strength again.

He had to stop her, he had to tell her. He searched for the words, fought for them, even though he knew what a blow they would be. Guilt rose again. My fault. My fault.

"I know I should ask why you've come, what you're doing here," Temple rattled on. "But I don't care."

"Yes, you do," he said quietly, but she paid no attention.

"You look tired, worn out. I'll bet you're hungry, too. Phoebe, go see what we have in the kitchen that you can fix for Lije. And make some coffee. We have real coffee," she told him. "With not an ounce of chickory in it."

Lije looked past her at Susannah. She knew he wasn't here to visit: Her gaze was full of apprehension and questions.

"How is your father? I wish he could have come with you," Temple added wistfully.

"He's here, Mother. Outside." He saw the shock overtake her expression—and the fear that followed. "He's been shot. Deu is with him."

Temple swayed. She had lived so long in fear of this day that, for a moment, she couldn't react further. The words she had dreaded to hear had actually been said.

But he was alive. The Blade was still alive.

"Where is he? Take me to him."

Struggling under The Blade's leaden weight, they carried him into the house and up the stairs to the master bedroom. When they had maneuvered him onto the bed, Temple sent Phoebe downstairs to fetch her medical basket.

"Sorrel, I want you to bring those bandages we planned

to take to the hospital at Fort Gibson." She pushed her daughter toward the door. "And be quick about it."

"How did it happen, Lije? There's been no word of fighting in the area." Eliza carefully untied the sling that supported his bandaged left arm and shoulder.

Lije hesitated fractionally, then replied, "A Union patrol jumped us. He took a bullet in the shoulder. It broke the bone. Deu and I set it the best we could, but there wasn't much we could do. He was shot in the back. The bullet is still in there." He saw no reason to mention Kipp right now.

Temple dropped the boot she had pulled off his foot at the same instant that Eliza turned to look at Lije. A second later, she retied the sling. "Help me roll him onto his side and remember to be careful of his shoulder."

"Where are my scissors?" Temple went to look for her sewing basket. "We'll have to cut his shirt and jacket off of him."

Within minutes the clothing lay in pieces on the floor. Eliza took one look at the wound low in his back and said, "He needs a doctor, Temple."

"The closest one is at Fort Gibson," Lije said. "As soon as the Union army finds out he's here, they'll arrest him and hold him prisoner."

"Master Lije is right," Deu inserted. "Those Union soldiers would like nothing better than to get their hands on one of Colonel Watie's troop officers. Master Blade is getting a reputation to match the colonel's."

"Then we'll have to take the bullet out ourselves." Temple stared at her husband's lean, muscled back. His skin, the color of teakwood, looked smooth, except for the dark hole that was so close to his spine. Somewhere inside was a bullet.

Temple could feel herself shaking and knew she had never been so afraid in her whole life.

"Temple, are you sure—" Eliza began.

"Yes!" Temple whirled on her, rigid and pale with determination and fear.

Eliza paused, then said quietly, "Very well, I will do it. Susannah, you can help me."

"He is my husband. I—"

"Exactly." Smoothly and efficiently, Eliza took charge. "Lije, you and Deu help me shift The Blade onto his stomach. We will need more light, Temple. It would be a good idea to close the drapes, too. We wouldn't want a passerby to wonder what we're doing up at this hour of the night."

After the bullet was removed and the wound bandaged, Eliza announced, "His breathing seems good. His pulse is weak but steady. I don't think we can expect more than that yet. What he needs now is rest and quiet."

Lije lingered by the bed while Eliza gently shooed everyone else, save Temple, from the room. He looked down at his father, jaws clenched, his insides all knotted up, a hand squeezing at his heart. On the bed table was the porcelain basin in which the tweezers, a small knife, and blood-soaked pads of cotton cloth were lying. The bullet was there as well. Lije picked it up. It was still sticky with drying blood. He looked at it for a long second, then curled his fingers around it; making a fist.

"He will be fine, Temple," Eliza murmured somewhere behind him.

"Yes." The tautly whispered response, riddled with anxiety and uncertainty, sliced through Lije like a saber.

With the deadly bullet still clenched in his fist, he glanced one last time at his father, then turned and moved away from the bed. His mother stood at the foot of it, her hands wound tightly around the tall, carved bedpost, her gaze riveted on The Blade. He wanted to offer some comfort and reassurance to her but, feeling none himself, he laid a hand on her shoulder as he passed.

Pausing in the outer hall, he reached back and pulled the

door after him. When it was inches from the casing, he heard his mother speak and stopped to listen.

"I am tired, Eliza," she murmured tightly. "I am tired of it. Do you realize how long I have been going through this? Not wondering *if* he were going to die, but *when?*"

"I know."

Showing no indication that she had heard the quiet reply, Temple continued. "How many days, months, and years have I spent alone, wondering where he was, whether he was still alive? Every time he left . . . every time I told him goodbye, I knew it might be the last time I would see him, that there were those who wanted revenge for that treaty he signed nearly thirty years ago. Thirty years, Eliza. I have been worrying about him for all these years and now he lies there. Maybe this time, he really will die. Oh, God, I don't want to lose him." She choked on a sob.

"Of course, you don't."

There was the sound of a long, indrawn breath and the whisper of a sigh. "I have told myself so many times that it will be all right; now I'm not sure I believe it anymore."

"He will make it," Eliza insisted. "I don't know why I believe that, why I feel so certain of it, but I do. You have to believe it, too. He will need you."

"I know."

Hearing the sound of soft footfalls on the stairs, Lije moved away from the door, leaving it ajar. Susannah paused near the top of the steps.

"I was on my way to find you," she said. "Phoebe fixed you something to eat. It's in the dining room."

Lije nodded and followed her down the stairs to the dining room. His glance strayed to the empty chair at the head of the table. His father's chair. A plate of food, a side dish of cornbread, silverware, a cup, and a molasses pitcher were all arranged before the chair immediately to the right of it. Lije pushed it all to the other end of the table and sat down.

It was a sight that tore at Susannah. Something more was

wrong. She had known it the instant she saw Lije and he told them about The Blade. She doubted that he'd said more than a dozen words since. All the while Eliza had been removing the bullet, Lije had simply stood there, holding a candle close, saying nothing, showing nothing.

Yet, somewhere beneath that grim-lipped silence, Susannah sensed a rage that went beyond justified concern for his father's condition.

Smothering a troubled sigh, she crossed to the sideboard. "The coffee smells good, doesn't it? Shall I pour you a cup?"

He nodded.

She pulled his cup closer and filled it while Lije drowned his cornbread in a pool of dark molasses. As she started to set his cup back in front of him, Susannah saw the bullet lying on the table. A chill of revulsion shivered through her.

"Heavens, where did that come from?" She went to snatch it up, but his hand closed over it first. She looked up and met the cold challenge of his eyes.

"I'll keep it."

Susannah drew back, straightening. "Lije, don't. He's alive."

He picked up the bullet and rolled it around with his fingers, staring at it. "Kipp is dead."

"Kipp?" she said in a startled echo. "Where? When?" Then the full import of his words hit her, and she sank into the nearest chair. "Oh, my God, you're saying The Blade was shot by—How—" She knew what to ask, but she couldn't get the words out.

There was a small, vague shake of his head. "Kipp must have been with the Union patrol that jumped him. I didn't see what happened." His voice held no emotion. "When Deu and I found him, he was still conscious. He said he had killed Kipp. He wanted me to tell Mother he was sorry."

"Did you—"

"No. She has enough to deal with now." Lije continued to finger the bullet. "The army can notify her about Kipp or the major can tell her himself if he recovers."

"Don't say it that way, Lije. He *will* recover."

Letting the silence build, he slipped the bullet in his vest pocket, picked up his fork, scooped some seasoned pinto beans onto it, chewed them, then washed them down with a drink of coffee.

Susannah watched him with worried eyes. Everything he did was too controlled, too emotionless. She could feel the frustration and tension building inside him. It was like being in a closed room and knowing a fire raged on the other side of the door. She could feel the scorching heat even though she couldn't see the smoke or hear the roar of its flames.

"You haven't told me everything that happened, have you, Lije?"

His upward glance was cool and brief. "I told you everything I know."

"Did you?" she persisted.

His look came back hard and sharp. "I wasn't there." His voice was abrupt and full of guilt. A thick, angry sigh broke from him, and he pushed the fork onto the plate and rocked back in his chair, hooking an arm over its straight back and grabbing up his coffee. "I wasn't there," he repeated into his cup and took a quick swallow of coffee, then lowered the cup, staring into it. "I should have been with him, but I wasn't. It's because of me he's lying up there."

"Why? Where were you?" Susannah asked in a low, prompting voice.

"I took a detachment out to scout for enemy patrols." The line of his mouth turned grim with the memory. "I knew Kipp was back in the Nation. I saw him when we attacked the supply train at the Cabin Creek crossing. I knew he would be looking for his chance to come up against the major . . . my father. I thought—" He bit off the rest of his words, his mouth closing in a taut line.

"What did you think?"

A sigh spilled from him. He tipped his head back and stared at the ceiling. "I thought if I took the point, I could spot Kipp first. I thought—" With a shake of his head, he dismissed that thought and brought his chin level again, rocking forward and shoving his cup onto the table. "I was gone too long, rode too far in front. I should have known Kipp would slip in behind me. I should have stayed with the major. I should have been there. It's my fault."

"That is the most ridiculous thing I have ever heard!" Susannah came to her feet and swept away from the table. She slammed the coffeepot on its hot pad and whirled back to meet Lije's startled look. "What happened was tragic, but you are in no way to blame for it, Lije Stuart."

"You don't understand," he began with impatience.

"That is obvious. Just what would you have done if you had been there?" she demanded, hands on her hips. "Thrown yourself in front of your father, taken the bullet that was meant for him? Then you would be lying in that bed upstairs, and your father would be berating himself." She saw his rejection of her words and sighed in frustration. "Be realistic, Lije. Even if you had been with him, there may not have been anything you could have done to prevent what happened."

"I'll never know that, will I?"

She pressed her lips together, then tried again. "That bullet in your pocket came from Kipp's gun. *He* is responsible for your father lying in that bed. No one else."

He picked up his fork again and proceeded to eat. Susannah watched him, waiting for him to say something. After the third bite, Lije remarked, "I didn't think I was hungry, but this tastes good. Better than the hardtack and jerky I ate this morning."

Susannah pulled a chair out and sat down. "You are deliberately changing the subject, aren't you?"

He ignored that and said in a blandly conversational tone, "Did you ever learn how to shoot that derringer of yours?"

Surprised by the question, Susannah frowned. "Derringer? Who told you I had a derringer?"

"Rans Lassiter, a lieutenant with the Texas Brigade." He gathered a forkful of the molasses-soaked cornbread.

Susannah hesitated, conscious of her own quickening heartbeat. "He said he knew you."

It had been nearly a year ago, yet her memory of him remained fresh and sharp. "I have often wondered. Is he still in the territory?"

"His unit returned a couple weeks ago or so."

"Then he has been away."

Lije treated her to a slow, assessing look. "You made a very definite impression on him."

"Did I?" She tipped her head down to hide the sudden glow of pleasure she felt.

"He swung by Oak Hill on one of his patrols. On his return, he told us it had been burned to the ground. A few days later we learned you and Eliza had come here."

Susannah was briefly warmed by the news that Rans had come by to see her. Then another thought intruded. "Did he give you my message about Diane?"

Once again Lije's jaw tightened. "He did."

"She's here, Lije. At Fort Gibson," Susannah told him. "She came to take care of her father after he was wounded."

"I saw him get hit." Lije cut off another chunk of cornbread with his fork, never looking up to meet her eyes. "How is he?"

"Better. He returned to limited duty last week." She hesitated, then knew she had to tell him. "He was hit in the left arm, Lije. They were able to save it, but the damage appears to be permanent."

"His arm is crippled?" He concentrated on the last few bites of food on his plate, pushing at them with his fork.

"Yes," Susannah said, then hurried to add, "It's the risk a man takes when he goes to war. Jed said so himself."

Lije nodded, then laid down his fork and gathered up the cloth napkin, wiping his mouth with it. "Tell Phoebe supper was good." He pushed out of his chair.

"Where are you going?"

"To check on the horses, make sure Deu has them safely out of sight." He moved toward the door.

"Lije, aren't you going to ask about Diane?" Susannah challenged. "Don't you want to know how she is? Isn't there anything you want me to tell her?"

He began to walk away.

"Lije," she began in protest.

"What can I say?" The question exploded from him, harsh with anger, but Susannah saw that beneath the anger there was pain. "That I still think about her? What good would that do either of us? I have a responsibility that puts me in direct opposition to her wishes. But she doesn't see it that way. She won't understand that I have to do what I believe is right." He stopped, recognition flickering across his expression that he had revealed too much. "It's old ground, Susannah. Leave it alone," he said and walked out.

Temple sat in the armchair positioned next to the bed, her eyes closed in exhaustion as she drifted in that state that was neither wakefulness nor sleep. She awakened with a start to the sounds of thick moans and rustling sheets. Her glance flew to the bed where The Blade stirred, his face twisted in a grimace, his fingers digging and clawing at the covers, moans coming from him in deep, grunting breaths.

She moved quickly to his side, running a hand over his brow to check for a fever. "Sssh, my love," she whispered.

"Pain . . . my back . . . leg."

She turned to her basket of medical supplies on the bed table and took out the bottle of laudanum. She fumbled briefly with its cork, then carried the bottle to his lips, cradling the back of his head in her hand.

"Take this." She poured a little into his mouth. "It will make the pain better." She spoke to him like a child. "Now, drink a little more. There, that's good."

While she waited for the drug to take effect, Temple moistened a cloth and bathed his face and neck. Several minutes passed before the groans subsided. His eyes opened slowly and tried to focus on her through the glaze of pain and opiate.

"Temple?" he mumbled uncertainly.

"I'm right here," she said, forcing a smile.

"Sorry . . . didn't mean to . . ."

"Sssh, don't talk now. Rest."

Dutifully, he closed his eyes.

"How is he?" Lije stood in the doorway, a dim figure in the guttering candlelight.

"Fine," she whispered, then tucked the covers around him and moved away from the bed toward Lije, her hands clasped in front of her, her fingers twisting in silent worry. "It's the pain. I gave him some laudanum. He should rest comfortably for a while." A rooster crowed. She glanced at the closed drapes, then back at the bed. "What time is it?"

"It's dawn." Lije stayed in the shadows, beyond the reach of the faint light. "You need to get some rest. I'll sit with him."

Temple shook her head. "I couldn't sleep."

"You need to try. He'll need your strength."

"I know, but—" Again Temple looked back at the bed.

"If there's any change at all, I'll wake you immediately."

Temple hesitated, then nodded. "Very well, but only for two hours."

"I'll wake you."

He waited until she left the room, then crossed to the bed. The faint, soft light of early morning filtered through the drapes. Lije blew out the candles and sat down in the chair next to the bed, taking up his vigil and rolling the bullet around and around between two fingers.

❦ 21 ❧

Restless, every muscle coiled with tension, Lije shoved on his campaign hat and headed out the door, no longer able to endure the sight of his father in pain. In the last thirty-six hours there had been almost no change in The Blade's condition. Lije would have been heartened by that, except for the intense pain that set in as soon as the laudanum began to wear off. His father was crazed with it.

Lije paused on the rear porch steps and inhaled a deep breath, trying to cleanse the nameless rage that seethed inside. The sun stood high in the sky. The first brown leaves of autumn tumbled across the grass, chased by a brisk afternoon breeze.

With narrowed eyes, he looked around. Nothing stirred; nothing moved. Once this plantation would have bustled with activity at harvesttime. Now there were no workers in the fields, no livestock in the pastures, no smells of newly mown hay, no rattle of cider presses. Instead, he saw sagging fences, empty Negro quarters, rusting equipment, and one wily old rooster strutting near the edge of the woods.

He pushed off the back porch and struck out toward the Negro quarters where the horses were hidden. He hadn't taken three strides when Sorrel called to him from the back porch, her voice tentative, "Lije?"

He swung back, mentally braced to be summoned back inside. "What is it?"

She stood on the porch, one arm hooked around a pillar. "Are you leaving now?" she asked with rare timidity.

"No," he breathed the word in irritation. "I'm going to check on the horses, make sure they have plenty of water."

"May I come along with you?"

He studied her for a silent moment, his lips coming together in a tight, grim line. Solitude was what he wanted—time alone to curse and rage and sort through the tangle of emotions that had his nerves on edge. But Sorrel was too quiet, nothing like the spoiled, tempestuous little sister he remembered. In fact, since his return, she had hovered in the background like a shadow.

"Come along if you want." His words were clipped, grudging.

Lije pivoted and again struck out for the cabins. He heard the swift, light patter of her footsteps behind him as Sorrel hurried to catch up. As soon as she drew level with him, she slowed and walked silently at his side, eyes down.

The horses were stabled in the burned-out shell of one of the cabins that had been hit by lightning the previous year. Lije waded through the tall, dry weeds to the side of the cabin, lifted aside the dead tree limbs that penned the horses, and stepped through.

A big-boned roan gelding lifted its Roman nose, snorted once at the sight of Lije, and went back to tearing at the sheaf of meadow grass at its feet. The other two flicked an ear at him and continued to eat. A check of the water buckets showed they were half full. Lije moved among the horses.

"Which one is yours?" Sorrel ventured closer, taking care where she stepped.

"I've been riding the roan."

She stepped beside the roan and ran a hand over its neck. "What happened to your horse Jubal?" she asked with quiet curiosity.

"He was shot out from under me last February." Lije examined a saddle sore on the chestnut's back.

"What's this one's name?"

"I haven't bothered to give him one." He picked up the chestnut's right front leg and cleaned its hoof with his knife. He didn't bother to tell her that, in war, the horses were dead too soon to name—either from enemy bullets, broken legs, or sickness. Counting Jubal, he'd had three mounts die; two others were back at Boggy Depot recovering from wounds.

"I would call him Red Smoke. That's what he looks like."

Lije grunted a nonanswer and picked up the next foot, the smell of horsehide, ash, and dung rising strong all around him.

"Lije?" Again, there was that tentative note in her voice, turning it all soft and uncertain and troubled.

"Yes." He glanced around to find Sorrel staring at him with dark, haunted eyes.

"Is Father going to die?"

"No." His answer came sharp and quick, and a certainty flowed through him the instant he spoke.

"But he could, couldn't he?" she said, all wrapped in gloom.

"He could," Lije admitted, but he no longer believed it.

Her chin quivered. "It would be my fault if he did."

Straightening, Lije frowned, an eyebrow shooting up in surprise.

"Because"—she screwed her face up, fighting to hold back the tears that suddenly welled in her eyes—"I wished he were dead. I said"—she hiccoughed back a sob—"he deserved to die for all the homes he'd burned, the food he took, the people he killed. I said you should die, too, but I didn't mean it. I didn't. I didn't," she wailed.

Lije went to her. "Of course, you didn't." At first, she was stiff when he put his arms around her. He threaded his fingers through her red hair and forced her head against his chest. She sagged against him and wept in earnest. He let her cry. "You aren't to blame, Sorrel." The bullet was in his shirt pocket. He could feel the outline of it against his skin. "You had nothing to do with what happened."

"But I *wished* it," she murmured brokenly.

"How old are you now, Sorrel? Eleven? Twelve?" He tried to remember.

"Almost twelve," she admitted, her tears subsiding, but she continued to hide her face in his shirt front.

"Almost twelve." Drawing his head back, he hooked a finger under her chin and lifted it. Using a thumb, he wiped at the tears on her cheek. "Then you're old enough to know wishing doesn't make it so. You can't make anything happen by simply wishing it. It's only when you *act* on the wish. And you didn't, did you?"

"No."

"It was just something you said when you were upset, wasn't it?"

Sorrel nodded, watching him closely.

"I've been upset a few times—and said things I didn't mean. I was always sorry afterwards . . . just like you," he added with a faint smile.

"I'm sorry." She sniffled back her tears.

"I know." Lije paused, catching the noisy rustling of someone walking through the tall weeds outside.

"Lije?" Susannah called softly. "Are you in there?"

"Yes." He set Sorrel away from him and whispered to her, "Better get those tears wiped up. We don't want to explain to Susannah why you were crying." He left Sorrel rubbing the sleeve of her dress over her face and went to meet Susannah. "Did you need me?"

"Yes," she said with thinly disguised agitation. "Would you help me get the mule hitched? I have to go to the fort."

"Why?" Lije came back quickly. "Is the major worse?"

"It isn't that—we're almost out of laudanum. Temple's had to increase the amount and the frequency of the dosages just to keep the pain at a level The Blade can tolerate. Now it doesn't look like there will be enough to last through the night. I'm going to get more."

"How?" Lije frowned.

"I don't know," Susannah admitted with a vague shake of her head. "I'll make up something to tell the doctor. If I have to, I'll steal it. But I can't let The Blade suffer like that."

"No." In that, Lije was in total agreement.

The mule halted in front of the hospital. Susannah wrapped the reins around the wagon brake and bundled her skirts aside to climb down from the seat, then froze, a frisson of alarm shooting through her when she saw Alex walk out of the hospital. In all the many scenarios she had imagined during the ride to the fort, she hadn't considered the possibility she might encounter him. Reverend Cole, yes. Diane, yes. But not Alex.

"Alex, what are you doing here?" She let her surprise show as she swung to the ground and turned to meet him.

"I could ask you the same question." His mouth quirked in one of his familiar smiles, but there was something cold and hard in his gaze that chilled her.

"You aren't hurt, are you?" Susannah rushed to avoid an answer, her mind racing. Lije had told her that Kipp was dead, but instinct warned her not to let Alex know that she knew. She shot a glance at the hospital, the thought suddenly occurring to her that Lije might be wrong. "Is it Kipp? Is he—"

"My father is dead."

After that instant of doubt, his confirmation was like hearing the news all over again. "No," Susannah murmured.

"I brought his body back to the post yesterday. He was buried at sundown." His words were emotionless, as if all feeling had been crushed from them.

"Alex," Susannah said in genuine sympathy and reached out, gripping his arm in a gesture of comfort. "I am so sorry."

His eyes narrowed in their study of her, unnerving in their directness. "Aren't you going to ask how he died?"

"How?" she repeated, startled by the unexpected question and all that it implied. Had Alex been there? Had he seen what happened? Why else would he ask such a thing? "I just assumed—wasn't he shot by rebels?"

He considered her reply for an agonizingly long minute before he nodded, his mouth twisting in a bitter and cynical line. "Yeah, by rebels. The Blade will be pleased when he learns my father is dead, won't he?"

"I wish you wouldn't say things like that, Alex. Your father is dead. Let all that hatred die with him."

"Yeah." For the first time, his gaze shifted away from her. "My company is going out on patrol again tomorrow. Reverend Cole said he would go see Temple, let her know about my father."

"There's no need for him to make the trip all the way out to Grand View. I know how busy he is here. Let him know I'll tell her."

He nodded, then stepped to the wagon box. "What have you got back here?"

"Some old linen we tore up for bandages. Reverend Cole mentioned that, sadly, there is always need for more." The bandages alone were a flimsy reason to come to the fort. Aware of it, Susannah sought to change the subject. "You never said why you were at the hospital."

"I stopped to see a friend of mine," he said, then flexed his shoulders in a sudden restlessness. "Look, I'm supposed to be at the stables. I'd better get back before I'm missed. Give my regards to Granny El and Sorrel."

"I will."

Susannah watched as he moved off in the direction of the stables. The instant he was out of sight, she shuddered with relief and gathered up the bundled bandages, her excuse for coming in the event she ran into Diane.

Armed with the knowledge gained from working as one

of Diane's volunteers at the hospital on three previous occasions, Susannah hurried into the building. She bypassed the wards where she might run into Diane and went straight to the supply room and small dispensary.

To her relief, she recognized the orderly on duty, a short, stocky man with muttonchop whiskers. "Private Cosgrove, how are you?"

He looked up, his muttonchops lifting with the quickness of his smile. "Well, Miss Gordon, it's good to see you. Miss Parmelee didn't mention you would be helping out today."

"Actually, I came to the post on another errand, but I wanted to drop these bandages off while I was here."

"What am I thinking?" He slapped a hand to his forehead in dismay. "Lieutenant Gordon was your brother, wasn't he? Aah, you have my sympathies, Miss Gordon. I guess you'll be visiting his grave while you're here."

"First, I want to see the doctor on another matter. Is Major Clark busy?"

"Aren't you feeling well?" His study of her instantly turned clinical.

"Not me. My mother. Is Major Clark busy?"

"He's back in his office, writing his reports. I'll take you to him."

After the orderly ushered her into Adam Clark's office, Susannah wasted little time on pleasantries before she launched into her carefully rehearsed story of her mother's fictitious fall and subsequent severe pain in her lower back.

"In her lower back, you say?" Adam Clark frowned thoughtfully.

"Excruciating, at times—so much so that she almost screams with it. And my mother is not a woman given to histrionics."

"I see," he murmured and proceeded·to question Susannah exhaustively about her mother's condition. Had she noticed any swelling? Was her mother running a fever? Was there any numbness or loss of feeling in her feet or legs? Did she have any tenderness in the abdomen?

In her mind, Susannah applied the questions to The Blade. She was able to answer "No" to all of them.

"Interesting." Adam Clark continued to frown while he absently packed fresh tobacco in his pipe. "There must be an injury to a nerve that's causing this pain."

"We had some laudanum on hand that gave her relief, but it's almost gone now. It will be by tonight," she explained. "That's why I'm here—to see if you could give me more."

"Of course, of course. Come with me." Laying his pipe aside, he rose from his chair.

Fifteen minutes later, Susannah climbed into the wagon, a tin of morphia tucked deep in her dress pocket. By Major Clark's calculation, there was enough to last a week, when given in the prescribed amounts. Her mission accomplished, Susannah slapped the reins across the mule's rump, and the animal broke into a reluctant trot. Adam Clark lifted a hand in farewell as the wagon rolled by, but Susannah was too intent on getting home to notice.

Nor did she see Diane and Reverend Cole emerge from the hospital tent when she drove past it.

"As John Wesley said, 'Cleanliness is next to godliness,'" Reverend Cole remarked to Diane.

"You should make that the theme for your sermon to the refugees this Sunday. It may encour—" Diane broke off to stare after the wagon. "Wasn't that Susannah?"

Reverend Cole turned to look. "I believe you're right. I wonder what she was doing here?"

Adam Clark strolled over to them. "Reverend Cole, Diane." There was extra warmth in his voice and his smile when he addressed Diane. "Beautiful day, isn't it? It's not likely we'll have too many more of these. Winter is right around the corner, I'm afraid."

"It is," Diane agreed absently. "Tell me—was that Susannah who just left?"

"Yes."

"I wonder why she never stopped to see me."

"She was in a hurry to get home to see her mother, I imagine," he remarked and frowned thoughtfully again. "By all accounts, her mother took a nasty fall."

"Eliza?" Reverend Cole said in instant concern.

"From what Susannah told me, nothing was broken; there was no indication of internal injury. But she's experiencing severe pain. Excruciating, at times. Obviously, there was some nerve injury. I sent some morphia with Susannah. That should relieve it."

"Do you think it's serious?" Diane asked.

"It's hard to tell. Hopefully, it's something complete rest will cure," Adam replied. "Susannah promised to keep me apprised of her mother's condition."

Twilight purpled the sky and deepened the shadows around the house when Susannah finally made it home. As the wagon rolled to a stop, Lije stepped from the shadows to meet her. "I was beginning to wonder what happened to you. Did you get it?"

"Enough for a week," she said as Deu appeared and climbed onto the wagon.

"I'll see to the wagon and mule for you, Miss Susannah."

"Thank you, Deu." She handed him the reins and moved to the side where Lije waited to lift her down. "How is he?"

"The same." Together they walked swiftly to the house.

The others converged on Susannah the minute she walked in. She responded to their flood of questions by producing the tin from her pocket.

"Thank God," Temple murmured, reaching out to Eliza in relief.

"It's morphia," Susannah told them. "Major Clark warned that it's a stronger painkiller than laudanum and needs to be given in the amounts specified."

"Did you have any trouble getting it?" Eliza asked.

"None. He believed my story about your fall—thankfully,"

Susannah added, with a relieved smile, then hesitated. "But I did see Alex." She felt Lije's gaze instantly sharpen on her.

"You did!" Sorrel said in excitement, then complained, "I wish I could have gone to the fort with you. I—"

Susannah ignored her. "I have some bad news, I'm afraid. Kipp was killed."

A moan of grief and protest came instantly from Temple. Eliza put an arm around her, sorrow darkening her own eyes. "We must pray that after so many years of knowing only hatred, Kipp has at last found peace."

With his own thoughts far from being that charitable, Lije turned and went up to his father's room. Phoebe sat close to the bed, a spoon in one hand and a bowl of soupy mush balanced in the other. His father reclined against propping pillows, breathing in those much-too-familiar moaning breaths, his eyes closed.

"Is he eating?" Lije glanced at the bowl of mush.

"Some." But Phoebe's expression indicated it was very little.

"I'll feed him." He crossed to the bed to take her place. "You go on downstairs. Tell my mother that I'll stay with him. She can take her meal with the rest of the family."

Phoebe surrendered the bowl and spoon to him. "You have to make him eat now, or he won't have the strength to get better."

He saw the worry in her eyes and nodded. "I will." He sat down, dipped some mush on the spoon and carried it to his father's lips. "Eat some of this," he said as Phoebe slipped quietly out of the room.

The Blade's eyes opened to mere slits. "Lije?" His voice was a scratchy whisper.

Lije immediately pushed the spoon between the parted lips. "It's me. Now eat this." He pulled the spoon back, drawing it over the upper lip to scrape the mush from it. He waited, watching for The Blade to swallow that before he dipped more onto the spoon.

"Never knew . . . could . . . hurt so bad."

"Eat. Don't talk." Lije pushed another spoonful into his mouth and waited again, giving The Blade a chance to rest between bites.

After three more spoonfuls, The Blade forced his eyes open again and struggled to focus on Lije. "Your mother . . . Kipp?"

He didn't have any trouble piecing together what his father was trying to ask. "She knows Kipp is dead, but that's all she knows. As far as I'm concerned, that's all she needs to know. It would only hurt her." He scooped another portion of mush onto the spoon. "Let her think what she likes. Kipp's dead. You're the only one now who knows what happened."

"Alex . . ." A frown puckered his forehead.

Lije halted the spoon an inch from The Blade's mouth. "Alex was there?"

There was a faint, barely perceptible nod. Lije swore under his breath and pressed his lips together in a tight, angry line. He knew in his gut that Alex would never keep quiet about it. Never.

"Wait a minute." Lije stiffened in sudden suspicion. "Who shot you? Was it Kipp? or Alex?"

"Don't know . . ." His head rocked slightly. "Kipp, dead. . . . Must'a been . . . Alex."

"Alex." Lije felt the anger and bitterness grow inside him. It wasn't over. Kipp's death hadn't ended anything.

❦ 22 ❧

A brooming wind swept out of the northwest, pushing dust and leaves and assorted debris before it. Now and then, a strong gust shook the horse-drawn buggy traveling along the Texas Road. Squinting her eyes against the blowing dust, Diane held onto the side rail with one hand and kept the other firmly on her hat.

"We are nearly there." The wind whipped away the sound of Reverend Cole's voice, diminishing its volume. "I'm glad. There's a storm brewing."

Diane looked up with a frown. "There isn't a cloud in the sky."

"Not yet." He nodded to the west, indicating the line of dark clouds on the rim of the horizon.

"It seems too late in the year for a storm." But she had lived in this country much of her life and knew thunderstorms could occur at any time of year, even winter, although rarely. This was only September.

"But the air has that warm, heavy feeling even with the wind." Reverend Cole spied the turnoff to the Stuart home and swung the buggy horse onto the lane.

The angling wind was at their backs now, pushing them along. The buggy's calash broke the force of it. The relief was instant and welcome. Letting go of her hat, Diane relaxed for the first time in miles. The buggy horse snorted its pleasure and picked up its trot, as if sensing their destination was directly ahead.

It was. There, at the end of the lane, stood the Stuart house, framed by wind-lashed trees and partially obscured by the haze of blowing dust. Diane stared at it, memories swirling up, dangerous memories, too vivid, too bittersweet.

Before the ache took hold, Diane said, "I hope Eliza is better."

The reverend nodded. "This fall she took is one more reason why I wish they would come live near the fort. In treacherous times such as these, it isn't safe for three women to live alone so far from aid."

"Temple won't consider leaving her home."

"As long as she stays, Eliza and Susannah will remain with her. They are three very stubborn women."

Diane preferred to think that they had learned to be independent and self-sufficient, traits she found very admirable.

The buggy came to a stop in front of the house. No one stepped out to greet them. The only sounds were the loud rush of the wind through the trees, the rustling of leaves, the clack and clatter of branches rubbing together, and the occasional snap of a limb breaking.

Reverend Cole cast a considering glance around the grounds and remarked, "As glad as I am that the slaves have been freed, it still seems odd to drive up to this house and have no one run up to tend to your horse."

He laid the reins down and climbed out of the wagon, unfolding his long, lanky frame, then reached back for the basket of foodstuffs and set it on the ground. Finally, he extended his hand to assist Diane.

The instant she stepped from the shelter of the buggy, Diane was again subjected to the sting of blowing dust and the tug of the wind at her hat. Again, she clamped a hand over it and hurried with the reverend to the front door. As she reached for the brass knocker, the door swung open.

Sorrel stared at them in surprise. "Reverend Cole. Diane. I thought I saw a buggy outside so—Susannah never mentioned you were coming."

"She didn't know." Diane smiled. "May we come in?"

"Of course." Sorrel stepped aside to admit them, then pushed the door shut behind them. A gust of wind rattled the windows as if to protest its exclusion.

"Here." Diane took the basket from Reverend Cole and handed it to Sorrel. "Will you take this to Phoebe?"

"What is it?" She held it up, trying to peer under the cloth that covered it.

"Some tins of fruit from the sutler's store and a smoked ham my father found tucked away in the back." Diane absently smoothed back the wisps of hair the wind had tugged loose.

"Real ham?" Sorrel sighed with pleasure. "I can't remember the last time we had any."

"We came to see Eliza," Reverend Cole inserted quietly. "Where is she?"

"Granny El? She's upstairs in mother's room. I'll—"

"Thank you, I know the way," Diane said and moved toward the stairs. Reverend Cole trailed a step behind her. Sorrel hesitated, then broke into a run toward the back of the house, carrying the basket. Halfway up the stairs, Diane wondered aloud, "I wonder why Eliza is staying in Temple's room instead of her own?"

"No doubt there is a logical explanation," Reverend Cole replied with unconcern.

"I'm sure there is, but I can't think what it is. Eliza is a woman who likes her own things about her, not someone else's."

The door to the master bedroom stood open a few inches. Diane rapped on it and received an instant response.

"Who is it?" It was Eliza's voice, reassuringly strong and sharp in its challenge.

"It's Diane. Reverend Cole is with me. May we come in?"

"Diane." There was a thread of relief in the reply. Then came a sound like a troubled sigh. "Yes, come in."

More curious than ever, Diane walked into the room and came to an abrupt halt when she saw Eliza standing beside the bed, looking neither in pain nor ill.

"Eliza, what on earth—I was told—" Diane heard the distinctive click of a hammer uncocking behind her.

Diane swung around and went motionless. Lije stood against the wall behind the door, a revolver in his hand, pointed at the ceiling. Her gaze locked with his, and instantly she remembered all that had passed between them, all the passionate, compelling, and disturbing reasons they had loved and fought against that love. His presence had always revived old longings and hunger, and a sense of incompleteness that she had never been able to ignore. It still did.

He had lost weight, she saw. His face was thinner, giving a gauntness to his cheeks and hardening his features. His body was all lean, long muscle, toughened by the harsh demands of war. The shaggy ends of his glistening black hair curled onto the collar of his shirt. He had never looked more glorious to her.

"Lije," she whispered and almost ran to him, but the coldness in his eyes registered, reminding her of all the things that stood between them. The wind howled down the chimney, a mournful sound that tore at her. "What . . . What are you doing here?"

A low moan came from somewhere in the room. Lije stepped away from the wall and shoved the revolver in the holster strapped to his side, automatically fastening the flap over it as he ripped his glance from her and sent it slicing to the bed.

"My father was hurt." He walked past her straight to the bed.

Turning, Diane saw The Blade lying in the bed, his face twisted by pain. Temple hovered anxiously at his side, along with Susannah. At that moment Diane realized how completely she had blocked out everything, allowing nothing and no one to exist except Lije. Even now a part of her wanted to go on looking at him.

To make up for it, she bustled into action, pulling the pins from her hat, discarding it, the pins, her shawl and reticule on a nearby dresser. "What happened? How was he hurt? Shrapnel? A bullet?"

"He was shot," Temple answered.

"Where?" Diane crossed to the bed, joining Temple on the opposite side.

"In the left arm and again in the back," Susannah told her. "We were about to change the dressings when we heard voices downstairs."

"You gave us quite a scare." Eliza looked pointedly at Reverend Cole.

"I regret that." The kindness of compassion was in his glance. "But when we learned Susannah had told Adam you were injured, we grew concerned for your well-being. Now, of course," he paused and glanced back to The Blade, the compassion in his look intensifying, "I fully understand why Susannah told such a story."

"It was the only way I knew to get morphia for him."

"Of course, of course." He nodded in understanding. "Now, what can I do to help?"

"We were about to roll him on his side," Lije said. "He can help some, but it would be easier on him if you could give me a hand turning him. Watch his arm, though."

"His arm is broken?" Diane noticed the crude splint that immobilized it.

"Yes, but it's a simple fracture. There was none of the serious damage your father suffered," Temple told her, watching anxiously while Lije and Reverend Cole carefully rotated The Blade onto his right side. "It looked like the bullet ricocheted off the bone and came out the side of his arm after breaking it."

"What about the wound to his back?" Diane asked, then stepped forward when Temple began to remove the dressing over it. "Let me help with that."

Lije watched her, studying the pale, honey gold sheen of her hair and the deft sureness of her fingers.

From the moment he had recognized her voice, he had realized time had diminished none of his feelings for her; rather, it had intensified them. That angered him.

After the dressings had been removed, Diane leaned forward to inspect the wound. "It appears to be healing nicely."

She smiled in approval, drawing his glance to the alluring curve of her lips. He remembered the taste of them and the heat of their kiss. Even as the old longings surged through him, he checked them, ruthlessly.

"That opinion comes from your vast store of knowledge on the subject, does it?" he mocked, aware she didn't deserve such treatment, yet unable to stop himself.

Her glance flicked to him, a quick spark of anger showing in her eyes before her lashes came down to veil it. "I have had some experience with wounds lately," she replied in an even voice.

Reverend Cole spoke up in warm praise of her. "Diane spends part of every day at the hospital, tending to the needs of the sick and wounded."

"A beautiful angel of mercy gliding from bed to bed, laying cool cloth on one soldier's fevered forehead, holding the hand of the next," Lije mocked, resorting to sarcasm in order to overcome the jealousy that twisted through him.

The reverend gave him an indignant look. "You are very much mistaken, Lije, if you think her assistance is limited to such things."

"You are wasting your breath, Reverend Cole," Diane said in a gentle rebuke. "Lije prefers to regard me as the spoiled and pampered type who would never deign to turn her pretty little hand to menial tasks." Her voice was deliberately light, turning his ridicule back on him. "I shouldn't wonder that he thinks I would faint at the sight of blood. He chooses to forget I was raised a soldier's daughter. Spoiled, I may have been, but pampered, I never was."

Wisely, Lije said nothing. There was no excuse for the things he'd said to her, no justification, except that his mind was doing cruel things to him, reminding him of the way she had once felt in his arms and the love she had given him— reminding him that he would never again know these things. He felt the loss of it all over again.

In silence he watched while she applied a fresh dressing to the wound. There were no wasted motions, no fumbling. She did it expertly and neatly.

When she finished, Lije studied her with new respect. "Where did you learn to do that?"

"When casualties arrive from a battlefield, the doctors and orderlies are grateful for extra hands to help staunch the flow of blood from a wound. It truly doesn't matter to them that an attractive face might go with those hands." Her voice was all warm and honey-smooth, but her eyes shot fire, making it clear that she hadn't forgiven him for his earlier attack.

"You must have helped with many casualties," Lije said without rancor.

The fire went out of her eyes as she sobered. "Too many. Both at Fort Scott and Fort Gibson." She swung her attention to The Blade. "If you are ready, let's shift him into a more comfortable position so he can rest."

Again Reverend Cole joined Lije in gently lifting and turning The Blade, laying him flat. Despite the care they took, the movement drew a loud groan from The Blade as he grimaced with the pain.

Temple stroked his cheek in comfort. "Sssh, it's over. You rest now," she murmured and drew back, lacing her fingers together in tight worry. "I gave him a dose of morphia before we started, but the wound causes him so much pain."

"It's gotten better." Lije clung to the positive. "A few days ago he would have been screaming with it when we moved him."

"Be glad that he has any feeling, even if it is pain, Temple," Diane remarked, and Lije knew instantly from her tone that Jed Parmelee had lost not only the use of his arm, but all feeling in it as well.

"You're right, of course. I'm sorry." Temple turned to her. "How is your father?"

The corners of Diane's mouth dented in a quick smile. "Frustrated to be behind a desk, chafing to get back in action, and lobbying to be reassigned to his regiment at every opportunity."

Sorrel rushed into the room, then caught herself and slowed to a more ladylike pace. "Phoebe is fixing tea. She asked if you wanted it served in the parlor."

"The parlor will be fine." Temple's reply was almost lost in the sudden blast of wind that shook the house.

"Listen to that," Eliza declared with an amazed shake of her head. "As fiercely as the wind is blowing today, you would think it was March."

"There's a storm coming. Reverend Cole and I noticed the bank of clouds on the horizon as we were driving up." Diane paused, her glance running to the reverend in silent message. "I'm afraid our visit will have to be a short one if we hope to return to the fort before the storm breaks."

"You will stay for dinner, won't you?" Temple protested. "If you waited until early afternoon, you would still beat the storm. Surely, it can't be traveling that fast."

"Why don't we continue this discussion in the parlor?" Eliza suggested and began herding everyone toward the door.

When Temple hesitated to glance uncertainly in the direction of The Blade, Lije spoke up, "I'll stay here. You go ahead."

Temple touched his arm in thanks. "Good. I don't like leaving him alone."

But it was the quick look of relief and gratitude from Diane that Lije noticed. She was as eager to escape the strain of his company as he was to escape hers. After all these months apart, being with her again brought all the more sharply home the way things were—and never could be again.

Lije stood beside the bed, his gaze fixed on his father as he listened to the fading murmur of their voices. It was easy to pick out Diane's from among them. Too easy. Lije started to walk over and close the door to shut out all sound of it, then changed his mind and sat down in the chair by the bed.

He was alone, haunted by the image of her in the room tending to his father's wound, her eyes filled with tender compassion. He breathed in and swore the fragrance of her lingered, mingling with the other smells of the sickroom.

Lije dug the bullet from his pocket and rolled it between his fingers, then leaned back in the chair and stretched his long legs out. But he could not get comfortable. He fixed his gaze on his father and watched the slow rise and fall of his chest as The Blade slipped deeper into a drug-induced sleep.

In silence, he waited for the time to pass, his fingers worrying constantly with the bullet. Every now and then he caught the smoky drift of her laughter, low and alluring, coming from the parlor area below, and his fingers would tighten their grip on the bullet. Outside the wind prowled.

The voices below grew louder, their direction changing, moving out of the parlor, their chatter nearly masking the sound of footsteps in the outer hall. His head came up, his glance shooting to the doorway, muscles tensing for an instant. But the footsteps approached from the direction of the servants' rear stairway; their quiet tread belonged to Deu. Lije relaxed his guard.

A moment later Deu walked in. "Miss Temple sent me to sit with Master Blade. She said you're to come downstairs and have dinner with the family."

Lije shook his head. "I'm not hungry."

"Miss Diane brought a big slab of smoked ham. Phoebe fixed it for dinner. One whiff of it will make your mouth water. You go get yourself some, Captain." When Lije started to refuse again, Deu added, "Sitting across the table from Miss Diane can't be any worse than facing a whole line of Yankee soldiers with those new repeating rifles—or Miss Temple when she finds out you aren't coming down."

Sighing heavily, Lije rolled to his feet. But it wasn't the thought of his mother's anger that swayed him. It was the realization that there wasn't much difference between being in the same room with Diane and being one floor above. Each was its own hell.

The others were already seated when Lije entered the dining room. Diane was on his mother's left. She looked up with only mild interest when he came in. Lije clamped his teeth together. All right, he thought savagely, if she can play that game, so can I.

"Sit down, Lije." Temple gave him a quick, smiling glance. "Nathan was about to give the blessing"

He walked directly to the empty chair at the head of the table and pulled it out. "Since the major can't join us, I'll sit here in his stead."

Recovering from her initial surprise, Temple instructed Phoebe to change the place setting. Lije sat down. Temple nodded to the reverend to begin.

"Almighty Father, bestow your blessings on those gathered here at this table, and . . ."

Lije tipped his head and watched Diane, her head bowed, her hands clasped in prayer. Again he was moved by the perfection of her beauty, the delicate line of her chin and the strong curve of her cheekbone. Her hair had the yellow gleam of sunshine, and her face was like ivory with a blush of rose beneath. Her lashes were long and, like her eyes, lethal. But she was no demure, genteel lady. She had too much laughter in her, too much lust for life; she was ready to do and to dare. That was what had attracted him from the first, much more than the power of her beauty. It was what still pulled him. Her pride and her passion, the strength of her character. He cursed her for it.

". . . name, Amen," Reverend Cole concluded.

"Amen," Diane echoed and lifted her head, her lashes sweeping up to reveal the clear, untroubled blue of her eyes. He cursed her for that, too, and removed his napkin from the table and unfolded it with a slight snap.

Phoebe carried in a tureen of potato soup and set it before Temple. "Have you, by chance, seen Shadrach lately?" Eliza directed her question to Diane as she passed her soup bowl to Temple.

"My father arranges to see him regularly. Shadrach keeps him apprised of all the happenings in the regiment. Of course, our striker fills us in on all the gossip that Shadrach feels is inappropriate to tell an officer," Diane replied, with a definite sparkle of laughter in her eyes.

"Shadrach was always very circumspect about such things." Eliza took the filled bowl from Temple and passed it to Susannah, beginning the chain until all the bowls were filled.

"Did you know that Shadrach is teaching about a dozen other colored soldiers to read and write during his off-duty times?" Diane dipped a spoon into her soup and took a taste. "Mmm, delicious."

"Yes, it is," Eliza agreed. "It doesn't surprise me in the least that Shadrach is teaching others. No offense to you, Temple, but he always was my best student," she declared, then sighed. "I miss him, but I am proud of him, too."

"You have reason to be proud of him. And Ike, too," Diane added when Phoebe returned to collect the soup tureen. "My father insists that he has never commanded better soldiers than the men in his Kansas First Colored Volunteers. At the battle of Honey Springs two months ago, they held the center, the most important position in the Union line, and withstood a charge of a Texas brigade, then attacked the rebel line and broke it. Afterwards General Blunt himself commended their courage and valor. He said they had fought like veterans and stated that he had never seen their coolness and bravery surpassed." Phoebe stood a little straighter, her eyes bright with pride for her son. "That's high praise from the general," Diane told her. "And well-deserved, too. The regiment lost some good men at that battle."

"Good men were lost on both sides that day," Lije pointed out, drawing her glance.

For a moment tension filled the room. The war with all its divisive loyalties threatened to color the entire meal.

Then Diane smiled with a mocking humor. "I had forgotten we had a rebel at the table. I will watch my words with more care."

"I doubt it," Lije returned dryly, drawing smiles all around. The uneasiness dissolved.

"He knows you too well, Diane," Reverend Cole observed. "Which reminds me—Eliza, do you remember that temperance meeting," he began, and the conversation became centered on shared memories of the past.

The soup dishes were soon cleared and the main course served, bringing a lull to the conversation. "Isn't it amazing how everyone stops talking the minute their plates are full of food?" Diane remarked.

"Food as delicious as this deserves our full attention." Susannah scooped another bite of sweet potato on her fork.

"It is good," Temple agreed, "especially this ham. It's so seldom we have meat for the table that this is a real treat."

"Now that the major is improving, I'll do some hunting, see if I can't change that," Lije said.

"I saw deer tracks behind the stables the other morning," Sorrel told him.

"That's a good indication there's game in the area." But he didn't think it would be wise to do any hunting on the plantation. It was too close to the Texas Road. A passing patrol might decide to investigate the sound of a single gunshot. "Although I don't think fresh venison is going to taste nearly as good as this ham."

"Then you do like it," Diane remarked in a voice that was much too innocent. "I'm glad. I was afraid you might have trouble swallowing Yankee ham."

"You're mistaken, I'm afraid." Lije smoothly speared another chunk of ham with his fork. "As tender as this is, it's definitely rebel ham. Some Yankee must have stolen it from a Confederate, so be careful that *you* don't choke on it."

Diane tipped her head back and laughed. The sound of it was like the trumpets at Jericho, tumbling all his carefully erected defenses. At that moment Lije wanted to snatch her from the chair and carry her off somewhere, anywhere, just as she had asked him to do all those years ago. But he hadn't been able to do it then, and he couldn't do it now, not when his father lay helpless in the second-floor bedroom.

The food on his plate became suddenly tasteless. Lije refused the steaming apple cobbler Phoebe had prepared for dessert and excused himself from the table to check on his father.

"How is he?"

"Resting." Deu picked up the meal tray. "He ate nearly all his food. I think he would have eaten more, but he got tired. That's okay, though. He's started eating again, and when a man starts eating, that's when he starts getting better. It never fails." Taking the tray, Deu left the room.

Restless, Lije wandered over to the window. The wind had died to a stiff breeze. High up, clouds scudded across the ocean of blue sky, announcing the advance of the changing weather pattern. He watched them for a long time—until he heard the quick tap of footsteps on the stairs and the distinctive rustle of long skirts.

Tensing, he swung to face the door. Diane walked through the opening, saw him, and paused, her chin lifting fractionally in response to the challenging stab of his gaze.

"I came to get the shawl and hat I left on the dresser," she stated.

Lije nodded, aware it wasn't his permission she was asking. As she went to retrieve them, he moved away from the window and came around the bed.

"I take it you and Reverend Cole are leaving now."

"Yes. Deu went to bring the buggy around." Diane collected her things and turned.

Lije stood in her path. "What will you do when you get back to the fort?"

"What will I do?" She frowned, puzzled by the question.

"Don't pretend you don't understand me." Impatience riddled his voice. "You and I both know capturing one of Watie's top officers would be quite a coup for the Yankees. Are you going to tell your father the major is here?"

Stung by the cold accusation in his voice, Diane reacted with anger. "Truthfully, the thought hadn't crossed my mind until now. But there isn't anything you can do to stop me, is there?" she challenged. "You can't keep me here. If you did, you know my father would immediately send out a patrol to search for me. He knows where I am, which means this is the first place they would come to look. And you can't spirit your father away after I leave. He's too weak to stand, let alone sit on a horse. Your hands are tied, aren't they?"

"Will you tell?"

"I should. He's a Confederate. A traitor, the same as you are." She tried to hold on to her anger, but too many other emotions crowded in. She half-turned to escape his prying eyes. "But sometimes . . ." Her voice thickened; she stopped and tried again. "Sometimes it's hard to think of you as the enemy, Lije. Sometimes, I—" She paused again. Evasion would have been simple for her, but an innate honesty impelled her to finish the sentence. "Sometimes, I miss you so much." She looked back at him with an outpouring of pain and love and longing.

He reached out and drew her to him, pinning her arms between them and crushing her hat and shawl. He hadn't meant to touch her. That was his last coherent thought before he covered her lips with his in a rough and desperate kiss. Her throaty moan spilled into his mouth like a rich, drugging wine.

Needs and desires too long suppressed claimed him. He pulled the shawl, hat, and reticule from her fingers, and gave them a toss, not caring where they landed. Her hands instantly curled around his neck, her fingers clawing into his hair as she returned the raw pressure of his kiss and demanded more.

He couldn't resist her. He felt her tremble as he touched, tasted, and tempted. His breath caught on her name. Pain and power, they were both tangled together in his need for her. She made him hurt and made him soar just by being in his arms.

"You don't know how hard I've tried to forget you," he told her, his voice thick, husky. "But you've been there, at the edge of my every thought. I've never stopped wanting you. Needing you."

"I'm glad," she murmured and tugged his mouth back to hers.

She was pulling something from him, drawing something out of him. His mind was swimming in the mist of his needs as his searching fingers found the buttoned front of her burgundy traveling suit and tugged the buttons free from their holes. Beneath, she wore a lace-trimmed, ivory chemise that went all the way to her throat, as erotic to him as the lowest décolletage. Arching her back, he tore his mouth free to fasten it on her breast, suckling greedily through the cotton.

The pleasure of it, dark and damning, lanced like a saber through his system. He heard the gasping cry she made and went back to swallow it, filling his palms with her breasts, his thumb discovering the wet material where his mouth had been.

His busy mouth never paused, moving from cheek to jaw to ear and back again. His breathing was heavy and ragged. "Every minute, every hour, every day, I've wanted you."

She went soft against him for an instant. Then she pulled back. "I've wanted you, too, Lije." Her voice fell to a throaty whisper. "More than you'll ever know." Reaching up, she cupped a trembling hand to his face. "I want us to be together. Now. Forever. And we can be," she said with growing confidence. "Your father belongs in a hospital, under a doctor's care. Take him to Fort Gibson—"

"No." He caught her hand and pulled it down from his face.

"Give it up, Lije," she urged, her tone insistent. "The South can't win. Not anymore. Fort Smith is already in Union hands. The rebel armies are being driven farther and farther south all the time. You don't have to stay with them. You can come to the fort and do as so many other Cherokees have done—join the Union army."

"No. I can't do that. I won't do that."

"The war is lost. Why go on fighting?"

"I'll go on fighting as long as he does." He jerked his head toward The Blade.

Diane pulled free and took an angry step away. "Why must you be so stubborn?" With shaking hands, she proceeded to button the front of her suit.

Lije never moved. "Are you going to tell your father?"

She froze for an instant, then her shoulders sagged and a long breath rushed from her. "You don't know how tired I am of making decisions." She looked back, her glance running to him with longing and regret. "Sometimes I wish you had never let me leave this house, that you had never let me pack my things. You could have persuaded me, Lije. You could have convinced me. I loved you so much, I would have stayed. You knew it, but you never even tried. Why, Lije?"

"Because," he said, "you would have grown to hate me for it. More than that, you would have grown to hate yourself. You can't abide weakness, Diane. Not in someone else. And not in yourself."

She dragged a breath in and let it out in a long, long sigh. "I wish I could say you were wrong."

"I know."

"Do you?" She turned, her head lifted, her control back, a touch of sadness hovering on her lips. "I wish you would quit this fighting while there is still time. There's no more reason for you to protect your father. The feud is over now. Kipp is dead."

In answer, Lije took the bullet from his pocket. "Eliza dug this out of my father's back." She looked at it and glanced up in silent question. "It came from Alex's gun."

"Did The Blade tell you that?"

"Yes."

"You think Alex will come after him now that Kipp is dead." She looked at him with sudden understanding.

"I can't be sure. And I can't take the chance he won't." He put the bullet back in his pocket.

"It's clear that nothing has changed. This feud is still more important to you than I am," she stated, all stiff and armored with pride.

"If that's the way you choose to look at it."

"It's the only way I can look at it." She walked over and retrieved her crushed hat, shawl, and reticule from the floor, then took a step toward the door and paused. "As for the other—when I get back to the fort, I'll do this much. I won't volunteer any information about The Blade. But if I'm asked, I won't lie."

She walked out of the room. Lije held himself stiffly, listening to the voices below exchanging farewells. The front door opened and closed. She was gone. The set of his jaw became hard as he turned and walked over to the bed.

The Blade groaned in his sleep, stirred, and sucked in a sharp breath, grimacing in pain. His eyelids fluttered for a moment. Then he stretched a leg out beneath the covers and groaned again. The morphia was wearing off.

Lije took a pill from the tin his mother kept in the medical basket beside the bed. Using the mortar and pestle on the nightstand, he ground the pill into a powder and dissolved it in a small amount of water. He cupped a hand be-

hind The Blade's head and gently lifted it, pressing the glass
to his lips.

"Drink this. It'll stop the pain."

"No," The Blade groaned and tried to turn his head away.

"Come on. You'll feel better after you drink this."

Again there was that small movement of refusal. Lije
lowered the glass and frowned. "You don't want to take
this?"

"See what I can . . . stand." The slurred words were pushed
through teeth gritted against the pain. "Makes . . . my mind
swim. . . . Too weak." He breathed in labored breaths. "Worse
than . . . drunk. No good . . . like this."

"All right." Lije lowered his head back onto the pillow
and set the glass on the night table. "We'll wait. Let me
know if it gets too bad."

There was a small nod. The Blade opened his eyes and
struggled to focus on Lije. "Later . . . got to stand . . . got to
see . . . if I can."

"Later," Lije promised.

He closed his eyes, a heavy sigh rushing from him as he
drifted back into a stupor induced by the drug and the pain.
He mumbled once, "Dangerous here. . . ." It was the first indication that he was aware of how exposed and vulnerable
they were.

❧ 23 ❧

The thwack of an axe blade biting into wood rang through the afternoon stillness. The black mare swiveled an ear at the sound, then carefully picked her way along the muddy lane, avoiding the puddles left by two days' worth of rain. Alex idly studied the house directly ahead. No black mourning draped the front door, but he wasn't sure what that meant and urged the mare into a lope. The mare immediately rocked into the gait and splashed through a puddle, snorting her displeasure at the spray of muddy water.

"Alex! Alex, wait!"

He pulled up and looked back, catching sight of Sorrel clumping through the woods on his left, wearing a pair of heavy boots two sizes too large. Smiling at his luck, he swung the mare around and rode back to meet her. He could always count on Sorrel to tell him anything he wanted to know.

She waited for him on the grassy verge at the lane's edge, all breathless and excited. "What are you doing here, Alex?"

"I stopped by to deliver your birthday present." It had seemed as good an excuse as any for coming. Alex had never visited his family without a reason.

"It isn't my birthday yet."

"But I may not be able to get away when your birthday does come around. So I thought I'd better give you your present while I had the chance." Alex dismounted and unfastened the flap of his saddlebag and took out a small package wrapped in brown paper.

"Are you being sent away again?"

"Not that I know about, but with the army, you can never be sure." He turned and offered the package to her. "Sorry, I didn't have any fancy ribbon to tie around it."

"That's okay." Sorrel took it from him with undisguised eagerness, then turned her bright eyes on him. "May I open it now?"

"Sure." Alex grinned and watched as she ripped the paper off. Her mouth opened in a big O, and her eyes grew nearly as big when she saw the gold locket and chain inside. "Do you like it?"

"It's beautiful," Sorrel whispered. "It's the most beautiful thing I've ever had." She paused long enough to fling herself at him and give him a quick hug, then went back to admiring the locket.

"If you open it up, there's a place inside where you can put a picture or a lock of hair." Alex had already removed the strands of black hair the locket had previously contained. All in all, the cloth-wrapped bundle he'd taken from the Meynard family had proved to be a good haul. In addition to nearly thirty dollars in gold coin, he was now the owner of a lady's brooch, a pair of garnet earrings, and a fancy gold watch fob.

"Alex." Sorrel darted him a worried and perplexed look. "It has somebody's name on the back of it."

"I got it from the sutler," he lied. "I guess he took it in trade for some food. The minute I saw it, I knew the perfect young lady who should be wearing it. Turn around and I'll fasten it for you."

Satisfied with his explanation, Sorrel surrendered the ends of the gold chain to him and turned, lifting the mass of long red hair off her neck so he could hook the chain. As soon as the clasp was secured, she proudly swung back to face him. "How does it look?"

"Beautiful," he replied absently, and Sorrel immediately peered down at it. The axe rang again. Alex glanced in the direction of the sound. "So what are you doing out here in the woods?"

"I was helping Deu chop and stack firewood so we'll have plenty for winter." She fingered the locket, continuing to admire it.

"Deu." Alex stiffened, his glance slashing to her face. "What's he doing here? Did something happen to your father?" He waited for the look of sorrow to leap into her expression.

"He got shot. Deu and Lije brought him home—last week, I think it was."

"He's alive?" The first current of unease skittered through him.

Sorrel nodded and heaved an exaggerated sigh of relief, smiling. "At first I was afraid he was going to die, but he's getting better. Lije helped him to stand up yesterday. Mother was furious when she saw them. She made him get right back in bed."

Cold with shock, Alex stared at the house, his mind racing in sudden panic. The bastard was alive. His shot hadn't killed him. Why hadn't he made sure The Blade was dead? He would come gunning for him now—the same as he'd come after his father. And Lije would be with him.

He had to get out of here. Alex grabbed up the reins.

"Let's go to the house, Alex." Sorrel touched the locket and tried to give off an air of poise and maturity. Inside, she felt positively heady with delight. Jewelry. No one had ever given her jewelry as a present before. It wasn't a gift for a child; it was what you gave an adult. "I want to show everybody my birthday present."

"Sorry, I have to leave." He stuck a foot in the stirrup and swung onto the mare.

"But why? You just got here," Sorrel protested.

"I know." He gave her a quick, stiff smile. "But remember I told you I just came by to drop off your present. I have to report back to the fort before dark, and I still have to ride over to my father's farm and check on things, to see whether Watie's marauders have burned the place yet."

"They wouldn't do that," Sorrel said quickly, but she knew better. Marauders had looted and burned her grandfather's house.

His mouth twisted viciously. "They'd do it in a heartbeat, Sorrel. In a heartbeat."

He touched a spur to the mare and rode off. Sorrel watched him a moment, then turned and hurried to the house. She had barely taken three steps inside the house before her mother called out, "Sorrel, you'd better not be tracking in this house with those muddy boots."

"Honestly, Mother, I am not a child anymore. I took my boots off before I came in," she declared with airy dignity, then walked over to the gilt-framed mirror to admire her locket. "Come see what Alex brought me for my birthday."

"Alex?" Temple came from the rear hall. "Is he here?"

"Not now. He had to leave." Sorrel gazed at her reflection, turned this way and that to watch the play of light across the locket's gold face. When she caught sight of Temple in the mirror, Sorrel turned and held out the locket. "See what Alex got me. Isn't it beautiful?"

"It's very beautiful," Temple agreed. "But your birthday—"

"Alex knew it wasn't my birthday yet, but he wanted to give this to me now in case he was sent somewhere else. You know how the army is." Sorrel feigned an adultlike knowledge of such things.

Lije came down the stairs. "Did I hear you say Alex was here? What did he want?"

Sorrel bristled at his tone. "He didn't *want* anything. He came to see me and give me this present." Touching the locket, she turned back to the mirror again and smiled at the sight of it around her neck.

"Why didn't Alex come to the house?" Temple wondered.

"Because he had to go check on Uncle Kipp's farm and make sure everything was all right there, then be back to the fort before nightfall." Sorrel paused as a thought occurred to her. "Although it's his farm now that Uncle Kipp is dead, isn't it?" She felt a twinge of guilt that she hadn't thought to tell Alex how sorry she was about his father.

"What did he say? Did he ask you any questions?" Lije came up behind her, his reflection joining hers in the mirror. The hostility and distrust in his voice were unmistakable.

Sorrel reacted to him with instant anger. "I hate it when you talk like that about Alex. You don't like him. You've never liked him, but I do. Why can't you leave him alone?"

"Sorrel," Temple murmured in reproval.

She turned on her. "But it isn't fair. Alex came to bring me this locket, and I was so happy—and now, he's ruined it!" She ran off in tears.

Lije watched her, a troubled frown furrowing his brow. Maybe Alex's visit was as innocent as she said. Maybe.

❦24❧

"Miss Temple. Miss Temple." Phoebe hurried into the bedroom, struggling to catch her breath after running up the back stairs. "Yankee soldiers—they're marching up the lane."

"Is Lije back?"

"No," she said, still breathing hard. "He must still be off hunting."

"Got to get . . . out of here." Still half-drugged by the morphia Temple had given him hours ago, The Blade tried to raise up on an elbow. But the combination of pain and weakness defeated the attempt. He collapsed onto the mattress, blanching nearly white, his face twisting in agony. "Can't . . . let them find . . . me."

"You're not going anywhere until we get this bandage tied. Finish it for me, Eliza." Temple went to the window to look for herself.

"The Blade's right, Temple. We have to get him out of the house."

"It's too late. They're almost here now." Temple stared at the column of Negro infantry, led by a trio of mounted white officers. "We could never get him out without being seen. We'll have to hide him." She swung away from the window and scanned the room. "Under the bed. It is so obvious, maybe they won't think of looking there."

"We don't know why they are coming here, Temple. We don't know that they will search the house," Eliza reasoned.

"We can't chance it. You and Phoebe get him under the bed. I'll go downstairs and . . . greet them." Stall them was what she really meant.

Maybe Eliza was right. Maybe it was only a guilty conscience that made her think the soldiers were here to look for The Blade. Maybe it was only some sort of courtesy call. But she was afraid to believe that.

Outside, Temple stood directly between the veranda's two massive Doric columns. As the officer at the head of the small party drew nearer, Temple fixed what she hoped was a pleasant smile on her lips. Suddenly, she couldn't believe her eyes. Her smile was no longer forced.

"Jed." She ran to meet him, not even waiting until he had halted his horse. She caught the bridle and held the animal's head as Jed Parmelee dismounted, his left arm making a bunch beneath his uniform jacket, its empty sleeve pinned up. "This is a surprise . . . a wonderful surprise. I don't have to ask how you have been. I can see for myself that you are doing well."

"And I can say the same about you, Temple." He took her hand and raised it to his lips, bowing slightly.

"You did that the first time we met in Washington." Temple smiled at him, and at the memory. "I remember I thought you were so gallant . . . and handsome." She admitted the latter with a certain coyness, feeling briefly young and flirtatious.

"And I thought you were the most beautiful woman I had ever seen," he replied, quite seriously. "You still are."

She released a soft, throaty laugh. "What a shame there isn't a band nearby so you can teach me the waltz again."

"And your husband, too, so he could glare at me while we dance."

"Yes." The blue of Jed's uniform suddenly registered, and Temple felt a wariness creep through her.

Deliberately, she glanced away from the house, as if The Blade was somewhere out there in the countryside instead of hidden away upstairs. She turned back, conscious that Jed watched her closely, and she wasn't sure why.

"You must be thirsty from your ride. Your men, too. Phoebe!" She called over her shoulder for the black maid, then said to Jed, "She can show your men where the well is. You come inside with me." Temple tucked her hand in the crook of his elbow, hoping that she wasn't inviting the fox into the chicken coop. "You can stay for dinner, can't you? Phoebe is fixing dessert, dumplings swimming in blueberry juice." She chattered away, trying to fill the silence as she walked him to the veranda. "Eliza will be so happy to see you—"

"Temple." Jed stopped short of the front door. "This is not a social visit."

Her heart was thumping loudly when she faced him. "You are here on army business?" It took every bit of her control to meet his gaze with a degree of curiosity.

His hesitation seemed to confirm her fear, but she wouldn't let it show, instead widening her eyes and feigning innocence.

"The army has received certain information that leads us to believe your husband, a major in the Confederate army, is here."

"What?" Temple drew back from him. It wasn't difficult at all to pretend to be shocked and alarmed. "That isn't true."

"Then"—Jed paused, his glance flicking briefly past her—"perhaps you could explain why Deu is here. We both know your husband never goes anywhere without him."

"Deu?" Temple looked back and saw him standing only a few feet away. For an instant their eyes locked, sharing the same feeling of panic and regret. It had never occurred to her that Deu's presence would give away The Blade. "The Blade sent him here to help me," she lied quickly, desperately. "He knows how difficult it has been for us—"

"It's no use, Temple. I have orders to search the house and grounds. . . . I'm sorry."

She tilted her chin a little higher. "If those are your orders, Major, then, by all means, search the house. But you won't find my husband. He is not here."

When Jed turned to signal his men, Temple fled into the house, needing these few precious seconds to stop her mad shaking. She couldn't let Jed suspect how frightened she was about his search. As long as he had a doubt in his mind, he might not be thorough—she might be able to distract him.

Hearing footsteps, Temple turned. Eliza and Phoebe came down the stairs as Susannah entered the foyer from the hall. Sorrel was right behind her, dark eyes bright and questioning. "Why are the soldiers here, Mama?"

"What do they want?" Eliza echoed.

"They know he's here." Temple moved quickly to the base of the stairs.

Startled, Susannah murmured, "How?"

"I think someone recognized Deu, I—" The instant the front door opened behind her, Temple hurriedly changed what she was about to say. "I said that he wasn't here of course. But Jed explained that he was obliged to search the house just the same." The house echoed with the tramping of dozens of feet. Momentarily, she glanced at the black soldiers pouring into the house, then focused on Jed. "If there must be a search, I am relieved you are conducting it, Jed. I know you will not allow your soldiers to tear my home apart. There is so much ransacking and looting going on—on both sides."

"They have their orders" was all he said, but she could tell by the way he avoided meeting her eyes that he was uncomfortable with his mission. It gave her hope.

Eliza gasped. "Shadrach." She swept past Temple to go to the slender black soldier standing in the foyer with the rest. Lowering his rifle, Shadrach smiled back and removed his forage cap, revealing the quantity of gray that now silvered his curly dark hair.

"Miss Eliza."

"It is so good to see you again," she declared. "You look splendid in your uniform, Shadrach."

"You are looking well, too."

"I know."

Ike, who stood a few feet from the grand staircase, paid no attention to the conversation between Shadrach and his former mistress. His eyes were on his mother. She stood rooted to the stairs. There had been joy in her eyes when she first saw him. But it had too quickly dissolved into dismay when her glance flickered to the blue uniforms of the soldiers surrounding him.

In many ways, her reaction was the same as his father's had been when Deu saw him outside a minute ago—an initial happiness, followed almost instantly by an expression of hurt and silent accusation. And in both their faces, there was fear.

The Blade was here. Ike could see it in their eyes. They had hidden him somewhere. Now they looked at him like he was the enemy . . . like he had turned against them. They weren't going to talk to him; they weren't even going to ask how he was; they weren't going to give him a chance to explain that he hadn't known they were coming to Grand View until after they had marched out of the fort.

Yes, he knew every nook and hidey-hole in this house, every floorboard that squeaked and every hinge that groaned. But couldn't they see that he was only following orders? Why did they have to make him feel guilty about being here?

Then the white lieutenant began barking orders, his sharp voice snapping Ike to attention. The men were divided into squads of three and assigned a given area of the house to search systematically. Ike was relieved when he and his two partners were sent to the second floor. There were few hiding places in the upstairs rooms and even fewer capable of concealing an adult. They must have hidden The Blade in the basement storeroom, or in that old root cellar near the double log cabin.

He was certain, that is, until he saw the almost panicked look on his mother's face and the way her eyes pleaded with him.

Ike felt sick inside. The Blade was upstairs. He knew it as surely as if she had come right out and said so. He started up the steps, his feet dragging as if they were bound with shackle and chain. He reminded himself that he was a soldier in the Union army. He was doing his duty. But he wished his momma wouldn't look at him like that.

With an effort Temple tore her gaze away from Ike as he followed the other soldiers noisily clumping up the stairs. She had been there the night he was born. She had laid him in Phoebe's arms. Surely he couldn't . . . he wouldn't give The Blade away if he found him. But the color of his uniform was the same as Jed's, and she remembered that, however reluctantly, Jed always followed orders—just as he had that long-ago day when he had forced the members of her family to leave their ancestral home of Gordon Glen and marched them to the detention camp to await their removal West.

Her heart was in her throat when she turned back to Jed. She saw how closely he watched her and knew he had to be remembering that, too. She mustn't let him see how frightened she was.

"Phoebe, bring some coffee to the drawing room," she said, then smiled at Jed. "If it wouldn't be considered consorting with the enemy, we would be happy to have you join us, Jed."

"A moment ago, it was Major Parmelee," he reminded her.

"A moment ago I was upset with you because I thought you didn't believe me when I said The Blade wasn't here. I forgot that, even if you did believe me, you would still be obliged to carry out your orders. You are a soldier. It is your duty. I shouldn't have taken it personally, Jed. Will you forgive me?"

He hesitated a split second, then smiled. "Of course."

"I knew you would understand." Temple breathed a little easier and led the way into the drawing room.

From all parts of the house came the sounds of searching soldiers, most of it muffled by the thick walls. But it was the noises from the second floor that kept Temple on the edge of her chair, nerves tense. Making idle conversation was an ordeal.

Ike paused outside the master bedroom, struggling with the feeling that he had no right to enter it without permission. Yet his buddies were already inside, beginning their search of the interior. He reminded himself he wasn't a slave anymore; he was a soldier with orders to search the house. He walked into the room.

He looked around. The last time he had been in this room, he had helped carry Kipp here, wounded after that battle at Pea Ridge in Arkansas. They had laid him on the bed, and he had listened to Alex tell about the fighting. He had thought the Yankee soldiers would be coming soon to free him. He was free now, but sometimes it was hard to stop thinking like a slave. Even now he felt uncomfortable being in this room without permission.

There was a basket on the floor by the nightstand. Drawn by its vaguely familiar shape, Ike walked over and picked it up. Miss Temple's medical basket. What was it doing here? Then he heard a sound, like someone breathing in sharply. It came from close by. Both of his companions were on the opposite side of the room.

He didn't know why he did it, but he knelt down and lifted the white lace ruffle that skirted the bed. Cautiously, he looked under it. When he saw the long dark shape of a body, he opened his mouth to call the news. Then he found himself staring at a pair of tortured blue eyes. The Blade was looking at him, his face twisted with pain, sweat rolling off it. He had something in his mouth. At first Ike thought they had gagged him with a leather strap of some kind. Then he realized that The Blade was biting down on it, the muscles in his jaws all ridged with the effort to hold back any sound of pain. He was hurting. He was hurting bad.

Slowly, Ike let the ruffle fall back in place. A sob of frustration lodged in his throat. He tightened his grip on the rifle in his hand. He couldn't do it. He couldn't turn him in. He knew he should. The Blade was the enemy. He didn't owe him anything. So why couldn't he say it? Why couldn't he shout that he had found him? That's what any other soldier would do. He stood up and stared at the bed.

"Find anything, Ike?"

He hesitated, then shook his head and started toward the door, avoiding their eyes.

After a three-hour search of the house, grounds, Negro cabins, and outbuildings, the young lieutenant reported to Jed that they had found nothing. Almost immediately, Jed turned to her, and Temple had to suppress quickly the shudder of relief.

"My apologies, Temple, for disrupting your morning this way."

"If you are truly sorry, you will stay for dinner." She was anxious for him to leave—for all of them to leave, but she didn't want it to appear that way.

"Perhaps another time . . . under more pleasant circumstances."

"We will look forward to that."

As he rode away, Jed was more than a little relieved that he hadn't found The Blade at Grand View. He had hated to be the one conducting the search for him—just as he had hated to be the one commanding the detail that had forced Temple and her parents from their home in Georgia. He was glad that this time, at least, he hadn't had to hurt Temple. She had been through enough.

* * *

As soon as the soldiers were out of sight, Temple hurried into the house. Susannah waited for her. "Are they gone?"

Temple nodded and closed the door behind her, then sagged against it for a moment, weak with relief. "I saw them turn onto the Texas Road. They're on their way back to the fort."

"Thank God," Eliza murmured with sincerity.

Regathering her strength, Temple pushed away from the door. "Have you checked on The Blade? Is he all right?"

"He's fine, Miss Temple," Phoebe said from the top of the stairs.

"Where's Deu?" Temple crossed to the stairs. "We may need his help getting The Blade back into bed."

"The last time I saw him, he was outside. I'll go find him." As Susannah turned to leave, Deu entered the foyer from the rear hall.

"I don't know where you've got Master Blade hid, Miss Temple, but I wouldn't be too quick to get him out," he warned. "I just saw two riders out back by the stables."

"That's impossible." Temple froze, one hand on the newel post and one foot on the step. "All the soldiers left. I saw them."

"Are you certain there were two?" Susannah asked quickly. "It might be Lije."

"There were two, and they were trying to keep out of sight so I didn't get a good look at them." He turned to Temple. "The Yankees are cagey. They could have sent another detachment to surround the place in case Master Blade tried to slip out."

"I'm going out and have a look," Susannah announced, her shoulders squared with determination.

"But if there are—" Eliza began in protest.

"I'll bring back a load of firewood."

"I'm going with you," Temple said. "Eliza, you and Sorrel keep watch out the front windows. Phoebe, let The Blade know he'll have to stay in hiding a while longer. Deu—"

"Master Blade would want me to go with you, Miss Temple."

"Three people to fetch a load of firewood will look ridiculous."

"Then I'll make like I'm going to do some chopping."

"Who cares how it looks," Susannah declared with impatience and set off for the backdoor. Temple and Deu quickly followed her.

The minute they stepped outside they heard the muffled pounding of hoofbeats on grass. Susannah halted, alarm shooting through her nerves. A horse and rider came around the corner of the detached kitchen at a gallop.

"Lije," Temple whispered in relief beside her.

But it was the second rider on a short-coupled bay who claimed the whole of Susannah's attention. Almost a full year had passed since she last saw him, but she recognized Rans Lassiter instantly. The sight of him was like an intoxicant running through her bloodstream, making her feel suddenly warm and giddy.

Lije piled out of the saddle as his horse plunged to a stop short of the back steps. "What was Parmelee doing here? What did he want?" He shot the questions at Temple.

"He was looking for your father. Somehow he found out he was—"

"Diane," he said in a savage mutter and hurled an angry look in the direction of the distant fort.

Temple shook her head. "You can't be sure of that. I think someone recognized Deu and guessed The Blade had to be here, too. In any case, they didn't find him." Rans dismounted, drawing her glance. "When Deu caught a glimpse of you down by the stables, we thought they were coming back to look again."

"Not to worry, ma'am," Rans told her. "One of my boys is following the Yankee column to make sure they don't take the notion to double back. The rest are fanned out along the perimeter."

"Captain Lassiter of the Texas Brigade," Lije said by way of introduction, the troubled scowl never leaving his face.

Rans nodded to her. "A pleasure to meet you, Mrs. Stuart." Then his gray eyes at last turned their attention on Susannah, a warmth entering them that snatched at her breath. "It turned out to be a lucky thing we crossed paths with Lije while he was out hunting. As soon as I mentioned we'd spotted a detachment of infantry headed this way, we hightailed it straight here."

"I'm glad," Susannah murmured, her pulse quickening under the steady regard of his eyes.

His mouth quirked. "Not half as glad as I am," he replied and released a long sigh of satisfaction. "You're a feast for hungry eyes, Susannah." He stepped closer and caught her hand, raising it to his lips. A thrill quivered through her when he brushed his mouth over her fingers.

"Deu, get the horses saddled and bring them up here," Lije ordered abruptly. "Lassiter, I'll need you to give me a hand with the major."

"Why?" Temple said in alarm. "What are you going to do? Where do you think you're going to take him?"

"It isn't safe here. Not anymore," Lije told her, a grimness in his expression. "If Diane hasn't told them he's here, she will now. They'll be back. And the next time they'll turn this house upside down until they find him."

"But he's in no condition to travel," she protested.

"He's better than he was when I brought him here."

"No. I'm not going to let you move him."

"Lije is right, Mrs. Stuart." Rans stepped in before the breach between them widened. "If your husband stays, it's almost a certainty he'll be taken prisoner. But if he leaves with us, we can escort him safely through the Yankee lines and see that he gets to a reb hospital. The major is a valuable man. We'll look after him."

"I—" Temple groped for an argument, then turned away in defeat, fighting tears.

Lije moved past her toward the house. He paused at the door and glanced back. "You coming, Lassiter?"

"In a minute," he said, his gaze swinging to Susannah.

She barely noticed when Temple followed Lije into the house. She was conscious only of Rans and the growing ache inside. "Can't you stay?" She crossed to him. "Wouldn't it be safer to wait until nighttime and leave under the cover of darkness?"

He shook his head. "It would be too risky to linger here very long, much as I would like to. Too many Yankee patrols use the Texas Road, and this place is too close to it. Every minute we stay here increases the chance my men might be spotted, and we'd find ourselves fighting to escape. We have to leave now—as soon as we can." He curved his arms around her waist and drew her closer, as if holding her was the most natural thing in the world. "It seems every time we meet, I barely have a chance to say hello before I have to say good-bye. This is a helluva courtship for you."

"Is that what it is? A courtship?" Susannah asked, her voice all breathless.

"It is to me." He rubbed his cheek against the side of her hair. "I love the smell of your perfume, that fresh, clean hint of sandalwood. It makes me think of sunshine and spring days." He stroked a hand over her back. "We'll have those days together, Susannah. I swear that to you." He drew back and cupped a hand to her face. "Right now, all we have is this minute. It has to be enough."

"It is," she whispered, loving him totally, completely.

"The hell it is," he muttered and kissed her hard and quick, then pulled away and walked into the house.

Within the hour, they had lifted The Blade onto the back of a horse. Lije swung up behind him and reached around him to collect the reins. Rans stood in the stirrups and released a shrill, loud whistle. A dozen riders—two dozen—poured from their hiding places in the surrounding trees and converged on the pair.

Lije checked to make sure Deu was mounted, then he tipped his head to peer at his father's profile. "Are you ready?"

The Blade nodded, still grimacing with the pain. "Let's go."

"He's hurting, Eliza," Temple murmured brokenly.

"He'll be fine." She curved an arm around Temple and rubbed her shoulder in comfort as Lije moved the horse out at a walk.

Rans reined his mount over to the back veranda, hooked an arm around Susannah's waist, and scooped her up to plant a hard, needy kiss on her lips. Then he let her slide to the ground.

"I'm coming back to collect my dance," he told her. "You'd better save one for me."

"I will," she promised, both a little dazed and a little dazzled.

He touched his hat to her and backed his horse away, then swung it after Lije. His men fell in behind him. Amidst the clatter of hooves and the groan of leather, Susannah heard him whistling. Even though she could only hear snatches of the tune, she knew the song was "Oh Susannah."

Sorrel glanced sideways in curious wonder. "Are you in love with him, Susannah?"

"I'm not sure, but I think so." She smiled at the thought, secretly pleased by the idea. It was crazy, but it also felt very right.

The house was silent. There was no sign of movement anywhere around it. Again, Alex scanned the run-down shanties of the Negro quarters and the plantation outbuildings. Nothing except some chickens scratching in the dirt.

The buggy was still in the barn. He had checked that already. They had to be around somewhere. Maybe the vegetable garden. He climbed onto the black mare. Keeping to the trees, he rode around the manor house to the plot of ground near the river. Phoebe was stooped over a shovel, digging potatoes.

"Where is your mistress?" Alex halted the mare close to the fence and made no attempt to check her nervous dancing.

"She's in the orchard, picking apples."

He started to ask her about The Blade, then thought better of it. He reined the mare away from the fence and kneed her into a canter, heading for the orchards.

The Blade had been here. He knew that. But the soldiers hadn't found him when they searched the plantation three days ago. Why? Where had they hidden him? Was he still here? Had he died? The questions had tormented him for days now.

A mule stood hitched to a wagon in the shade of the apple trees, its tufted tail swishing lazily at the buzzing flies. Alex slowed the mare to a walk and turned off the dirt track onto the tall yellow grass that carpeted the orchard. Almost immediately, he spotted Temple and Susannah, both on ladders picking apples.

Then, he spied Sorrel strolling back to the wagon, a basket of apples in hand. He rode up as Sorrel took the apples one by one and placed them in a wooden crate in the back of the wagon. The last one she kept, brushing it off and biting into it, reaching up to catch the juice that rolled down her chin.

"Are you supposed to be eating that?"

Caught unawares, Sorrel whirled around, guiltily hiding the apple behind her back. She recognized him and broke into a smile. "Alex. What are you doing here?"

"What does it look like?" He dismounted and walked to the back of the wagon. "I came to visit my favorite cousin. But I see your mother has put you to work picking apples."

She wrinkled her nose in dislike. "Mama is determined that the raiders aren't going to get all of the fruit this year. Want one?" She gestured to the crate. "They taste best like this, all warm from the sun."

He took a ruby-skinned fruit from the box, but he didn't immediately bite into it. "How is your father?"

"He's fine as far as I know." She shrugged and crunched again on her apple.

"What do you mean? Isn't he here?"

"No. He left two—or was it three days ago?"

"Then he recovered from his wounds." This meant The Blade would be after him now. Not necessarily right away. The Blade would pick the time and the place—unless Alex got to him first.

"He was still in a lot of pain," Sorrel paused to lick the apple juice from her fingers. "Mama was upset."

"Why?"

"I don't know. She just was."

"I wonder if she found out," he mused aloud.

"Found out what, Alex?" The voice was Temple's.

He turned sharply, surprised to find her standing behind him. Did she know? Should he tell her?

"I didn't hear you come up," he stalled, trying to decide.

"Sorry. I didn't mean to startle you." She walked over to the wagon and lifted her basket onto its wooden bed, then paused and wiped her hands on the front of her work apron. "Now, what was it you wondered if I knew?"

"How my father died?"

She looked at him with sudden wariness. "You told Susannah he was killed."

"He was murdered, shot down in cold blood . . . by The Blade."

"No." Susannah walked up. "I don't believe you!"

"It's true," Alex stated, his eyes going cold. "I was there. I saw it all."

"No," Temple murmured and looked away, her shoulders slumping.

"First he shot the gun out of my father's hand, then he ordered me to throw mine away." His voice was thick with bitterness. "He said, 'You're a man who deserves to die, Kipp.' And then he shot him."

"If that's true, why didn't you tell me this before?" Susannah demanded.

"I wasn't sure you'd believe me."

"I'm not sure that I do now."

"But she does." Alex smiled and pointed to Temple.

Horror-struck by the possibility, Sorrel turned to Temple. "Is it true, Mother? Did he kill him? Is my father a murderer?"

When Temple failed to answer, Susannah rushed in. "Sorrel, you have to understand there is a war going on. Your father and Kipp were on opposite sides. During a war, people get killed. That doesn't make it murder."

"But you heard Alex. Uncle Kipp didn't have a gun, and he shot him anyway," Sorrel said with a sob in her voice. "He knew who Kipp was and he killed him. It wasn't the war!" She turned and ran, tears of shame streaming down her cheeks.

❦25❧

Massive bouquets of wild azaleas and fragrant honey-suckle stood once again in the great hall of the former Cherokee Female Seminary. Its doors were thrown open this night to host a military ball. The red, white, and blue of the Union flag, prominently displayed, echoed the colors in the bunting that draped the bandstand where musicians from Fort Gibson played.

Officers in full dress uniform whirled their partners in an ever-moving circle around the dance floor. As far as Adam Clark was concerned, none of the ladies in attendance was as lovely as the woman he held in his arms, none more alluring even though the necklines of their gowns dipped daringly low. The illusion of décolleté was there in Diane's blue satin gown, but a sheer lace netting of silver and blue threads discreetly covered the swell of her breasts and the bareness of her shoulders, culminating in a highruffed collar of satin at the throat.

"You do realize that I am the envy of every man here," he said, needing to have her look at him.

"Is that right?" she murmured, her lips curving.

"A smile. I finally coaxed one from you."

"I haven't been very good company tonight, have I? I'm sorry."

"You should be sorry," Adam informed her. "After all, you're in the arms of the most skillful and graceful dancer this side of the Mississippi," he proclaimed and immediately, deliberately, stepped on her toe. Diane laughed, almost in spite of herself. "Now, that is the music I've been waiting to hear all evening."

"You are hopeless, Adam."

"No. I am never without hope." That was the wrong thing to say. He saw it immediately as the laughter withdrew from her eyes and again, she became preoccupied. She had been that way ever since they arrived. Something was bothering her.

When the song ended, he slowly came to a stop, then hesitated, unwilling to let go of her. Around him other couples acknowledged their partners. Adam stepped back and did the same, bending slightly at the waist, then offering his arm to escort her from the floor. But the instant he turned toward Eliza Gordon and her daughter, Susannah, he knew he didn't want to take Diane back to them. He wanted to keep her to himself a little longer and find out what was troubling her. This moodiness wasn't like Diane. His Diane was vibrant, full of life and laughter, rarely subdued.

"Let's take a walk outside," he suggested.

"You should ask Susannah for the next dance."

"Reverend Cole can dance with her."

"Reverend Cole?" Her surprise quickly turned to a barely suppressed smile of amusement. "Can you imagine him dancing with his two left feet, holding himself stiff as a board? Or should I say . . . Bible?"

Adam laughed, catching a glimpse of the Diane he knew so well. But, as before, it didn't last. "No, I truthfully can't imagine that. But I don't think Susannah will be unduly troubled if she sits out another dance. I'm convinced she accepts

my invitations out of a sense of duty. Her heart's not in it any
more than mine is." He steered Diane toward the outer door,
conscious that she offered no objection.

"No. I think her heart is elsewhere."

As they walked outside onto the seminary's columned
portico, the band struck up a military two-step. The lilting
air drifted after them into the darkness. A warm breeze wandered over the front lawn. A lopsided moon beamed down,
lighting the night and the towering brick columns. Together
they strolled to the far end of the colonnade. Diane idly trailed
a hand over the bricks as she turned and faced the lawn, gaz-
ing across it.

"You are very quiet tonight," Adam observed. "Want to
talk about it?"

"About what?"

"Whatever it is that you have on your mind. I promise I'll
be a good listener."

"You always are." There was a certain wryness in her
voice.

"Talk to me. What's bothering you?"

"I don't know." Her shoulders lifted in a vague shrug.
"Maybe it's just all this—you in your dress uniform and me
in my best gown, music playing in the background, people
dancing, laughing . . . pretending the war doesn't exist. How
can they do it? How can we do it?"

"We all need to escape from the war and the tension once
in a while or we'll go crazy. It's been a long winter." With little action, he could have added.

The inactivity, the waiting, and the wondering had made
everyone restless and edgy. Other than a rare encounter with
an odd patrol, it had been too quiet in the area. A dozen times
Adam had wanted to believe the war was winding down, the
South was beaten. But he couldn't shake the feeling that this
was the lull before the storm. Even though the rebels couldn't
win, they wouldn't quit.

"After all the misery we've been through these last three

years, we are entitled to some gaiety, Diane. Even if it's only for one night."

"Perhaps. But here we are waltzing while not far away people are suffering. Reverend Cole talked to one of the rebel prisoners the other day. The man told him that down in the Red River country of Texas, people are hungry. I don't want to think what it must have been like for them this past winter with little food, clothing, or shelter, and almost no medical supplies. It must have been horrible."

"We aren't in much better shape. The rebels couldn't launch a winter campaign, but neither could we."

"It isn't the same."

"Isn't it?"

"You know it isn't. Sometimes I wish—" She stopped and sighed heavily. "I don't know what I wish anymore."

"Like all of us, you wish the war would end."

"Except it's never going to end. Never. Because the hate won't. I'm so tired of it, Adam."

When she felt the touch of his hands, Diane swayed into his arms, desperately wanting and needing the things his arms and lips offered. She ached to be loved, to be comforted and cared for, to have her worries kissed away and her emptiness filled.

He did all that with the caressing stroke of his hands and the eagerness of his mouth. She took and took—and demanded more, her fingers sliding into the curly ends of his hair, forcing him to increase the pressure. Greedily, she took everything he had to offer, and the tears rolled from her eyes because she had nothing to give. She had already given everything to Lije.

Fighting the tears and the pain, she broke off the kiss and flattened her hands against his chest to push back from him, keeping her head down. "I'm sorry, Adam. It's too soon."

"Too soon?" he repeated huskily, his hands tightening to prevent her from completely pulling away from him. "Am I supposed to believe that after the way you kissed me?"

Slowly, she lifted her head to look at him. "It's true. I didn't want it to be, but it is."

Stark pain flashed in his eyes a second before he took a deep breath and willed it away. "I can wait. I've waited this long." He stepped back, releasing her. "I think a short stroll is in order before we go back inside."

"I think so, too." Like him, Diane wasn't ready to rejoin the other party guests.

Making good her escape from the hall, Susannah slipped outside the seminary unnoticed. If she had to smile and make polite conversation with one more person, she would scream. She knew she shouldn't feel that way. It was a party—a ball. Dancing and idle chatter were naturally part of it.

She paused in the deep shadows by the door and glanced both ways. To her left, a couple wandered across the moon-silvered lawn, moving slowly in her direction. Recognizing Diane and Adam Clark, Susannah walked swiftly to her right, keeping to the dense shadows close to the building. She didn't feel like explaining her desire to be alone.

After she had rounded the corner of the building unseen, she slowed her steps and started down the long side colonnade, the taffeta of her copper gown whispering softly around her. The music from the hall carried clearly into the night air, a muted serenade, which oddly failed to soothe her restlessness.

Almost absently, Susannah recalled her school days here at the seminary. She had always thought she would come back here to teach. But it was closed now, like all the rest of the schools in the Nation, because of the war.

But she didn't want to think about the war. Instead, she made herself remember the last time she had heard the fort's military band play. It had been here at the seminary, too, but outside on the rear lawn near the blackjack woods.

Drawn by the memory and the dark mass of trees that

loomed ahead of her, Susannah left the shelter of the colonnade and moved across the lawn. The night breeze wandered
over the bareness of her shoulders. She briefly wished she
had stopped to retrieve her shawl, but then it would have been
obvious she was going outside, and that young lieutenant
would have repeated his earlier invitation to take her for a
moonlight walk. She knew she should have been flattered by
his interest, but instead she wished he would leave her alone.
And she wished, too, that he hadn't complimented her on the
perfume she had worn.

It only reminded her of Rans Lassiter. She would be better off to forget him. Six months had passed, and she hadn't
seen or heard from him. She wasn't sure what she expected,
but it certainly wasn't silence. Maybe he hadn't meant the
things he had said. Maybe it was only talk—a trick to steal a
kiss. Maybe she was simply a fool.

She heard someone whistling and glanced back to the
seminary, regretting that she was out here in the open, easily
seen. Then she recognized the tune, "Oh Susannah." Her heart
leapt in excitement. The sound came from the woods. Rans.
It had to be him.

Casting one quick glance over her shoulder to make sure
she wasn't seen, Susannah caught up her taffeta skirt and ran
quickly into the well of black shadows at the edge of the
woods. A dark figure in a slouch hat left the concealment of
the trees and stepped forward to meet her.

"Rans."

The moonlight gave a silver gleam to his gray eyes as he
smiled at her. "I believe this is my waltz, Miss Gordon."

By the time she realized it was a waltz the band was playing, he had swept her into his arms and guided her into the
first series of steps. "What are you doing here?"

She still felt stunned, as if this were a dream. She was
half-afraid if she closed her eyes, Rans would be gone when
she opened them. Yet the arm at the back of her waist and the
fingers gripping her hand were no illusion.

"I heard the Yankees were having a cotillion tonight. When I stopped by your house, your colored maid Phoebe said you were here. I couldn't let those Yankee officers have every dance with you."

Susannah suddenly remembered the hall was filled with blue uniforms. "Rans, what if one of them sees you? Don't you know practically every Union officer from the fort is present?"

"As a loyal Yankee, you should do your duty and sound the alarm," he said in that mock-solemn way of his.

"I am serious. You are crazy to come here like this."

"That's what my men said."

"You should have listened to them. It isn't safe here."

"I'm here just the same." His voice had a slightly angry edge to it. "Can't you say you're glad to see me?"

"I am glad to see you, Rans. I—"

With a barely muffled groan, he pulled her against him and brought his mouth down hard against her lips, effectively cutting off the rest of her sentence. Desire surged through her, ignited by the hungry demand of his kiss. There was nothing tender about his passion or its need. It burned and scorched and seared. And Susannah responded with the same sense of urgency and desperation.

Breathing raggedly, he dragged his mouth from her lips and ran it across her jaw to the perfumed hollow below her ear. "God, how I've missed you, Susannah."

"I missed you, too," she whispered, her voice throbbing like the rest of her.

"I've needed you. You don't know how much I've needed you." His mouth seemed to be all over her at once, kissing her eyes, her cheeks, nuzzling her throat, and nibbling at her shoulder. Rocked by pleasure, she could hardly concentrate on the things he was saying. His mouth and hands excited every part of her. "I would have written, but there wasn't a safe way to get a letter to you." He rubbed his lips across hers. "If this war ever ends . . ." He groaned again. "Dammit,

Susannah, I can't make any promises. I don't know if I'll get through it alive, but if I do—"

"I know. I know." She dug her fingers into his hair and forced him to kiss her. She didn't want to talk about death and dying when she felt so alive.

A whippoorwill called from the woods, then repeated its mournful cry more stridently. With an effort, Rans caught hold of her arms and held her away from him. "I have to go, Susannah." Yet he didn't release her as his smoldering gaze traveled over her face, down her neck, and over the bareness revealed by her off-the-shoulder gown. "I'll see you again . . . when I can. Believe that."

"I do." She trembled with the longings he had aroused.

"Captain," a rasping whisper came from somewhere in the blackjack trees, pitched low and insistent. "Come on."

"Yes." But still his hands wandered over her naked shoulders, then trailed along the plunging neckline of her gown.

"Dammit, Captain," came the voice again.

"Rans, please go before they catch you here," Susannah pleaded.

With his hands cupped around her neck, he kissed her hard and quick. "'Don't you cry for me,'" he sang softly into her mouth; then he was gone, swallowed by the dense shadows.

She listened to the soft rustle, but she couldn't tell if it was Rans or the breeze stirring the leaves. She smoothed a hand over her gown and struggled against the sensation that she had lost something.

Hearing the clop of hooves, she turned toward the seminary. A mounted detachment of Union soldiers rode into view. A patrol. She said a silent prayer that Rans and his company would avoid detection, then shuddered when she considered the risk he had taken coming here to see her. He loved her. He hadn't said it, but she knew it. Smiling, she started back across the lawn to the seminary—and the ball.

❧26❧

Flat Rock
Indian Territory
September 16, 1864

Lying belly down on the lip of a prairie ridge, The Blade scanned the Union haying station through his spyglass, then made another, slower sweep of the black soldiers cutting and stacking the hay. Beside him were Generals Watie and Gano, the latter of the Texas Brigade and, by date of rank, the commanding officer of the combined Confederate force of some two thousand men stretched along the Texas Road.

"Depending on how many scouts they have out, I'd say there's between a hundred and a hundred twenty-five men down there," The Blade guessed.

Again, their orders for the expedition were simple: cut off the supplies to the Union garrison at Fort Gibson and some sixteen thousand refugees encamped there.

As The Blade started to lower the spyglass, someone caught his eye. He focused on the black soldier cutting hay. It was Ike, Deu's son. He remembered lying under that bed, ripped with pain, and Ike's face, his eyes, looking at him without raising one word of alarm.

A sickening tightness knotted his stomach when he heard General Gano order an advance party forward to cut off any retreat to the fort. Slowly, he lowered the glass. Outnumbered nearly twenty to one, the men at the hay camp didn't have a chance. Ike didn't have a chance. And there was nothing he could do about it. Nothing.

Shadrach paused to wipe the sweat from his face. Ike glanced at him and laughed. "Poor Uncle Shad, if they haven't got you weeding in the garden, then you're out here stacking hay. I'll bet you never figured when you joined the army, you'd be doing so much fieldwork. Instead of going from a house nigger to a soldier, you went to a field nigger."

Before Shadrach could respond, the bugle sang across the field. "It looks like we're back to being soldiers, Ike."

They hurried back to camp. An enemy force of an estimated strength of two hundred had been sighted near the haying station.

"Two hundred, hell," Ike muttered. "There's closer to two thousand of them. I counted six artillery pieces." He looked at Shadrach for a long second, then said, "We're in for the fight of our lives, Uncle Shad. They already have us cut off from the fort." Shadrach made no reply. "Did you hear what I said?"

"I heard," he answered slowly, hearing also his nephew's desperation. "Since it looks like we're already dead, there is no sense in worrying about dying."

Now it was Ike who was silent, his gaze sober. There was much Shadrach wanted to tell him—about life, freedom, and being black. He wanted to remind him they weren't dying as slaves, but as soldiers fighting for the freedom of every black. He wanted to tell him it was all right to die for that, but the words sounded too high-minded, too noble, especially when the feelings inside him were quite humble.

A faint smile lifted the corners of Ike's mouth. He briefly

clamped a hand on Shadrach's shoulder. "We aren't going to die cheap, Uncle Shad. They're gonna pay a high price for us."

Shadrach smiled back as scattered musket fire broke out. A line of rebel skirmishers advanced on the ravine. The battle had begun. Shadrach wondered how long they would hold out.

The sun sat up there watching, a golden globe in the September sky, as the rebel infantry advanced in formation. Everything seemed to be shades of gold, from the long prairie grass and the ricks of hay in the field to the butternut color of the clothes the Johnny Rebs wore. Shadrach adjusted the rifle more comfortably against his shoulder and waited, his mouth and throat dry. He thought about his sister Phoebe, and he thought about Eliza. He thought about the school that would never be built.

Two hundred yards away, the Confederate infantry opened fire, and there wasn't any more time for thinking. Out of the golden landscape came an eerie, ripply sound that raised the hair, the terrible high, thin scream of the rebel yell. The ground vibrated under the thundering hooves of charging cavalry.

For half an hour they turned back charge after charge. Then, spotting a weakness in the rebel line, the Union captain ordered any man with a horse to mount up. They were going to try to break through. It was a desperate attempt to save some part of his command from annihilation, though there were horses for barely half the men.

When Ike hesitated, Shadrach snapped gruffly, "You heard the captain. Get on your horse."

"I can't." Ike turned from the sight of the jug-headed bay sprawled on the ravine floor and grimly faced the rebel front. "My horse is dead. I guess I'll stay here with you. I didn't really like the idea of running away."

In all, sixty-five of the one hundred twenty-five Union soldiers galloped out of the ravine. For a few minutes, it looked as though they might make it. The rebel line sagged and faltered under the weight of their unexpected charge. More rebel cavalry raced up to reinforce the line, and the fighting grew savage. Riderless horses by the score, both Yankee and rebel, added to the confusion.

"Do you think any of them got through?" Ike wondered.

"A handful maybe. I don't know." Shadrach paused to reload and glanced at the remnants of their unit. Except for the white lieutenant now in command and a few white infantrymen, they were mostly colored soldiers. Yet, the expressions on all their faces were the same—grimly desperate and haunted by death.

The rebel army launched another assault, attacking the ravine from all sides as before. A bullet tore through the fleshy part of Ike's right arm. Blood flowed from the wound, soaking his sleeve. But Ike couldn't afford to take the time to bandage it. The fighting was too intense.

Moments later, in his side vision, Ike saw the force of a bullet spin Shadrach around. "Uncle Shad." He scrambled toward him. But Shad was already turning, struggling to get back into firing position.

"I'm okay," Shadrach insisted as blood oozed between the fingers of the hand that he clutched to the wound in his chest.

With an effort he raised his rifle and took aim again. Ike hesitated, then followed suit. For two hours, they held them off, then ran out of ammunition.

"Scatter," the lieutenant ordered, "and save yourselves the best way you can."

"Come on, Shad." Ike pushed back from the wall of the ravine, holding his wounded arm.

"No." Shadrach didn't move. It hurt too much to move . . . to breathe. The bullet wound on the left side of his chest wasn't bleeding much, but the pain was agony. "You go. I have a few rounds left. I'll keep them occupied while you and the others slip away."

"I won't leave you. Come on. We'll go together." When Ike lifted Shad's left arm to help him up, Shadrach nearly blacked out from the pain.

"No, don't," he moaned. "You have to leave me, Ike. I'm not going to make it anyway. I've been hit in the lung. For God's sake, go."

"Uncle Shad." Ike knelt beside him, a hand reaching out helplessly.

Shadrach saw the anguish in his eyes and tried to smile. "It's all right. Go on. Your mother will never forgive me if anything happens to you."

"Dammit, Shad, you have been more like a father to me than my own. You always understood," he said thickly.

"And you have been like my son. We're a lot alike, I guess." Shadrach smiled and continued to draw in quick, shallow breaths, the pain slowly ebbing. "But I was born before my time. This is your time. You take it and make something of it . . . something we can both take pride in. Now get out of here before they come again and you lose your chance."

Ike hesitated a full second longer, then took off down the ravine at a crouching run. Slowly, gritting his teeth against the new pain, Shadrach eased himself into a firing position and waited for the end to come, praying it wouldn't be so for Ike.

The Confederates rushed the ravine again. Two went down before his rifle; then it was empty. Shadrach tried to rise up to grapple with a charging infantryman, but a bullet struck him in the chest. He lay against the bank, staring at the sun hanging heavy in the afternoon sky. The sight of it filled his vision.

Golden, it was so golden.

The Blade walked his horse over to Shadrach's body and looked down. Inside he felt flat and a little dead himself. War destroyed more than people. It had a way of turning memories into bittersweet things and twisting beliefs to a point where a man questioned whether fighting was worth the cost.

"Did you know him?" a voice drawled.

With an effort, The Blade pulled his gaze away from Shadrach and focused it on the Texas captain to his right. Noting the quizzical look in those gray eyes, The Blade belatedly remembered the question Rans Lassiter had just asked and nodded an affirmative. "I knew him."

Resting his hands on the pommel of the saddle, Rans Lassiter glanced at the bodies that littered the ravine. "They put up a helluva fight for so few."

"Yes." As yet, The Blade hadn't found Ike's body. Had Ike been among the dozen or so riders who made it through the line back at the very start of the fight? He hoped so . . . for Deu's sake.

"Anything wrong, Major?" Rans Lassiter tipped his head to one side, a watchfulness about him.

The Blade realized he had been staring through the Texan and quickly let his glance slide to the blood-soaked kerchief tied high around the man's arm. "Better have somebody look at that wound," he said, and reined his horse away. Black smoke billowed from the burning ricks of hay in the field.

At one of the pools of water, runoff from the Grand River, Lije dismounted and let his horse drink from it. Noisily and greedily, the horse sucked up the brackish water, its neck and sides caked with drying sweat from the afternoon's repeated charges.

Absently, he hunched a shoulder forward and wiped his mouth across it, breathing in the pungent smell of sweat and powder smoke. Lifting his gaze, he let it sweep to the columns of smoke rising from the hay field.

Above the distant shouts from the former Federal camp

came the drum of hooves. Lije turned as a sergeant rode up. The man reined in short of the pool.

"We covered the whole area around the ravine," he reported. "There's no more hiding out, or we would've spotted them."

"Post your sentries and have the rest of the men return to camp," Lije said.

With a nod, the sergeant rode off. Lije gathered up the reins to his horse and prepared to remount. The unpleasant but necessary task of searching for survivors was over. As he swung into the saddle, he heard the plopping sound a frog makes diving into the water. His horse snorted and pricked its ears at the rushes along the left side of the runoff pool. A small arcing wave spread across the pond's surface, part of a concentric ring that had its beginnings in the tall grassy reeds.

Cautiously, Lije studied the area, aware that his horse continued to watch it. In war a man learned to obey his instincts; sometimes they were all that kept him alive. Slowly, Lije unholstered his gun and walked his horse around the pool, keeping to the thick grass and soft ground to muffle the sound of its hooves.

When he neared the very edge of the rushes, a head surfaced in the center of them.

"Step out. Now!" Lije drew back the hammer on his revolver. The man jerked his head around, and Lije stiffened in recognition. "Ike."

Ike stared back, water lapping softly around his neck. Lije's mind flashed to his boyhood times when the two of them had grown up together. Then he thought of Deu and Phoebe.

He eased the hammer forward and holstered his gun, then glanced at the lowering sun. "Once it's dark, you should have a couple hours before the moon comes up," Lije said softly. "Luck to you, Ike."

He didn't look back as he swung his horse away from the pool and headed to camp. All the way, he kept telling himself he had done the right thing—the only thing he could. Dammit, he owed Ike at least a chance.

Spotting The Blade near the lip of the ravine, Lije rode over to make his report. The Blade didn't glance around. "We secured the perimeter," Lije began, then saw Deu in the ravine below, kneeling beside the body of a colored soldier and gently folding the dead man's arms across his chest. He frowned. "Who—"

"Shadrach," came the grim answer, followed by a heavy sigh and a turn of the head as The Blade surveyed the other bodies scattered over the ravine, his jaw clenched.

Lije guessed what his father was thinking. "You won't find his body." Instantly, he had The Blade's full attention, his probing gaze sharp with question. "You can tell him Ike's alive."

"How—"

"Let's just say I know and leave it at that."

The Blade nodded slowly in agreement. A hint of a smile glimmered in the blue of his eyes. Lije smiled back, then turned his horse and started for camp.

When night swallowed the last rays of twilight, Ike dragged himself out of the rushes. Shivering and half-numb with soaking-wet cold, his arm wound throbbing, he crawled away from the pool, making as little noise as possible. There were sentries somewhere. He had to get past them. He had to get to the fort.

On his belly Ike crawled through the long grass, gritting his teeth to keep them from chattering. Thirty yards from the pool, Ike spotted the first guard and inched his way past him, sweat breaking out on his forehead and lip. He kept crawling until he was certain he was out of sight of them, then staggered to his feet and struck out for the fort, heading south. Sometime, close to morning, the palisades of Fort Gibson loomed before him. Wounded, exhausted, and cold to the bone, Ike stumbled the last few yards to the gate.

"I made it, Uncle Shad," he whispered when the guard on duty challenged him.

Later Ike learned that of the one hundred twenty-five men at the haying station at Flat Rock Ford, nineteen survived. In the mad dash for freedom by the mounted troops, fifteen had made it. Three others besides himself had successfully hidden either in the long prairie grass or in the runoff pools from the Grand River, then sneaked through the enemy lines at nightfall.

Two days later the same Confederate force that had wiped out most of his unit struck the supply train at Cabin Creek, attacking shortly after midnight. One hundred wagons were burned and another one hundred thirty were captured by the rebel army, along with a million and a half dollars in cargo.

By the time Ike had recovered from his wound, his regiment was transferred to Arkansas, first to Little Rock, then Fort Smith. In early spring of 1865, the telegraph chattered with the news of Lee's surrender at a place called Appomattox. Then it clattered again with the tragic word of President Lincoln's assassination. But the war was, for all intents and purposes, over. One after another, the armies of the Confederacy gave up the fight. On June 23, 1865, Brigadier General Stand Watie surrendered his troops at Doaksville, the last Confederate general to do so.

Brown leaves raced across the lane in front of Ike's horse, tumbling over one another in a helter-skelter game of tag. Ike ignored the uneasy dancing of his horse and gazed at the house. From a distance it looked as grand as its name implied, but the closer he came to the big house at Grand View, the more signs of neglect he saw.

Four days ago—the end of October—he had been mustered out of the army. He had come home to see his mother, but he was none too sure of his welcome. He rode around to the kitchen at the rear of the house. Smoke curled from the chimney. Ike dismounted and looped the reins around the branch of a bush, leaving the horse to crop at the tall grass.

He stepped inside and saw a woman standing at a work-table, her back to him. Then she turned, wiping her hands on her apron. It was his mother—older, heavier, grayer, but she still possessed full cheeks and big doe eyes. She stared at him in shock.

Hastily, Ike removed his hat and held it uncertainly in front of him, nervously fingering the brim. "Hello, Momma."

"Ike?" Phoebe took a step toward him, still with a look of doubt. "It is you," she cried and ran to embrace him, then tearfully framed his face in her hands. "I thought I was dreaming, but you're here. You're truly here."

"I wasn't sure you'd want to see me. I . . ." He fumbled over the words, fighting the blur of tears in his own eyes and the happiness that choked his throat.

"Not want to see my own boy? I'm your mother." She drew back to look at him, still holding his arms as if he might slip away. She smiled, almost teasingly. "At least, you're not wearing that awful blue uniform anymore." She clutched at him again, unable to contain her happiness. "Just wait 'til Miss Temple sees you. And Eliza." Taking him by the hand, like he was a little boy again, Phoebe led him into the main house and called loudly, "Miss Temple! Ike's here. He's come home!"

Within minutes he was engulfed in more welcomes as Temple, Eliza, Susannah, and Sorrel swarmed around him. None of this was what he had expected, not after the way he had run away to join the army. Before he knew it, he was sitting at the table with a plate of food in front of him.

The knife and fork were in his hands, but he couldn't take that first bite. "Momma, I have to tell you about Uncle Shad. He—"

"We know," Eliza inserted. "Jed—Major Parmelee told us about him . . . about his bravery."

"He was brave, Momma. He was about the bravest man I know."

"He always was. Gracious, when I think of the way he used to sneak into that school to get the lessons you left for him, Miss Eliza . . ." Phoebe shuddered expressively, then smiled. "Our mammy would have whipped him within an inch of his life if she had found out. But that didn't stop him. He was determined to get an education."

"I know," Ike murmured.

She reached over and affectionately squeezed his hand. "I wish your father were here."

"They'll be home soon, Phoebe," Temple assured her.

Ike hesitated. "I . . . wouldn't count on that, Miss Temple."

"Why?" Her look of alarm bordered on fear.

"They're fine," he said quickly. "I saw them last month in Fort Smith when they attended that meeting with the Federal commissioners. I didn't get to talk to them, though, but they were all right."

"Why won't they come home? The war is over."

"Miss Temple, you have to know there's a lot of bad feelings between the Cherokees who fought for the Union and the ones who fought for the South . . . especially after the commissioners told the delegates from all the Indian Nations that they had forfeited all rights to their tribal lands and annuities when they joined the Confederacy. The whole Cherokee Nation is being held accountable for the actions of Stand Watie and his rebels, even though half the Nation remained loyal to the Union cause. They have to make a new treaty, give up some of their land and their rights, and guarantee Cherokee citizenship to former slaves."

"You're saying that . . . it's not safe for them to come back—that there might be reprisals?"

Ike nodded, wondering if she knew how devastating the

war had been to the Nation. Within the boundaries of the Indian Territory, most of it had been fought on Cherokee soil. Practically anywhere a man rode, he would find charred ruins, fields choked with weeds, and abject poverty where there had once been prosperity. From what Ike heard, only one other area had suffered more damage than the Cherokee Nation, and that was the swath of burned ground Sherman had left behind him in his march to the sea. Ironically, much of that burned ground included the Cherokee's former homeland in Georgia.

"Temple, it isn't that they don't want to come home—" Eliza began.

"I know," she retorted crisply, fighting against the despair she felt. It seemed the feuding was never going to end. Never.

"Maybe I shouldn't have said anything," Ike murmured.

"Nonsense. It is always better to know these things," Eliza declared, clasping her hands together and resting them on the tabletop in an attitude that dispensed with the subject. "You haven't said what your plans are, Ike, now that the army has discharged you."

"I don't know. I'm not sure." He shrugged, then glanced at his mother. "I met this girl in Fort Smith. Her name is Ginny. I think you'd like her. She's almost as pretty as you."

"Now you sound like your father with all that sweet talk." But Phoebe beamed at him just the same.

"I thought I'd go back, maybe find me a job, save up some money to go along with what I've got left of my army pay, and get a place of our own somewhere."

"Why don't you bring her here?"

"No, Momma. I'm a free man now. I want to work my own land, have my own place. I have to. I know you don't understand that, but I promised Uncle Shad."

PART III

The houses and cabins had been burned. Fields had grown up into thickets of underbrush. The hogs and cattle, which the soldiers had not killed, had gone wild in the woods and canebrakes. People had to start life anew—build log cabins, clear ground, plant crops, build fences.

—Mrs. Mary Cobb Agnew,
Cherokee

✄ 27 ↝

Sorrel wrestled another ear of corn off its stalk and tossed it into the cart with the others. Her whole body prickled with sweat as she paused and lifted the hot weight of her long red hair off her neck. It gave her little relief. There wasn't a breath of air stirring anywhere.

"How can you stand it, Susannah?" There was her aunt, methodically moving down the adjacent corn row, pulling brown-silked ears off the stalks, completely oblivious to the heat. "I am positively melting.

Susannah smiled at her sympathetically. "We're almost done. Only two more rows."

"I think I hate corn." Sorrel gazed at the mound of ears in the cart, certain if she never looked at corn again, it would be too soon.

"Think about how good a cool bath will feel when we're finished here," Susannah suggested.

"If I can last that long." With a heavy sigh, Sorrel turned back to the corn row, only to be distracted by the steady clip-clopping of a horse's hooves. "Someone's coming." She stepped out of the corn rows to look down the lane. The air shimmered like liquid glass, blurring the rider on the black horse. The instant Sorrel spied the white star on the horse's forehead, she knew who it was. "It's Alex!"

She ran to meet him, her bonnet slipping off and dangling down her back, held only by the loosely tied ribbons around her neck. When she stopped beside the mare, she was out of breath and smiling widely.

"You're home. You're finally home." Sorrel waited for him to dismount. At almost fourteen, she was much too grown up to hurl herself at him in a childish hug, but she had to touch him, so she rested her hands on his shoulders and raised up to give him a quick kiss on the cheek, then stepped back. "I'm so glad you're back. I've missed you."

"I've missed you, too."

"I'm still wearing the locket you gave me." She reached inside the neck of her dress and lifted it out to show him. "I wear it all the time."

Alex glanced at it and remembered the trove of gold coins and jewelry he'd taken with it. They had not been the last items of value that he'd "confiscated" from someone, rebel or otherwise. In one way or another, he had managed to get and spend a considerable amount of money during his time in the army. One of his more profitable schemes had been to force local farmers to sell him their corn at a fraction of its value, then sell it to the army himself. He'd made a tidy sum for a while, but all of it was gone now.

"The locket looks good around your neck. Does your father know you wear it?" It amused him to think how irritating the sight of it would be to The Blade, knowing that Alex had given it to her.

"No." She tucked it back inside her dress. "He and Lije haven't come home yet, although Mother expects them back anytime now that a new treaty has been signed. Did you hear that Chief John Ross died in Washington?"

"I heard."

"Everyone says his nephew William Potter Ross will be elected principal chief when the National Council meets in November."

"Probably." Unlike his father, Alex had no interest in the Nation's politics. All he knew was that if The Blade was for it, he was against it.

"Have you been to your farm yet? Someone told Mother that the cabin is in awful shape, all the windows broken out, a hole in the roof. If you want, I'll come help you fix it up."

"Thanks, but I plan on selling the place if I can find somebody to buy it."

"Why would you do that? I know it's too late to plant anything this year, but next spring—"

"I'm not cut out to be a planter, Sorrel," he told her. "I am not about to spend most of my life staring at the back end of a mule. It isn't me. It never was. If I had to sit around and watch crops grow, I'd go crazy."

"But, if you sell the farm, what will you do? Where will you live?"

"I haven't decided." He reached out and stroked the mare's neck. "I still haven't seen any horse than can outrun this little lady. I thought I might head up to Kansas or Missouri, someplace where her reputation isn't known, and pick up some money racing her."

Sorrel gave him a long, thoughtful look. "I know why you're leaving. You don't have to pretend with me, Alex. It's because of my father, isn't it?" she stated with grim conviction. "You think that when he comes back, he'll come after you, that he'll try to kill you the same way he killed your father."

"I don't think it—I know he wants me dead." But Alex had plans of his own for The Blade. He had thought long and hard about avenging his father's death. In retrospect, Alex was glad The Blade hadn't died when he shot him. It would have been too quick, too easy, especially when he remembered the years his father had spent waiting and wondering when The Blade was going to make his try for him. It had eaten

Kipp like a cancer. Alex had decided it would be poetic justice if The Blade had to do some waiting and wondering of
his own. The day would come, though, when Alex would kill
him—as cold-bloodedly as The Blade had killed Kipp. But
he would pick the day, not The Blade.

"But that has nothing to do with me leaving," he told Sorrel. "Your father isn't driving me away. I'll be back. You can
count on that. I just need to get some money in my pockets
first."

"I don't care whether you have money."

He tipped his head back and laughed. "But I care. You take
care of yourself, Sorrel, and you keep wearing that locket."

He climbed back into the saddle, tossed Sorrel a salute,
and reined the black mare around to head up the lane to the
Texas Road. He felt good inside, so good that he wanted to
throw his head back and laugh.

Seeing the open road before them, the mare pushed at the
bit. "Feel like running, do you?" Alex chuckled and eased
the restraining pressure. The mare broke into a canter.

A mile farther, the mare lifted her head and pricked her
ears at the dust haze ahead of them. Alex eyed it curiously,
then caught the low, steady rumble of sound. At first he thought
it was a supply train, then he heard the bellow of a steer and
knew it was a trail herd. The drives to northern markets had
begun again.

He traveled another quarter mile before he spotted the point
men riding in advance of the lead steers. He was close enough
now to hear the drum of hooves and the clatter of the steers'
long horns cracking against each other. He swung the mare
off the road and pulled up to let the herd pass.

One of the point riders split off from the other two and
cantered up the road. But it was the cattle Alex watched, an
idea forming. In Kansas City, Sedalia, or Saint Louis, a steer
would sell for twenty or thirty dollars. That river of horns
represented a fortune.

Up along the Kansas border, some less-than-scrupulous

"cattle brokers" would pay eighteen dollars a head, no questions asked. During the last couple of years of the war, stealing cattle and selling them to the Kansas brokers had been a lucrative operation, and the authorities had looked the other way. The last Alex had heard, it was still going on. A man could make a lot of money at it. A helluva lot of money. And he'd been planning to head for Kansas anyway.

With the last ear of corn picked, Susannah headed for the house. There was time enough to shuck it later in the evening when it would be cooler. Right now, she wanted a bath and change of clothes. Using the front of her apron, she blotted the perspiration from her face and neck. Tired as well as hot, she tried not to think how much quicker she might have finished if Sorrel hadn't run off to see Alex, then not come back when he left. Fourteen was a difficult age.

She glanced down the lane and saw another rider approaching. "This is certainly our morning for visitors," she murmured.

The dancing heat waves distorted the shape of the horse and rider, concealing his identity. Then Susannah heard the whistling and stopped.

The horse broke into a canter. She stood stock still, unconsciously holding her breath, waiting for the image to either disappear or break through the heat ripples. Suddenly there was no more doubt in her mind. It was Rans!

She ran to meet him. He vaulted from the saddle and caught her up in his arms, swinging her around and bringing his lips down to crush hers. When her feet were back on the ground again, she wrapped her arms tightly around him as she kissed him with hungry ardor.

Even after they both came up for air, she couldn't seem to get enough of him, greedily running her hands over his face and into his hair, letting her lips taste and explore the saltiness of his jaw and neck. He smelled of dust, sweat, and cattle, but Susannah knew she had never breathed an aroma more wonderful.

"You are here," she whispered shakily against his skin. "I was beginning to think I would never see you again."

"Didn't you get my letter?" His hands moved up and down her back, stroking, kneading, and caressing her.

"The one telling me your father was in trouble and you were going home?" It was the only letter she had received from him.

"Yes."

"That was last year, right after the war ended."

"I guess it was. So much has happened I lost track of time." He rubbed his mouth across her forehead, his breath running moist and warm into her hair. "The ranch was sold for back taxes. My father died right after that. I think losing the place killed him."

"I am sorry," she murmured.

"Dear God, I've missed you, Susannah." His arms tightened around her.

"I missed you, too. But you're here now. Nothing else matters."

"I can't stay," Rans told her. "I'm taking a herd up the trail to Iowa. It'll be the end of November or the first of December before I make it back. It seems like I'm always asking you to wait, but will you?"

"I don't know why you even bother to ask. You know I will."

He kissed her long and hard.

✣ 28 ✣

Grand View
Cherokee Nation
December 1866

Outside the parlor window, white flakes swirled and sparkled in the bright sunlight, an illusion of falling snow created by the wind blowing away crystals from the frost-crusted trees on the lawn. Diane concentrated on a new flurry of flakes that danced and whirled beyond the glass panes and worked to block the feelings of envy that knifed through her.

"Shall we drink a toast to the newly engaged couple?" Jed Parmelee's question was met with a chorus of agreements.

Drawing in a quick, steadying breath, Diane turned back to the group and raised her glass of sherry, conscious that her smile was a little too bright. "To Rans and Susannah." The tightness in her voice was thankfully masked by the others.

She took a sip of wine, her glance straying to the couple on the sofa, sitting as close together as propriety would allow. Diane remembered too well when she and Lije had acted like that—in this very room. She remembered, too, the heady excitement she'd felt whenever he was near.

When the laughter and clamor of congratulations were over, Jed asked, "How did your cattle drive go, Rans?"

"Not as well as I'd hoped," he admitted with a sigh. "I did get top dollar in Iowa, but I lost almost two hundred head to raiders. They jumped the herd a few miles south of the Kansas border. By the time I paid all the costs on the drive, I didn't make as much money as I'd hoped." Rans swirled the sherry in his glass and briefly met Susannah's smiling look. "What we need is closer markets.

"The East is crying for beef, and longhorns are running wild in Texas by the hundreds of thousands. Those steers represent the only money we have. Hard cash is scarcer than angels' wings in Texas. I don't have any choice but to try to make another drive next year." His gaze shifted to and moved soberly over Susannah's face once again. "It's going to take a couple more drives before I can afford a place of my own—our own."

"Have you considered building a ranch here in the Nations, Rans?" Although Eliza tried, her question sounded anything but casual in its interest. "I know it is terribly selfish of me, but I am not looking forward to traipsing all the way to Texas to see my grandchildren."

"Truthfully, I hadn't, Mrs. Gordon."

Diane didn't want to listen to more talk that spoke of home, husbands, and family. As unobtrusively as possible, she wandered over to the marble-fronted fireplace to stare into the crackling flames. She knew it wasn't the talk that bothered her nearly as much as witnessing the intimacy between the young couple.

Diane found it unsettling to discover how much she longed for it herself. Standing there, she could almost feel the sensation of Lije's lips on hers and his strong hands moving over her body. She hadn't expected to ache with desire like this, not after all these months. Time should have dulled such feelings. But they remained as sharp and powerful as ever. Unconsciously, Diane shuddered with the force of those longings.

"Are you cold? I can put another log on the fire."

She spun around, surprised to find her father at her side. "No, it was nothing." She held the sherry glass in both hands, her fingers loosely linked around it, her glance running back to the greedy, leaping flames. "It was just ghosts from the past."

"We toasted your engagement to Lije in this very room, didn't we?" he said quietly.

"That was a long time ago." Diane kept her voice low-pitched so the sound of it would not carry beyond his hearing to the others.

"The war is over, Diane."

She shook her head. "It's too late."

"Not if you don't want it to be."

She smiled at him. "It's too late," she repeated with a soft finality.

"Tell me, Major," Reverend Cole began, then broke off with a rueful look. "I beg your pardon—Jed. I fear I will never get used to your being a civilian again. Have you adjusted to life out of the military?"

"Regardless of what he tells you, he misses it." With the ease of long practice, Diane donned the role of the charming officer's daughter. "I am waiting for the day when he walks in with a bugle, in hopes I'll learn to play it so that he can once again awaken to Reveille, be summoned to the mess, and retire to bed with Butterfield's Lullaby echoing through the night."

"A bugle," Jed repeated with a mock-serious expression. "An excellent idea. I should have thought of that."

Diane smiled and lifted her shoulders in a hopeless shrug. "Do you see what I mean?" Everyone laughed.

"Seriously, Jed," Temple said. "I know the Council gave you permission to remain in the Nation and open a general store, but have you chosen a location yet?"

"We have." He beamed a bit with satisfaction. "As luck would have it, I learned the other day that a trader in Tulsey Town, over in the Creek Nation, wanted to sell out. Diane and I just returned from there."

"You bought it," Temple guessed.

"We did," Jed confirmed. "The location is a good one, and I have a feeling it may prove to be ideal. Since the new treaty gives the railroad companies the right of way to enter the territory, it will be only a matter of time before one of them starts laying track. I'm convinced that Tulsey Town will be along any east-west line that's laid."

Eliza released a troubled sigh that carried throughout the room. "I don't think I like the idea of railroads coming through."

"Why not?" Jed raised an eyebrow in sharp question. "Look at the business they'll bring and the market for local goods they'll provide."

"But look at the white settlers they will bring, too. We don't need any more," Eliza stated decisively.

"Mother," Susannah laughed in protest. "Will you listen to yourself? A minute ago you were encouraging Rans to start a ranch here."

"Yes, but he is marrying into the Nation—the same way I did."

"But what about Jed and Reverend Cole?" Susannah chided. "Are you saying they shouldn't be here?"

"I think, I speak for Jed when I say that"—Nathan began—"I don't think I would be happy living anywhere else. For most of thirty years, I have lived here in the Nation. This is my home. It's where my friends are . . . and the people I care about."

"I agree." Jed lifted his sherry glass in an acknowledging salute.

"I didn't mean the two of you particularly," Eliza insisted. "It's only that . . . I can't forget what happened with the Georgians. They didn't stop at merely coveting the land they saw. I would hate to see history repeat itself."

"Everyone in this room feels the same way, Eliza," Jed assured her quietly.

Rans turned his head. "I hear horses outside." He rose from the sofa and moved to the front window.

"Horses?" Temple questioned just as she heard the sound of the front door opening and the heavy tread of footsteps in the foyer. She started for the archway. "Who could be calling at this hour?"

From the foyer came Phoebe's joyful shriek, "Deu! You're home!"

Temple breathed in sharply, afraid to believe what that meant. Her hopes had been dashed too many times. But she had to find out. She grabbed up the hem of her skirts and rushed into the foyer. She saw The Blade and faltered, stunned by all the silver in his black hair. Then her gaze darted to the faint white scar on his bronze cheek, and a second later her eyes locked with the deep blue of his. There was such intense longing in them, such need—an echo of everything she felt— that they pulled her across the space that separated them. Totally oblivious to everything and everyone, Temple went into his arms.

Drawn toward the foyer as everyone else was, Diane paused in the parlor's archway, a hand gripping the casing for support, her gaze riveted on Lije's smiling face. She had been thinking about him too much, wanting him too much. It hurt to see him. It hurt even more when he noticed her and the smile left his thin, hard cheeks.

He shifted his glance to the right of Diane, where her father stood. His eyes narrowed, and she knew he was looking at that empty left sleeve and the bulge under her father's coat. Lije jerked his gaze away from the sight and turned, his lips curving in a stiff smile to greet Susannah.

Diane stole a glance at her father. He stared at the foyer scene, a look of pain in his eyes. For a moment Diane didn't understand. She looked back, trying to see what he saw. There was Temple, pressed against The Blade's side, radiant with happiness. Diane then recognized the cause of his anguish and felt sympathy when he pivoted and walked back into the parlor.

Watching Temple and The Blade together, Diane experienced a fresh wave of envy and bitterness. She should have been welcoming Lije with the same joyous abandon. But he had ruined any chance of happiness for them. She almost hated him for that.

Everyone drifted toward the parlor archway. Good manners dictated that Diane remain there to greet the returning pair. Good manners and pride. But it was his daughter The Blade noticed first.

"You have grown into a beautiful young lady while I've been away, Sorrel." His smile brought a tender warmth to his eyes.

"You've been gone a long time." She offered no smile in return.

"I guess we have." The Blade nodded, sobering.

Lije stepped up. "It looks like we came back just in time to keep an eye on all the eager young men who will come to call."

"Don't tease, Lije," Sorrel retorted sharply and spun away to walk back into the parlor.

"Welcome home, Major." Diane spoke up quickly before the moment became too awkward. But she was conscious of two things—the way Lije avoided looking at her, and the way Temple clung to The Blade's side. "I'm pleased to see you looking well."

"And you look even more beautiful than before, Diane," he said, then glanced past her. "I see you are out of uniform again, Jed."

"Permanently, this time," Jed replied as The Blade moved past Diane to enter the parlor, with Temple on his arm.

Gathering her poise, Diane turned to acknowledge Lije, but he eliminated the need with a curt nod, then brushed past the pair to join the others in the parlor. She swung around to face the room, her gaze following him for an instant before it encountered Sorrel. All her attention was focused on her parents, a mixture of envy and accusation on her face. Diane looked at Temple again and sighed in confusion.

"Are you all right?" Eliza touched her arm.

"I don't understand how Temple can be so happy," she admitted at last.

"Surely it's obvious—The Blade is home."

"I know, but . . . he killed her brother. How can she forget that?"

Eliza smiled. "She loves him."

Diane considered her answer for a moment, her glance straying to Lije. "No." She shook her head. "It can't be that simple. Love isn't enough."

"If love isn't, then what is?" Eliza countered with a touch of impatience, then smiled and patted Diane's arm. "One of life's greatest lessons—one of love's greatest lessons—is to learn to forgive what you can't forget. A long time ago Temple learned those two beautiful words 'I forgive' the hard way. To love is to forgive a wrong. Perhaps you should talk to Reverend Cole about it," she suggested, then patted her arm again and moved away to let Diane think about that. Turning to The Blade, Eliza broached one of her favorite subjects, asking, "Did Sorrel tell you she is one of the top students in her class?"

"No, she didn't mention it. Congratulations." The Blade smiled at his daughter.

"Thank you." She allowed the smallest smile to show, but Lije noticed the wariness didn't leave her eyes. He didn't have to guess who was to blame for this less than warm welcome. It had to be Alex.

"Eliza deserves some of the credit for Sorrel's achievements," Temple said. "She tutored her all through the war until the schools opened again. I've been checking into preparatory schools so we can enroll her in one after she graduates this next June."

"Next June," The Blade mused. "It hardly seems possible."

"The school is going to have a graduation ceremony. Anybody can come." Sorrel paused, her chin lifting to a defiant angle. "I am going to invite Alex."

Lije glanced at the gold locket around her neck, a present from Alex. "Alex is around then. I wondered. Is he living at Kipp's old place?" he asked, much too casually.

"No," Temple began.

"He went to Kansas," Sorrel informed him.

"Kansas?" Lije frowned in surprise. "What's he doing there?"

"He said nobody in Kansas knew how fast Shooting Star was, so he was going to go there and win some money racing her."

"Then he still has his racing mare."

Sorrel nodded. "And she's still lightning fast. There isn't another horse in the whole territory that can beat her."

"There may be one," Rans said.

"Where?" Sorrel challenged.

"One of the raiders who jumped our herd was riding a black horse that was the fastest thing I'd ever seen."

"You were hit by raiders?" Lije asked, instantly alert.

Rans nodded. "Just south of the Kansas line. It was the smoothest operation I've ever seen. They struck around midnight, stampeded the herd, and drove off about three hundred head. Once we got the main herd stopped, a bunch of us went after them. It was close to dawn when we caught up with them—or thought we did." A gleam of wry humor appeared across his bronzed and hardened features. "I guess I should have been suspicious when they didn't put up much of a fight, but there were only two of them and six of us. So I wasn't surprised when they threw a couple half-hearted shots at us and took off. We gave chase—I thought we were going to catch them. Then this guy on the black horse took off. I was ready to swear that horse had sprouted wings the way it streaked across the prairie. The other rustler was spurring and whipping his horse for all he was worth, but that black horse just left him in his dust. It was a sight to see," Rans declared with another wry look.

"And the cattle?" Lije prompted.

"We drove them back to the main bunch. After the stampede, it took us two days to round up all of the strays. When I did a tally, I found I was still almost two hundred head shy. We made another sweep of the area, and that's when we discovered they had split the stolen cattle into two bunches and left a plain trail with the smaller one for us to follow. It was a clever plan, very clever."

"As I recall," Reverend Cole said into the silence that hung over the room, "Alex rode a black horse."

The remark was made in all innocence, but Lije had already suspected a connection. "It's probably coincidence." He wasn't convinced of that, and, judging from Susannah's expression, she wasn't either. "I'm afraid, though, the war has turned some men into hard cases and taught a lot of others about stealing and killing. Do you remember Frank James?" he said to Rans. "He rode with Quantrill during the war."

Rans nodded. "He had a younger brother Jesse who joined up with Bloody Bill Anderson's guerrillas."

"They robbed a bank in Libertyville, Missouri, last February. They've robbed a couple more since then. Last week I heard Cole Younger had joined their gang. Another one of Quantrill's men."

Diane came around to stand next to her father by the fireplace. Lije knew the minute she moved away from the arch. It was more than the whisper of movement she made. It was an awareness of her that licked through his senses every time they were in the same room.

"Not many people mourned when Quantrill was killed in Kentucky during the last days of the war," Jed remarked.

"You're right there," Lije agreed. "The Confederacy may have given him the rank of captain, but the Union put the right brand on him—outlaw."

"I imagine the time you spent in the Light Horse taught you to recognize the lawless element," Reverend Cole said.

"You recognize them by their actions, much as it is in your line of work, Reverend. A man isn't a sinner until he sins. Even good men can go bad." He looked straight at Sorrel. "Sometimes it's the lure of easy money—like the James boys robbing a bank. Sometimes it's out of revenge. Sometimes it's a thirst for power. And sometimes the people you least expect turn bad."

Suspicions. That was all he had about Alex. Lije tried to convey them to Sorrel. She idolized Alex. She always had.

"I may be wrong," Eliza paused and tipped her head to one side, a bit amused and a bit smug, "but I have the distinct impression from your last remark that you intend to seek your old assignment with the Cherokee Light Horse."

"You aren't wrong. In fact, I already have."

"You aren't serious," Temple said in protest. "You've just arrived home—"

He held up a hand to stop her. "I don't have to report for duty until after Christmas."

"Thank goodness," Temple declared with feeling.

"Speaking of home," Jed Parmelee inserted. "It's time Diane and I were leaving."

"So soon? Can't you stay for supper?"

Jed shook his head. "I'd like to get back to Tahlequah before nightfall. We're going to be very busy the next few days with all the packing and arrangements that need to be done."

"Jed has bought a general store in Tulsey Town," Reverend Cole explained.

"We hope to be settled in by Christmas," he said. "If you're up that way, drop in and see us. With a store to run, I doubt we'll be able to get away very often ourselves."

"You are coming to my wedding, aren't you?" Susannah said in tone that warned she wouldn't take no for an answer.

"When is it?" Diane asked, breaking a self-imposed silence that had lasted from the time she had greeted The Blade until now, a fact Lije noted.

Rans and Susannah both answered her question at the same time. But Rans said, "June," and Susannah said, "March."

Jed laughed. "Which is it? March or June?"

"March," Susannah stated and gave Rans a warning look. "I have waited for you as long as I'm going to wait. We're getting married in March, here at the house, and Reverend Cole will perform the ceremony." Taking his agreement for granted, she turned back to Jed and Diane, a quick smile lighting her face. "I also want you to be my maid of honor, Diane. You will, won't you?"

Diane hesitated, the memory of all her own wedding plans rushing back with sharp poignancy. She glanced at Lije, but he stared at the floor. She knew then just how wide the gulf was between them. She knew no way to bridge it.

"I would be proud to be your maid of honor, Susannah. Thank you for asking me."

After a round of leave-takings, Diane walked out into the brisk December air, bundled in her warm winter cape and gloves. The sun had melted the frost from the trees, leaving a glisten of moisture on the branches. The diamond sparkle of water droplets was almost as beautiful as the glazing frost had been. But Diane was too absorbed by her own thoughts to notice.

Jed offered her a steadying hand into the buggy, then climbed in beside her. As soon as the horsehide blanket was tucked around their legs, he tapped the horse with the reins and they set off. Diane let her gaze drift sightlessly over the barren winter landscape, unaware of the lengthening silence and the questioning looks from her father.

At last Jed said, "You're awfully quiet, Diane. Care to tell me what's on your mind?"

She responded with a vague, troubled shake of her head, then murmured, "I think I've made a terrible mistake. And I don't know what to do about it." She still loved Lije, but she had been the one who broke the engagement, the one who pushed him away. She wasn't sure he would ever trust her again, believe her again.

Lying in bed, completely naked, with only the thinness of a bedsheet covering her, Temple felt wonderfully wicked and sinful. She loved the feeling. Inside she was all smooth and warm, like honey on a hot day. She snuggled closer to The Blade and rubbed her cheek against his shoulder. His arm tightened slightly in response. Temple smiled and let her hand travel up his flat stomach to his chest. His body was still hard and lean, and she still enjoyed caressing it.

She listened to the soft crackle of flames in the master bedroom's fireplace, recalling how passionately he had just loved her, leaving no doubt about how much he had missed her, how much he wanted her, and how much he loved her. He had erased all her aches and the emptiness she had experienced for so long.

When she felt his hands stroke her ribs, she whispered, "What are you thinking about?"

"Pork."

She sat up. "Pork!" She glared at his laughing blue eyes. "Blade Stuart, I ought to—"

Chuckling, he caught hold of her wrists and pulled her down on top of him, his glance sliding to the ripe mounds of her breasts now lying heavily on his chest. "That ham I had at dinner tonight was the first I've tasted since before the war."

"What about me? You haven't tasted me since before the war either," she reminded him tartly.

"I swear I didn't enjoy the ham nearly as much as I enjoyed you. Does that satisfy you?"

He was laughing at her, and it made her angrier. "No," she flashed. "You should never have made the comparison in the first place."

"I didn't. You did."

"Then why did you mention it?" she demanded.

"Because I remembered that pork is in short supply in Texas. It's practically worth its weight in gold. We have a lot of rebuilding to do, Temple, and like everyone else, we don't have hard cash to do it with. In Texas you can trade fifty or a hundred pounds of bacon for a full-grown steer, seed, or anything else we need. I noticed some hogs down by the barn when I rode in. How many do we have?"

"Six that are big enough to butcher."

"That's a start." He smiled and ran his hands up her arms, curving them around her and pulling her the rest of the way down. Contented again, Temple nestled her head on his chest and listened to the low rumble of his voice. "I've been thinking about some things Lassiter said at the table tonight. We don't have enough Negroes—or have the money to hire more—to get the fields all plowed and replanted this spring. But there is plenty of grass and water on the Verdigris River northwest of here. We could put a good-sized herd of longhorns there, fatten them up. Then, in November when the ban is not in effect, drive them to Kansas. I wonder if I could talk Lassiter into going partners with me on it. I like him. He's a good man."

"I agree." Absently, she traced the mark on his shoulder left by the bullet wound, his remarks starting her thinking about some of her own plans for rebuilding. "If you did that, we could use the blacks we have working for us to reopen the sawmill. People will need lumber to rebuild their homes."

"That's a good idea." He sounded surprised. "Did Parmelee suggest that?"

"As a matter of fact, no one suggested it. I thought of it myself." Slightly irritated by his attitude, Temple raised her head to look at him. "Who do you think has been running Grand View these last five years? Under the circumstances, I think I did a good job of it. At least you had something to come home to, which is a lot more than a lot of people can say."

"A lot more," he agreed soberly. "To be truthful, Temple, I don't think I could have done better. Looking around, seeing all that you have saved—it hurts a bit to realize that you don't really need me."

"I do need you. I will always need you." Tenderly, she cupped his cheeks in her hands. "And I didn't really do all this alone. Eliza helped a great deal . . . and Susannah and Sorrel."

At the mention of his daughter's name, he frowned. "Sorrel wasn't exactly happy to see me, was she?"

Temple hesitated. It was wonderful lying here with him, talking about the future. She didn't want to spoil it by dredging up the ugliness of the past. But how could she not? He'd have to know sooner or later.

"What is it?" He watched her.

She laid her head back on his chest and pressed herself a little closer against him. "We know how Kipp died."

She felt his stillness, his chest ceasing its even rise and fall. Then he sighed. "Alex told you. I should have guessed." His arms tightened their circle around her as he buried his mouth in her hair and murmured, "Dammit, Temple, I wanted to spare you that. You have got to believe that I didn't want it to happen. I tried to avoid it. If he hadn't pulled that gun—"

Stiffening, she raised herself up. "Alex said he wasn't armed."

"Kipp had a gun—a small pocket revolver—hidden inside his jacket. Alex was standing behind him." The Blade studied her with narrowed eyes. "When Kipp pulled that gun, I had no choice but to shoot him. Temple, you didn't really believe I killed your brother in cold blood?"

"I . . ." she looked down at his smooth bronze chest. "I kept remembering that Shawano wasn't armed either."

Tucking a finger under her chin, he lifted it. "No, my father wasn't armed, but Kipp was."

"I believe you," Temple whispered. "And Sorrel will, too, when we tell her what really happened."

"Why should she? She doesn't know me. She looked at me tonight like I was a stranger. After five years I suppose I am to her."

"But we can't let her go on thinking you are a murderer."

"Then tell her if you want. Maybe it doesn't make sense to you, Temple, but I want to let the past die. I am tired of the fighting, the killing, and the hate. It's finally over, and I want to leave it at that." He captured a lock of her long, black hair and fingered it idly.

"Yes, the war at least is over."

"Kipp is dead. Maybe the feuding is over for us, too."

"Do you think so?" A wistful note crept into her voice. "What about Alex?"

"It's over as far as I'm concerned," The Blade stated.

"I hope Alex feels the same way." But Temple was skeptical. "It would be such a relief for all of us."

"It would, indeed," The Blade said, ending on a heavy breath. "Like you, I would hate it if Lije was still faced with it after I'm gone."

Something in his voice sent a shiver through Temple. To banish it, she immediately sought to lighten the moment by teasing, "Gone? Just where do you think you're going now?"

"Nowhere," he told her. "Nowhere at all. I'm home, Temple. I'm finally home. And this time, I promise I'm not going to leave you again."

"No." She pressed her hand against his lips. "Don't make any promises. You're here now, and that is enough."

"I love you." He pulled on her hair, bringing her down to kiss him.

❧ 29 ❧

Grand View
Cherokee Nation
March 1867

Outside the sun blazed down from a crystal blue sky and the air was warm with spring. Inside the house, a throng of guests milled about, their numbers spilling through the rooms, their voices filling the entire house as they laughed, talked, and offered their congratulations to the new bride and groom.

"Susannah is such a beautiful bride, isn't she?" Eliza beamed proudly at her daughter.

"She is, indeed." Lije sipped at his punch and glanced in the direction of the newlyweds, but the image of Diane standing next to Susannah during the ceremony continued to preoccupy him. She'd worn a gown of sky blue, which accented the slenderness of her waist and the porcelain fineness of her skin.

"The ceremony was lovely," Eliza murmured, then sighed. "I wish Will could have been here."

"He would have liked Rans."

"Yes." She brightened at the thought. "I know I have no say in it, but I do approve of her choice in husbands."

Lije simply nodded and took another sip of the punch, not tasting it at all. The endless chatter of voices, the crush of guests, and the strain of making polite conversation annoyed him.

"It's wonderful that so many people came," Eliza remarked, "although I do wish Jed and Diane had come sooner so we could have visited before the wedding. Have you spoken to her?"

Lije felt the probe of her speculating glance and stared into the glass cup. "No. We have nothing to talk about." He bolted down the punch and wished it was whiskey. Punch couldn't relieve the vicious tension that coiled inside him like a snake.

"How do you know that if you haven't talked to her?"

"Don't meddle, Eliza." With barely checked hostility, he set the empty cup on the refreshment table. "If you'll excuse me, I think I'll step out and get some air."

The nearest exit was the front door. Lije made his way to it, dodging the tall vases of yellow forsythia sprays in the foyer and threading his way through the crowd, nodding stiffly to those who spoke to him, but never stopping. Outside, the restlessness pushed him to the far end of the veranda. From there he surveyed the collection of wagons and buggies that clogged the drive.

He loosened the knot of his striped silk tie and tugged at the throttling tightness of the boiled collar around his neck until he unhooked the top button. Taking a cigar from his pocket, he lit it, then leaned a shoulder against the corner pillar and gazed cheerlessly across the lawn.

The prattle of voices and tittering laughter from inside the house spilled onto the veranda. Lije blocked it out, not wanting to catch the sound of Diane's voice inadvertently. A breeze, soft as a breath, swept away the spiral of blue smoke from his cigar and made the tip glow. He lost himself in contemplation of the silver gray pattern of its ash.

A board creaked near him, breaking his reverie. Lije jerked his head around and saw Diane standing there, studying him. A brutally intense longing shot through him.

Abruptly, Lije broke eye contact and pushed away from the pillar, turning to leave. "I didn't know you were out here."

"I wasn't." Her simple reply, with its wealth of meaning, stopped him. "When I saw you here, I knew this was probably the only chance I would have to speak to you alone before Father and I have to leave."

"What is it you want?" His own insatiable needs made him short with her.

Her lashes lowered. Lije waited for them to lift, for her eyes to flash him one of her amused and provocative glances. But her gaze remained downcast, her head slightly bowed. At that moment, Diane looked fragile, breakable. Then she pushed her chin up and looked at him with a frankness he hadn't expected, a rigid pride holding her stiff.

"I had hoped you would come by the store to see . . . us," she said.

"The Creek Nation is out of my jurisdiction."

"Tulsey Town isn't far from Rans and Susannah's ranch in the Outlet. Rans often stopped at our store for supplies while he was building their cabin there. You could come by when you go to visit them."

"For what reason, Diane? What would be the point?" he challenged.

She started to answer him, then swung away to face the vehicles parked in front of the house. Lije looked away as well, but his gaze was drawn back to her, attracted by the sheen of sunlight on her hair. She wore it intricately twisted at the back of her head, a style that accented the slender curve of her neck.

"You have no idea how many times I have rehearsed this," she began, a light undertone of self-deprecating humor in her voice, "or how many clever and witty things I thought of to say. Now, they all seem foolish and phony."

Lije clamped the cigar between his teeth, then forced himself to relax and take a puff. The smoke burned his tongue.

"Say it in plain words, then." Impatient and annoyed, he tossed the cigar into the grass.

"In plain words—I want to make things right between us. I want this, awkwardness to end. We have known each other too long—since we were children—"

"I can't be your friend, Diane. We went way beyond that."

"I know. But surely we can put the past behind us."

The uneven cadence of hoofbeats pounded across the afternoon air as a pair of riders cantered their horses toward the house. Lije focused instead on Diane.

"The past will always be with us," he told her. "It can't be changed."

"But the way we look at it can be changed," Diane insisted. "We can change. I have. I understand so much more than—"

The front door opened, distracting Lije. Sorrel rushed onto the veranda, then checked her headlong pace and proceeded with a fourteen year old's version of mature dignity. But her expression held a child's bubbling excitement. Lije's attention instantly shifted to the dismounting riders. He didn't have a clear view of their faces, but Lije was willing to bet one of them was Alex.

"Lije, don't shut me out," Diane said, a snap of frustration in her voice. "We need to talk—"

He cut her off. "Not now."

She started to argue, then noticed the way he pushed his coat aside and felt for his holstered gun. Only he wasn't wearing one. "What is it? What's wrong?" Looking over her shoulder, she saw Sorrel with two men. "It's Alex, isn't it? You think he's here to cause trouble, don't you?" Diane guessed, sensing the potential for danger.

"He is trouble." Lije gripped her elbow and steered her toward the front door. "Go inside and warn my father that Alex just arrived."

Diane moved quickly into the house while he approached the front walk where Sorrel stood with Alex and a man whom Lije didn't recognize.

Tall and whipcord lean, the stranger had chestnut hair and a smoothly chiseled face. It was too smooth, Lije thought, like a face carved from stone and given no expression. But the man's eyes never stopped moving, their glance darting here and there, taking in everything—the way an animal's did when it entered strange new territory. His dark brown coat hung unbuttoned, one side pulled back to reveal the holstered gun strapped around his middle. On the revolver's walnut butt were the joined initials *MB*.

The initials on the gun immediately nagged at Lije. He'd heard something, read something about that. When or where, he couldn't recall.

"Well, Cousin Lije," Alex greeted him with a wide smile, but his eyes mocked. "How are you?"

Lije didn't waste his breath on pleasantries. "What brings you here, Alex?"

"He came for Susannah's wedding," Sorrel said in quick defense, her expression both determined and defiant.

"That's right." Alex smiled again. "But Sorrel tells me the ceremony is already over. I guess that means I'll have to be satisfied with congratulating the new bride."

"Susannah will want to know you're here. Why don't you go tell her, Sorrel?" Lije suggested, not letting his attention stray from either Alex or his companion.

Sorrel hesitated. "You are coming in, aren't you, Alex?"

"Shortly," Lije answered for him.

"All right. I'll go tell her." With a rustling whirl of her organdy skirts, Sorrel left them to go back inside.

Alex tipped his head to one side, his look cocky and taunting. "Was there something you wanted to tell me, Cousin Lije?"

"Who's your friend?"

"Didn't I introduce him? This is Mel Brandon. He's a cattle broker."

The pieces clicked. "Brandon, you say? That's funny. I read a flyer the other day on a man called Morgan Bennet, a known cattle thief. He's wanted in Missouri for robbing a bank and killing one of the tellers. He fits your friend's description—right down to the gun with initials on the butt."

"Is that a fact?" The man smiled, unconcerned.

Alex shook his head in mock amazement. "That is what you call a truly strange coincidence."

"According to the flyer, two other men helped this Morgan Bennet rob the bank. The descriptions of them were vague," Lije said. "It couldn't be that one of them was you, could it, Alex?"

Alex grinned, his eyes turning defiant. "And if it was, what then, Cousin? That bank was robbed in Missouri. You can't arrest me for that. I haven't broken any laws here in the Nations, so you can't touch me."

"No, by law I can't," Lije admitted. "But I can point out that you and your friend are overdressed for the party. Why don't you leave your gun belts on your saddles? I wouldn't want you to feel out of place."

Alex hesitated, then shrugged and unbuckled his gun belt. After a moment Bennet, alias Brandon, did the same. When both weapons were tucked securely inside their saddlebags, they faced Lije once more.

"Are you satisfied now, Cousin?" Alex grinned. "Sorrel's going to be wondering what happened to me."

"Keep away from her, Alex."

He laughed. "What can I do? She likes me. She'd be hurt if I ignored her. I can't be that cruel."

"You don't care how she feels."

"She'll never believe that." He grinned and glanced at Bennet. "Ready?" The man nodded. "Then let's go to the party. Lead the way, Cousin."

Lije shook his head and stepped to the side. "You go first, Alex. I prefer you in front of me." For an instant the mask slipped, and Lije was treated to a look of glittering malevolence, an expression that was strongly reminiscent of Kipp. At that moment, Lije was sure beyond any doubt that Alex had no intention of letting the past die.

Out of pure devilry, Alex stayed longer than he planned, mixing and mingling, laughing with this person and that. He was amused by the way neither Lije nor The Blade let him out of his sight and the way The Blade's Negro servant stuck closer to him than a noontime shadow.

Jed Parmelee and his daughter Diane had just left when Alex finally wandered over to Sorrel. "We have to be going now. Are you going to walk me out to my horse?"

"Of course, I will." She beamed with quick pleasure.

Alex offered her his arm and glanced over, deliberately catching Lije's eye when Sorrel slipped her hand under the crook of his elbow. He almost laughed out loud at the sudden stiffening in Lije's demeanor.

When they reached the horses, Sorrel took her role as hostess seriously and turned to Alex's companion. "It was a pleasure to meet you, Mr. Brandon."

"Same to you, miss." He nodded and untied the reins to his horse.

Facing Alex once again, she took his arm to draw him aside. "Before you go, there's something I need to tell you," she said, darting a quick glance at Bennet, making it clear she didn't want him to overhear.

"Sure." Alex walked a couple of steps away with her and smiled when he noticed Lije watched from the veranda. "What's on your mind?"

"It's something Mother told me—about when Uncle Kipp died."

"What about it?" He stopped smiling.

"She said that Uncle Kipp had a gun hidden inside his jacket, and that when he pulled it out, that's when my father shot him. She said you couldn't see the gun because you were standing behind Uncle Kipp."

Little frissons of shock sprayed through him as Alex recalled the pocket revolver his father always carried. He had forgotten about it. Was that what happened? Had his father pulled out his pocket gun?

He glanced sharply at Sorrel. "You don't believe that, do you?"

"It could have happened that way, couldn't it?"

"Sure it could have, but it didn't." He deliberately scoffed at the idea. "I saw everything that happened, and my father didn't have a gun. The Blade made up that story so your mother wouldn't think he was a cold-blooded murderer."

"Then . . . it isn't true?"

"I told you I was there. I saw it." Alex paused and gave her a hurt and bitter look. "There's no way I can prove it. And nobody's going to take my word over his. Not even you." He turned on his heel and walked over to the mare.

"Alex, wait." Sorrel hurried after him and caught his arm. "I believe you."

"I hope you do." He gave her a long, sad look. "A man gets lonely when he has no one who cares about him or believes in him."

"I care about you, Alex. You can always count on me."

He reached out and fingered the gold chain that held her locket. "You take care of yourself and keep wearing this."

"I will," Sorrel promised and stepped back as he gathered up the mare's reins. "Where are you going now? When will I see you again?"

"I don't know, but if you ever need me, contact old Joe Washburn over at Salina. He'll get a message to me wherever I am."

"Mr. Washburn at Salina," she repeated to fix it in her mind.

"That's our secret now. Don't you be telling anybody." He stepped into the stirrup and swung onto the mare.

"I won't. You can trust me, Alex."

Lije waited on the veranda, his impatience growing. The only thing that kept him from charging out there and sending Alex on his way was the certain knowledge that Alex deliberately delayed his departure just to irritate him.

At last Alex wheeled the mare around and rode off. Sorrel waved to him, then turned and started back to the house. When she saw Lije, her steps faltered a bit. Then, with a slightly combative jut of her chin, she continued onto the veranda.

"What are you doing out here?" she challenged.

"Keeping an eye on you." Which was half-true. "What did Alex have to say? You two talked a long time."

"It was personal. It had nothing to do with you."

"Sorrel, you be careful around Alex. He isn't the kind of man you think he is."

"You don't know him the way I do."

"But I may know more about Alex than you do," Lije countered. "He's traveling in some bad company, Sorrel. That man with him, the one who called himself Brandon—his real name is Morgan Bennet. He's wanted in Missouri for robbing a bank and killing a teller. He had two men with him when he held up that bank. One of them was described as tall and slim, with black hair and dark eyes."

"You're trying to say that was Alex, aren't you?" she accused. "But that description could fit a lot of other people, too. You'll never make me believe it was Alex. He wouldn't do that."

Irritated by her blind faith in the man, Lije went on the attack. "What kind of work does he do, Sorrel? Where does he get his money? That was a new store-bought shirt and coat he was wearing, and he had a new saddle on the mare. How did he pay for them?"

"He probably won the money racing Shooting Star," she

retorted, her eyes snapping with temper and outrage. "He didn't steal it."

"He's using you, Sorrel. He's using you to get back at the major, trying to turn you against him, against all of us. And he's laughing at you the whole time, knowing you'll believe anything he says. He doesn't care about you."

"That's a lie!" she raged. "Alex cares about me. I'm the only one he can trust, the only one who believes in him. You're making all this up to make him look bad. But it's a lie. It's all a lie!"

She stormed off. Lije began to go after her, then stopped and sighed in frustration and disgust. Sorrel was at the rebellious age when she challenged the opinions of her elders in an attempt to assert herself. The more he spoke against Alex, the more he made him a martyr in her eyes. Instead of tearing Alex down, he was elevating him, turning him into a romantic figure who was horribly misunderstood by everyone but Sorrel.

The Blade came out. "Did Alex leave?"

"A few minutes ago." Lije nodded and glanced after Sorrel. She was still on the veranda, a rigid and defiantly proud figure staring down the lane, a hand clutching the locket at her throat. Lije cursed softy when he saw that.

"What's wrong?" The Blade divided his curious glance between Sorrel and Lije.

"I tried to warn Sorrel about Alex, but she wouldn't listen," he said, then told The Blade about his earlier confrontation with Alex and the outlaw Bennet, what he knew and what he suspected.

"Naturally, she didn't believe you."

"She called me a liar. I don't know how to reach her. She's so upset and angry now . . ." He let the rest trail off in a sigh and shook his head.

"I'll go talk to her."

"Good luck," Lije said with skepticism and headed back inside.

Sorrel continued to stare at the lane, but The Blade noticed the mutinous tilt of her chin that signaled her awareness of his approach. When he stopped beside her, she threw him a sideways glance. The sparkle of temper in her eyes was so reminiscent of Temple that he almost smiled.

"I suppose you've come to tell me what a terrible, evil man Alex is, too." Her low voice vibrated with anger.

"Lije told me you were upset. You'll have to forgive your brother. He still tends to see you as his little sister, someone he needs to watch over and protect. He doesn't realize that you'll be fifteen in a few more months—a grown young lady, intelligent enough to figure things out on her own."

"You're just complimenting me because you think I can be flattered into believing all those things about Alex," she retorted.

This time The Blade didn't hide his smile. "I was speaking the truth. But you have proved you're intelligent enough to recognize that."

"Like Alex, I suppose," she said with an undertone of sarcasm.

"I'm not here to talk about Alex."

"Oh?" She turned and arched an eyebrow in a show of mocking skepticism that would have done Temple proud. "Then why are you here?"

"Two of Rans's friends from the old Texas Brigade brought a fiddle and a banjo, and your grandmother is dusting off the piano keys while the others clear a space in the parlor for people to dance." Even as he spoke, the first ripple of notes came from inside the house. "I thought I would ask a certain beautiful young lady to dance with me." He half-turned and presented his arm to her. "Would you do me the honor of being my partner?"

Sorrel hung back, eyeing him warily. "You don't really want to dance with me."

"Oh, but I do." He took her arm and threaded it through the crook of his. He'd had few chances to be a father to his daughter these last few years. He was certain if he had been around more to give her the attention she needed, she wouldn't have turned to Alex. He wanted to make up for that. "I can hear people now whispering to each other, who is that lovely young lady dancing with The Blade Stuart? Finally someone will say, That's his daughter Sorrel. It will be one of the proudest moments in my life."

"You're just saying that to make me feel good." But there was a betraying glow of pleasure in her eyes.

"No, it makes *me* feel good," he told her, then paused a beat. "Shall we?"

"Very well," she said primly. "But you may as well know that I still don't believe all those things Lije said about Alex."

The Blade threw his head back and laughed.

❦ 30 ❧

Stuart/Lassiter Ranch on the Verdigris River
Cherokee Nation
June 1867

The liquid in the bucket shimmered a light, iridescent green. Lije scooped some of it up in his fingers, feeling its slickness as it slipped between them to drip back into the bucket. He took a deep smell of it, then touched the tip of his tongue to it and looked at Rans.

"Remind me never again to take two days off to help you. I don't care how shorthanded you are, Rans."

"You didn't take time off to help me. You came to track down an empty rumor that Alex was up here."

"But I stayed to help you." Lije picked up a rag and wiped the thick liquid from his fingers. "It's oil, all right."

"That's great. That's just dandy," Rans muttered. "We sink a deeper well to increase our water supply and look what happens. Tell me what in hell am I supposed to do with it?"

"You could do what that fellow from Pennsylvania did after the war. He pumped the oil out, separated the salt water from it, put the rest in containers, and sold it for lamp fuel or cattle dip."

"You can't be serious. Do you know how much time that would take?" Rans said in disgust.

"I wasn't serious."

"I sure as hell hope not," Rans declared, then sighed and shook his head. "I guess we might as well joke about it. We sure as hell can't drink it."

Lije nudged the bucket with the toe of his boot. "You could fill a couple hogsheads with it and use it here on the ranch for fuel and wagon grease."

"I can do that—after I sink a new well."

A horse whinnied in the corral. Its ringing call was quickly answered by the whicker of a second horse somewhere on the prairie. Lije frowned and ran a searching glance to locate the second horse.

To the south, no more than a half mile distant, a horse and buggy laid a swath through the tall buffalo grass. A saddle horse was tied behind the buggy, and two men on horseback ranged alongside.

"Looks like you have visitors," he told Rans.

Together they watched the small party draw closer. "Isn't that The Blade?" Rans said.

Lije nodded, his attention zeroing in on the second man with one arm. "Jed Parmelee is with him." Simple logic told him Diane rode in the buggy. Uneasiness leapt through his system like lightning.

When the buggy rolled to a stop near them, Deu was at the reins with Diane next to him. Rans stepped up to greet them. Lije felt the same urge, but he resisted it and kept his distance.

"Diane, how are you?" Rans smiled a welcome. "Susannah will be glad to see you. She's been starving for the sight of another woman. I think that's half the reason she's so anxious for us to leave tomorrow for Sorrel's graduation."

"I wouldn't be surprised. It can be lonely for a woman out here," Diane said, then looked at Lije, a question and more in her eyes. "After our talk at Susannah's wedding, I thought you might come by the store."

"I've been busy." He didn't admit that he had been tempted to do just that. At least a dozen times he'd considered saddling his horse and riding to Tulsey Town. Cold reality had always set in. With nerves raw, Lije turned to her father. "Good to see you, Jed."

"Same to you, Lije." He swung out of the saddle and stepped to the ground.

Rans came over to shake hands with him. "Who's minding the store while both of you are away?"

"My old striker Amos Johnson has come to work for us. He and his wife are looking after things."

"I stopped by the store on my way here and convinced Jed and Diane to ride along with me." Saddle leather creaked as The Blade dismounted. "I had a feeling Susannah might be ready for company about now. This way we can all travel together tomorrow." His glance slid to Lije. "What did you find out about Alex?"

"No one's seen him around here."

"I expected that," he said. "How is the new well coming?"

"It isn't. We tapped into an oil spring." Rans looked with grim disgust at the bucket of crude oil. "I'll have to dig another one."

"My news isn't much better." The Blade paused and glanced at the buggy. "Deu, why don't you drive Diane up to the house. Tell Susannah we'll be along directly."

Lije felt the quick assessment of Diane's gaze before Deu slapped the reins and the buggy lurched forward. When it had pulled past him, he turned and watched it for a second as the buggy rattled toward the wood-frame house sitting by itself in the empty expanse of prairie.

"What's your news?" Rans's question pulled Lije's attention back to The Blade.

"Old Johnny Scott was killed three days ago. Beaten to death."

"Johnny Scott, the old whiskey peddler?" Lije frowned in surprise. "Before the war, I must have trailed that man a dozen times or more. He was a cagey old rascal. I never got close to him." Lije had a moment's regret for the old man's passing. "I always figured he'd die drinking his own bad whiskey. I guess somebody was after his gold."

"What gold?" Rans looked from The Blade to Lije.

"Scott had a cabin just across the line in Arkansas, not far from Dutch Mills," Lije explained. "If you believe all the stories, he buried the gold he made smuggling whiskey somewhere in the woods behind his cabin." His gaze centered on The Blade. "Why do I have the feeling Scott's death has something to do with Alex?"

"A neighbor of Scott's saw two men ride past his house right around dark. He didn't get a good look at the men, but one of them was riding a black mare with a white star. The old man was found dead the next morning, and fresh tracks of two horses were found in his yard."

"Was the gold taken? Do they know?" Rans asked curiously.

"There were holes dug in the woods, and a couple of rusty iron pots were found nearby—empty, of course."

"Then all those stories about buried gold may have been true after all," Lije mused. "Does Sorrel know about this?"

"She knows, but she's convinced Alex had no part in it. According to her, there must be dozens of black mares with white stars in the territory There's no proof the neighbor saw Alex's mare."

"She wouldn't believe it if there were." Lije said in disgust.

"No," The Blade agreed. "Alex has cast some sort of spell over her. The only way I know to break it is to keep her away from him. I don't want him near her again."

"That may not be wise," Lije warned.

"Wise or not, I don't trust him. The man's a thief and a murderer, and I don't want him near my daughter."

Lije couldn't argue with that, but Sorrel would. He knew that, too.

"We aren't going to solve any problems standing around here," Rans said at last. "We might as well head to the house and get washed up for dinner."

"You go ahead." Lije knew how small the house was. It would be even smaller with Diane in it. "I have a few things to finish here."

He dallied outside as long as he could, then went to the house and killed more time washing his hands and face, all the while listening to and for the occasional sound of Diane's voice. He splashed his face with cold water one last time, then wiped it dry.

When Lije finally walked into the house, everyone was seated at the wooden table. Two chairs remained empty, one beside Diane and the other one at the far end next to Susannah. Lije made the long walk to the latter. His muscles felt knotted, and his nerves were on edge.

A platter of roast beef, a basket of homemade bread, bowls of hominy, roasted onions, fresh green beans from Susannah's garden, and parsnips, dishes of pickled beets and corn relish, and jars of honey, horseradish, and butter all made the rounds of the table. Lije filled his plate, the chink and clatter of dishes and silverware jangling his nerves. He speared the first bite of green beans.

"Let me cut that for you." Diane's quiet voice ripped through him. His glance shot to the far end of the table where Diane calmly sliced her father's meat into bite-sized pieces.

Unembarrassed, Jed Parmelee leaned back in his chair to give her room. "As useless as this arm of mine is, there are times when I wish the surgeon had sawed it off. I never thought I would consider it a nuisance, but that's what it has become. Especially in the summer when it gets hot. If I wrap it against my side the way I usually do, the heat makes a rash. If I rig it in a sling, the cloth rubs my neck raw. And if

I let it dangle, it flops in my way." It was all said with more bemusement than rancor.

Diane chided him in mock reproval, "Complain, complain, that's all you ever do." Jed chuckled as Diane returned his fork to him. "There, you're all set." She picked up her own utensils. "Actually I am constantly amazed by how well Father has adjusted to the use of only one arm. Believe me, he can do more things with one arm than most people can do with two. Of course, his right arm is as strong as two."

"I know what you mean," Rans spoke up and proceeded to tell them about a friend of his in Texas who had lost a leg in the war and been blinded in one eye. "You should see him work cattle. I still don't understand how he stays in the saddle."

The food turned tasteless in Lije's mouth. Changing. Diane had talked about changing. But one thing would never change— Jed Parmelee would never regain the use of his arm. It would always serve as a reminder of just how far apart their beliefs had taken them.

He ate the food on his plate, drank his coffee. The minute Susannah rose to clear the table, Lije excused himself and walked out of the house.

On the porch that ran the length of the house, he stopped and breathed in deeply, his nerves quivering from the strain of the last hour. When he heard the creak of the door hinge, followed by light footsteps, he stiffened and shoved his hat on his head, moving toward the steps.

"Lije, wait." The sound of Diane's level voice was like a rope cast around him, pulling him up short. He fixed his gaze on the green grass prairie that rolled to the far horizon, its vastness dwarfed by the immense sky. She came up behind him. "I hoped we might talk."

Hardened with grimness, Lije looked back to meet her gaze. "About what?"

"Us," she replied evenly.

"There is no 'us,' Diane. Not anymore."

She dropped her gaze. "That's very definite."

"What did you expect me to say?"

"I don't know," she admitted. "I . . . I received a letter from Adam Clark last week. He was the physician at the fort during the war. He's been mustered out and gone back to Abilene to take over his father's practice. He's asked me to marry him."

"Congratulations." He pushed off the porch steps and headed across the yard.

Diane came after him and swung ahead to block his path. She held her head high; her eyes sparkled with determination. The combination accentuated the pride and strength of will Lije had always admired in her.

"I haven't accepted his proposal yet, Lije," she told him, then challenged, "Have you thought at all about what I said at Susannah's wedding?"

His breath ran out in a silent, humorless laugh. "I've thought about it, but my opinion hasn't changed. I can't be your friend. I told you before—we went past that."

"I know we did. But it would be a beginning, Lije."

He shook his head, visualizing the hell of being with her and not taking her in his arms, of watching her smile and not kissing her.

"Have you forgotten your father's arm was crippled in a battle against my regiment, Diane? Have you forgotten just how far apart we have drifted since the war began?"

"I haven't forgotten, but the war is over, Lije."

"Yes, the war's over." Lije nodded. "But the feud isn't, Diane. Alex is still out there."

Impatience and disdain flickered in her eyes for an instant; then she collected herself "I know you still regard Alex as a threat. Heaven knows he's turned into a dangerous criminal, capable of anything."

It was her brief hesitation, her careful choice of words that told Lije she didn't believe—she didn't believe the old feud still had meaning. It hurt that she didn't understand, that she didn't accept it as valid.

But maybe it was best. He thought of his mother and the years of agony she'd gone through, fearing for his father's safety. He didn't know how long the fight with Alex might drag on. There was no way he wanted Diane to go through the anguish his mother had suffered.

"Lije?" Diane frowned, confused by his lengthening silence. "Did I say something wrong?"

"No, you're absolutely right, Diane. Alex is capable of anything."

"Then—"

"Maybe you should accept your doctor's marriage proposal. Right now I can't deal with what's between us. I have too much unfinished business. There's too much going on. I haven't got the time to find out if there's anything for us to salvage."

"Not salvage," she objected to the word. "Something to build on. I won't settle for less."

"You'd better go see if your father needs you," he told her. "I have work to do."

As he walked off, Diane watched him, confused, hurt, and a little frightened. She knew she might have lost the last chance to rebuild her relationship with Lije. But there was still Sorrel's graduation. She'd wait until then before making any decisions regarding her future.

ᴄᴏ 31 ᴏᴅ

Grand View
Cherokee Nation
June 1867

Lije drove the carriage around to the front of the house and swung to the ground. The sun was high in a sky of pure blue and the air had that warm, lazy feel of summer to it. In the trees, a wren warbled in a musical burst.

Deu came up in the buggy. "Master Lije, will you tell Phoebe I'm out here waiting for her?"

"I'll tell her." Lije headed for the house.

Eliza bustled into the foyer, saw Lije, and paused. "Is the carriage out front?"

"Ready and waiting," Lije confirmed. "Where's Phoebe? Deu's outside waiting for her."

"I'll tell her." Eliza crossed to the rear hall and traveled its length to the butler's pantry. Phoebe was there. "Deu is outside," Eliza told her while pulling on an ivory glove. "Are you ready?"

"Yes, ma'am." Phoebe tucked the ends of the checkered cloth around the sides of the large basket, then used both hands to pick it up by its wooden handles.

"How nice you look, Phoebe. Is that a new hat?" Eliza studied the small-brimmed hat perched atop Phoebe's curls. A spray of blue flowers, the same color as her dress, adorned the brim.

"Yes." Beaming proudly, Phoebe reached to touch it. "Deu bought it for me. He said today was a special occasion, and I needed to have something special to wear."

"I completely agree." Eliza fitted the glove snugly to her fingers, then tugged its mate onto her other hand. "Now you tell Ike that as soon as Sorrel's graduation exercises are over, Nathan and I will come directly to his school. We should be there in plenty of time for the dedication ceremony."

"He will be so glad to have you, Miss Eliza."

"Not as happy as I will be. It's a wonderful thing he is doing, dedicating the school to Shadrach. As his former teacher, I wouldn't miss this ceremony for anything." Eliza smiled proudly, conscious of the tears that threatened to fill her eyes.

"Ike said he was only making Shadrach's dream come true. Shadrach always wanted to build a school for colored children. It's only right for it to be dedicated in his memory."

"Indeed." Eliza nodded in firm agreement, then briskly gathered herself up. "You mustn't keep Deu waiting any longer. We will see you at the school."

Eliza moved off, retracing her steps, her thoughts crowded with a thousand memories. But there was no time to dwell on the past. There was still Sorrel's graduation to attend first. She walked straight to the parlor where the others were gathered—The Blade, Reverend Cole, Jed Parmelee, Diane and Lije, Susannah and Rans.

"What are we waiting for?" Eliza paused in the archway.

"Temple and Sorrel haven't come down yet," Susannah explained.

"What's keeping them? We'll be late." With an impatient frown, Eliza turned to face the staircase.

Sorrel appeared at the top of the curved stairs, dressed in

her white graduation dress, a lilac sash around her waist, her flame gold hair caught up with a matching ribbon. Temple was behind her.

"Here they come now," Eliza told the others. "Good, we're all ready."

Diane moved to the archway and paused next to Eliza, looking up. "You look beautiful, Sorrel."

"She does, doesn't she?" Emotion tugged again at Eliza as she watched the young girl—no, she was a young woman now—come down the steps, moving with a regality and grace that reminded Eliza of Temple. Something glittered on her dress. The sparkle caught Eliza's eye.

"What's that you're wearing, Sorrel?" She crossed to the base of the stairs for a closer look and gasped in surprise when she recognized the silver sword-shaped pin with pearls and an amethyst crowning its hilt. "The kilt pin." Eliza's eyes misted as she glanced past Sorrel to Temple. "You gave it to her."

"I wanted Sorrel to have it, and this seemed to be the perfect day to give it to her." Reaching up, Temple lightly ran a smoothing hand over her daughter's fiery tresses. It was a mother's caress, a brief clinging to a child who had become a woman.

The Blade came to stand by the stairs. "That pin has been in the Gordon family for over a hundred years. You should be honored your mother gave it to you."

"I am," Sorrel replied. But Lije noticed it was the gold locket around her neck that she reached up to touch. The locket Alex had given her. He stifled a sigh of irritation when he heard footsteps outside on the veranda. The front door opened, and Lije stiffened.

"Alex, you came!" Sorrel launched herself toward her cousin.

The Blade caught her arm before she could sweep past him. "What are you doing here, Alex?" he demanded as Lije pushed past Diane to stand next to his father.

"Let go of my arm! You're hurting me," Sorrel protested.

The Blade ignored her attempt to twist free. "You haven't answered my question, Alex."

"I'm here for Sorrel's graduation." Alex grinned back at him, satisfaction and confidence gleaming in his black eyes. "She invited me."

"Sorrel made a mistake. You're not welcome here," Lije told him.

"No!" Dismay and shock riddled Sorrel's expression. "I asked him to come."

The Blade ignored her. "Get out, Alex. And don't come near my daughter again." Lije watched surprise, disbelief, and anger chase themselves across Alex's face, a redness rising in his neck. "Don't make me repeat myself," The Blade warned.

Alex hesitated a moment longer, flashed a look of pure hatred at The Blade, then reached backward for the doorknob. "No!" Sorrel strained toward him, but he ducked his head, avoiding her, and slipped out the door. In a fury, she turned on The Blade. "How dare you order him to leave? This is my graduation. I can invite whomever I want!"

"Not him." He relaxed his grip on her arm.

She tore the rest of the way free. "If you won't let Alex come to my graduation, then I am not going."

"Sorrel, you don't mean that." Temple moved toward her.

"I do!" she flashed. "I won't go."

"But everyone is here. Jed and Diane came all the way from Tulsey—"

"Alex came a very long way, too, but *he* ordered him to leave." Sorrel waved a hand at The Blade. "You can tell them to go away, too. There isn't going to be any graduation!"

"Sorrel," Temple began in a reasoning tone, but Sorrel swept past her and ran up the steps. Seconds later, the door to her bedroom slammed shut. After the heated shouting, the ensuing silence was thick. "I'd better go to her." Temple gazed up the long staircase.

"Let her be," The Blade said. "She's too angry to listen to anyone right now."

"You don't think she really meant it, do you?" Diane murmured.

The Blade released a long sigh and shook his head. "Truthfully, Diane, I wouldn't be at all surprised if she did."

An hour later it became apparent that Sorrel was not coming out of her room—at least, not in time to participate in the graduation exercises. Lije drove Nathan and Eliza to the dedication ceremony at Ike's school.

The ceremony, like the one-room schoolhouse built with lumber from the Stuarts' sawmill, was a simple one. Afterward, Lije stood at the back of the room and watched Ike as he accepted the congratulations and the heartfelt expressions from the dozen or so Negro families who filled the room. Ike looked proud and a little nervous, but mostly eager and determined.

When the last well-wisher had moved on to the refreshment table, Ike noticed Lije standing at the rear of the room. He hesitated a moment, then made his way past the long wooden tables and benches that served as desks until he reached Lije.

"I'm glad you came," Ike said, a little stiff and reserved.

Lije felt the awkwardness, too. "I'm glad I came, too." He glanced around the room. "This is quite an accomplishment."

Ike looked around, sobering. "It isn't much. Someday I hope to have proper desks and enough primers and slate boards for all my students. And I don't have—"

"It's a beginning, Ike." The minute he said the words, Lije realized he was referring to more than the school. He looked at Ike with new eyes. "Shadrach would be proud of this. He would be proud of you. You are your own master now."

"Yes, sir, I am." He met Lije's gaze squarely, a glint of challenge in his dark eyes.

"That was a helluva stand you and your company made at the hay camp. A lot of brave men died that day alongside Shadrach. I'm glad you weren't one of them."

"Me, too," Ike replied, swelling a bit with pride.

"Someday we need to get together and trade war stories. I don't think I'll ever forget the sight of you boys charging across Cabin Creek."

"I don't reckon I will either," Ike agreed with a laugh. "The sound of that rebel yell was enough to make a man's blood freeze. Were you at Elk Creek when—" He broke off the question as his wife came up, claiming attention.

"The Radleys are leaving," she told him. "They said they'd be enrolling both of their boys. I thought you'd want to speak to them before they left."

"I'll be right there," he said, then turned back to Lije, a mixture of regret and uncertainty in his eyes. "I guess we'll have to leave the war talk to that 'someday' you mentioned."

"I'll look forward to it." Lije hesitated, then held out his hand. Ike looked at it for a long second, then gripped it in his own. They shook hands, for the first time man to man.

During the ride back home to Grand View, Lije reflected on that moment. He had attended the dedication out of a sense of duty, but he discovered that he came away from it feeling good inside. Good about Ike, and good about himself.

He dropped Eliza and Reverend Cole off at the house and drove to the stables to put the carriage and the team away. When he walked back to the house, Lije noticed the fluttering of a curtain in the opened window of his sister's bedroom. Sorrel was still up there, all right, no doubt fuming over what she considered the injustice of The Blade's actions. Her misguided loyalty to Alex irritated Lije. He wished he could shake some sense into her.

Centimeter by centimeter, the sunlight streaming through the window crept across the floor and up the wall. Sorrel sat on the bed and watched it with a fixed stare. Every tightly coiled nerve and muscle in her body threatened to snap under the strain of waiting for the sun to go down. The urge to pace the room was strong, but she didn't give in to it. She didn't want to make any sound that could be heard below for fear they would become suspicious when the noises stopped.

Her empty stomach increased its gnawing pangs of hunger. Sorrel pressed a hand against it, trying to still its rumblings, then ran a hand further down her stomach onto the black material of her riding skirt. It had to be close to suppertime. Why weren't they eating yet?

A second later she tensed at the sound of footsteps on the stairs. She turned her head to watch the door, listening intently. The tread was light, signifying a woman's footsteps. They were slow, not quick and brisk like Susannah's or Diane's. It could be either her mother or her grandmother. Each of them had come to the door once that afternoon and tried to persuade her to talk.

Again the footsteps stopped outside her door. There was silence, a hesitation, then a knock. "Sorrel." It was her mother's voice that called to her. "Sorrel, you have stayed in there long enough." Sorrel deliberately didn't answer right away. "Sorrel, supper is ready. Come down and eat something."

"I'm not hungry."

"Will you stop being so stubborn and come out?" There was an edge of impatience in the demand.

"Go away and leave me alone."

"You are acting like a child."

Sorrel could have easily argued that they were the ones treating her like a child, telling her who she could see and who she couldn't.

"Sorrel?" Her mother knocked at the door again.

Sorrel ignored it and waited for the silence to end. Finally, she heard a heavy sigh, then footsteps, this time retracing their path to the stairs. She listened until she could hear them no more, then got up and tiptoed to the door, careful not to let the heels of her riding boots strike the floor.

Leaning against it, Sorrel pressed an ear to the small crack where the door butted up to the frame. She could hear voices, muffled and indistinct, but she couldn't tell which one of the downstairs rooms they came from.

Minutes passed. Each felt like an hour. Then came the clatter of silverware. She waited a little longer to make certain everyone was in the dining room eating. Slowly, Sorrel turned the key and unlocked the door. She opened it a crack and listened again, then peered out to see if the hallway was clear.

Stealthily, she slipped out and pulled the door closed behind her. She glanced at the main staircase, then headed in the opposite direction to the backstairs. She crept down, hugging the wall, expecting any moment Phoebe would appear. Somehow she managed to sneak past the kitchen without being seen.

Safely outside, Sorrel walked swiftly and confidently toward the stables. Her plan was a simple one. She would ride to Washburn's place near Salina. If he wouldn't tell her where Alex was, then she would persuade him to get a message to Alex, telling him she was there. If her parents wouldn't let Alex come see her, then she would go to him. But they weren't going to stop her from seeing him.

The first stars glittered in the purpling sky as Alex walked the black mare through the shadowy woods. He spotted the house lights and stopped to dismount. He tied the mare's reins to the trunk of a tree, patted her neck once, then crept forward.

He crouched next to another tree and studied the house. Every time he remembered the way The Blade had ordered him to leave, anger and utter humiliation burned within him. Frustrated by his impotence, he knew he had had no choice but to leave. There had been too many of them: The Blade, Lije, Lassiter. They'd had him outnumbered. The Blade had gone too far this time. And he was going to pay for it. He was going to pay for everything.

A light shone from the study window. Alex moved a few

feet to his right to get a better view. Someone was in there, and it was likely The Blade. Was he alone? Alex hesitated. If he was, what better opportunity could there be?

Temple sighed dispiritedly and glanced at The Blade. "Lije thinks we should bash the door in and drag Sorrel out by her hair. I'm half-tempted to do just that. This has gone on much too long. Why can't she see that you sent Alex away for her own good? You didn't do it to spite her." She was nearing the end of her patience with their daughter, yet The Blade appeared to be resigned to the situation. "Why aren't you more upset with her?"

He shrugged, but there was a hint of weariness in the gesture. "Maybe I've gotten used to it. All my life I have been condemned because I acted for the good of others. Why should my daughter react any differently than everyone else has?"

Dismayed by his comparison and the defeat in his voice, Temple swung around to face him, feeling his hurt as clearly as if it were her own. "I never condemned you. I know you did what you thought was best for everyone. And what you did today—ordering Alex to leave—that was right, too. I know that."

"I hoped Sorrel would—" He broke off the sentence, his shoulders sagging. "It doesn't matter what I hoped. The reality is that she has locked herself in her room. She's up there now—hating me for what I did."

"Don't say that." She cupped his strong face in her hands and made him look at her. "It isn't true. She may be very angry with you, but she still loves you. I know she does. Look at how many times I ranted and raved at you over the years. There were times when I was so mad I wanted to throw something at you—"

"I think you did a time or two." A smile tugged at the corners of his mouth.

"The point is—no matter how angry I was, I never stopped loving you. Sorrel loves you, too. Even now. You have to believe that."

She looked so earnest, so irresistibly lovely that The Blade couldn't help but smile. He leaned down and tasted the fullness of her lips. The honey-wild flavor of them hadn't faded with the passing years. For a moment his blood ran fast and strong with a young man's intoxication as he fell in love all over again with this proud, spirited woman who could satisfy him as no other ever had. When their lips warmly parted, he gathered her to him, wrapping his arms around her and resting his chin on the top of her hair.

"I do love you," he said, conscious of the strange contentment that could be found in simply holding her.

"I should hope so."

He chuckled softly at the hint of reproval in her voice and let his arms come away, releasing her. "It's odd," he murmured thoughtfully, moving away toward his desk. "I always expected Sorrel to cause us grief over a man, but I never once suspected that man would be Alex."

"Who would?"

There was a light rap at the door. The Blade pivoted, hope springing that perhaps Sorrel had finally emerged from her room. "Yes? Come in."

Deu entered carrying a tray laden with a coffee service and a small plate of cold chicken in paste, pickled walnuts, and asparagus spears. "I noticed you didn't eat very much at supper this evening, so I thought you might like a little something before you went to bed." He set the tray on the desk. "I thought you might want to join him, Miss Temple, so I brought along an extra cup and some silverware for you."

Temple gave no sign she heard him as she stared at the food. "Sorrel hasn't eaten all day, either. I'll fix her a tray. Perhaps I can bribe her into unlocking the door." Briefly, she arched an eyebrow in The Blade's direction. "It's certainly better than Lije's suggestion of breaking it down."

Personally, The Blade thought Lije's idea had a better chance for success, but he kept that to himself as Temple left the room. When Deu started to leave, The Blade waved him back. "Sit down and have a cup of coffee with me . . . if you have the time."

"I always have the time, Master Blade." Deu walked over to the desk and filled both cups with coffee.

"Speaking of time—don't you think it's time you dropped the 'master'? You're a free man, Deu. I'm not your master anymore." The Blade moved to sit in the mahogany-and-leather chair behind the desk.

"I know, but I've called you that for so long, it just comes out." Deu carried his cup over to an easy chair in front of the desk. "But the funny thing is"—he eased himself onto the seat cushion—"I never really felt like a slave. I know I was, but . . ."

"I know. Somewhere along the line, I stopped thinking of you as one, too." The Blade cut off a piece of the cold chicken, but when he tried to raise it to his mouth, he couldn't do it. The sight of the food reminded him of Temple—and Sorrel. Sighing, he laid the knife and fork across the plate. "What am I going to do about that girl up there, Deu? How can I make her understand about Alex? I can't talk to her. She won't listen."

"It's always like that with children. You were lucky with Lije, but—you take Ike, for instance. I remember when he ran away and joined the Union army. I couldn't believe he would do such a thing. I was upset and hurt that he hadn't stayed here to look after his momma and Miss Temple." Deu shook his head at the memory. "We tried to raise him right, but I thought we failed. Look at him now, though. I couldn't be prouder of him than I was today at that school. Someday you'll feel the same way about Sorrel. You just wait and see."

"I hope you're right."

"I know I am. She's a good girl who's a little mixed up now." Hearing footsteps pass by the study door, Deu set his cup on the desktop and pushed out of the chair. "That sounds like Miss Temple. I'll go carry that tray up for her, then come back."

The Blade watched the study door close behind Deu, then

looked at the food on the plate before him. Sighing, he pushed it aside and picked up his coffee cup. Rising from his chair, he stood behind the desk for several seconds, then wandered to the side of it, conscious of the cool breeze blowing in through the open window.

Hugging the shadows, Alex crept along the wall toward the study, his gun drawn. He thought he heard voices coming from the room and flattened himself against the wall, feeling the blood slugging heavily through the vein in his neck. He listened, but there was only silence now. He inched closer to the windowsill, then crouched down to peer inside.

The Blade was standing in full view, calmly sipping coffee from a china cup. No one else was in the room. Slowly and carefully, Alex edged himself into position. The Blade started to turn toward the window and Alex ducked out of sight. He waited, afraid to breathe, listening intently for the sound of footsteps approaching the window. None came. There was no sound of any movement. Warily, he stole another peek inside. The Blade was still in the same place, his back to the window. Alex smiled.

Lije walked out of the drawing room and noticed a movement on the staircase. He turned, half-hoping it would be Sorrel, but it was his mother, a third of the way up the stairs, struggling with a food tray.

"Let me carry that for you, Mother."

"You don't have to do that, Master Lije. I was just coming to help her." Deu crossed to the staircase.

"Lije, is that Deu I hear?" Eliza called from the drawing room. "Ask him to tell Phoebe to bring us some coffee?"

"Go ahead, Deu. I'll carry the tray for Mother." Lije relieved her of it. "Am I right in assuming you're taking this to Sorrel?"

"Yes." Temple continued up the staircase with Lije. "She hasn't eaten all day. Maybe this will entice her to unlock the door."

"I wouldn't get your hopes up."

When they reached his sister's bedroom, Lije stood to one side while Temple knocked on the door. "Sorrel? I've brought some food."

Silence.

"Sorrel, I know you're in there. Will you please answer me?" She waited again for a reply that never came. She knocked again, louder. "This has gone on long enough, Sorrel. You proved your point. You didn't go to the graduation. It's over. Now I want you to unlock this door immediately."

Lije frowned, suspicious of the continued silence from inside. "Try the door."

"It's no use," Temple answered irritably and reached for the knob. "She has it lo—" But it turned under her hand. She cast a startled glance at Lije, then pushed the door open and swept into the darkened room. "Sorrel?"

Lije was right behind her, his glance skimming the black shapes as he set the tray on the vanity table. Even before his mother lit a candle, he knew Sorrel wasn't there.

"She's gone." Temple breathed the words in shock.

"Damn her," Lije muttered softly.

"Where would she go?"

"To find Alex, where else?" he snapped and silently cursed his sister for being thirty kinds of a fool.

From downstairs came the sound of a muffled report. Lije swung toward the door.

"What was that?"

He bolted from the room without answering his mother's question.

A curl of blue smoke drifted from the muzzle of his gun as Alex watched the arching jerk of The Blade's body. He

pitched forward, falling heavily to the floor, the cup flying
from his hand. Alex smiled coldly. It was done. The Blade
was dead.

To his amazement, the body moved. The Blade was trying to push himself up on his hands. The bastard wouldn't die.
Angrily, Alex squeezed the trigger, sending another bullet
plunging into the man on the floor. It drove him down. But
was he dead? This time Alex had to be sure. He swung a leg
through the open window and started to climb into the room.

At that instant, the door burst open and Deu charged inside,
stopping abruptly when he saw Alex straddling the windowsill. Alex fired instinctively, thumbing two quick shots at the
Negro before he hurriedly dodged back through the opening
and took off at a run.

With Rans at his side, Lije rushed into the study. The others crowded in behind them. He faltered briefly at the sight
of his father motionless on the floor with Deu struggling to
crawl to him. The curtain at the window fluttered from the
breeze blowing in.

Kneeling beside his father, Lije felt for a pulse. There was
none. A tightness gripped his chest, painfully squeezing all
the air out of his lungs. For an instant, Lije bowed his head,
closing his eyes and doubling his hand into a fist.

Above the jumble of other voices, he heard his mother
scream, "No!"

He rose, catching her and stopping Temple before she
reached The Blade. The stark terror in her eyes stabbed him
like a knife. He shook his head. "He's dead, Momma."

"No! He can't be!" She pulled free and fell to her knees
beside the body.

Frozen, Lije watched her, barely noticing when Eliza
brushed past him to go to Temple. Abruptly, he turned away,
fighting the waves of rage that swept through him.

"Lije," Rans called sharply to him. "Deu is still alive."

Rans had an arm under the old man's shoulder, support-ing him as Susannah tried to staunch the flow of blood from the wound in his chest. Lije knelt down beside them. Deu's eyes were closed. He made a weak attempt to open them.

"Master Bl . . . Blade?" His voice was a thready whisper as he tried to focus on Lije. Lije shook his head, unable to say the words again. Deu moaned. "I should . . . stayed with . . . him. He . . . he wanted me to."

"Deu, who shot you? Did you see who it was?"

There was a small, affirmative nod of his head in response, then he moistened his lips and framed the word. "Alex."

"Alex? It was Alex?" Lije had to be sure.

Deu nodded again.

"That is enough, Lije," Susannah warned as a sobbing Phoebe crowded close. "He's too weak, and I can't stop the blood. Mother, go fetch Temple's basket while I keep pres-sure on this wound."

But Lije had what he needed. He stood up, surprised at how calm he felt inside. He crossed to the gun cabinet and removed one of the gun belts. After checking to make sure the revolver was loaded, he strapped the belt on, took one of the carbines, and grabbed a supply of ammunition. When he turned to leave, Diane stood before him.

"The feud—I never really understood." Her eyes were filled with tears and hot with anger. "You have to get him. You must go after Alex, or it will never be over."

Her words rushed through him like a reviving wind, fill-ing him, lifting him. *She understood. A* deep tenderness swelled up inside him, making this a moment to be savored. But there was no time. No time.

He cupped the smooth curve of her cheek in his hand. "Stay with my mother."

Diane nodded. "You come back to me, Lije Stuart."

"I will." Lije turned to leave, but Rans was there in his way. He brushed past him straight out the study doors.

In the foyer, Rans grabbed his arm. "What do you think you're doing, Lije?"

"I'm going after Alex."

"Dammit, you can't. Think of your mother."

"I'm thinking about my sister," Lije snapped. "She's gone—probably to find Alex. I have to get to him before she does."

"I'll go with you." Rans released Lije's arm.

"No. Stay here." Lije glanced back at the study. "The family will need you." He went out the door.

A keening wail broke from the study. Rans swung from the door, his jaw clenched on the helpless feeling that swept through him. He strode back to the room, arriving just as Eliza came running with Temple's medical basket. Phoebe was on the floor with Deu cradled against her, rocking back and forth as she cried. Susannah turned to them, her hands wet with blood, Deu's blood. Her eyes were filled with grief, appeal, and apology.

"I . . . couldn't stop the bleeding," she murmured. "The bullet must have severed an artery." There was sadness in every line of her body, but she didn't cry. Somehow Rans had known she wouldn't. The others needed her strength right now, not her tears. He put an arm around her shoulders, offering her a measure of comfort before she had to do the same for them.

At the same time Nathan and Jed helped a softly weeping Temple to her feet and gently drew her away from The Blade's body. Eliza went to her. "After . . . all these years, Eliza," Temple murmured brokenly. "After all these years . . . it finally happened."

"I—I know, Temple." Eliza's voice wavered. "I know."

Temple looked around a little blankly. "Now Lije has gone after Alex. Oh, God." She clutched at Eliza's arm. "It's history repeating itself all over again with Lije."

"He'll come back, Temple," Diane stated with certainty. "Lije will come back."

When Temple saw Phoebe reluctantly lay her dead husband onto the floor, she went to the grieving woman. "Phoebe." She waited for her to rise. They looked at each other for several tearful seconds. "I am sorry, Phoebe." Temple gathered her into her arms and hugged her tightly. "I am so sorry."

༼ 32 ༽

Alex galloped the mare for five miles, trying to put as much distance between himself and Grand View as he could. He approached a small settlement and slowed the mare to a walk, taking a back trail that cut off ten miles.

Instinct warned him to keep riding north and not slow up until he was beyond the Kansas border. But all his supplies and most of his share of old man Scott's gold were in the cabin hideout east of here, in the rugged hills of the Boston Mountains. Morgan Bennet waited for him there as well.

For a mile, Alex walked the mare over the rough trail. When the moon came up to silver the path, he pushed her into an easy gallop for another three miles. Walk one, gallop three; Alex kept that combination until he neared the intersection with the main road. Halting short of the road, he dismounted in the cover of some trees and checked to make sure the road was clear.

He started to loosen the saddle cinch, then heard the rhythmic three-beat tattoo of a cantering horse. Instantly, Alex moved to the mare's head and placed a hand over her nose. He watched the moonlit road.

A lone rider appeared and cantered into the path of the moonlight. Alex stared in disbelief. It was Sorrel. How? Why? Did she know about her father? She couldn't.

He hesitated a second longer, then swung into the saddle and rode onto the road to intercept her. She pulled her sorrel gelding in sharply, showing alarm.

"Sorrel, it's me. Alex."

"Alex?" She laughed in relief. "I was coming to find you."

"Does your family know where you are?" he asked warily.

"No," she said with a defiant toss of her head. "They think I'm still in my room with the door locked. After you left, I refused to go to the graduation. While they were eating supper, I snuck out. They won't miss me until morning."

Alex knew they would miss her sooner than that. He couldn't send her home . . . not now. He wished he hadn't stopped her, that he had let her keep riding. But that wouldn't have worked either. She knew about Washburn—and Washburn could point them to the cabin. He had to take her with him.

"I have a cabin about ten miles from here. We'll go there." Alex swung the mare around and pointed her up the road.

"A cabin? I didn't know you had a cabin, Alex."

There were a lot of things about him she didn't know. He planned on keeping it that way.

Sorrel stood on the small porch of the two-room log cabin built against the side of a steep hill. The morning sun was full on her face, the air fresh and cool. She tore off another chunk of jerky with her teeth and chewed it while Alex finished tying the supplies on the packhorse.

"I never thought jerky could taste so good," she said. "I guess you have to be hungry."

"I guess so." He tossed her a smile, then patted the packhorse on the neck.

"Why do we have to leave so early?"

"You want to go to Kansas City, don't you? It's a long ride, and the longer we wait, the longer it will take."

"I know." Sorrel tried to smile. Last night, going to Kansas City with Alex had sounded fun. But she knew her parents would be wondering where she was—worrying about her. Alex said she could write them and let them know she was all right. Still . . .

"Alex," Morgan Bennet called from the lower edge of the clearing. "We got company coming up the trail."

Curious, Sorrel followed Alex when he walked over to look down the hill at the switchback trail. It was dark when they had arrived here last night. Sorrel hadn't realized the trail could be seen from the clearing. She recognized the rider the same instant that Alex did.

"It's Lije," he announced grimly.

"We can make it out the back way before he gets here," Morgan said.

"No. He would be too close behind us."

Sorrel bit at her lower lip, fully aware that Lije was coming after her. They must have discovered she was gone sometime last night. Out of the corner of her eye, she saw Morgan's hand pull the revolver from his holster.

"We'll fix that." He leveled it at Lije.

"No," she breathed in shock. At the same moment Alex reached out to push the hand down.

"I have a better idea." Alex backed away from the vantage point and turned toward the cabin. "I'll hide the horses behind the cabin. Morgan, you get in the back room. Sorrel, you get Lije in the cabin, tell him you're alone, that we're not here. But stay on the right side of the room out of the way. I'll sneak around front. We'll get the drop on him." His hand was at her elbow, propelling her back to the cabin.

"What are you going to do?" Sorrel murmured uncertainly.

Alex shot a quick glance at Morgan, then smiled. "Tie him up and leave him so he can't follow us—at least not until he gets the knots free. What did you think we were going to do? Kill him?"

"I wasn't sure." She looked at Morgan, remembering the way he aimed his gun at Lije.

"You mean that back there?" Alex said, his grin taking on a joshing quality. "Morgan was only going to spook his horse and hopefully get him thrown. A man on foot in these hills is in for trouble. His feet would be covered with blisters before he walked out of here. Don't worry, Sorrel. Everything will be all right. You leave it to me and Morgan—and stay on the right side of the room. Okay?"

"Okay." She nodded, none too certainly.

"Go in the cabin. When he rides up, call him inside."

Still Sorrel hesitated, watching Morgan Bennet as he moved quickly and quietly inside the cabin. She remembered all the things Lije had told her about Bennet. It made her even more uneasy.

"Alex . . . maybe I should go back with Lije."

"What?" For an instant his black eyes glowered at her. She felt the faintest shiver of fear. It startled her. Then Alex dipped his head. When he looked at her again, there was hurt in his expression. "I thought you wanted to be with me. I wanted to take you places and show you things. You're the only family I have, Sorrel, the only one who cares about me. But, if you would rather be with them . . ."

"It isn't that, Alex," she hurried to assure him. "I don't want to cause trouble for you."

"I want to do this."

"And I want to go to Kansas City with you."

He looked relieved. "Better get in the cabin before Lije comes."

"All right." She moved toward the door.

"Remember," Alex called softly. "Morgan will be in the back room, but don't let on he's there."

She nodded and stepped inside. She glanced around the room, taking in the chinked-log walls, the stone fireplace, the crude wooden table and chairs, and the narrow bunk where she had slept last night. She went over to it and sat down. Its thick straw mattress and rope springs weren't nearly as comfortable as the feathery softness of her own bed at home, but last night, she had been too tired to care. She laid a hand on the lumpy mattress and shuddered, wondering if there were lice in it. The place was filthy.

She didn't understand why Alex had a cabin in the hills. The land wasn't good for anything. It was too rocky for farming, and there wasn't enough graze for cattle. It looked like an outlaw's hideout. Suddenly, Sorrel wondered if everything Lije had said about Alex was true. She touched the locket around her neck.

Stones clattered outside, dislodged by hooves as Alex led the horses behind the cabin. Sorrel stiffened, apprehension tightening her muscles. She looked at the dirty blanket that hung in the doorway to the cabin's second room. Morgan was behind it. Morgan and his gun. She felt a chill curl down her spine.

A jay shrieked in the trees outside. Sorrel jumped and gripped the edge of the bed.

At last she heard Lije's horse on the trail. She knew he wouldn't see the cabin until he rounded the rocky promontory. By then he would be in the clearing. She forced herself to lie down on the crude cot and pretend to be asleep. Pretend everything was all right, that everything would be all right.

She closed her eyes and listened, trying to track Lije's approach to the cabin with her ears alone—the creak of saddle leather when he dismounted, the faint scrape of his boot on the gravel when he moved toward the cabin, the groan of a wooden step when he started up them, then nothing. She was certain he was inside the cabin, but she couldn't hear him anymore. She hadn't realized her brother could move so quietly, so stealthily. Why didn't he call out? Why was he being so cautious? She couldn't stand the suspense any longer. She stirred, pretending to wake up.

When she opened her eyes, he was three feet inside the door, his narrowed eyes suspiciously scanning the room. He had a gun in his hand, the hammer cocked. For an instant, he looked remarkably like her father, but without the scar on his cheek.

"Lije." She sat up, pretending to brush the sleep from her face. "What are you doing here? How did you know where to find me?"

"Where's Alex?"

"He isn't here," she answered quickly, then worried that maybe it was too quickly.

"What's back there?" He gestured to the blanket covering the doorway.

"Nothing," Sorrel lied and hated herself for it.

The feeling intensified when Lije glanced sharply at her as if doubting her words. "Come on," he ordered and beckoned her to him. "You're getting out of here."

Sorrel stood, not knowing what else to do or how else to stall him. Then, in a flash of motion, the blanket was flung back, and Morgan stepped out with a gun in his hand.

"Look out!" But the booming report of Morgan's gun muffled her warning shout.

Almost simultaneously, Lije's gun bucked in his hand. The two explosions blended together into one deafening roar. In shock, Sorrel saw Morgan slammed against the wall by the bullet that plowed into him. He tried to bring his revolver up to bear again. Again the air reverberated with the thundering discharge of Lije's weapon, and Morgan slid down the wall, his legs crumpling under him, a look of shock on his face.

"Lije." Sorrel turned, relieved to see him standing upright, but her relief quickly changed to alarm when she saw his hand pressed against the top of his arm, blood oozing from the cracks between his fingers. "You've been shot."

She took a step toward him, but he waved her back with his gun, the whiteness of pain showing around his jaw. "Where is Alex?"

"Right here, Lije. Alex stood in the doorway, his revolver

aimed at Lije's back. His smile was frightening. Lije stiffened and started to turn, but the ominous click of a cocking hammer checked the movement. "That's right—don't move. Sorrel, take his gun."

She hesitated, again unsure of what to do. She stared at Lije, vaguely unnerved by the sad, pitying look he gave her. "I'm sorry," she whispered and moved closer to take his gun. He handed it to her butt first.

"Now, move away from him, Sorrel," Alex ordered.

When she backed up, Lije said, "I should have known you would be behind me, Alex."

"Wait for me outside, Sorrel." Alex stepped to the left of the doorway and motioned for her to go out.

"Stay here, Sorrel." Lije lifted his head slightly, but he didn't look around. "I want you to know he'll be lying when he tells you I made a try for his gun, and he had to kill me."

Sorrel stared at Alex, waiting for him to deny it. Instead, he snapped, "Turn around, Stuart."

"No. You're going to shoot me in the back just the way you killed my father."

"What?" Dazed, Sorrel looked at him. "Father is dead?"

"I don't know what you're talking about," Alex growled. "Get out of here, Sorrel."

"You know what I'm talking about," Lije taunted. "You made the same mistake the last time."

"Shut up!"

"Deu didn't die right away, Alex. He lived long enough to identify you."

Deu was dead, too? Alex had killed Deu and her father? No. Her father couldn't be dead. He couldn't be!

"You've said enough," Alex leveled the long barrel of his revolver at Lije's back.

Dear God, he was going to kill Lije, too. Without thinking, Sorrel lifted the gun in her hand and pointed it at Alex. "Alex, no." Her voice wavered, but she managed to hold the gun steady. "Don't. Put the gun down . . . please."

For an instant, Alex froze at the sight of the gun in her hand. He glanced from it to her, then smiled crookedly. "What do you think you're doing with that? You won't shoot me."

She swallowed nervously. "I'm not going to let you kill my brother, Alex." To enforce her statement, she pulled the hammer back, using both thumbs.

His smile grew wider, along with his confidence. "You won't shoot, Sorrel." He turned back to Lije, centering his attention on him. "Not me."

She caught the faint movement of his trigger finger and squeezed with her own. The revolver jumped in her hands as the loud report vibrated against her eardrums. Through half-closed eyes she saw Alex stagger to one side, then slowly fall.

"Alex!" She dropped the gun and ran to him, falling to the floor beside him.

His eyes clung to her, pain and confusion in their depths. "Why?" he murmured faintly. "Why?"

"I had to," she sobbed. "Don't you see I had to?"

"I . . . trusted you."

Then came that sound, that horrible, never-to-be-forgotten sound of a long, rasping breath expelled, followed by absolute silence.

"Alex." She threw herself onto him and sobbed.

A hand pulled at her. "Sorrel." Lije's voice came from far away. "Sorrel, there isn't any more you can do for him."

Still weeping, she let him pull her upright. "I had to, Lije," she said again. "I couldn't let him shoot you. I had to."

His right arm went around her and pulled her to him. "I know." He pressed her head against his shirt and let her cry. "I know."

At last Sorrel drew back and wiped at the tears with her hand. She glanced back at Alex's body. "Is it true, Lije?" she asked in a thick, broken voice. "Is Father really dead?"

"Yes." He smoothed a hand over her hair.

Her face scrunched up, tears rising again. "Why? Why did he have to die? It isn't fair, Lije. It isn't fair."

"I know."

"But you don't understand. I never had a chance to tell him I loved him. And I did love him. Truly, I did, Lije," she sobbed.

"He knew that. I swear to you he knew that," Lije told her, his own voice thickening with grief and pain. "Come on. Let's go home." He turned to lead her outside.

Sorrel pulled back. "Wait." She reached behind her neck and fumbled briefly with the chain's clasp, then pulled the locket from around her neck and tossed it back. It fell in the shadows near Alex's body. "I don't want it anymore."

It was close to dusk when they returned to Grand View. Rans saw them coming up the lane. By the time they reached the house, everyone was outside waiting for them. Lije dismounted first and walked around to help Sorrel down. Wordlessly, Temple rushed to embrace her.

Lije stepped back and turned. Diane came to him, more slowly, her gaze traveling over him in careful examination. She saw the blood-stained kerchief tied around his arm.

"You're hurt."

"Not badly," he said, then reached out to gather her into his arms. For the moment he simply wanted to hold her and let the rightness of it spiral through him.

"Alex?" she said in question.

"He's dead." He rubbed his cheek against her hair. "It's over. This time it's finally over."

She shuddered and pressed closer. "I love you, Lije."

"I love you, too." He lifted his head to look at her, his eyes lazy and warm. "Marry me?"

Her breath caught, then escaped in a laughing sigh. "I thought you'd never ask."

More by Bestselling Author

Janet Dailey

Bring the Ring	0-8217-8016-6	$4.99US/$6.99CAN
Calder Promise	0-8217-7541-3	$7.99US/$10.99CAN
Calder Storm	0-8217-7543-X	$7.99US/$10.99CAN
A Capital Holiday	0-8217-7224-4	$6.99US/$8.99CAN
Crazy in Love	1-4201-0303-2	$4.99US/$5.99CAN
Eve's Christmas	0-8217-8017-4	$6.99US/$9.99CAN
Green Calder Grass	0-8217-7222-8	$7.99US/$10.99CAN
Happy Holidays	0-8217-7749-1	$6.99US/$9.99CAN
Let's Be Jolly	0-8217-7919-2	$6.99US/$9.99CAN
Lone Calder Star	0-8217-7542-1	$7.99US/$10.99CAN
Man of Mine	1-4201-0009-2	$4.99US/$6.99CAN
Mistletoe and Molly	1-4201-0041-6	$6.99US/$9.99CAN
Ranch Dressing	0-8217-8014-X	$4.99US/$6.99CAN
Scrooge Wore Spurs	0-8217-7225-2	$6.99US/$9.99CAN
Searching for Santa	1-4201-0306-7	$6.99US/$9.99CAN
Shifting Calder Wind	0-8217-7223-6	$7.99US/$10.99CAN
Something More	0-8217-7544-8	$7.99US/$9.99CAN
Stealing Kisses	1-4201-0304-0	$4.99US/$5.99CAN
Try to Resist Me	0-8217-8015-8	$4.99US/$6.99CAN
Wearing White	1-4201-0011-4	$4.99US/$6.99CAN
With This Kiss	1-4201-0010-6	$4.99US/$6.99CAN
Yes, I Do	1-4201-0305-9	$4.99US/$5.99CAN

Available Wherever Books Are Sold!

Check out our website at **www.kensingtonbooks.com**